SINS
OF THE
FLESH

Colleen McCullough

Simon & Schuster

NEW YORK   LONDON   TORONTO   SYDNEY   NEW DELHI

Simon & Schuster
1230 Avenue of the Americas
New York, NY 10020

First Simon & Schuster hardcover edition November 2013

SIMON & SCHUSTER and colophon are registered trademarks
of Simon & Schuster, Inc.

For information about special discounts for bulk purchases,
please contact Simon & Schuster Special Sales at
1-866-506-1949 or business@simonandschuster.com.

The Simon & Schuster Speakers Bureau can bring authors
to your live event. For more information or to book an event,
contact the Simon & Schuster Speakers Bureau at
1-866-248-3049 or visit our website at www.simonspeakers.com.

Interior design by Rory Panagotopulos

Manufactured in the United States of America

1 3 5 7 9 10 8 6 4 2

Library of Congress Cataloging-in-Publication Data is available.

ISBN 978-1-4767-3533-7
ISBN 978-1-4767-3536-8 (ebook)

For KAREN QUINTAL

All the many loyal and loving years are deeply appreciated.

Here's hoping there are just as many more to come.

Thanks, pal.

SINS
OF THE
FLESH

MIDNIGHT, SUNDAY/MONDAY, AUGUST 3–4, 1969

H e had no idea it was midnight. In actual fact, he didn't know whether the sun was shining or the stars were twinkling. Nor could he work out how long he'd been here, so timelessly did time pass. One moment he had been free, smiling with happiness, at the center of a world that had opened its arms wide to embrace him; the next moment he had fallen into a sleep so deep that he remembered not even the tiniest fragment of a dream.

When he woke he was here, to live a different life. Here, in a big, featureless room that contained a padded toilet and a plastic water bubbler that produced a slim fountain whenever he put his foot down on a button in the floor below it. So he could drink, and he had a tidy place in which to excrete. Here only had one color: a dirty beige, not from squalor but from the poor lighting of one dim bulb, center-ceiling behind a tough glass case wrapped in steel rods.

He was stark naked, though he wasn't hot, and he wasn't cold. Everything was oddly soft—the floor and the walls sighed and gently gave way wherever he touched them, akin to leather squabs on a car seat. What at first he thought were seams around the bottom of the walls turned out to be the exact opposite of seams: tucks, as if this cushioning surface were rammed down inside a crevice, together with the edges of the floor. No matter how he tried to dig with his fingertips, the fabric refused to move one single millimeter.

Soon his ravenous hunger became the be-all and the end-all of his entire existence, for though he could always drink, and as much as he wished, he had no particle of food. At times, coming in and going out of the sleeps, he vaguely remembered a taste of food, and understood that he was fed something that sat in his belly like a coal of such glorious warmth and comfort that even the most fleeting memory of it caused him to weep.

His panics belonged to differently befogged and shrouded periods, when he had screamed on and on and on, crashed against the walls, flailed his fists against those yielding surfaces, howled like an old dog, bleated and bayed and bellowed and bawled. No one ever answered. All he heard was himself. Emerging from the panic exhausted, he would drink thirstily and sleep the sleep of the dead, featureless, his last thought the hope of food.

He had nothing to do, nothing to look at—not even a mirror! Nothing to pass the time, he who had passed so much of it gazing at his own reflection, marveling at the perfection of his beauty. All he had to do to get what he wanted was to smile. But in here there was no one to smile at. Just one little chance to smile, that was all he needed! A smile would get him out—no one could ever, ever, *ever* resist his smile! A smile would get him food. It always came in his sleeps, the food, therefore he must go to sleep smiling.

He was weakening, it seemed the way a snail dragged itself around, with mind-numbing slowness and enormous effort, a visible labor just to hold the house of his life up off his head, for if it slipped, he was gone like a drop of slime on a white-hot stove. He didn't want to part with his beauty yet! Or his smile!

"Why are you so cruel?" He smiled. "Who are you?"

This time his awakening brought changes: he was still hungry, and he was in pain.

No glowing coal of food lingered in his belly—it hadn't fed him! But at least the pain said he was still alive, and it wasn't agonizing— more an ache in the groin. One of the things he couldn't fathom was its attention to his groin, stripped of all hair, since it had never, as far as he knew, subjected him to any kind of abuse. This wakening's pain made him doubt, and he groped for his penis; it was there, unharmed. No, the soreness was behind it, in his ball-sack. *Something was wrong!* Each testicle should roll under his fingers as if it were free inside the sack, but no testicles rolled. His ball-sack was empty. *Empty!*

He shrieked, and a voice spoke from every square inch of the room, impossible to pinpoint.

"Poor eunuch," it cooed, dovelike. "You did well, my poor eunuch. No bleeding. They came out as easily as the stone out of a fleshless avocado. Snip, snip! Snip, snip! No balls."

He screamed, and went on screaming, long shrill wails of grief and despair that finally died away into gibberish; and from that he passed to a silence flirting with catatonia, moving not the tiniest muscle. The pain was dying away to nothing, more bearable than the pain of no food, and even that didn't matter the way it had before the discovery of his neutering. Without his manhood, there was nothing to smile about. An utterly weary hopelessness moved into his soul and took up residence there.

Though he didn't know it was midnight, the savage hack of Time's scythe that shoved Sunday the 3rd into the past and Monday the 4th into the present, he suddenly knew there would be no more food. Curling up to hug himself, arms around his knees, he gazed across the vast expanse of the floor into a dirty beige eternity.

The chair came down out of the ceiling behind him, descending silently to a halt with its foot platform still a meter short of the floor. Had he turned his head, he would have seen it and the person who occupied it, but he didn't turn his head. Everything that was left of him was focused on his contemplation of eternity, though he was a long way off dying yet. A complete authority on the matter, his observer estimated that he had about forty days left before the very last flicker of life snuffed out. Forty days of ecstatic conversation and study—but how interesting! He *still* wore a kind of a smile. . . .

The chair lifted itself back into the ceiling while the dying man on the floor continued to plumb his perspective on eternity.

MONDAY, AUGUST 4, 1969

"I told you, Abe, I told you," Delia said, "but you and Carmine were being typical men— wouldn't listen to a woman, oh, no!"

She and Abe were sitting in a booth at Malvolio's waiting for their lunch, and Abe had miscalculated his moment: Delia's gauzy outfit of mustard yellow and coral pink had seemed tame to him, an indication that today's Delia was placidly bored. But her reaction to his news said otherwise; Abe heaved an internal sigh and revised his mental chart labeled DELIA CARSTAIRS.

"It's taken this one to convince me," he said in undefeated tones. "Until now, the evidence was insufficient."

"No evidence, but no guts either," she said, disgusted.

"I don't see why you're crowing so loud," he said.

"Minnie is coming with our omelets," she said in the voice of a prissy schoolmarm, "and I propose we eat before we discuss."

Ah, that was it! Delia was plain hungry! Meekly Abe ate. Luigi's summer cook produced superb Western omelets, and Delia hadn't grown tired of them yet. Which didn't mean Abe's mental chart of Delia could stay unamended. The real problem was, did he modify CLOTHES, COLOR or FOOD, and how much ought he to cross-index? A very complicated mental chart, Delia's.

The eating dealt with, Delia leaned forward, her bright brown jewels of eyes glittering. "Enlighten me," she commanded.

Abe began. "Same as James Doe. Gus has named him Jeb Doe

4

until he's identified—if he ever is. I know you maintained James Doe was related to the four earlier bodies, but decomposition did *not* permit any positivity, whereas Jeb Doe does." His cigarette kindled, he inhaled with obvious pleasure. "Gus hasn't posted Jeb yet, but the preliminary examination is uncannily like James. The body was found on Willard two blocks farther out than Caterby, where Little San Juan has taken to dumping trash. No apparent cause of death, except that starvation sure played a part in it. His testicles had been removed some weeks prior to death."

"Cause of death will be starvation," Delia said confidently, "and the perpetrator is a multiple murderer, you must admit that now. Jeb and James Doe are preceded by four John Does whose bones we've found. My guess is that there are a lot more than four."

"If so, not in Holloman. We've looked back twenty years, and found nothing before John Doe One in 1966." Abe puffed away luxuriously, then gazed at his dwindling cigarette in real grief. "Why do they go so fast?"

"Because you're quitting, Abe dear, and you can't have your next ciggy until after dinner tonight. Are you sure there are no other John Does elsewhere in Connecticut?"

"At this moment, yes, but I'll have Liam and Tony repeat our enquiries." Abe smiled wryly. "At least we can be pretty sure no bodies will turn up in idyllic rustic settings."

"Yes, this chap definitely thinks of his victims as garbage the moment they're dead." Delia put her hand on Abe's arm when he rose to go. "No, let's stay here a minute more, please. I love the air-conditioning."

Abe sat with the alacrity of a trained husband. "It's cool, yeah, but the smoke torments me," he said plaintively.

She gave a mew of exasperation. "I love you dearly, Abraham Samuel Goldberg, but you have to get through kicking the habit, and in one respect Jews are like Catholics—they find it easier to suffer one torture when they have to suffer more than one. Well, I am not sweltering in County Services just so you can, a, swelter, and b, with-draw simultaneously. Set your mind where it ought to be—on Jeb Doe, not the Marlboro Man."

"Sorry," he muttered, wrestling a grin. "If Jeb Doe's cause of death is starvation, then we know that the last two Does were defi-nitely starved to death, as well as emasculated. In turn, it suggests an MO for all of them. Gruesome!"

"Yes, quite horrible," said Delia, grimacing. "It's a very un-usual way to murder because the degree of premeditation is truly formidable—I mean, it takes weeks if not months, and can be stopped at any time. While it may not be messy, it's certainly the op-posite of most murder."

"You mean it's colder than ice, harder than steel?"

"Yes, whereas murder of its very nature suggests passion and rage," said Delia, frowning.

"How would anyone light on starvation as a modus operandi? You'd need a dungeon." Abe's freckled face betrayed dismay. "We have had our share of underground premises in Holloman lately."

"Exactly!" Delia cried, excited. "Starvation is a Middle Ages form of murder. Endowed with dungeons galore, the less civilized mon-archs indulged in starving people to death. Aunt Sophonisba of-fended the King and the King threw her into a dungeon where—oh, how *could* it have happened?—they forgot to feed her. However, the victims were almost always women. Sort of murder by proxy, which lessens the guilt."

Cigarettes forgotten, Abe stared at her, intrigued. "I hear you, but am I getting the correct message? Are you implying that our Doe murderer is a woman? Or that the victims should be women?"

Delia went wildly tangential. "Confining the word 'homosexual' to the male of our species while putting lesbians on a back burner, may I say that while a number of homosexuals may feel like women trapped inside men's bodies, I believe the majority do not? After all, homosexuality isn't exclusively the preserve of human beings. Ani-mals practice it too," she said.

Abe's luminous grey eyes mirrored his brain's confusion. "Are you saying these are homosexual murders? What *are* you saying?"

"I'm saying the killer is definitely not homosexual."

Abe continued to stare at her, mesmerized. How did Delia's mind work? Greater intellects than his had failed to find the answer to that question, thus he was able to view his defeat with equanimity. "So you're hypothesizing that the four John Does, James Doe and Jeb Doe are all the work of the same heterosexual killer?"

"Definitely. Come, Abe, you think the same."

"After Jeb, the same killer, yes. Heterosexual? Search me."

"The real question is, how long ago were his trial runs?"

"Easing his way into his MO, you mean?"

"I do indeed." Delia gave a wriggle of anticipatory delight. "James Doe was your case, Abe, so I need filling in."

"The consensus of opinion at the time was that it was a homosexual murder, pure and simple. But after Liam and I had a talk with Professor Eric Soderstern, we had to can that," Abe said.

There were many occasions, thought Delia, when being a minor police department in a small city could possess unexpected bonuses. The Holloman PD had all the resources and expertise of one of the world's greatest universities at its fingertips; these included the Chubb University Medical School professors of psychiatry. Dr. Eric Soderstern, a famous authority on the psychology of homosexuality, had been consulted in Abe's need.

"The prof said that castration of the victim indicated rape was the precipitating factor for murder, not homosexuality. We'd gotten nowhere with our enquiries among Holloman's homosexual contingent." Abe's beautiful smile appeared. "We were also told that with this new decade coming up and so many guys coming out of the closet, homosexuality was taking a new lease on life with the word 'gay.' We have to educate ourselves to say gay rather than homosexual."

"I've heard gay around a little," said Delia. "It goes back at least as far as Oscar Wilde. But continue, dear."

"Anyway, now at least we had a reason for the gay community's ignorance—apparently James Doe wasn't a homosexual and his murder had no gay aspects. Instead, we had to ask ourselves if he might have raped someone."

"Perhaps he was homosexual, and raped a male?"

"Delia! That implication I don't need!" Abe glowered at her, "Hot weather and you don't mix, lady. I need a smoke."

"Codswallop, of course you don't. You're down in the mouth, Abe dear, because the discovery of Jeb Doe does rather put the kibosh on rape theories of any kind. The killer lives for the act of murder, and has to be regarded as a multiple. His reasons for castration will be absolutely individual, not due to some Freudian generalization." Delia arose in a mustard and coral cloud. "Come on, let's see if Gus has done the autopsy."

They stepped out into the August humidity, up near saturation point, and gasped.

"There's method in my madness," Delia said cheerfully as they descended to the Morgue, one floor below ground. "Everywhere in the ME's is air-conditioned." Her face saddened. "It's still a wee bit of a shock, not seeing Patrick's cheeky face. He seemed to resign his coroner's duties overnight."

"You can't blame him."

"No, of course not. But miss him, I do."

Gustavus Fennell had stepped into Patrick O'Donnell's shoes as Medical Examiner, a decision that had pleased everybody in the aftermath of Patrick's sudden illness, a particularly malevolent arthritis. To have replaced a forceful, vital, pioneering man like Patrick with another of the same sort would have led to all kinds of wars, internal and external, whereas dear old Gus (who in fact was neither very old nor very much of a dear) knew all the ropes and could be relied upon to run the Medical Examiner's department smoothly. Lacking his retired chief's good looks and charm, Gus had gotten along as Second-in-Command by consciously playing the second lead, as Commissioner John Silvestri was well aware. Now, after three months as ME, the real Gus was starting to shed his veils in an intricate dance that would, Silvestri knew, finally end in revealing a gentle yet obdurate autocrat who would push his department onward and upward with extreme efficiency.

Like Patrick, Gus enjoyed performing criminal autopsies, the more complicated or mysterious, the better. When Delia and Abe walked, gowned and booted, into his autopsy room, he was just stripping off his gloves, leaving an assistant to close for him. If the cause of death were unknown and might conceivably have a contagious factor, he worked masked, as he had on Jeb Doe.

Mask off, he led his visitors to several steel chairs in a quiet corner of the room, and sat with a sigh of relief. His face and hair, stripped of their coverings, were displayed as—no other word would do—nondescript. Mr. Average Everything, to which add, fade into the wallpaper. However, his slight body had a wiry strength its proportions belied, and his face said its owner could be trusted. That he had certain crotchets Abe and Delia knew: he was a strict vegetarian who forbade smoking anywhere in his department, and if circumstances deprived him of his two generous pre-dinner sherries or after-dinner ports, then mild-mannered Dr. Fennell became a hideous Mr. Hyde. His passion was bridge, at which he was an acknowledged master.

"Unless the fluid or tissue assays come back to show some toxin—I doubt they will—the cause of death is simple starvation," Gus said, kicking off his chef's clogs. "My feet are so sore today, I don't know why. The testicles were enucleated about six weeks before death, by someone who knew exactly how to do it. There was nothing in the alimentary canal that I could call a food residue, but he wasn't dehydrated."

"Water, Gus? Or fruit juice, maybe?" Abe asked.

"Nothing but plain water is my guess. Certainly nothing with fiber of any kind in it, or indigestible end products. If he were given plain water the starvation metabolism would proceed smooth as silk, and it did. There were no substances under his nails."

"May we have a look at him?" Delia asked.

"Sure."

Delia and Abe moved to the dissecting table, where the body now lay unattended.

Thick, waving black hair, cut to cover the neck and ears but not long enough to be tied back, they noted; it was almost the sole evidence of normality that the corpse displayed, so dynamic were the ravages of a metabolism forced to digest itself to obtain sustenance. The skin was very yellow and waxy, stretched fairly tautly over the skeleton, which showed in vivid detail.

"His teeth are perfect," Delia said.

"Good nutrition and fluoride in the water supply. The latter says he wasn't raised in Connecticut." Abe shook his head angrily, balked. "I'll get Ginny Toscano to flesh out the skull for me, no matter how bad her hysterics are. Jeb needs an artist's sketch."

"Haven't you heard? We have a new artist," said Delia, first with this news too. "His name is Hank Jones, and he's a child just out of art school with a cast iron digestion, absolutely no finer feelings, and a macabre sense of humor."

"A child?" Abe asked, grinning.

"Nineteen, bless him. Ethnicity—you name it, he has at least a drop of it in his veins. His hobby is drawing cadavers at the Medical School, but I met him in our parking lot sketching Paul Bachman's 1937 Mercedes roadster. He's gorgeous!"

"Gorgeous I can live without, but if he doesn't mind the sight of a nasty dead body, he's worth knowing," Abe said.

"Those who've seen his work say he's good." Delia raised her voice. "Gus, does starvation make body hair fall out, or has someone depilated the poor little blighter?"

"The latter, Delia," Gus answered. "He wasn't hirsute by nature, but what body hair he had was plucked. Further to hair, his head hair has been dyed black, which was also true of James Doe. The natural color was fairish, for James as well as Jeb. Both had very blue eyes, and skins that tanned well. Bone structure—Caucasian." Gus spoke from his chair, still waggling his feet.

Delia and Abe continued to cruise around the table, curiously unsettled by Jeb Doe, who was far from the most horrible body either had ever seen, yet had a power to impress beyond most victims of a violent end. His smell was oddly wrong, which Abe, better educated scientifically than Delia, put down to the beginnings of decay minus some of the usual murder concomitants—no blood, vomitus, open rot. Delia simply thought of it as an utterly bloodless murder, as murder by inches over months. Jeb's body didn't look moist or damp, and the head, with its black mop of hair, was a terrifying sight, the skull showing fully under its wrapping of veined skin, which of course gave it the death grin, emphasized by a pair of brown lips drawn back and up in a rictus. Appalling! The eyelids were closed, but Jeb had been gifted with dense, long dark lashes and arched, definitive brows. Nothing about the body suggested mummification—those, Abe and Delia had seen aplenty.

Finally, convinced Jeb Doe had nothing more to tell them, Abe and Delia thanked Gus and departed.

Detectives Division was a trifle scattered through the big police presence in County Services, but Carmine's (and Delia's) end was easier to access from the ME's domain by taking the first flight of stairs or elevator; she started up with a wave, leaving Abe to wend his way to his end alone, and grateful for that—with Delia, you never could tell where the conversation might go, and he wanted to hang on to his current thoughts undeflected. Her technique was oblique or tangential because she never saw things as mere mortals did, but that, of course, was exactly why Carmine so valued her. And, he amended, be fair, Abe Goldberg! You value her just as much.

Carmine had taken Desdemona and their sons to visit his old pal, the movie mogul Myron Mendel Mandelbaum, in Beverly Hills, and wasn't due back for three weeks. He had bribed Delia by giving her permission to work on a series of missing women that had been bothering her for months, and telling her that the usual crimes and suspects were safe in Abe's hands, so butt out unless Abe orders you in, okay? Since she had never dreamed of having a whole month to ride her hobbyhorse, Delia took the unspoken implication philosophically, and left Abe alone. The however-many Doe victims seemed likely to blow up into a big case, but it would continue to move at a snail's pace for some time; she wasn't *needed* there.

Abe collected Liam Connor and Tony Cerutti on his way through, then, settled in his desk chair, gave them the news that the four Johns and James Doe had a new member of the family, Jeb.

"Looks like Professor Soderstern's rape theory is out," said Liam sadly. "Are we back to homosexual?"

"If we are, no nancy-boys or pansies, understood? Homosexual or the prof's word, gay," said Abe severely. "However, castration says not, unless the perpetrator is a fanatical homo-hater."

"Then as a theory it stays in," Tony Cerutti said. He was young, handsome, and still a bachelor, related to Commissioner Silvestri, Captain Delmonico and about a third of the Holloman PD, and while he could be impatient and tactless, he was an excellent detective whose speciality was street crime. "The homo-haters hate the ones who hide their inclinations because they marry and have kids. Then about ten years later the wife wakes up that she's married to a queer—I can't use that either? Anyway, she's all screwed up, the kids are screwed up—yeah, castration can fit into the picture just fine if her father or her brother is—uh—offended. Can I say offended?"

"Don't be smart, Tony," Abe said calmly.

"You're talking about a different age group, Tony," said Liam, a quiet, understated man who formed an ideal contrast to Tony. Married, he never brought his domestic woes—if, indeed, he had any—to work, and had few prejudices. "The Doe victims are too young to have wives and kids. It does have to stay in our list of possibles, though. If a guy's wife knows he's homosexual and goes along with

12

it, okay, but if he has deceived her, the results when she finds out are bound to be messy in all kinds of ways."

"But messy to the point of a string of murders?" Abe looked skeptical. "I suggest we look at militantly anti-homosexual movements, including Neo-Nazis and assorted racial screwballs. Racial prejudice is usually linked to other social prejudices."

"We can't exclude a solitary psychopath," Liam said, frowning. "One at a time suggests one perpetrator."

"Definitely."

Tony's eyes were closed, a sign of deep thought. "*Who* done it won't be easy to find," he said in his attractively gravelly voice, "but *where* might be. Did Gus find evidence this latest Doe was gagged for long periods of time?"

"The mouth tissues were unbruised."

"So wherever he was held was soundproof twenty-four-seven for at least a couple of months. Shades of Kurt von Fahlendorf, huh? A lot of the work looking for *where* has been done relatively recently looking for Kurt," Tony said eagerly. "We need to take a look at those files, then we'll have a list of possibles."

"The Does must have screamed the place down," Liam said.

"But we have a list of places to check," said Abe, pleased. "With Delia head down, tail up on the trail of her Shadow Women, she won't mind lending us her plans and schematics of Holloman—they'll be a help too. If we were on a classic paper trail, I'd bring her in, but this is secret compartment stuff." Abe rubbed his palms together; his speciality was locating secret compartments.

Carmine Delmonico had a daughter old enough to be a pre-med student at Chubb's Paracelsus College, but he saw nothing of Sophia during school vacations. Her mother had left Carmine to marry the movie mogul Myron Mendel Mandelbaum while Sophia was still a baby; the marriage had quickly foundered, but not the bond between Myron and his step-daughter, with the result that Sophia had grown up with two fathers, each of whom adored her. It was generally understood that the girl would fall heir to Myron's empire one day, but in the meantime her inclinations led her in the direction of medicine; during school semesters she lived with Carmine and his second family in Holloman, and during vacations she lived with Myron on the West Coast. A brilliant, capable and down-to-earth young woman, she was sufficiently detached from her biological father's spell to see how she could best help him, and proceeded to do so.

After the birth of their second son, Alex, only fifteen months later than his brother, Julian, Carmine and Desdemona had run into trouble; Desdemona suffered a post-partum depression made worse by her streak of obsessiveness. A health administrator whom Carmine had met during a case, Desdemona refused to concede her weakness, and thus was slow recovering. At which point Sophia stepped in. His wife, said Sophia to Carmine, needed a long rest being pampered, and since she wouldn't be separated from her sons, they too must become a part of her rest-and-recreation holiday. The result was that Carmine took Desdemona, Julian and Alex to California at the end of July; they were to stay in Myron's enormous mansion for as long as Sophia felt necessary, though Carmine would have to return to Holloman when his annual leave was up. That Desdemona consented to such a colossal upheaval was hard evidence that, in her heart of hearts, she knew she needed a long rest. The little boys were no problem in that world of make-believe Myron could tap at will; with so many treats, excursions and people at their beck and call, they didn't need to badger Mommy, who could enjoy them without being bullied or dominated as she had been in Holloman.

Knowing all this, Delia could settle to her task in peace and quiet; the Shadow Women were elusive, and continued to defy analysis. Six cases considered open in only the loosest way, certainly not urgent; cases that enabled her to quit work on time every day, and count on free weekends. That was important at the moment, for Delia had made two new friends, and looked forward to her leisure hours very much.

*   *   *

She had met Jessica Wainfleet and Ivy Ramsbottom near Millstone Beach at the beginning of June, when they combined forces to rescue a cat stranded up a tree, yowling piteously. Of course when the creature was thoroughly satisfied that all three women had genuinely risked their necks on its behalf, it descended daintily of its own accord and vanished in a tabby blur. Jess and Ivy had laughed until they wept; Delia laughed until she had a stitch in her side. This feline practical joke had occurred very near Delia's condo, so they had repaired to the condo to drink sherry, send out for pizza, and make mutual discoveries about each other. Jess and Ivy had been friends for years. Each lived in the region; Jess had a small house a block behind Delia, and Ivy lived in Little Busquash, a cottage on the huge grounds of Busquash Manor, the great pile atop Busquash Peninsula just to Delia's west.

"But you outclass both of us, Delia," said Jess with a sigh. "I'd kill to have a condo right on the beach—top floor too!"

"A bequest from a rich aunt I didn't even know I had, some luck, and some useful relatives," Delia said happily. "Yes, I have everything I want."

"Except a husband?" Jess asked slyly.

"Oh, dear me, no! I don't want a husband. I like my life as it is—except that I am in need of two new chums."

All three women were spinsters; in America, very rare, even for lesbians. Though Delia sensed no undercurrents suggesting *that*, thank the Lord! It had broken up several new friendships, for Delia was conservative in her social attitudes, and disliked sex rearing its (to her) ugly, destructive head. Simply, she was one of those lucky women whose sexual urges were neither powerful nor frequent. Her self-image was of an eccentric, and she cultivated it assiduously, helped by a patrician Englishness she also made capital out of. The sooner after meeting her that people adjudged her eccentric, the better, as far as Delia was concerned.

Ivy Ramsbottom was an extremely tall woman, though not at all obese; her exact height she declined to give, but Delia put it at about Desdemona's height, six feet three, and deemed Ivy of the same athletic bent. There the comparison faded; Ivy had curly corn-gold hair, fine features and cornflower-blue eyes. She was so well-dressed that only Gloria Silvestri eclipsed her. Her casual walk-on-the-beach-in-early-summer costume was so perfect that not even a mad scramble after a cat had mussed it.

"Clothes are my trade," she said to Delia, manipulating her pizza slice so deftly that it wouldn't have dared drip on her sweater. "I manage my brother's clothing businesses."

"What sort of clothes?" asked Delia, who adored dressing only a little less than police work.

"All varieties these days, though he started out among the forgotten women, as he calls them—women who are too tall, too fat, or disproportionate in some way. Why should they be doomed to dismal or unfashionable things? A tiny segment of one percent of women wear clothes well anyway. I can only think of Gloria Silvestri, Mrs. William Paley Jr., and the Duchess of Windsor, though a number of women can pass muster, and a few almost make it to the top. However, the majority of women look like something the cat dragged in."

"I quite agree!" cried Delia.

"But most of all," said Ivy, continuing, "he's famous for his bridal gowns. I manage Rha Tanais Bridal in person."

"Rha Tanais is your brother?" Delia asked, squeaking.

"Yes," said Ivy, amused.

"Different name?"

"Ramsbottom is not euphonious," Ivy said with a grin. "Gown by Ramsbottom doesn't quite get there, somehow."

"Gown by Rha Tanais is far more exotic."

"And Rha Tanais *is* exotic," said Jess, laughing. "But come, Delia, why should a mere purveyor of clothes be more exciting than a psychiatrist like me or a detective like you?"

"The sheer fame, no other reason. Fame is exciting."

"I concede your point, it's a valid one."

Jess Wainfleet was forty-five years old, a slender woman with a good figure for clothes, since she wasn't busty; most men would have called her attractive rather than pretty or beautiful, despite her small, fine, regular features. Her black hair was cropped very short, her make-up restrained yet flattering, and her creamy-white skin endowed her with a certain allure. Her chief glory was her eyes, dark enough to seem black, large, and doed.

By rights Delia should have met Jess somewhere along the way, but she never had, a curious omission. Dr. Jessica Wainfleet was the director of the Holloman Institute for the Criminally Insane, always called the Holloman Institute (HI) for short. It had begun 150 years earlier as a jail for dangerous criminals, and so was off the beaten track to the north of route 133, set in fifteen acres walled in by bastions thirty feet high that were surmounted at intervals by watchtowers fifteen feet higher again. Soon the locals called it the Asylum, and though from time to time efforts were made to scotch the unofficial name, it remained the Asylum. In the explosion of infrastructure building that had gone on after the Second World War it underwent extensive renovations, and now housed two separate but allied activities; one was the prison itself, tailored for incarceration of men too unstable for life in an ordinary prison, and the other was a research facility in its own building. Jess Wainfleet headed the research facility.

"Brr!" said Delia, mock-shivering. "How do you work there and stay sane yourself?"

"Most of my work is clerical," said Jess apologetically. "I deal with lists, rosters, schedules. Interesting, however, that both of us are in a criminal field. I get scads of would-be PhDs wanting to interview this or that inmate, including a few who turn out to be journalists." She snorted. "Why do people assume you must be a fool if you sit behind a desk?"

"Because they equate a desk with a bureaucratic mind," said Delia, grinning, "whereas in actual fact," she went on in casual tones, "I imagine that at this moment you're being self-deprecating. There are some first-rate papers come out of HI—even detectives keep up with the literature on certain types among the criminally insane. Sorry, my friend, you're found out. Lists and rosters? Rubbish! You see and follow the progress of inmates."

Jess laughed, hands up in surrender. "I give in!"

"One of my jobs in Detectives is to chase bits of paper, I admit. Not a sexist directive, but self-appointed. I have a mind just made for statistics, plans, tabulations, the written word," Delia said, anxious to explain. "My boss, Captain Carmine Delmonico, is another who reads, though his forte is the oversized tome. We do notice the work of places like HI, and it's a real pleasure to meet you, Jess."

By the end of June the three were fast friends, and agreed that when 1970 rolled around, they would go on vacation together to some alluring destination they could wrangle about for months to come. They met at least twice a week to talk about nearly everything under the sun, their favorite meeting place Delia's condo. Little Busquash was a strenuous uphill walk for the other two, and Jess's place, she confessed, was wall to wall papers.

Why neither Jess nor Ivy had ever married was not discussed, though Delia thought it was because they, like she, lived inside their minds. If Delia had ever questioned her own taste in clothes she might have wondered why clothes weren't talked about either, but it simply didn't occur to her that Jess and Ivy avoided the subject of clothes out of affection for their new pal, who they soon saw was at perfect peace with the way she dressed.

Removing the 8 × 10-inch photographs from each of six very thin files, Delia lined them up on her desk in two rows of three, one row above the other, so her eyes could take in all of them at once. Each was a studio portrait, unusual in itself; most file photos of missing persons were blow-ups of smaller, casual shots. Under ordinary circumstances the portrait artist's name or studio would be indicated somewhere on the back of the paper: a rubber stamp, or an ink signature, or at the very least a pencil mark of some kind, But none of these photos held a clue as to its portrait artist, just an area on the back of each where a pencil mark had been erased, and never in the same spot—two were near the center, one high to the left, a random business. Paul Bachman and his team hadn't been able to discern a residuum.

1963 TENNANT, Margot. Thirtyish. Brown hair, brown eyes. Average height and shape. 3/23 Persimmon St., Carew.

1964 WOODROW, Donna. Thirtyish. Red hair, green eyes. Average height and shape. 222c Sycamore St., Holloman.

1965 SILBERFEIN, Rebecca. Thirtyish. Fair hair, blue eyes. Average height and shape. 12th fl., Nutmeg Insurance Bldg.

1966 MORRIS, Maria. Thirtyish. Black hair, black eyes. Average height and shape. 6 Craven Lane, Science Hill, Holloman.

1967 BELL-SIMONS, Julia. Thirtyish. Blonde, blue eyes. Average height and shape. 21/18 Dominic Rd., the Valley.

1968 CARBA, Elena. Thirtyish. Peroxide blonde, brown eyes. Average height and shape. 5b Paterson Rd., North Holloman.

Apart from their average height and shape and the fact that each looked to be about thirty years old, the six missing women had little in common physically. Hair and eyes went from near-black to near-white, with red and brown thrown in—or so the studio portraits indicated. 1965's Rebecca Silberfein was the fairest; her hair was a streaky natural flaxen blonde and her eyes so pale and washed out they looked whitish. Her nose wasn't long, but it was broad and beaky. Maria Morris, blackish of hair and eyes, had a very olive skin and a crookedly flat nose. 1964's Donna Woodrow had really green eyes, the color of spring leaves rather than the more usual muddy combat tinge, and her carroty hair was definitely not out of a dye bottle—no henna highlights. She had, besides, a fine crop of camouflaged freckles. None of them could be called beautiful, but none was unattractive, and none gave off a smell of the streets. The fashion of the times meant hair styles bouffant from back-combing, and heavily lipsticked mouths tended to hide their natural shape, but everyone connected with the case had reason to thank each woman's impulse to have a fine photograph of herself in color. Only why leave it behind?

The shape of the skull was similar in all six cases, suggesting Caucasian of Celtic or Teutonic kind. Allowing for the hair, the cranium looked to be very round, the brow broad and high, the chin neither prominent nor receding. About the cheekbones it was harder to tell, due to weight differences and, probably, how many molars were missing. Sighing, Delia pushed the photos together.

Nothing was known about these six women save their names, an approximate age, faces, and their last known addresses. Notification of missing person status had been extremely slow, depending as it had upon individuals engaged in an occupation wary of creating fusses—landlords.

Delia sighed again, aware that sheer over-familiarity with the case carried its own, very special, dangers.

Starting with Mary Tennant in 1963, each case followed an identical course. Tennant had rented the top floor of an old three-family house in Persimmon Street, Carew, very early in January of that year; she signed a one-year lease and paid, in cash, her first month's rent, her last month's rent, and a damages deposit of $100. If she had a car it must have been randomly parked on the street, as no one knew it or was aware of its existence. As a tenant she was remarkable in only one respect: she was extremely unobtrusive. No one ever heard her music or her TV or noises of her moving around; she passed people on the stairs in silence, and never seemed to entertain visitors. The details furnished by the rental agency were scant: she had said she was a secretary, gave two written references and a driver's license in verification, and presented so favorably in an anonymous kind of way that the agency never bothered checking. Most three-family houses saw the landlord living on the premises, but Carew was a student-resident district, so Tennant's landlord owned fifteen three-family houses, and used his realty business as a rental agency. When July's rent came due on the first of the month, Miss Tennant didn't pay it, and ignored the agency's reminders. This led to the discovery that Miss Tennant had no telephone—amazing! Several personal visits to her home by the clerk delegated to handle the affair never found Miss Tennant there, and thus matters stood when August arrived. She was now well and truly in arrears, and no one could remember seeing her since June.

The delinquency now attained a certain urgency, for early September saw the new academic year's influx of students pour into rental agencies looking for furnished accommodations: Miss Tennant had to go, and go fast. In mid-August the realtor went to the Holloman PD and requested that he be accompanied to Miss Tennant's apartment by a police officer, as enquiries suggested she hadn't been seen since June, and her rent was overdue.

Missing Persons leaped to the same conclusion the Realtor had, that Miss Margot Tennant would be found inside her apartment, very dead: but such was not the case. A faint and noisome smell proved to emanate from the refrigerator, where two-month-old fish and meat were in a slow decay. Miss Tennant's few possessions were removed from the premises and stored until garnishment proceedings saw them auctioned to pay rent and damages, the latter to the refrigerator. Said possessions were meager: a chcap radio, a black-and-white TV, a few clothes and a cigar box of imitation jewelry—no books, magazines, letters or other private papers. Thanks to the refrigerator, they didn't fetch enough to pay what the missing Mary Tennant owed.

Each year since had seen the same pattern. Locations were scattered all over Holloman County, but the renting was always at New Year or scant days after, and June the last rent paid by the missing woman before the six-to-eight-week period leading to a report with Missing Persons. The few things in common lent the task of finding the missing women a nightmare quality because the differences only pointed up the similarities.

Missing Persons had handed the Shadow Women to Detectives

and Carmine Delmonico when the third woman vanished from her studio flat on the twelfth floor of the Nutmeg Insurance building; now the total had escalated to six. "Ghost" was the sobriquet of a famous case, therefore couldn't be applied to the missing women, but Delia had suggested "Shadow" as apt, and the Shadow Women they became.

Something was going on, but what on earth could it be? The Commissioner, John Silvestri, found the case fascinating and kept tabs on it through his regular breakfast meetings with his detectives; since she was his blood niece, Delia yearned to be able to produce something brand-new to offer him, but thus far the pickings were nonexistent.

One promising hypothesis had been promulgated by Silvestri's wife, Gloria, who was the best-dressed woman in Connecticut. She decided that each woman was having cosmetic plastic surgery, and that in her own identity she was too well known not to be hounded and embarrassed if news of the surgery leaked. So she became a Shadow Woman for six months.

"As you well know, John," said Gloria, stroking her smooth, un-scragged throat, "any woman in that predicament would *die* sooner than confess, even if the price is a murder hunt."

"Yes, dear," said the Commissioner, dark eyes twinkling.

"The cops never find any clothes worth wearing, do they?"

"No, dear."

"Then that's it. They're all movie stars and socialites."

"I appreciate your submitting your theory to me in writing, dear, but why have you signed it Maude Hathaway?"

"I like the name. Gloria Silvestri sounds like old vaudeville programs and fish on Fridays."

Enquiries produced no professional cosmetic plastic surgeon operating in the vicinity of Holloman, though the Chubb Medical School had plastic surgeons aplenty, but attached to a famous burn unit. What Maude Hathaway's effort said was that no stone would go unturned.

* * *

Delia had long passed beyond practical considerations. Her mind had fixed on the reason why any reasonably attractive woman in her late twenties to early thirties would voluntarily isolate herself from her fellow human beings? Not that Delia was fool enough to exclude the possibility that obedience was ensured by a hostage situation like the kidnapping of a beloved man, woman or child, but that stretched the chain laterally as well as added to its length, and the more people were involved, the greater the chances of a situation falling apart. If not a hostage situation, then a death threat of some kind? Yet wouldn't a woman tortured by worry about a loved one have a telephone in her house? None of the Shadow Women had telephones. Was there a set of rules involved? That hinted at a genuine mania, psychopathy, an utter absence of morals, ethics, principles. Easy enough to impose for a short period, but six months of living under the rigid quasi-mathematical torture of rules was a very long time indeed unless the subject had first been exhaustively brainwashed, which seemed impossible. Had the Shadow Women been jailed for long enough to turn them into semi-zombies? No, because what people they had met had seen them as nice, conversable, *ordinary.* Prison left visible scars.

There was something Delia called a "gibber factor," though only a Jess Wainfleet would fully understand what she meant by the term. To Delia, no human being was truly inviolate, meaning that he or she could not be broken. Everyone had a breaking point wherein mental torture caused the mind to snap. The human being shattered into small pieces, unable to cope. In Delia's world, they became a "gibbering idiot"—her father's phrase—and resigned their hold on sanity. Six months of relentless mental torture would trigger the gibber factor, Delia was sure, yet what evidence was there that the Shadow Women had spent six months under relentless mental torture? The answer: there was no evidence. Each woman, she was sure, had commenced her strange six-month isolation voluntarily, and nothing left behind in the rented premises suggested that July and early August were any different from the earlier months.

That told Delia each of them owned an average intellect; that they were satisfyingly entertained by whatever their radio and television broadcast, and that if they read at all, it was newspapers, magazines and throw-away paperbacks. If they played solitaire or dominoes or did crosswords, any evidence was gone, and that probably meant they hadn't. Everything left behind was cheap, ordinary and uninspiring: over-the-counter medicines, supermarket cosmetics. After Mary Tennant, no perishable foods were left behind, and none of the six had left household cleaners or a stock of plastic bags. Had someone cleaned up? If so, no attention had been paid to fingerprints, for the same set was found all over each apartment, presumably the occupant's. None was on file with any large agency—a dead end.

Plenty of people vanished for a few months, then turned up unwilling to give an explanation; Missing Persons was full of files solved that way—by the subject—and from thence were sent for permanent storage to the Holloman PD repository out on Caterby Street. But no matter how innocent a disappearance might be, the file on closure was a fat one, thanks to biographical data accumulated as the investigation ground on, always too slowly to please the relatives. Whereas the Shadow Women were thin files, devoid of biographical data; none had a past, none seemed likely to have a future. Certainly no one had ever come forward with information about any Shadow Woman, and the date was rapidly approaching for 1969's victim to bob to the surface.

They rented at the beginning of January, paid first and last month's rent, vanished by the end of June, and were invaded by the letting agent in mid-August, two weeks after the last month's deposit was exhausted. Which was why Carmine had put her on the case. August. Who would 1969 be? By now every Realtor in the county was aware of the Shadow Women, and taking immense pains with the details of any rentals in early January. Two likely names had come up at the time, but neither turned out a possible candidate; whoever she was, her rental must have fallen down a crack. That was usually

24

the way, Delia reflected. Monday the fourth day of August today, a matter of ten to fifteen days to go. . . .

She glanced at her watch. An hour more, and she'd scoot. The pathetic little bunch of skinny files needed their photos back inside, but suddenly she decided to take them instead to the new police artist, Hank Jones.

Then she noticed a file Carmine had withdrawn from Caterby Street, and realized that he must have left it for her to look at as well. Yes, he'd clipped a note to it that said "Our most famous Missing Persons file." Oh, it was old! 1925. Sidetracked, Delia pulled it forward and opened it upon an 8 x 10 black-and-white head shot of a very beautiful young woman: Dr. Eleanor (Nell) Carantonio. An up and coming young anesthesiologist at the Holloman Hospital, Dr. Carantonio had failed to turn up to give a morning's scheduled anesthetics, and was never seen again.

A haughty, white-skinned face framed by fashionably shingled black hair, with dark eyes that managed to flash fire even in the picture. . . . No Shadow, this! An opinion borne out by reading the forty-four-year-old file, which revealed circumstances very different from the Shadows. Dr. Nell's profession was known, her life an open and unimpeachable book, and she was wealthy. Since she left no will, her nearest relative, a first cousin named Fenella (Nell) Carantonio, had had to wait over seven years to take possession of two million dollars and a huge mansion on the Busquash Peninsula. Eleanor—Nell. Fenella—Nell. No trace of the young woman's body had ever been found, from 1925 to this day. Age twenty-seven when she vanished. The second Nell was nine years her junior, and her only known relative.

No help or guidance there, said Delia to herself, picked up her photos and got to her feet. Off to the ME's air-conditioning and the artist the ME's and PD shared. As she walked Delia continued to think about the most baffling puzzle of them all—why did the Shadow Women have studio portraits of themselves? And why had the portraits been left behind?

She was convinced the women were dead, but no bodies had ever come to light, and she had excellent reason to know that even the most bizarre methods of getting rid of bodies had been thoroughly explored. If a body were considered as over a hundred pounds of meat and fat plus some really big bones, then the disposal of that body was every killer's worst nightmare.

Sadly (for Delia was a woman who adored flamboyance) what her case seemed to be boiling down to was rather humdrum. A killer who prowled in search of shy, retiring, very ordinary women, and, having found one, did whatever his fantasy prompted before taking her life, then managed to dispose of her invisibly. The rental of apartments was a year-round activity, and in a student town many of them were let furnished. The dates were *his* kinks, had nothing to do with the women. Delia was obliged to admit to herself that she was automatically drawn to the more extravagant explanations of these rare cases that made no sense. In the cold blast of air that assaulted her as she went around in ME's revolving doors, she decided that the Shadow Women would end in a shabby, dreary manner satisfying no one. What an indictment her adjectives and adverbs were! Humdrum, shabby, dreary. Lives were being taken, and she was cataloguing the method of their taking on a scale graduated in degrees of glamour! Well, she knew why: it kept Delia the detective on her toes, whipped up energy, enthusiasm. Flippant it may be, but as a technique it worked a treat.

Ginny Toscano had attained sixty, and was retiring, which led to some quiet cop cheers; when she had started out as the police artist the work had been far more, to use her word, "civilized." Some of what she was asked to do these days she found beyond her stomach or her talents, for the world—and her job—had changed almost out of recognition. And the very moment that a new artist was hired, Ginny used up the time until her birthday on annual leave.

The big studio and its accompanying laboratory/kitchen had been tastefully decorated in shell-pink, institution oak and off-white, but when Delia entered she found hardly a morsel of Ginny remained. I hope, thought Delia, that the poor dear is having a wonderful time in Florence!

The walls were almost completely papered in unframed posters of landscapes not from this Earth, their skies transected by sweeping curves of what looked like Saturn's rings, or holding two suns as well as several moons, while the foregrounds were soaring multicolored crystals, or weird mountains, or erupting volcanoes, or cascades of rainbow-riddled fluid. One depicted a robot warrior mounted on a robot *Tyrannosaurus rex* at full trundle, and another was the famous half-buried Statue of Liberty from *Planet of the Apes*. Fabulous! thought Delia, bewitched.

In the midst of this other-worlds environment a thin young man was working on the top sheet of a slab of paper with a dark German pencil, his models clipped to the top of his architect's table, well above the paper block: a series of photographs of Jeb Doe, with one of James Doe at either end of the row.

"Bugger!" Delia cried. "Lieutenant Goldberg beat me to it."

He looked up, grinning. "Hi, Delia."

"Any chance you can squeeze me in too, Hank?"

"For you, baby, I'd squeeze to death." He put his pencil down and swiveled his high chair to face her. "Sit ye doon."

In Delia's estimation he had one of the most engaging faces she had ever seen—impish, happy, radiating life—and his eyes were unforgettable—greenish-yellow, large, well spaced and opened, and surrounded by long, dense black lashes. His negroidly curly hair was light red and his skin color that of a southern Chinese. His head was big but his face, delicately fine-featured, tapered from a high, wide brow to a pointed chin; a dimple was gouged in each cheek, this last a characteristic that made Delia weak at the knees. *He* made Delia weak at the knees—Platonic, naturally!

If it were impossible to gauge all the kinds of blood in his veins, that went doubly so for his voice, unexpectedly deep and quite lacking an accent that pinned his origins down; he didn't roll his r's like an American, clip his word endings like an Oxonian, drawl his a's like an Australia, reverse his o's and u's like a Lancastrian, twang like a hillbilly—she could go on and on, never reaching an answer. To hear him talk was to hear traces of every accent, adding up to none. No arguments, Hank Jones bore investigating.

Delia laid out her six photographs on a vacant corner of the bench at her side; Hank wheeled over to study them closely.

"I'm not sure that I need a drawing," she said, "as much as I need an expert opinion. The idiotic hair-do fashion makes it hard to assess the shape of the cranium in the first three, but it seems to me that it's likely to be quite round. In fact, I came to the conclusion that if I were to go on bone structure alone, in all six cases I could be looking at the same skull, despite the differing noses, eyebrows and cheeks. Actually, I want you to shoot down one of my more potty ideas— that these six women are in fact all the same woman, someone highly skilled in the use of prostheses and stage makeup. If her true eyes were light in color, she could achieve any color with contact lenses, and wigs and hair dyes in the Sixties are a piece of cake. So tell me I'm baying at the moon, please! Shoot me down!"

His own eyes lifted from the six photographs to rest on her face thoughtfully, and with considerable affection. He didn't know why he had taken one look at her in the parking lot and liked her so much, save that his eccentric soul recognized a partner in crime. That day she had been wearing a tie-dyed organdy dress in strident scarlet admixed with mauve and yellow; it was miniskirted at midthigh and displayed her grand piano legs clad in bright blue tights rendered queasily opalescent by the sheerness of their weave. Though in Hank's judgment the outfit's finishing touch was a pair of black lace-up nun's shoes, which she told him owned both comfort and pursuit power. One day, he vowed, he would paint well enough to capture the character and lineaments of her face, from the mop of frizzy, brassy hair to the mascara-spiked lashes and the beefy nose; but how could he ever manage the mouth, so lipsticked that little streaks of red crept up into the fissures around it and made it look as if sewn shut with bloody sutures? Though she flirted with grotesquerie, she deftly avoided it by the force of her personality. Yes, she was definitely his kind of eccentric—only where did fact leave off and fantasy begin? Hank suspected that might take a long time to discover. In the meantime, the journey was going to be fun.

Today something had gotten her down. He had never seen her so dismally dressed. Wasn't she enjoying life without the Captain?

After fifteen minutes by the clock, Hank put the photos in a pile and handed them to Delia.

"Very similar skulls, but each one is different," he said. "I can see why you concluded they're the same skull, so I may as well start with the matches. The ethnic group is northwestern European, with eyes set the same distance apart and near-identical orbits. Jeez, how I hate the air brush! I had to zap each one with my X-ray vision to find the true edge of the orbit, but I did, baby, I did! Eyes being the windows of the soul. . . . You based your same-skull hypothesis on the orbits and the zygomatic arches. But—*but*—the nasal bone and cartilage structure is different skull to skull—the width of the mouth—the height of the external auditory meatus—and the maxillary bone sprouting the upper teeth. The lower down the face, the more marked the differences become. Tendons and ligaments attach to their sites on the skull in highly individual ways. The differences in faces always go clear down to bone somehow. I hate to be flyin' the Spitfire put your fuselage on the ground, honey-baby, but you are smokin' wreckage in a Flanders field."

He thrust his face close to hers and dropped his voice to a whisper. "Maybe I did shoot you down on the skull, but I'd swear on my collection of Blackhawk comics that the same guy snapped all the photos—he's wall to wall idiosyncrasies with a camera."

"Really?"

"My Captain Marvel comics too it's the same guy, and he ain't no professional. Good camera, no lighting but Nature."

"No one has spotted that," Delia said, very grateful. "We did think each woman had her portrait done by someone rather fly-by-night, but it's a hugely over-populated field, photography, and we thought each one different enough."

"Not in the ways that count," Hank said positively.

"Oh, this is wonderful! It really, really helps."

"How?" Hank asked, eager to learn.

"I won't bore you by going on at length about how tenuous our theories have been—we've felt at times like dogs chasing their own tails. All that link these six disappearances are conjectures a good lawyer could demolish in a minute as wishful thinking. There *are* common elements: each follows the same calendar, was noticed for six months, then vanished leaving a few cheap possessions behind and the landlord out of pocket for two months' rent. That's it!" Delia clutched at her hair, growling. "However, Hank, there's a smell about it that tells us the Shadow Women *are* linked, that foul play *has* been done, and that only one perpetrator is involved. In reality, they're six entirely separate cases with no tangible evidence connecting any one of them to any other. Each woman left just one unusual thing behind—a studio portrait of herself. Hank, you've broken fresh ground for us, you've told us that the same person took all six Shadow portraits. As a lead it mightn't go anywhere, but that's not what's so important about it. Its significance lies in the fact that it tells us the six cases are definitely linked, that the similarities are neither accidental nor coincidental."

She waved the photos triumphantly. "Dear boy, you're an absolute brick! An idiosyncratic amateur photographer, at that! Thank you, thank you, thank you!"

And she was gone.

Hank stared after her for a moment, cast into the state of minor fugue Delia inspired in many. Smiling and shrugging, he wheeled his high chair back to the sloping drawing board and its slab of paper. Working on the Jeb Doe skull because his was the freshest corpse, Hank found the 6B pencil he had worn to the required slant of tip, and chuckled to himself.

From A to Z in a second, he thought: stripping the flesh off Delia's heads to come at a skull, now laying flesh on Jeb's skull. Man, what a cool way to earn a living! Sure beat imparting a white sparkle to teeth in an advertising agency, and how close had he come to that, huh? Who said learning anatomy from cadavers was a waste of time compared to a life class? If he hadn't snuck into the Med School dissecting labs, he wouldn't be here at all.

TUESDAY, AUGUST 5, 1969

T hough the darkness was too stygian to permit his having any idea of the size of the place he was in, Abe Goldberg, sensitive in such matters, knew that it was immense. He was sitting in one of a row of what felt like theater seats, thrust there by the willowy young man who had met him at the front door; said willowy young man had led him through an incredible house, down a ramp, opened a door onto this night, and whispered "Wait!"

A voice spoke, weary and resigned. "Light it."

Part of the blackness became a purple pool that illuminated a huge gold throne occupied by a naked, sexless dummy, and spread far enough to reveal the inner edge of a couch to one side.

Silence reigned. Someone heaved a melodramatic sigh, then the weary voice spoke again.

"This may come as a shock, Peter, but the truth is that you couldn't light your own farts."

A different set of vocal cords screeched, the noise overridden by His Weariness, who went on as if uninterrupted.

"I know this is a musical comedy, Peter, but this song-to-be is curtain down on Act One. It's the hit of the show—or so the authors insist." The voice gathered power. "King Cophetua is smitten, Peter darling, smitten. *Smitten!* Servilia the slave girl has just told him to fuck off, danced away warbling for her shepherd-boy with no notion in her empty little head that he's really an Assyrian wolf using her to descend on King Cophetua's fold. Are you following me? Have you gotten the general gist? King Cophetua is blue, blue, *blue!* That doesn't mean you have to light him blue, but why in Ishtar's name have you lit him purple? What you've created looks like Beelzebub's boudoir drenched in sicked-up grape juice! Mood, Peter darling, mood! This isn't lighting, it's blighting! And I am vomit-green!"

The screeches had dwindled to sobs of distress, the dominant voice seeming to feed off them until it lost all its weariness. Suddenly it shouted, "Lights up!" and the entire space in which Abe was marooned sprang into glaring relief.

Abe stared at what he presumed was an entire stage in nude disarray, a full forty feet high; its upper half was a grid of rods, rails, booms, rows of lights on thin steel beams, gangways, and walls solid with boxes, machinery, rods. The wings, he was fascinated to discover, communicated as one space with the back of the stage. His mechanical eye discerned hydraulic rams—expensive! No amateur playhouse, this, but the real thing, and constructed with a disregard for cost that put it ahead even of some major Broadway playhouses. Though it wasn't a theater; audience room was limited to perhaps fifty stall seats.

The owner of the voice was approaching him, the willowy man at his side, no doubt to fill him in. Abe gazed in awe.

Easily six and a half feet tall, he was clad in a black-and-white Japanese kimono of water birds in a lily pond, and wore backless slippers on his feet; gaping open as his legs scissored stiffly, the kimono revealed close-fitting black trousers beneath. His physique was too straight up and down to be called splendid, yet he wasn't at all obese. What my Nanna would have called "solid" thought Abe: a basketballer, not a footballer. Feet the size of dinghies. Tightly curly corn-gold hair, close-cropped, gave Abe a pang of envy; Betty had finally managed to push him into growing his fair, thinning hair long enough to cover his ears and neck, and he hated this modern look. Now here was an internationally famous guy sporting short-back-and-sides! This guy had no wife, so much seemed sure. His facial features were regular and were set in an expression suggesting a kind nature, though looks were treacherous; Abe reserved judgement. The eyes were fine and large, an innocent sky-blue.

How, wondered Abe, am I to reconcile his aura of kindness with his waspish tongue? Except, of course, that the rules of conduct in the theater world were rather different from others, he suspected. The artistic temperament and all that.

Mr. Willowy was now moving toward the weeping form of Peter the lighting blighter, clucking and shushing as he went.

On his feet, Abe stuck out his right hand. "Lieutenant Abe Goldberg, Holloman PD," he said.

One huge hand engulfed his in a warm shake, then the Voice sat down opposite Abe by pulling a fused section of seats around. Something flashed as he moved; Abe blinked, dazzled. He wore a two-carat first water diamond in his right ear lobe, but no other jewelry, not even a class ring.

"Rha Tanais," he said.

"Forgive a detective's curiosity, sir, but is Rha Tanais your original name?"

"What an original way to put it! No, Lieutenant, it's my professional name. I was christened Herbert Ramsbottom."

"Christened?"

"Russian rites. Ramsbottom was probably Raskolnikov before Ellis Island, who knows? I ask you, Herbert *Ramsbottom?* High school was a succession of nicknames, but the one everybody liked best was Herbie Sheep's Ass. Luckily I wasn't one of those poor, despised outsiders picked sometimes to literal death." The blue eyes gleamed impishly. "I had wit, height, good humor—and Rufus. Even the worst of the brute brigade had enough brain to understand I could make him a laughing-stock. I racked my own brain for a new monicker, but none sounded like *me* until, as I browsed in the library one day, I chanced upon an atlas of the ancient world. And there it was!"

"What was?" Abe asked after a minute's silence, appreciating the fact that (a rare treat in a detective's working life) he was in the presence of a true raconteur with considerable erudition.

"Family tradition has it that we originated in Cossack country around the Volga and the Don, so I looked at the lands of the ancient barbarians to find that the Volga was called the Rha, and the Don was called the Tanais. Rha Tanais—perfect! And that really is how I found my new name," said Rha Tanais.

"You'd have to be a professor of classics to guess, sir."

"Yes, it's a mystery to the world," Rha Tanais agreed.

Abe glanced across to where Mr. Willowy was concluding his ministrations to Peter the lighting blighter, and looking as if he was about to join them. This remorseless glare gave the lie to Abe's impression of youth; Mr. Willowy was an extremely well preserved fortyish. At six feet he seemed short only when he stood next to Rha Tanais, but no other word than "willowy" could describe his body or the way he moved it. Coppery red hair, swamp-colored eyes, and wearing discreet but effective eye makeup. Beautiful hands that he used like a ballet dancer. Such he had probably been.

"Come and meet Lieutenant Abe Goldberg!" Tanais hollered, muting his tones as Mr. Willowy arrived. "Lieutenant, this is my irreplaceable other half, Rufus Ingham." Suddenly he burst into bass-baritone song, with Rufus Ingham singing a pure descant.

"We've been together now for forty years, and it don't seem a daaay too long!"

A bewildered Abe laughed dutifully.

"Rufus didn't come into the world so euphoniously named either," Tanais said, "but his real name is a secret."

Rufus cut him short, not angrily, but quite firmly—which one was the boss? "No, Rha, we're not talking to Walter Winchell, we're talking to a police lieutenant. *Honestly!* My name was Antonio Carantonio."

"Why try to hide that, Mr. Tanais?"

"Rha, my name is Rha! You mean you don't know?"

"Know what?"

"This is *The House!* Carantonio is *The Name!* Abe—I may call you Abe?—the story has passed into Busquash mythology by now, they even tell it on the tour buses. I'm sure the Holloman police department must have files in the plural on it. In 1925, before Rufus and I were ever thought of, the owner of this house and a two million dollar fortune vanished from the face of the earth," said Rha Tanais in creepy tones. "After seven years she was declared dead, and Rufus's mother inherited. The original owner was Dr. Nell Carantonio, and Rufus's mother was yet another Nell Carantonio."

"I'm Carantonio because I'm illegitimate," Rufus interjected. "I have no idea who my father is—my mother put him down on my birth certificate as first name, Un, and second name, Known."

Rha took up the narrative. "Fenella—Rufus's mother—died in 1950, but unlike the original Nell, she did leave a will. Antonio Carantonio IV—Rufus—got the lot." He heaved one of his sighs, both hands flying into the air. "Can you *imagine* it, Abe? There we were, a couple of sweet young things, with a positive barn of a house and carloads of money! Fenella had quintupled the first Nell's fortune *and* kept the house in repair. Our heads had always been stuffed with dreams and we'd made good beginnings, but suddenly we had the capital and the premises to do whatever we wanted."

"And what did you want?" Abe asked.

"To design. Glamorous clothes for so-called unattractive women, first. Then bridal gowns. After that came stage costumes, and finally production design. Wonderful!" Rha caroled.

"Wonderful," Rufus echoed on a sigh.

"Let's get out of here and have an espresso," said Rha.

Shortly thereafter Abe found himself drinking superb coffee in a small room off the restaurant-sized kitchen; its chairs were upholstered in fake leopard skin and were replete with gilded carvings, the drapes were black-and-gold-striped brocade, and the floor was a black-spotted fawn marble. All it needs, thought Abe, is Mae West.

"The nice thing about Fenella—Nell the second—is that she approved of gays," said Rufus. "She was a good mother."

"Stop chattering, Rufus! Let the man state his business."

Abe did so succinctly, unsure whether rumors about the six Doe bodies had ever penetrated as high in homosexual strata as this one, since neither he nor his team had ever approached Rha and Rufus, but all worlds gossip. "I'm going to have at least two likenesses of the later Does shortly, and I'm here to ask if you'd mind looking at them," Abe concluded. "One thing has emerged—that the Does were what my niece calls drop-dead gorgeous. Expert opinion says they weren't—er—gay, but they were all around twenty years of age, and likely to be seeking careers on the stage, or in film, or maybe in fashion. Mrs. Gloria Silvestri said I should talk to you."

Rha's face lit up. "Isn't she *something?* She makes all her own clothes, you know, so I take her around the fabric houses. Unerring taste!"

"Let the man state his business, Rha," said Rufus softly, and took over. "I know what she was thinking. We always have scads of young things passing through and learning the trade. At seventy miles from New York City, Holloman is an ideal jumping-off place before hitting the urban nightmare. Girls and boys both, we see them. They stay anything from a week to a year with us, and I'm glad you found us first rather than last. We might be able to help, but even if it turns out we can't, we can keep our ears and eyes open."

Down went his empty coffee cup; Abe stood. "May I come back with my sketches when our police artist has finished?"

"Of course," said Rha warmly.

On his way to the front door, Abe had a thought. "Uh—is Peter the lighting blighter okay?"

"Oh, sure," said Rufus, he seemed taken aback that anyone should remember a lighting blighter. "He's sucking a stiff Scotch."

"Did you add the theater onto the house?"

"We didn't need to." Rufus opened the front door. "There was a ballroom out the back nearly as big as the Waldorf—I ask you, *a ballroom?* Debutantes running amok in Busquash."

"I daresay they did back in the late 1800s and early 1900s," said Abe, grinning, "but I can see why you gentlemen would find a theater stage far handier. Thanks for the time and the coffee."

From a window the two partners in design watched Abe's slight figure walk to a respectable-looking police unmarked.

"He's very, very smart," said Rufus.

"Definitely smart enough to tell a sequin from a spangle. I suggest, Rufus my love, that we be tremendously co-operative and astronomically helpful."

"What worries me is that we won't know anything!" Rufus said with a snap. "Gays aren't the flavor of the month."

"Or the year. Never mind, we can but try." Came one of those explosive sighs; Rha's voice turned weary again. "In the meantime, Rufus, we have a pool of sicked-up grape juice to deal with." He stopped dead, looking thunderstruck. "*Gold!*" he roared. "Gold, gold, gold! When the richest king in the world is blue from unrequited love, he does a Scrooge McDuck and rolls in gold, gold, gold!"

"Open treasure chests everywhere!"

"A waterfall of gold tinsel!"

"He'll have to roll on a monstrous bean-bag of gold coins, that won't be easy to make look convincing—"

"No, not a bean-bag! The pool of gold dust at the bottom of the tinsel waterfall, numb-nuts! He *bathes* in his sorrow!"

Rufus giggled. "He'll have to wear a body suit, otherwise the tinsel will creep into every orifice."

Rha bellowed with laughter. "So what's new about that for Roger Dartmont? Shitting gold is one up on shitting ice-cream."

Still chuckling at their shared visions of Broadway's ageing star, the immortal Roger Dartmont, Rha Tanais and Rufus Ingham went back to work, imbued with fresh enthusiasm.

Abe went straight to see Hank Jones as soon as he returned from his interview with the design duo.

"How's it going, Hank?"

The pencil kept moving. "A proposition, sir?"

"Hit me."

The pencil went down. Hank flipped his left hand at two drawings of naked skulls side by side on his drawing board. "A black-and-white pencil sketch won't do it, sir. James and Jeb will have different faces, but the sameness of the medium will diminish the differences and make the similarities overwhelming. They're very much the same type, what I call a Tony Curtis face. I have to play up each man's individuality! D'you get my drift, sir? Tony Curtis is a type."

"Make it Abe, Hank. You're as much a professional in your line as I am in mine, so formality's not necessary." What he couldn't say was that he was beginning to realize their incredible luck in finding Hank Jones, clearly too good for the job's pay and status. Not only was he an unusually gifted artist, he was also a young man who *thought*. In September he'd have to pow-wow with Carmine and Gus, then they could go to Silvestri to have Hank's status and pay improved. "What do you suggest?" he asked.

"That I paint them rather than draw them," said Hank eagerly. "Oh, not in oils—acrylic will do, it dries at once. Each Doe would have his natural color of hair, whatever the fashionable cut was that year, and the right skin tones. The eyes I'd do as blue, like Jeb's." Hank drew a breath. "I know speed is a part of my job description, but honest, I'm fast, even in paint. If you had a color portrait of Jeb and James at least, people's memories would trigger better, I know they would. But it does mean a few extra days."

Abe patted the artist on the back, no mean accolade. "Right on, Hank! That's a brilliant idea." He smiled, his grey eyes crinkling at their corners. "If you have a thoroughbred in the stables, don't hitch him to a wagon. Use your talents, that's what they're there for. Take as long as it takes."

"For Jeb, by Friday," said Hank, delighted.

On the dungeon front, things were gloomier. Liam and Tony were wading through possible sites for a dungeon, but after Abe's visit to Busquash Manor, they crossed it off their list; those gargantuan roofs hid not underground cells but a full-sized theatrical stage, complete with a trap room and pit below stage level. The whole area was in use, the acoustics superb—no, Busquash Manor was not a possible. When Kurt von Fahlendorf had been kidnapped they had ransacked Holloman County for a soundproof cellar, which made this new quest much easier. Most structures were listed, had been inspected then, and could be inspected again. The chamber where von Fahlendorf had languished had been filled in since. No local builder had installed a soundproof studio anywhere, and what new cellars had come into existence were just ordinary basements. War relics like gun emplacements hadn't changed, and theaters in a try-out city like Holloman containing three repertory companies and a faculty of drama were, like Busquash Manor, in constant use.

"This sucks," said Tony to Abe.

"It's here somewhere," Abe said stubbornly.

"Needles in haystacks," said Liam, as disgruntled as Tony.

"Paint on, Hank Jones," said Abe under his breath.

SATURDAY, AUGUST 9, 1969

I vy Ramsbottom had invited Delia to "a late afternoon and entire evening of entertainment"
at Busquash Manor, and Delia was bewil-
dered. The invitation had come out of the blue last Thursday, which
didn't give a girl much time to sort out what to wear when the hosts
were Rha Tanais and Rufus Ingham. Oddly, it had been Jess Wainfleet who explained it yesterday over lunch at the Lobster Pot.

"No, Delia, you mustn't decline," Jess had said.

"I think I must. I don't know Ivy's brother and his friend from a
bar of soap—if I came, it would look as if my reason for doing so was
vulgar curiosity."

"Believe me, it wouldn't. The short notice is unusual, except that
Ivy tells me the new musical Rha's designing is hopeless. As they're
party animals, Rha and Rufus throw a party on the slightest of ex-
cuses, and they like to mix and match their invitation list," Jess said,
sipping sparkling mineral water. "I met them first at one of their par-
ties, and Rufus, honoring my profession, I suppose, told me that every
social get-together needed a certain amount of abrasion to go well.
The recipe called for one stranger and several guests who set people's
backs up a little. Drop them into the mixture, said Rufus, and you
were guaranteed to have a memorable party." Jess grimaced. "My senior staff almost inevitably form the several guests who set people's
backs up—they're a serious bunch who only attend to please me."

"How extraordinary!" Delia stared at her friend, intrigued. "If
you know all that, why oblige your hosts?"

41

"Because they're two of the sweetest guys in the world, I love them dearly, and I love Ivy most of all." The big dark eyes held a softer look than Delia was used to seeing; clearly it mattered to Jess that her motives be understood. "I'm very aware of my less admirable personality traits, the worst of them being an abnormal degree of emotional detachment—common in obsessive-compulsives of my kind. My affection for Ivy, Rha and Rufus is important to me, I'd rather make them happy than please myself. So I push my senior staff to attend Busquash Manor festivities, even if they dislike it."

"It rather sounds to me," said Delia shrewdly, "as if you dislike your senior staff."

Jess's laugh was a gurgle, the eyes brimmed with mirth. "Oh, bravo, Delia! You're absolutely right. Besides, a Rha-Rufus party is a joy, and once they're here, my HI bunch wallow in them. What they hate is being yanked out of their routines."

"Then they're obsessive-compulsives too."

"They sure are! But please come, Delia."

"What should I wear?"

"Whatever you like. Ivy and I will wear eveningified things—Busquash Manor is fully air-conditioned. Rha and Rufus will be in black trousers and sweaters, but Nicolas Greco will look like an advertisement for Savile Row and Bob Tierney will be in black tie. My bunch will dress down rather than up, and favor white—a mute protest at being pressured into attending."

As a result of this lunch, Delia's curiosity was so stimulated that she phoned an acceptance taken by a secretary, and ransacked her several wardrobes for something interesting to wear to what sounded like a sartorial free-for-all. She *needed* a diversion.

The Shadow Women had repaid the strenuous efforts of her last few days with absolutely nothing. The photographer responsible for the portraits hadn't come to light, a sign of the times: the days when such a person had a shop kind of studio were gone save for an established very few. Nowadays prosperity was so widespread that any would-be artist could buy an excellent single lens reflex camera and advertise in the Yellow Pages. The difference in cost for wedding photos between one of these enterprising photographers and an established professional was slowly forcing the latter out of the market. So most of Delia's time had been frittered away in phoning the would-be photographers of the Yellow Pages. Some had come into County Services to look at the portraits, but none had admitted to creating them.

Driving up in her own red Mustang, Delia found that parking space was available within the imposing mansion's grounds, an expanse of tar marked with white lines and conveniently hidden by a tall hedge from the kind of landscaped garden that required no specialist attention or concentrated work: lawns, shrubs, an occasional tree. Once Busquash Manor had stood in ten acres on the peak ridge of the peninsula between Busquash Inlet and Millstone Beach, but at the turn of the nineteenth into the twentieth century it had been subdivided, and four acres sold off in acre-lot parcels. The house itself was enormous, though the attic windows of its third storey suggested this had been a servants' domain, leaving the family with two flights of stairs to climb at most. Excluding the third floor, Delia guessed there might originally have been as many as fifteen bedrooms.

She was more used to looking at the rear end of Busquash Manor, as this faced Millstone, where her condo sat at beachfront. A far less pleasing view, incorporating as it did an ugly acreage of sloping roofs that reminded her of a movie-theater complex in an outdoor shopping mall. From Ivy she had learned that the enormity of the roofs came from a genuine theater inside, mostly a gigantic stage. The house itself was built of limestone blocks and was plentifully endowed with tall, broad windows; where it really belonged, she decided, was at Newport, Rhode Island.

Inside, it revealed the unique eye and taste of its owners, though what in a lesser eye and taste would have been vulgarity here was lifted to a splendor that took the breath away. Had she known it, every piece of furniture and every drape had once adorned a Broadway stage in days when props had been custom-made by true artisans, and only the finest materials had been used. The colors were rich, sumptuous, and always uncannily *right*; there were chairs shaped like sphinxes, like lions or winged Assyrian bulls; walls turned out to be vast mirrors that reflected on and on into a near-infinity; one room was completely lined in roseate, beaten copper. Mouth agape, Delia trod across marble or mosaic floors, gazed at priceless Persian carpets, and wondered if she had gone through the looking glass into a different universe. No stranger to the trappings of wealth or to palatial houses, Delia still felt that Busquash Manor was an impossible fantasy.

Her nose was about level with Rha Tanais's navel; she had to tilt her head far back to see his face, lit from within by what she sensed were warmly positive emotions. He gave her a delicate crystal glass of white wine; one sip told her it was superb.

"Darling, you are magnificent!" he cried. "How dare Ivy hide you? Come and meet Rufus."

Who was already watching her, a stunned look on his handsome face. Organza frills upon frills in magenta, acid-yellow, orange and rose-pink. In shock, he stumbled to his feet.

"Delia darling, this is my other half, Rufus Ingham. Rufus, this is Ivy's friend Delia Carstairs. Isn't she magnificent?"

"Don't ever change!" Rufus breathed, kissing her hand. "That dress is *gorgeous!*" He drew her toward a striped Regency sofa and sat down beside her. "I *have* to know, darling—where do you buy your clothes?"

"The garment district in New York City," she said, glowing, "but once I get them home, I pull them apart and tart them up."

"It's the tarting up does it every time. What an eye you have—totally individual. No one else could ever get away with that dress, but you conquer it like Merman a song." He smiled at her, his eyes caressing. "Dear, delicious Delia, do you know anyone here?"

"Ivy and Jess, but I seem to have arrived ahead of them."

"Fabulous! Then you belong to me. D'you see the decrepit old gentleman posing under the painting of Mrs. Siddons?"

Rapidly falling hopelessly (but Platonically) in love with Rufus, Delia studied the elderly, debonair man indicated. "I feel I ought to know him, but his identity eludes me."

"Roger Dartmont, soon to sing the role of King Cophetua."

"*The* Roger Dartmont?" Her jaw dropped. "I didn't realize he was so—um—up in years."

"'Tis he, Delicious Delia. God broke the mold into a million pieces, then Lucifer came along and glued him together again, but in the manner Isis did Osiris—no phallus could be found."

Delia giggled. "Difficult, if your name is Roger." Her gaze went past Roger Dartmont. "Who's the lady who looks like a horse eating an apple through a wire-netting fence?"

"Olga Tierney—a wife, darling. Her husband's a producer of Broadway plays, including the abortion we're working on at the moment. That's him, the one in black tie who looks like a jockey. They used to live in Greenwich, now they have one of the islands off our own Busquash Point." Rufus's mobile black brows arched. "It's a gorgeous place—or would be, if Olga weren't one of the beige brigade." His voice dropped. "Rumor hath it that Bob Tierney is overly fond of under-age girls."

"An island," said Delia thoughtfully, "would be excellent."

Something in her tone made Rufus's khaki-colored eyes swing to Delia's face, expression alert. "Excellent?" he asked.

"Oh, privacy, sonic isolation, all sorts," she said vaguely.

"Delicious Delia, what does a ravishingly dressed lady with an Oxford accent do for a living in an Ivy League town?"

"Well, she might discuss Shakespeare with Chubb undergrads, or run a swanky brothel, or operate an electron microscope, or"—a wide grin dawned as she paused dramatically—"she might be a sergeant of detectives with the Holloman police."

"Fantastic!" he cried.

"I'm not undercover, Rufus dear, but I'm not advertising my profession either," she said severely. "You may tell Rha, but I would prefer to meet everyone else as—oh, the proprietress of that swanky brothel or that expert on Shakespeare. Once people know I'm a cop, they become defensive and automatically censor their conversation. Would you have been so frank if you'd known?"

A slow smile appeared. "For my sins, probably yes. I have a lamentable tendency to voice what I'm thinking—isn't that well expressed? I'm a parrot, I collect ways of saying things. But seriously, mum's the word. However, your desirability mushrooms with every new snippet of information you feed me. I *love* unusual people!" His face changed. "Are you here on business?"

She looked shocked. "Oh, dear me, no! I wouldn't be here at all if I didn't know Ivy. My police cases are as decrepit as Roger, I'm afraid, though I admit that a detective never doffs her deerstalker hat either. So when I hear something interesting, I file it in my mind. We have lots of old cases we can't close."

"Age," he said with great solemnity, "is the worst criminal of them all, yet perpetually escapes punishment. Ah! Enter the Kornblums! Ben and Betty. She's the one in floor-length mink, he's the one with the knuckle-duster diamond pinky ring. Betty is the sole reason to ban air-conditioning—it enables her to wear mink indoors in August. It wouldn't be so bad if she weren't addicted to two-toned mink—the *spitting* image of a Siamese cat."

"Does she keep Siamese cats?" Delia asked.

"Two. Sun Yat Sen and Madame Chiang Kai Shek."

"What does Ben do to earn diamond pinky rings?"

"Produce plays and movies. He's another backer. They used to have a penthouse on Park Avenue," Rufus said chattily, "but now they live in the Smith place—you know where I mean, tucked away inside a cleft of North Rock."

Delia straightened. "The Smith place, eh? Hmm! Privacy galore. Has Mr. Kornblum any sordid secrets?"

"He fancies ponies way ahead of Siamese cats."

"A gambler? An equestrian? A practitioner of bestiality?"

"Darling, you are delicious! The ponies he fancies are in the back row of the chorus."

"I thought they were called hoofers."

"No. Hoofers can dance well, they're in the front row."

"But Holloman isn't rich in chorus girls."

"That's what Betty thought too. What she didn't take into account was Holloman's thousands of beautiful girls at various schools. Ben attends classes on everything from typing to dancing to amateur photography."

The very large room was beginning to look populated; about twenty people were dotted around it engrossed in talk larded with laughter, witticisms and, Delia was willing to bet, gossip. They all knew each other well, though some on arriving behaved as if considerable time had gone by since last they saw these faces.

True to his word that she belonged to him, Rufus Ingham took Delia on a round of introductions, feeding her information so guilelessly that no one on meeting her had any idea that Rufus was steering the conversation to yield maximum results for a sergeant of detectives.

Perhaps due to her diminutive size, Delia wasn't sure she could ever make a close friend of Rha Tanais in the same way she knew she could of Rufus Ingham. It was just too much constant hard work encompassing someone that big. Political cartoonists sometimes drew General Charles de Gaulle with a ring of cloud around his neck, and Rha inspired the same feeling in Delia. Whereas Rufus provoked emotions that shouted a friendship as old as time; having met him at last, she couldn't imagine her life without him. Had Hank Jones been Rufus's forty, he would have ranked with Rufus; how strange, that in the space of one short summer she should have met two men of great significance to her, when it hadn't happened since her first days in Holloman. Women friends were essential, but men friends were far harder to find, as Delia well knew. Very happy, she let herself be introduced.

Simonetta Bellini (born Shirley Nutt) bowled Delia over. The principal model of Rha Tanais Bridal, she was tall, thin, and moved with incomparable grace; her genuinely Scandinavian-fair coloring lent her an air of virginal innocence even her skin-tight lamé tube of a dress couldn't violate. She could wear a hessian sack, Delia decided, and still look like a bride.

"Fuck, a spoiled shindig," she moaned as Rufus left to hunt fresh quarry.

"I beg your pardon?" Delia asked, bewildered.

"The creepy shrinks are coming. Rha says shindigs like this, the shrinks get to come, but they spoil the fun," Shirl said. "They look at the rest of us as if we're animals in a zoo."

"Shrinks do have a tendency to do that," Delia agreed, her antennae twitching. "Why do they have to be invited?"

"Search me," Shirl said vaguely.

According to Jess, Rha and Rufus asked the shrinks for their abrasive qualities, and according to Simonetta/Shirl, they were indeed perceived as abrasive. "You said shindigs like this one, Shirl—are there other kinds of shindig?" Delia asked.

"Oh, lots. But the shrinks only come to this kind."

The quintessential bride, thought Delia, has gauze inside her head as well as on top of it.

But as Rufus piloted her from guest to guest, Delia noted that Shirl's aversion to "the shrinks" was universal. So universal, in fact, that she began to wonder how true Jess's explanation had been. *Would* two such affable men honestly blight their shindig for the sake of mental stimulation? It didn't seem likely, which meant Rha and Rufus invited the shrinks to one kind of shindig to please Ivy, who begged the favor of them to please Jess. Thus far it was an ordinary party for about fifty people; drinks and nibbles were to be succeeded by a buffet, apparently, but people were still arriving. There were mysteries here, but they seemed to be centered on Ivy and Jess, whose home this was not; nor were Ivy and Jess footing the shindig bill.

While her body moved about and her tongue clacked acceptable banalities, Delia's mind dwelled on Ivy and Jess differently than it had until this moment in their friendship, just two months old. I see far more of Jess than I do of Ivy, she thought; some of that is free choice, I know, but some is definitely Ivy's doing—she travels to New York City frequently, she's committed to Rha and Rufus by blood as well as business, and she lives an uphill walk away. Jess lives around the corner, our professions are slightly allied, and our schedules permit lunches once or twice a week. And while Ivy isn't gigantic enough to be offputting for a midget like me, there's no doubt she's a Desdemona—borderline. So terrifyingly well-dressed! Funny, that Aunt Gloria Silvestri doesn't cow me when it comes to clothes, whereas Ivy does. There is an aloof quality to her—no, that's the wrong word. Opaque is better. Yet I like her enormously, which means the real Ivy hides behind someone she's not. Ivy knows pain, she's been hurt. I don't sense that in Jess, whose hurts have been professional, I would think—her sex militating against her abilities. Ivy's hurts have been of the spirit, the soul. . . .

Slender fingers snapping under her nose, Rufus laughing. "No gathering wool, Delicious Delia! I'd like you to meet Todo Satara, our choreographer."

He had been enjoying a joke with Roger Dartmont and his feminine counterpart in stage fame, Dolores Kenny; they moved off while Todo remained. Probably a stage name, she decided, since he didn't look Oriental: mediumly tall, balletic body movements, a face not unlike Rudolf Nureyev—Tartar? His vitality and sexuality left her breathless, even though he was past his dancing days. The look in his black eyes was disquieting; like coming face to face with a panther that hadn't had a meal in weeks.

"By rights Delia belongs to Ivy and Jess," Rufus said before following the famous singers, "but until they arrive, she's mine, and I'm not sure I intend to give her back."

What conversational tidbit could she throw at Todo to make him feel fed? "I admire great dancers so much!" she gushed. "The tiniest movement is sheer visual poetry."

He swallowed it whole, delighted. "We are what God makes us, that simple," he said, his accent pure Maine. "Actually you move pretty well—crisp and non-nonsense, like a competitive school-marm." The sinister eyes, glutted, assessed her. "You are very decep-tive, darling, under the frills you're extremely fit and, I suspect, fleet. I bet you do the hundred yards in no time flat."

With a mental salute to Hank Jones, she chuckled. "You're the second man with X-ray vision I've met inside a week! My best time for the hundred yards was astonishingly fast, but I was in training then. Oh, it was hard!"

"I could teach you some marvelous comedic dance routines."

"Thank you, kind sir, I can live without them."

"A pity, you have stage presence. Don't try to tell me you spend your leisure hours in a dreary beige room looking at television for mental occupation—I wouldn't believe you."

"You might be right," she said coyly.

There was a stir at the door from the hall; Todo Satara stiffened. "Oh, shit! Off-key fanfare, and enter the loonies."

Six people came in amid a cacophony of greetings, Rha and Rufus directing them where to put anything they didn't wish to carry, ex-changing kisses with Ivy and shaking hands with the rest, Jess in-cluded. That was interesting: an uneasy alliance between Ivy's family and Jess Wainfleet?

Ivy took the best dressed award, as usual, in a floor length co-balt blue crepe dress, but privately Delia thought Jess magnificent in crimson silk. The two of them standing together quite eclipsed the wives of the millionaires.

The other four newcomers were the shrinks, three of whom she had already met over a Lobster Pot lunch. Number four, she now learned, was a psychiatric nurse named Rose who had married Jess's senior assistant literally yesterday, and in consequence was Mrs. Aris-tede Melos. The two men wore white tropical suits, the two women knee-length white dresses—not precisely hospital gear, but definitely out of place in this peacocky house, its peacocky people. Well, they were shrinks, so they were playing some sort of mind game, Delia divined, and if as children they had been taught good manners, the lessons hadn't struck or stuck. They coagulated clannishly, and needed no encouragement to eat or drink; now that they had arrived, the buffet was opened.

Todo and Rufus took Delia to the buffet and heaped her plate with goodies: lobster, shrimps, caviar, crusty bread, indescribably tasty sauces, and the best company in the room. Then, all three plates filled, the three of them repaired to a small table having just three chairs. Ideal for talking, but not yet, she thought, her eyes as busy as her antennae, thrumming on full alert.

Dr. Aristede Melos, Jess's senior assistant, was a thin, dark man of forty-odd—strange, that nearly all the protagonists were around forty. His face was plain, his expression dour, and his eyes conveniently hidden behind thick-lensed glasses with horn rims. His brand-new wife was the bustling, cheery type, but looking into her pale-grey eyes didn't inspire much cheer, Delia felt. Rose's fair complexion would have benefited from pinker clothes; white simply bled her to a chalky effigy.

The other two shrinks were husband and wife: Dr. Fred and Dr. Moira Castiglione. They radiated a long marriage complete with a couple of kids. Delia knew that Jess valued the Castigliones more than she did Melos, whom she found stubborn and afflicted with tunnel vision. Moira was red-haired and hazel-eyed, had a plain face and little charm of manner, whereas Fred, a brown man, was outgoing and ebullient. He had the gift of seeming an intent listener, though whether he actually did listen was moot, for his eyes gave nothing away. Like most married couples in the same profession, they worked as a team, used each other to bounce ideas off, and had a conversational shorthand.

The meal ended, Todo excused himself, and Delia started to dig. "Rufus, exactly why do you and Rha invite Jess's shrinks to your shindigs, as Shirl calls them?"

"Ah, you've sensed the negative feedback."

"What rot! One would have to be dead not to sense emotions that strong. Your people dislike Jess's shrinks intensely."

"They do, which is unfortunate," Rufus said on a sigh. "It's all to do with music, with Jess's comfort, and ultimately with our duty as well as our love for Ivy. It goes back to 1962, when we invited Jess to an evening very much like this one. She went back to HI raving about it, and her senior staff got it into their heads that they should have been invited too. So they nagged."

"Over not being invited to a party thrown by people they didn't *know*? Jess's personal friends, unrelated to her work?"

"You'll understand better when the evening's over," Rufus said, "and I'd rather you experienced what's going to happen in the same ignorance Jess felt at the time, which is why I don't want to go into explanations this minute. Just take my word for it, Jess's shrinks felt left out in the cold, and thought they deserved to be let into the warm." He shrugged, looked wry. "A work situation can be uncomfortable when the people who consider themselves indispensable get it into their heads that they're unappreciated. They carped and nagged."

"Jess is a very strong and fairly ruthless woman," Delia said, unconvinced. "Senior professional staff behaving like children? As an explanation, Rufus, it's weak, though I don't doubt it's the one fed to you and Rha—and possibly Ivy too."

"Point taken. Personally I tend to think that Ari Melos or one of the Castigliones caught Jess out in a bureaucratic error she'd find embarrassing to explain."

"More likely, yes. Capital criminals incarcerated for life as insane provide institutions like HI with their patients, and the paperwork is a nightmare." Delia grinned. "You've whetted my curiosity, I'm dying to find out what's so special about this kind of shindig. I must confess that the arrival of the shrinks looks a little like cabbage moths invading an orchid house."

Jess and Ivy bore down on her; Rufus escaped.

"You both look sensational," she said, kissing Jess's cheek and, on a little upward leap, Ivy's chin.

"I'm sorry we were so late," Jess said. "A conference."

"On an August Saturday?"

"Or an August Sunday," Jess answered dryly. "Don't tell me it doesn't happen to you, Delia."

"Oh, I understand. I love Rha and Rufus."

"I knew you would," Ivy said.

"Maybe it was better that you meet Rha and Rufus without our moral support," Jess added, enigmatic black eyes gleaming. "It's easy to see you're in your element. Excuse me, girls, I see the great Dolores Kenny." And off went Jess, looking excited.

Despite her stunning appearance, Ivy seemed—unhappy?—unwell?—uneasy? Something was wrong, though Delia fancied it had nothing to do with Rha, Rufus, Jess or the shindig. Perhaps she felt caught in the middle of the situation Jess's shrinks provoked? But why should she feel that more than Jess did? No matter how she might have felt in 1962, when the contretemps occurred, by 1969 Jess obviously had come to terms with it.

Delia put her hand on Ivy's arm. "Are you well, dear?"

A pair of beautiful blue eyes fell to rest on Delia's face, a startled expression in their depths; then they began to fill with tears. The finely painted red mouth quivered for a moment, then Ivy visibly brought her unruly emotions under control, and smiled. "Yes, Delia, I'm well. But thank you for asking. You're a very perceptive person."

"I wouldn't go so far as to say that, Ivy dear, but I can tell when the people I'm fond of are troubled."

"Troubled . . . Yes, troubled is a good word for my state of mind. It's purely personal, and by tomorrow I'll be fine. Do you believe in right and wrong? I mean the kind of thing they used to teach us in first grade?"

"Before we understood the importance of grey, you mean?"

"Yes, exactly." She sipped her martini. "Let's go over there for a minute, do you mind? No one will notice us."

Curious and disturbed, Delia followed her towering companion to a Victorian love seat tucked in a corner and partially hidden by the graceful curling fronds of a belmoreana palm, and sat the opposite way to Ivy, yet heads together. How like the Victorians! she thought. Nether regions barred from each other, upper regions in close proximity. Keep the lovers chaste!

"What's the matter?" Delia asked, disposing of their glasses on the broad arm separating her from Ivy.

"I'm considerably older than Rha," Ivy said, "and Ivor, our father, was chauffeur, bodyguard, caretaker and God knows what else to the third Antonio Carantonio."

Considerably older than forty? Shocked, Delia stared into the face near hers, but couldn't see a single sign of age.

"I've lived in Little Busquash all my life," Ivy continued, oblivious to the sensations she was triggering in Delia. "Rha's and my mother was—was 'simple'—she couldn't read or write, and was barely capable of keeping house. When Antonio III died in 1920 and Dr. Nell inherited, Ivor kept on running things for her. Mind you, she was hardly ever there—university and medical school took priority. I loved Dr. Nell! When she disappeared my father was like a man demented, though I didn't realize until later that he had expected to be mentioned in her will, that all his frantic behavior was really just Ivor looking for a will. Well, there wasn't one, so he had to ingratiate himself with the new heir, Fenella—also Nell."

Delia looked about uneasily, not sure where this story was going, and beginning to wonder if it should be aired in such a public place. Ivy proceeded to confirm her impressions.

"My father was a very strange man. He was heterosexual *and* homosexual—" She broke off when Delia grasped her hand, looking surprised. "What is it?" she asked.

"Ivy, now isn't the right time or place for this. Are you free tomorrow? Could you come to lunch at my condo and tell me then?"

Relief made Ivy's face sag; all at once Delia could see some of those extra years, even if not enough. "Oh, yes! I'll come."

Smiling as she left Ivy to the attentions of a group of her models, Delia joined the Doctors Castiglione. No need to conceal her profession from them; thanks to Jess, they knew she was a cop.

"It's clear that you don't feel like a fish out of water here, Delia," said Dr. Moira. "You fit right into this menagerie."

"Is that how you see it? As a menagerie?"

"What Moira means," said Dr. Fred, "is that you're extremely clever and resourceful."

"Menagerie?" Delia persisted.

Dr. Moira sniggered. "A collection of queer animals, anyway."

And I begin to see why they are disliked, she thought; they patronize. I'll bet their qualifications are very ordinary, but does that include Ari Melos? Poor Jess! Public service salaries don't buy brilliant helpers. "Queer as in homosexual?" she asked.

"Queer as in peculiar," said Dr. Moira.

"Why come, if these are not your kind of people?"

The Castigliones stared at her as if she were—peculiar.

"Our abiding passion," said Dr. Fred.

"And that is?"

"Music. Moira and I are trying to put an HI orchestra together—I conduct, she plays violin. Music does indeed soothe the savage breast."

"Admirable," said Delia.

Dr. Ari Melos and his new bride arrived, each drinking red wine; Melos was very pleased to be here, but Rose looked to be out of her depth.

"A Rha salon is one of the high points of my year," Melos said, "and I can't wait for Rose to experience what she's only heard of until now. I wonder what treats there are in store?"

And grudgingly the Castigliones nodded.

Well, well, we move ahead, thought Delia; whatever it is has to do with music.

Todo Satara sidled up. Bent on being awkward? Delia got in first, hoping to divert him.

"How many of the Asylum inmates are HI patients, Doctor?" she asked, assuming an interested expression.

"All of them, if we wish," Melos said, apparently unaware of Todo's enmity. "However, at any one time I would say no more than twenty are actively participating in HI programs. You must surely know, Sergeant, that the M'Naghten Rules are so archaic a 'guilty by reason of insanity' verdict at trial is rare—the dementia goes on full display after the prison term commences. Anyone in the Asylum is clinically insane, which gives us a fascinatingly rich patient pool to draw from."

Todo pounced. "Scary work," he said. "How do you manage to keep your cool sitting in a session with a homicidal maniac?"

"Oh, really!" Melos exclaimed. "There speaks the ignorant layman. Sometimes I think the general public still believes that the warders wear suits of armor and keep the inmates at bay with high-pressure water hoses. Inmates are properly prepared for their sessions. If they need to be sedated, they are. It's not dangerous work, Todo—in fact, it's more likely to be boring."

Dr. Fred took over. "HI has state and federal funds, and has one aim: to remove violent, sociopathic crime from humanity's list of unacceptable behavior. One day we'll be able to cure the physiologically violent criminal."

"Oh, sure!" Todo sneered, looking militant. "It happens now, guys—some axe murderer is released as cured, and what's the first thing he does outside the prison walls? Kills more people with his trusty axe. Psychiatrists play God, and that's a very dangerous role."

But Melos and Dr. Fred merely laughed.

"Blame the press, Todo, not psychiatrists," Melos said. "No journalist ever wastes space on the thousands of successful cases. The one-in-a-million failure gets the publicity."

Dr. Moira chimed in. "Setting an inmate at liberty isn't under psychiatric control," she said. "The steps taken to release a patient considered a danger to the community are multiple as well as agonizing for all concerned. Boards, committees, panels, reviews, outside consultations, exhaustive enquiries, investigations and tests—it's a near-endless list." She looked complacent. "Besides, Asylum inmates aren't ever considered for release. HI is like Caesar's wife, above reproach."

Animation had crept in; the shrinks had undergone a sea-change now the subject was their work. If only, thought Delia, they could abandon their air of superiority, they might win a few fans, but they couldn't. Her eyes encountered Jess, also listening, and saw an echo of her own sentiments; Jess too deplored their snobbery.

"I've never cottoned on to the idea of using tax dollars to create a place like HI," said Todo, enjoying himself. "I mean, isn't it bad enough that public funds have to keep the criminally insane fed and housed, without also providing health services ordinary citizens can't afford? I hear that HI has a modern hospital capable of treating anything from a heart attack to cirrhosis of the liver."

Rose piped up. "But how can it be helped?" she asked, sure of her ground. "This is a civilized country, people have to be treated for their illnesses. But what hospital can cope with violent patients who can't be reasoned with? The Institute is a prison, and the general hospital side of it was installed to protect the community. Our psychiatric research unit is quite separate again, so is its funding." Her rather plain and ordinary face had become flushed.

The mother defending her young, thought Delia; she's new to this, and resents the criticism.

"There's no altruism involved, Todo," said Dr. Moira crisply. "Ours is a job that has to be done. The cost of long-term—no, life-long!—incarceration is so astronomical that we have to find some answers, or at least make the tax dollars go farther."

"Our work is immensely valuable to society," said Ari Melos. "In the long run, it's units like HI that will make the whole problem of the criminally insane a cheaper exercise."

I think, said Delia to herself, that I have just heard the same old arguments that come up every time these two disparate groups of people get together. Rha and Rufus invite them to please Ivy, who wants to please Jess, who wants to please her staff. And it's all to do with music.

Around six, while the sun was still lighting the sky brilliantly, blinds and curtains were unobtrusively drawn, plunging the big room into semi-darkness. A most alluring after-shave essence stole into her nostrils, the mark of Nicolas Greco, whom she'd met only in passing. The Rha Tanais Inc. accountant of the Savile Row suits, easily the best-dressed man Delia had ever seen, and, she suspected, as close to indispensable as people got.

"Rufus has issued stern instructions," said he, piloting her with a hand under her left elbow. "I am to put you in Fenella's chair—it has the best outlook."

People were taking seats all over the place, no system or method to it except for this one smallish armchair, which had a footstool and, across its padded back, a sign that said RESERVED. Placed in it, she had an uninterrupted view of one large, octagonal niche wherein a grand piano, a harp, drums, and music stands were located. Even Betty Kornblum of the Siamese cat wore an excited expression, and the shrinks, clustered together, were positively animated.

What had been an ordinary, if magnificent, party turned into what in Delia's days at Oxford had been called a "salon."

Rufus began it by playing Chopin on the piano well enough to entrance a Paderewski audience—glorious! Was *this* what he did for a living? One of the willowy waiters picked up a violin and Rufus passed to Beethoven's fifth sonata for violin and piano; you could have heard a pin drop, so rapt and quiet was the audience. Roger Dartmont sang, Dolores Kenny sang, and they finished with a duet. Todo danced with a group of the waiters, males for one dazzling athletic number, females for a voluptuous dance, then males and females together for something balletic and graceful.

With pauses and intermissions it went on for five hours, and by the end of it Delia fully understood why all the badgering to obtain invitations for the shrinks went on. To be privileged to witness such first-class performances in the cozy intimacy of a salon was memorable enough to, pardon the hyperbole, kill for. The evening would, Delia knew, live in her memory forever. If anything puzzled her, it was the arrogance of the psychiatrists, who didn't seem to grasp that they were being honored; rather, they seemed to think they were entitled. And that, she decided, had nothing to do with psychiatry. It was all to do with the mind-set of people who would, could they, ban all exclusivity from the face of the globe. A Rha and Rufus salon was exclusive, and they had managed to invade it. What did that make Jess?

"That was utter magic," she said to her hosts as she was leaving, "and I want you to know that I deeply appreciate your asking me to come. Truly, I don't take the privilege for granted."

Rha's eyes twinkled. "Rufus and I are greedy, darling," he said. "Concerts are *such* a bore! Parking—crowds—coughs—strangers a-go-go—and never exactly the program you feel like. Salons are a total self-indulgence. No grubby money changes hands, performers who love to perform get to do their thing—terrific!"

"Even the loonies wallowed," she said demurely.

"Poor babies! So ghastly earnest!"

"Were you a concert pianist, Rufus?" she asked.

"Never, Delicious Delia! Too much like hard work. No, I love to play and I keep my hands supple, but life's too full of variety to lay one's entire stock of sacrificial goats on just one single altar. I play to please me, not others."

"If you eat British stodge, I'd very much like to ask the pair of you to dinner at my place," she said, a little shyly.

"We'd love to come," said Rha, and looked wary. "Uh—what is British stodge?"

"Bangers and mash for the main course—I drive to a butcher outside Buffalo for the bangers—absolutely authentic! And for dessert, spotted dick and custard."

"How," asked Rha seriously, "could we possibly turn down a spotted dick? Especially with custard."

Delia handed Rufus her card. "Decide on a night, and call me," she said, beaming.

SUNDAY, AUGUST 10, 1969

J ess Wainfleet kept nothing of her professional life in the small house she owned one block behind the middle reaches of Millstone Beach; it was purely a gesture at the normality of having a private address. When HI had been built in 1960 she had fought to be let have an apartment on the premises, only to find her arguments overridden on the grounds that her own mental health was best safeguarded by living off-site. Once informed of the decision, she had accepted it with grace, and immediately acquired her house in Millstone, a shortish, cross-country drive from the Asylum.

The place did come in handy, she admitted; it was somewhere to put her enormous collection of papers, journals and books, it held her wardrobe of clothes, it had laundry facilities, and it was a mailing address. What it was not was a home: that was HI, for Jess was one of those people who literally lived for her work.

Within six months of HI's being finished, she had organized herself. A bathroom in close proximity to her suite of offices became exclusively hers; opening off it was a room originally intended as a rest and recuperation area for a member of the staff feeling under the weather, and this too Jess commandeered. To all extents and purposes the Director of HI was enabled to live on the premises provided neither bathroom nor rest room suggested that she was making a home there.

Riddled with complexes and well aware of the degree of her obsessive-compulsive psychosis, Jess had managed to make an iceberg of them; what showed was the tip, the rest successfully buried. It would not have been possible were she intimately involved with another person, but since her psychic weaknesses were benign and she had no intimate friend, her colleagues accepted her failings as they did their own—as part and parcel of the profession.

The only person who had ever broken through Jess's defensive wall was Ivy Ramsbottom, a fellow obsessive of about the same degree—everything compulsively straightened, catalogued and tidied, without going over the top into a clinical mania.

"The world is full of people like us," Jess had said to Ivy on first meeting, just after noting that Ivy's china-headed pins were stuck in their little cushion in a shaded pattern that turned them into a graduated rainbow. "It would kill you to stick a black-headed pin into that row of red ones, wouldn't it?"

A startled Ivy laughed, and owned that it would.

Jess had been walking on Holloman Green to take in the beauty of its copper beeches when her eye caught a fascinating picture framed by cuprous leaves: a jet-black shop window containing three unrealistically slender plastic mannequins, a bride and two bridesmaids clad in fabulous dresses. Above the black window it said in white letters Rha Tanais Bridal. Unable to resist, Jess had crossed the road and walked into the shop. It was a large premises whose changing booths were big enough to hold a client in a full crinoline, and whose dress racks were entirely devoted to wedding clothes.

An extremely tall, attractive woman in a modish purple dress approached her, smiling.

"You're here out of curiosity, not custom," the woman said as she shook hands. "I'm Ivy Ramsbottom."

"I'm Dr. Jess Wainfleet, a psychiatrist," Jess said bluntly, "and your window fascinated me. The crowds it draws! Even cars passing by slow down to a crawl."

"There's not a woman born doesn't yearn to be a bride. Come into my den and have an espresso."

That had been eight years ago. The friendship had bloomed,

mostly because of their shared obsessive tendencies—it was so good to have someone to laugh with about them! In Ivy, the type was pure, extending to meticulously straight notes on a refrigerator door and the pattern on the china facing all the same way, whereas in Jess it was joined by a manic quality that pushed her to work too hard, sometimes become impatient.

Of course by now Jess knew Ivy's story, and had been of help to her; the insights and sensitivities of her field made her the best kind of confidante an Ivy could ask for. If there was pain and sorrow in it, that was because Ivy couldn't reciprocate with the kind of advice Jess's problems needed. Those, she continued to bear alone and un-aided save for the act of friendship itself.

So after the salon at Rha and Rufus's place, Jess visited her house only long enough to change out of evening wear into an HI outfit of trousers and a plain blouse; then she went home: that is, she drove out to the Asylum.

First step was to patrol her kingdom, its shiplike corridors of rails and unmarked, anonymous doors; sometimes she opened one and entered a particularly beloved room, such as the neuro O.R. When she had agreed to take this job in 1959, she had insisted that HI have all the appurtenances of a general hospital; it cost money, yes, but general hospitals weren't geared for criminally insane patients in any way, especially security. So when an Asylum prisoner became ill, he was treated at HI, even including surgery or intensive care. Of course the O.R. was also used for experimental animal surgery, chiefly primates—how did one deal with the Todo Sataras of this world, with their tax dollars and inability to understand that trying to treat the violently insane in a general hospital ended up being more ex-pensive than an HI?

Finally, as the big clock on the wall opposite her desk said 4.47 a.m., she eased into the padded armchair behind her desk and opened the cupboard door that occupied her desk's right side. A safe with a combination lock came into view. Cupping her hand around the striated and sparsely numbered disc, she performed the necessary twirls back and forth until, with a faint "thunk" the last tumbler disengaged. Her hand dropped. A stupid thing to do—anyone trying to see her manipulate the disc would have to have eyes in the end of the chair arm, yet still she did it every single time. That was the obsession, of course. Like *knowing* no one's back was going to break because you trod on a crack—but what if someone's back *did* break? Therefore you stepped over the crack just to make sure. Rituals were so powerful, so stuffed with meanings that went all the way back to the apes.

"Language," she said as she lifted bundle after bundle of files out of the safe, "is an expression of the complexity in a brain. Like the verb 'want.' An animal can indicate want by making some physical movement or gesture of vocalization aimed at want fulfilment. 'I want it!' Only a human can actually say it, including indications of the degree of want, the specific kind of want, the niche want occupies. Without moving any muscles except those of the lips and tongue and upper airway. How do the pathways open up between an infant's saying 'I want!' and a mature adult's saying 'I want, but I can't have my want because to take it would destroy someone else's superior entitlement to it?' "

Her voice died to a mutter. "What, in the pathways to maturation, can possibly overcome the most primal urge of all—want? Oh, Jess, there is an answer, and you're the one will find that answer, you are, you are!"

It was a big office, and well furnished, but she hadn't lit the overhead fluorescents, just flicked on the green-shaded lamp goose-necked to her desk; the room's far corners were plunged into utter darkness, and unexpected shadows lurked, shook, trembled whenever the worker at the desk changed position. Something in Jess loved this encroaching blackness—as if she, and she alone, held it at bay; it was a harmless demonstration of power, and, being harmless, could be condoned. Mindless power—now *that* was something else again, never to be condoned.

Perhaps a hundred files lay on her desk, divided into smaller stacks cross-tied with differently colored, striped ribbons. Each ribbon was actually a code only she knew, nor was it written down anywhere. Inside her brain, the safest safe of them all . . . Her gradations were concerned with behavior, and progressed from most primitive to most sophisticated in reasoning ability. For other people, the trouble was that Jess's gradations followed the lines of her theories, which were unorthodox and highly individual. In that respect she was a poor colleague, a non-sharer. But this project, as she was at pains to point out, was extraneous to her work as Director, funded by a separate grant to her alone, and too contentious to be aired until she had more results.

"It goes on much deeper than language," she said aloud, her eyes on the coded stacks, "but it surfaces in language, and I must find the key words. The trigger words."

A head came around the door.

"Come in, Walter," she said, not glancing up.

"I'll bring you fresh coffee first, Jess."

He came back with a fine china mug of hot, excellent coffee and put it down in front of her, then sat in the visitor's chair with one bare leg draped over its padded arm. A tall man, he was in perfect physical shape, with wide shoulders, a flat belly, narrow hips and powerful legs; he wore a T-shirt and short shorts of a drab grey with no identifying marks. His blond hair was all there, said his frosted scalp, but he wore it in a Marine cut too short to let it have any character; all it really did was emphasize his bull's neck. Smooth and clean-shaven, his regular-featured face was as soldierly in its expression as his bearing was. A striking man, of the kind that a stranger, on meeting, would deem sterling. His name was Walter Jenkins, he was an inmate whose records were marked never to be released, and he was Jess Wainfleet's greatest triumph. Every member of the HI psychiatric unit knew he was cured, but they also knew that not their must eloquent arguments would ever give Walter his freedom. No one was prepared to take the risk of releasing him, even for an afternoon. Walter himself was well aware of this, and accepted his lot with equanimity. Prison was almost the only life he had ever known, and he knew when he was well off. Here at HI they had cured him, that was first and foremost, and here at HI he led an interesting life, was of use.

"Good party?" he asked, lighting a cigarette and passing it to her before lighting another for himself.

"Superb entertainment. Rufus played Chopin—you would have loved it. Roger Dartmont was there and sang—too much vibrato in his voice these days, of course, but still wonderful. Rha is hard to take, but his salons are worth the agony, even Ari admits it. Fred and Moira rather bleed—so much talent under one roof."

Walter's face betrayed no humor, but that was normal for him. His eyes, a clear and lambent aquamarine, dwelled upon her with undisguised—could it be affection? This woman had freed him from the horrors of a padded cell just a building away, and he was hers to command.

"Jess, you're too tired to deal with this tonight," he said, a hint of authority in his tone. "Have a nice long soak in the tub, and go to bed. I'll put these away for you."

"I *must* work!" she said fretfully. "Life is too short, I'll die before I decode it. I'm still looking for the trigger words."

"Shoo!" he said, getting up.

"Why are you always right?"

"Because you showed me how to be right. Go on, go!"

She plodded toward the door. "Has the bath overflowed?"

"Not yet, but it will if you dawdle."

"Good night, Walter. And thank you."

As she closed the door behind her he slid into her chair and checked that all the stacks were cross-tied in her inimitable style; those that were not, he cross-tied himself. Then he stared at one hugely fat file bound in a plain indigo ribbon: his file. Tomorrow she'd enter his actions of tonight in it—more pathways coming into existence.

Safe door wide open, he began to put the files away exactly as she had; the last one to join them was his own. Then he shut the safe door and spun the disc crazily. What would Ari Melos say if he knew that Walter Jenkins, the most dangerous prisoner in the Asylum, knew the combination to Dr. Wainfleet's safe, as well as having access to every code that opened every lock in the place?

On his way out, the green gooseneck lamp extinguished, Walter opened the door to Jess's illicit domicile: an empty bed. Yes, there she was, sound asleep in the tub! Flipping the water outlet, he took a big bath sheet from a rack, shook it out, and wrapped the naked body of his protectress in it. Carrying her without effort, he then toweled her dry on her bed, slid her cotton nightgown on, and finally tucked her up comfortably. She would wake in the morning having no memory of his timely intervention.

He didn't think of it as love. Walter Jenkins didn't feel as other people felt, nor have names for what he did feel. His was not a fantasy world, for Walter Jenkins didn't even know such a thing as fantasy existed. In fact, Walter's world was the distance of a universe away from the worlds of all other people, though he had no idea that this was so. What Jess had done for him was to teach a complete force of nature that inside his head there also lived an entity she called Reason, and, not knowing she had done so, provoked an emotion he called Pleasure. Pleasure was not the animal caged or the animal tamed; it was the enormous sense of wellbeing he experienced at realizing that people *thought* the animal caged or the animal tamed. His world had mushroomed in size, in feeling, in complexity. And he had discovered the exquisite pleasure of secrecy. Jess thought him cured. Walter had never felt sick. Jess thought him a miracle she had worked. Walter knew no miracle had been involved. For their worlds did not collide; they passed each other a universe apart.

In all outward respects Walter lived the life of a never-to-be-released prisoner who is utterly trusted, admired, even loved. So, having ensured that his protectress was safe, her findings hers (and his) alone, and established that all was well within HI, Walter went down one of the shiplike corridors to an anonymous door behind which were his special quarters, there to retire.

He didn't really sleep; instead, he retreated to a trancelike state that refreshed, and gave him an advantage over everybody else he knew, in that he was alert in a millisecond, ready for action. Walter Jenkins befuddled? Never happen!

Jess woke befuddled, and was grateful for it; this drowsy state meant that she had really slept for a change, and could approach a peaceful Sunday in her office with her files clear-minded from genuine rest. Vaguely she remember Walter's ordering her to bed, and smiled. When was he not there for her? Never, was the answer. It was increasingly hard to conjure up the vision of Walter before treatment had begun: a zombie conjoined to a shrieking maniac? He'd always been in terrible trouble, so much so that from his thirteenth birthday onward, all his offenses had been committed inside some kind of detention center. He hailed from the mountain states, which had tough prisons, but Walter was in a class all his own. After he snatched a guard and two prisoners, barricaded himself in a cell and tortured them to death, the only way men were willing to deal with him was at a distance; less care was taken over feeding tigers or gorillas in a zoo because they were more predictable. During the course of his last furor, he had literally torn a fellow convict into small pieces.

Having read about him in a journal in 1962, Jess Wainfleet worked indefatigably to have Walter Jenkins transferred to the Asylum. Crossing state and federal jurisdictions was nightmarish, but no prison wanted him, and the Asylum, specially renovated for the Walter Jenkinses of the penitential world in 1960, actually made money for the state by taking inmates, federal and state, from elsewhere in the country. Warden Hanrahan did a deal that saw the Asylum staff increased, and Jess Wainfleet got Walter Jenkins. The chief cause of her excitement lay in two factors: the first, that the neurosurgeons had decided he was not a candidate for prefrontal lobotomy, and the second, that, in order to establish the condition of his brain, he had been fully investigated with every test known during a heavily medicated trip to Montreal. As far as angiograms, pneumoencephalograms, ventriculograms and all the other tests could ascertain, Walter's brain was normal.

The story of Dr. Wainfleet's humanizing of this monster was legendary in certain circles, though it hadn't happened overnight. It took four years. At the end of those four years, Walter was a reasoning human being who couldn't be provoked into manic rage; he was highly intelligent, and a capable man who read good books, enjoyed classical music, and was intriguingly articulate. This last, his ability to talk well, was astonishing, for it indicated that, even in his worst furors, some part of his brain had still retained logical thought.

His "cure" was now almost three years old, and had seen no hiccoughs of any kind. His status as a trusted prisoner had progressed to his becoming an unofficial aide to Dr. Wainfleet, whose methods and techniques he knew even better than her fellow psychiatrists did. She had written a total of nine papers on him over the years and now used him as proof positive of her theories, which were all to do with forcing well-known neuronal pathways into channels far removed from their known functions. Of course she brought to her work on Walter one asset nobody else in the field could hope to match: her knowledge of cerebral anatomy, especially of nuclei and areas below the brain's neocortex. Jess Wainfleet was more than a psychiatrist. She was also a neuroanatomist and a neurosurgeon.

In a way, Walter was famous, though his kind of fame was that of a medical "first" and would never be sung to the multitudes. To Jess, Walter was the equivalent of splitting the atom.

Her safe was closed—bless Walter! If he hadn't come in, she would have gone to sleep at her desk surrounded by files only she (and Walter) had access to. Anyone might have raided them and used the photocopier. . . .

It was no one's business save hers what, for instance, Walter's I.Q.

was, or how her primate study of rage centers was going—a long, long list of data gathered here in these files alone. Hers was the overall command, and she intended to keep it firmly hers. In which resolution, Walter Jenkins was her most valuable ally.

Ivy arrived for lunch, though Delia had wondered whether she would, given the direction her confidances seemed to be taking at the salon. Still a little intoxicated by the music and the company, Delia hadn't gone to much trouble over her luncheon menu—just toasted cheese sandwiches, mineral water, and good coffee.

"It's changeover Monday tomorrow," Ivy said, professing rather grateful pleasure at the menu's simplicity, "and Rha is still in summer mode for the dresses. Jane Austenish sprigged muslin for the bridesmaids, though of course what Jane Austen called muslin is a far cry from ours. Mabel won't complain, but Mavis and Margo will whine dreadfully."

"Mabel? Mavis and Margo?" Delia asked blankly.

Ivy laughed. "The window mannequins, dear! Mabel is the bride, Mavis and Margo the bridesmaids. I *love* weddings!"

Yesterday's mood was entircly gone; today's Ivy was happy and content. That put Delia in a quandary: ought she bring the matter up, or leave it lie? Ivy's attitude suggested leaving it lie; Delia decided to see where today's conversation went, now the sandwiches were eaten and they were seated at the window.

"How long have you been at Rha Tanais Bridal?"

"Since it opened—fourteen years," Ivy said, face glowing. "It's every woman's big day, and I get to plunge into the middle of the plans, the arguments, the dreams, the impossibilities as well as the possibilities. Rha Tanais Bridal patrons don't just buy a wedding gown and something for the bridesmaids, you know. We mostly clothe the mother of the bride and the mother of the groom as well, not to mention have a whole department to coordinate color themes, recommend venues, give ball-park figures for cost. You have no idea how much people are prepared to pay to throw a wedding, and I always feel it's a part of my function to make sure they know what the cost is going to be."

"Well, it's a little like sending a child to college, isn't it?" Delia asked, fascinated. "There must be heaps of hidden expenses. I'm glad someone tells them what the bill is going to be before they really incur the debt."

"The loveliest weddings are often the less expensive ones, as a matter of fact. Big splashes scatter farther, and some of the places the water lands don't bear being on display."

A novel thought had occurred to Delia. "Ivy, do you actually attend the weddings?"

Ivy looked surprised. "If they're within reach, always. I keep scrapbooks and albums. The albums can be very useful, since a lot of brides don't have much idea what they want. I sit them down with a couple of albums of weddings in their price range and tell them to show me the look they like."

"And to think all of this originally started so a man could be sure his bride was an untouched virgin!"

"Well, isn't that another way of saying, that a man's children are his? To be sure of it, he must marry a virgin and then make sure she can't cheat on him," Ivy said.

"How depressing!"

"But a very human conundrum, you must agree, Delia. A man yearns to know his children are his, and tries his hardest to ensure it."

"Well, I don't think it's going to be long before there's an ironclad test for paternity," Delia said. "Paul Bachman of our forensics lab says the discovery of DNA and RNA are breakthroughs in all sorts of directions, and won't prove dead ends."

She looked at today's Ivy with a twinge of regret, for she had made up her mind; yesterday's subject had to be laid bare. "When I saw you yesterday, Ivy dear, you were very upset, and started to tell me about your father, Ivor. But when you told me that he was both heterosexual and homosexual, I cut you short—it wasn't the right place or time for that story. Now here I am today reminding you of your unhappiness for one reason only—I'm convinced you need to share whatever it is with *me*. Why that is, I don't know, but I want to hear the story. Tell me!"

To Delia's surprise, Ivy's mood didn't flatten or plummet; she looked relieved, even eager.

"Thank you for bringing it up, Delia. I confess that if you hadn't, I wouldn't have found the courage to broach it. Ivor! My terrible father. . . . The thing I find hardest to fit into my picture of him was our mother. I've racked my brains trying to find a reason why he, of all people, should have married an oversized simpleton, but I can't. He didn't treat her like a wife, yet he made no secret of the fact that she was his wife."

"Did you like her, Ivy? Did you call her Mommy?"

"Oh, I was so confused, Delia! Children have no parameters beyond their own experiences, and I never saw other children or even other adults than those who lived in Busquash Manor and Little Busquash. I was told this enormous, bumbling woman was my mother, but I called her Marm, which was what the servants called her. As to what I felt—she frightened me. Oh, not in a malignant way! But one couldn't really have a conversation with her, especially on a child's level. People think that's odd, they seem to believe Marm's own childishness would have made it easier to communicate with children, but it wasn't so."

"You remembered events that happened when Dr. Nell was alive, you said yesterday," Delia prompted.

"Oh, I remember events before Antonio the Third died in 1920!" Ivy said, adding years to her age that Delia just couldn't credit, looking at her. "Ivor was always in command, of Antonio, and then of Dr. Nell, and then, later, of Fenella, who was the second Nell. I told you that he went slightly crazy after Dr. Nell vanished, looking for a will that was never found, but once Fenella was installed, he came into his own again. Looking back, it's obvious that he had an affair with Dr. Nell, and another with Fenella, but he also had affairs with beautiful young men."

Fascinated but bewildered, Delia frowned. "Where did the beautiful young men fit into the scheme of things?" she asked.

"Ivor drew them to him like moths to a lamp," Ivy said. "I suppose he went somewhere they congregated and picked one out, then brought him home to Little Busquash. From the time that Dr. Nell inherited, my mother lived in Busquash Manor as a kind of helper or companion—maybe Dr. Nell pitied her, I don't know. Fenella let her stay, and that meant Little Busquash was always where Ivor conducted his affairs with the young men."

"Where did you live, Ivy?"

"In Little Busquash. I hated Busquash Manor, I think because it was where Marm lived, and to this day I hate that place! The Ivy you met there last night was the Ivy of Dr. Nell and Marm and Fenella. The moment I enter, the memories come back like women at a sale." Ivy smiled, her cornflower blue eyes tranquil. "Oh, except if I cook," she added. "Cooking makes the Manor bearable."

"Finish your story," said Delia. "You haven't, yet."

"You won't let go, will you? And yes, it isn't finished," Ivy said. "Marm became pregnant with Rha, who was due toward the end of 1929. About three months before that, Fenella was located, and inherited Dr. Nell's estate. Fenella was pregnant too—their babies were born about an hour apart on November second. Fenella's was Rufus. Marm died falling down the grand staircase when Rha was a few months old. Fenella took Rha and raised him with Rufus as a brother, so my contacts with the child Rha were limited. I was stuck in Little Busquash with Ivor and his current beautiful young lover—sometimes a female, more often a male."

"Which beautiful young man did you love?" Delia asked. "You may be statuesque, Ivy, but you're extremely attractive. If Ivor was bisexual, it's certain some of his young male lovers were too."

"Right on!" Ivy cried, striking her hands together. "His name was Lance Goodwin, he was as beautiful inside as he was on the outside—dark hair, dark eyes, an olive skin, a magnificent body. And a gentle, loving soul, Delia, that was what I really fell for! Of course he had aspirations to go on the stage—that was usually how Ivor caught them. People are so naive, especially beautiful ones. Lance's personality attracted Ivor even more than his looks did—he liked corrupting the innocent, so most of his young men were inexperienced. Perhaps that accounted for Marm as well? Ivor trying to corrupt someone infantile?"

"Yes, it's possible," Delia said, "but not provable."

"He succeeded in corrupting Lance, who ended in spurning me in favor of my father. Horrible, isn't it? I was devastated at the time, and cut my wrists. I was slow to recover."

"But eventually you did, except for visits to Busquash Manor."

"It helped that Ivor died in 1934."

"When did you get to know Rha and Rufus?"

"After Ivor died, though Fenella never loved me, and didn't encourage sibling intimacy. Really, I didn't get to know Rha and Rufus until after Fenella died in 1950. Since then, we've more than made up for the lost years."

"It must thrill you to be a part of Rha Tanais Inc.," Delia said, "not to mention the weddings."

"I could write a book about weddings," Ivy said, laughing.

"Why don't you?"

Ivy looked shocked. "No, never! The worst tragedies would make the most interesting reading."

"One doesn't think of weddings as tragedies, Ivy dear."

"I've seen two girls widowed before they could leave the church. One poor groom died of a heart attack at the altar, and one was shot dead by his wife's ex-boyfriend."

"Brr! The grubby side of life can intrude anywhere."

That set Ivy chuckling. "Delia dear, beneath the surface of the glossiest, most gorgeous wedding there simmers God knows what, from the groom's mother's resentment of the bride to the maid of honor's despairing she'll ever be a bride. For all that, I love my work, I adore my brother and his world, and I pity the grim compulsion in Jess that leads her to flog herself for, I suspect, few thanks."

"And how do you feel about Delia the Detective, who winkled your story out of you?"

"I love her, but I don't pity her."

And that, thought Delia after Ivy left in mid-afternoon, is a compliment. Interesting, that she pities Jess.

MONDAY, AUGUST 11, 1969

Awed and astonished, Abe Goldberg stared at the four acrylic portraits on the slanted drawing table. Depicting head, neck and base of the shoulders only, Hank Jones had made them the size of Rha Tanais's head, more generous than the customary 8 × 10-inch photograph. And how right the quirky young guy was! In color, opaquely rendered by what Abe suspected was a masterly hand, the four Does were *dramatically* different from each other despite the obvious similarities.

"James Doe's natural hair color had enough red in it to hint at freckles," Hank was saying, "so I gave him a powdering of them— not the awful freckles of a carrot-head, just the fainter ones of auburn hair. John Doe Three and John Doe Four both had a few strands of fair hair embedded in their skulls, which is why in the end I did four portraits—John Three, John Four, James, and Jeb. I did pencil sketches of Jeb as well, to let you see with your own eyes that color is far better."

"They're brilliant, Hank," Abe said huskily, dazzled by the vistas this Monday morning was opening up. He'd survived the whole weekend without a single cigarette, now here he was gifted with work of this quality—! Even his ears and neck felt great: he'd found time to have a decent haircut. Let the teenyboppers sport the Prince Valiant haircuts! Betty had been told that from now on he was sticking to short-back-and-sides.

The four Does had been epicenely beautiful, though age would have decreased the feminine in them as full maturity progressed. At twenty, a man was far from physiologically mature; he would be in his early thirties before he "set."

Jeb's hair was a 1969 style and length, mouse-brown streaked from the sun, and his skin was lightly tanned, his mouth full and dark reddish-pink; he had a crease in his right cheek and a dent in the middle of his chin, and his nose in the penciled profile Hank had also drawn was ruler-straight, an ideal length. The eyes, fringed with long blackish lashes, were a vivid blue beneath arched dark brows.

James was the auburn-haired one with the light sprinkling of freckles; his skin was pinker and more luminous, his nose an enviable retroussé, and his brows peaked rather than arched. Hank had given his eyes a touch of green, but they were still blue. He had a dent in his right cheek and a dented chin.

John Doe Four had blond hair, a darker skin, very blue eyes, a faintly aquiline nose, dimples in both cheeks, and arched brows, but had no dent in his chin. John Doe Three had streaky brown hair, a straight nose, blue eyes, arched brows, and dents in his right cheek and chin.

"I've done another one based on Jeb," Hank said then, his tone diffident, "but you can burn it if you like, Abe. It's the person I think the killer is trying to make them over into, if you get what I mean. Black hair, f'r instance. Seemed to me that he liked a dent in the chin and a dimple in the right cheek, and arched eyebrows ahead of peaked ones. I've given it the bluest of blue eyes, and I call it Doe the Desired."

Hank laid another painting down. He had tried to give it a personality, yet it curiously lacked one; the mystery was deeper than Hank's brushes could go. The drama of the coloring made the portrait spectacularly handsome, though it was unfired clay.

Liam and Tony stepped up to have their turns inspecting the board; neither said a word, just exchanged glances. This weird kid was a genius.

"I'll have Photography duplicate them," Abe said, "but I can tell you where the originals will wind up."

"In the files at Caterby Street," said Hank, unconcerned.

"Far from it. They're going to be a joint Christmas present from ME and Detectives to the Commissioner. His office walls need some decent art, and he'll be tickled that it's cop art."

"Abe too can brownnose," said Liam with a grin.

Busy placing blank sheets of tracing paper between each of the paintings, Hank went quite pink from pleasure. Wow! His art on the Commissioner's office walls!

They met Delia on the way to Photography.

"Down in the mouth, Deels?" Abe asked.

"Utterly. The studio portraits mean nothing, I'm sure."

"Cheer up, there's an answer somewhere."

Rha and Rufus prepared to receive Abe Goldberg, which chiefly consisted in making sure the hard rolls were freshly baked and the lobster salad perfectly seasoned; he was coming to lunch.

Feeling like an old hand, this time Abe demanded the grand tour of Busquash Manor, and was conducted everywhere.

"Having these premises turned out to be a godsend," said Rha as he led Abe around the top floor. "In its heyday it took thirty-three indoor servants to run the place—upstairs, downstairs, in milady's chamber, da de da de da. Six pairs of hands in the kitchen alone! This floor was a warren of pokey little rooms I'd sooner call oversized closets, though the sinful sexes were segregated—the butler was always a drunk, but the housekeeper was a prison warden who ruled with a rod of iron. When we inherited it had been closed up, but it was in good repair, and we found it a wonderful repository for our costumes—in fact, having this floor enabled us to go into the costume-hire business."

He opened a door that said VALHALLA to reveal racks of what Abe supposed were Viking outfits, complete to winged or horned helmets. "They get an airing every time an opera house puts on Wagner's *Ring* cycle," said Rufus. CRUSADES revealed knightly armor, including for several horses, and CAVALIER held the satins and laces of Stuart England. "Women's costumes are stored separately from men's," said Rha. "Opera houses in particular love us."

"Maintaining all this must be an horrific exercise," Abe said, staggered. "Cleaning, repairs, logistics—!"

"We own an apartment building in Millstone to accommodate our staff—one reason why we have a proper parking lot. Management don't live there, but there are always young people looking for work on the fringes of show biz, and they do learn things while they're here. Rha and I hold lots of classes."

"I never thought of you as a big employer, Rha."

"Few people do, but why should they, really?"

They sat in what Abe privately called the Mae West Room to eat lunch, drinking sparkling mineral water as well as coffee; then it was down to business.

"I need a blank section of wall or a screen about six feet wide," Abe said, patting his solid briefcase, "in something close to daylight. I'll stick them up with plasticene, guaranteed not to stain. Show me where, then leave me to it until I'm finished. I don't want you to get a snatched glimpse ahead of time, okay?"

"Okay," said Rufus gravely.

Having shown Abe a skylit hallway that ended in a blank wall ideal for his purposes, Rha and Rufus went off to clear away the lunch remains.

"Okay, I'm ready!" Abe called.

The pity of it was that the corridor was too narrow to see their faces full on as they gazed at the paintings; Abe had to content himself with antennae tuned to breathing, tiny movements, vibrations in the air. Not that it turned out to matter.

"Jesus!" Rha exclaimed.

"Jesus!" Rufus echoed.

"Who of these people do you know?" Abe asked.

"All of them!" Rha cried, and swayed. "I'm going to have to sit down, Abe. The bigger you are, the harder you fall. Please!"

Rufus moved against Rha's side and took a part of his weight, careless of Abe, shoved aside. "Bring the pictures," he said.

Half supported, Rha groped along the wall past several doors before Rufus opened one and led him into a sitting room that also functioned as a library; Rufus maneuvered him into a lounger chair, got his feet up and his knees bent, while Abe found a bar cart and poured cognac into a snifter.

"Here, Rha, drink a little. It'll brace you."

"Yes, Rha, drink it—*now!*" Rufus snapped. Over his shoulder he said to Abe, "He's like all huge people, there are pieces that don't work too well."

"A doctor?"

Rufus cast his friend a piercing look, then shook his head. "No, the brandy will do the trick."

"I'm sorry, I wouldn't have been so up-front if I'd suspected the pictures would come as such a shock. Honest, guys, it wasn't a cop trick, I wouldn't do that to people I'd broken bread with," Abe said, feeling wretched—but also triumphant.

"We know that," Rufus said, trying to smile. "Jesus, Abe, what a shock! Those delightful young men—they're *victims?*"

"Is Rha up to this? Should I come back later?"

"Fuck that!" said Rha, color stealing into his face. He let the foot of the lounger down and sat up straighter. "I'm fine, Abe, and I'd much rather we got this over now." He groped for Rufus's hand and clutched it. "Sit down, both of you. I'm fine, just give me a couple of minutes to get my breath back."

Sinking into a chair, Abe decided the time would go faster if both Rha and Rufus had a moment to compose themselves that was not focused on the Does. His bright eyes fixed on Rufus. "You don't seem too keen on your new Broadway musical production, am I right?" he asked.

"About as keen as an epicure on a piece of dry toast, and dry toast it is," Rufus said, getting Abe's drift. "The times are changing, Abe. Put on *Annie Get Your Gun* in 1969, and I wonder how big a hit it would be? *Hair* started a new trend, and the off-Broadway shows are becoming racier by the month. Sex and nudity are what people are beginning to want, though the authors of our production have a great track record and it won't lay an egg, that's for sure. If you asked Dr. Jess Wainfleet, she'd probably tell you that our brains are evolving to process information at an ever-increasing rate, so the old 'stop for a number' kind of show is dying. People want the action to continue through the number more and more. *West Side Story* had more than Romeo and Juliet going for it—Jerome Robbins made dance really exciting, and Bob Fosse has galvanized Broadway. *King Cophetua* feels old and tired to us, Abe, that simple. It's a 1950s kinda show."

"Enough, enough!" Rha said, and transferred his six-plus feet to an ordinary armchair.

"I'll send you and your wife best-seat tickets for opening night," said Rufus.

"Being 1950s show goers, we'll love it. Ready, Rha?"

"A bit weepy, but yes, I'm fine." Rha held out his hands and took the four pictures from Abe. He held up Jeb Doe. "This is Nick Moore. Age, about nineteen. He was with us for about six months, left last March to go to L.A. and try his luck with the movies." He waited for Abe to finish writing in his notebook, then held up James Doe. "This is Gene Bierbaum. Aged twenty-one. He was with us for—oh, three or four months last year, quit in September of 1968 after he successfully auditioned for a lead part in a play in Calgary, his home town. Quite a lot of our youngsters come from Canada." He held up John Doe Four. "This guy was a Canadian. His name was Morgan Lake. Age, as I remember, was just twenty. He was from Toronto, stayed with us for nine months, then went back north of the border. He would have quit about the end of 1967. Nic Greco will have all their details—Social Security numbers, W-2 form copies. We'll call him and make sure he knows to cooperate."

Abe scribbled busily, then stopped and looked enquiring.

Rha held up John Doe Three. "This isn't a spitting image, but would you say, Rafe Caron, Rufus?"

"Yes, I'd say that's Rafe," Rufus said quietly.

"Then he was with us early in 1967, left around February. He was about twenty. So ambitious he was frightening, I remember that about him. A dancer, and a good one, but cursed with skinny legs— he was forever trying to bulge up his calves. I think he went to the West Coast."

"None of these faces or names were in our Missing Persons."

"Frankly, it would have surprised me if they were," Rha said, looking quite himself again. "At that age, and looking like that, kids of both sexes have wanderlust. The early twenties are the years of looking for the big break, which of course can't come when they're so young—you have to work at your act and image, casting directors have to see your face enough times, agents take you on—the traps and pitfalls are legion. Always add five years minimum to the age at which success is said to have occurred. Rock stars are younger, but that particular specimen doesn't hang around stage doors and casting couches. And while it's usually the girl wannabees wind up the subject of journalistic tragedies, there are just as many boy wannabees come to grief. And I guess that these poor boys didn't even make beautiful corpses."

"Anything but," Abe said. "I take it that their parents may not even know they're missing?"

"Few of the kids who come through here even admit to having parents," Rufus said. "A career based on the face and figure is usually not parentally sanctioned. Moms and dads want their kids in steady jobs with promising futures. As a result, most leave under a cloud of disapproval, if not a bitter quarrel."

"Yes, I can see that. There's no one else you suspect might be missing?"

"No one springs to mind, Abe."

"How many of these youngsters pass through Busquash Manor in any given year?"

"In 1968, the total was forty-two. One stayed a week, the longest stayed ten months," Rha said. He began to get to his feet. "I'll call Nic Greco for you."

"In a minute. I have a fifth painting, of a hypothetical person no one thinks exists at all," Abe said, diving into his case for Doe the Desired. "Our police artist studied the changes made to the bodies of the young men, and produced a picture of the man he thinks the killer was seeing in his mind." Abe removed a big flat envelope and handed it to Rufus, closer to him.

This room too was well lit, including from a skylight, but as the envelope left Abe's hand there was a sudden wild flurry of rain drumming against glass; Rufus, Abe and Rha jumped at its unexpectedness, then Rufus laughed, as if ashamed of his jitters.

When the painting came out of its envelope it was Rufus's turn to look faint; he gave it to Rha and sank against Rha's shoulder, his face buried in the side of Rha's neck. Left arm around Rufus, Rha used his right to hold the portrait out.

"First name, Un, and last name Known," he said in a steady voice. "This is Mr. Un Known, Rufus's father."

Abe was holding out another brandy. "I'm truly sorry, Rha. I never realized my briefcase was so full of shocks. How do you know this is Mr. Un Known?"

"Go back to the foyer, take the corridor to the left of the grand staircase, walk along it to the end, and open the door with the inset panel of Sanderson roses. You'll be in Fenella Carantonio's room. Our copy of that is on the wall. Bring it back," said Rha, preoccupied with Rufus. "He'll be okay by the time you return."

Abe went out; Rha stroked the head of beautiful hair with a rhythmic tenderness that didn't vary until Rufus moved, sat up on the arm of Rha's chair and drew a breath.

"Oh, Rha, what are we going to do?" he asked, whispering it.

"Play it very cool, Rufus my love. *Very* cool!"

"Was it wise, to come out with it like that? I'm petrified, and you must be beside yourself."

"We have no choice but honesty, my dearest friend of all friends. Take your cues from me, we'll get through it. Un Known never existed, and his twin brother, No One, never existed either. We stick to the truth as we know it. It's my turn to be lucid, yours to be confused. Remember, *always the truth!* We can't afford to become entangled in lies."

"Give me a sip of that brandy."

When Abe returned he found Rufus still huddled against Rha, and sipping at cognac.

"Who is this, really?" he asked. "Someone must have posed for it, there's nothing dreamy about it. This is a real man."

The room he had been directed to locate was a lush boudoir of pinks, white, reds and gilt, its fabrics Sanderson roses, its furniture Louis Quinze, its carpet Aubusson; an intensely feminine retreat calculated to emasculate a man inside five minutes. Except for the portrait of Un Known, which hung in the midst of an area of whiteness, its dark and brooding presence at odds with all else, including the room's very spirit. It had been executed by one of those European painters who still understood and carried on the techniques of the Renaissance masters. That was not to cast Hank Jones into disrepute; they were the products of two very different schools. The older work, in oils and with museum-quality brush strokes, caught Un Known in ways Hank had not.

The man's hair was thick, black, lay straight back from his brow in natural waves, and finished on his collar. His ears were small, neat, and clipped against his head, and the bones of his skull belonged to Adonis. Richly tanned skin lent him a certain hardness he needed, so delicate were the curves of his mouth and the fineness of his nose; his cheekbones rivaled Julius Caesar's. Thin, arched brows sat beneath a broad, high forehead, and there was a slight dent in his chin, probably, when more relaxed, a crease in his right cheek also. The radical difference between Un Known and Doe the Desired lay in the eyes, which Hank had done a vivid blue, whereas Un Known's were dark enough to appear black. In the Fenella portrait, their effect was to transform Lucifer into Mephistopheles: sinister, stuffed with secrets, innately evil. Beauty at its most masculine and deadly.

"If you ever met him, you'd remember," Abe said, still awed.

"Sometimes I'm convinced I know him well, at others I'm sure I never met him," Rha said. "Given Fenella's age, and the fact that he's listed as Rufus's father, neither of us remembers."

"Fenella said that after she told him she was pregnant, he disclaimed responsibility and she never saw him again," Rufus said.

Abe studied Rufus's face, his own frowning and intent. "I can't see anything of Un Known's face in yours, no matter how hard I try. You're a good looking guy, but not in the same way. Do you take after Fenella?"

"Not really. She was very fair—that's her portrait at the top of the grand staircase."

"Then you don't resemble either parent."

"I'm a changeling, Abe," Rufus said with a grin. "I figure I must have been hers—she left me her entire estate. I loved her, but she was sickening a long time before her disease clamped down, so it was love at one remove, if you know what I mean. Rha and I were raised by nannies, nurses, governesses and tutors."

Abe's heart twisted. "Not much home life, huh?"

Rufus laughed. "We did have a home life, actually. We were born on the same day, and we always had each other. Because we're gay, you probably think we were molested as children, but we weren't. We think we were just—born queenly."

Not wanting to go there, Abe concentrated on Un Known. "So no one apart from Fenella ever knew this man?"

"All I can tell you is that an aura of fear surrounded him—everybody was afraid of him because they'd picked it up from Fenella. And Ivor was definitely around—another nasty piece of work. Rufus and I used to hide when he appeared."

A shudder in someone as big as Rha was impressive; Abe stared at a shuddering Rha in amazement. "So the one father you did know frightened the pair of you as well?"

"So much so that neither of us remembers Ivor either. If you showed us a photograph of Ivor, we wouldn't recognize him."

"Oh, that's sad!" Abe exclaimed, thinking of his own sons; life as a cop showed you almost every day how many bad parents the world contained, but he and Betty were determined their boys would prosper under the right mixture of freedom and discipline. So far it was working, but that was the key word—work. "How many of your people know about Un Known?"

"Anyone who stays more than a month is bound to know," Rha said. "We keep Fenella's room as a kind of shrine, and the more responsible kids get a week or two caring for it. They all see the portrait as out of place, and ask. Of course Ivy knows, Jess too. Long-term backers like the Kornblums and the Tierneys."

"Nic Greco," Rufus contributed; he still looked shocked.

"Do you tell the story when asked?"

"Warts and all," Rha said. "The whole Carantonio story is interesting, and Un Known is definitely its Mystery Man."

Rufus spoke again. "All four of your victims knew. Each of them had flicked a duster around Fenella's shrine."

"When and how did Fenella die?"

"In 1950. Rha and I were twenty years old. I was the principal dancer with a successful company called *Ballet Bohemia* and Rha had just opened his boutique a block from Bloomingdale's in New York City—*Rha Tanais*, no qualifications. It was for big women, he was in hock to the eyeballs, and he gambled his all on what he displayed in his shop windows. They were genius! The word got around faster than a brush fire. I was bored with ballet and wanted to work with Rha. The odd thing is that Rha's success happened *before* Fenella died, a matter of three months."

"Were you expecting to inherit, Rufus?"

The khaki eyes didn't change. "At the time, no. Fenella approved of our homosexuality, but not of our leaving Holloman. Well, she was dying, poor baby, and in one part of our minds we knew it, but we buried it. Oh, there was no quarrel, but we knew we had to get out of Holloman to make something of ourselves, and the curse of dying by inches is that you never really think it's going to happen at all. As for her money—she'd educated us at home and neither of us went to college—it wasn't *real*. She never spoiled us with expensive gifts or toys, and she didn't give us an allowance while we lived at Busquash Manor." Rufus smiled. "She couldn't have done better by us if she'd tried, which we don't think she did. We hit New York City at seventeen, worked our assess off, and had some luck."

"And Fenella's illness?"

"She had a wasting disease—the word they used was strange to us—demyelinating. The use of her body was gradually taken from her, until she ended in an iron lung. That occurred at our seventeenth year, and there wasn't anything we personally could do for her except sit by her bed. We're not proud of running away, but that's what we did—ran away. Death by inches over many years."

"How old was she?" Abe asked.

"She was born in November of 1908, the same day her father, Angelo Carantonio, was killed at a railroad crossing. So in May of 1950 she was forty-two years old." Rufus's face contorted. "She looked a thousand." Rufus gazed at Abe, a challenge in his eyes. "As far as I know, the police were never involved in her death. She'd been treated by a bunch of doctors for fifteen years."

"Thank you," Abe said, defusing Rufus's challenge with a winning smile. "I have to ask, honestly."

"Of course you do!" Rha cried. "Between your own case and that of the delicious Delia's, Abe, you're awash in missing persons of both sexes." He rolled his eyes ceiling-ward. "Well, haven't we all *died* to go missing at one time or another, as the bishop said when caught with the dancing-girl and both sets of knickers missing?"

"That," said Abe solemnly, "I'd give a lot to see. However, back to business. I'm adding Un Known and Dr. Nell Carantonio to our list of missing persons."

"May we have copies of the pictures, Abe darling?"

"Calling me darling is an arrestable offense, so don't."

"Oops!" from Rha, with an impenitent look.

"Oh, Jesus!" Abe waved his hands in the air, and departed.

Rha and Rufus stood in the foyer looking up at Fenella's huge portrait, of a thin, anaemically fair young woman emerging from clouds of wispy white tulle.

"What do we do now?" Rufus asked.

"What can we do?"

"At the very least, tell Ivy."

"That goes without saying, but there's no one else, is there?"

"Not in this present contretemps, anyway."

"Ivy will be terrified that it might all be dredged up again."

"If it is, it is," Rha said, voice hard. "There can be no shelter from the elements this time. Abe Goldberg is too good."

While Abe made full sail, Delia was miserably aware that she lay on her oars still waiting for a wind. She had established that the person behind the camera taking studio shots of her Shadow Women had no professional ambitions; he shot for his own records, for no other reason. Now she had nothing left to do.

After a lonely lunch she climbed into her cop unmarked and set out for HI and the Asylum, Jess having assured her that she was at a loose end herself, and would welcome company. Truth to tell, Delia felt like a drive, while Jess privately cursed time wasted on pleasantries.

As prisons went the Asylum was not large; the original asylum had seen its inmates shockingly crowded together, and there had been 150 of them; when the huge renovations were completed in 1960, a hundred cells held a hundred inmates, one per cell, in a rigid framework far more stringent than even high security prisons. This was not a place where inmates had contact with each other; their physical fitness was ensured by small multiple gyms, and they ate in their cells, most of which were padded. Now that a few drugs were available to damp them down, caring for them was less dangerous, but it was not a place any of its staff would have called nice, or safe, to work in.

It sat in fifteen acres of parklike ground, though the Asylum itself sat in two blocks, one to either side of the only gate, and HI sat three hundred yards down a sealed road in its own block; almost all of it was unused acreage. The reason lay in its walls, erected in 1836 by the inmates themselves, and so stoutly, thickly and impregnably that, even in 1960, by which time the land was valuable, no one in authority wanted to incur the cost of building new walls for a smaller area. The bastions enclosing the Asylum were thirty feet high, wide enough on top to take small wheeled vehicles, and contained ten watchtowers, each round in shape and twenty feet in diameter. At their base they were hollow, and in shape if looked down on from a helicopter, formed a teardrop whose thinner end saw the forest outside meet a relic of the same forest inside. A bleak place, it was a saucer that sat just within the Holloman County boundary on its northwestern side, where people had never much cared to live, between the dampness and the wind tunnel it formed whenever the wind blew from the inclement northern quarter. Allotment size around it stood at five acres, which meant forest hid all but its watchtowers from view.

The entrance was on Millington, and looked every inch the prison it was: a massive iron gate that opened only to pass buses, machinery and big trucks; a smaller gate for cars, vans and little trucks; and a turnstiled door for pedestrians that led through a short tunnel. In the back, interior side of the walls were various reception rooms and offices, their guards armed with both pistols and semiautomatic rifles. Handy, that the hollow walls and their bigger watch towers could be used.

Admitted when she showed her gold detective's shield, Delia

parked and then walked to her designated office, where she lodged her 9mm Parabellum pistol and her Saturday night special, and asked for Dr. Wainfleet in HI.

HI had been built from scratch, and contrived to look somewhat classier than most public structures, though it was uninspiringly rectangular in shape and not overly glassed. What glass there was probably had to be toughened and shatterproof, considering the patient kinds, which would make it very expensive. Instead, walls had been faced with interesting stone by an architect who liked to do that type of thing, so as a look, it worked.

The road down to HI from the Asylum curved and was deserted save for a patrol car cruising slowly past her going the same way; the only other soul in sight was on foot, and striding out toward her. Clad in a grey T-shirt and short shorts, he wore no shoes and seemed not to notice that the August sun was sending ripples off the gooey tar—the soles of his feet must be solid asbestos, she thought. A superb physical specimen with a military air about him, and impossible to think of as an inmate. Besides, inmates didn't have the run of the grounds, even were one permanently in HI care. A handsome man too, she added as he drew near, still straight-faced. But no, he was after her! Three feet from her he stopped and nodded.

"Sergeant Carstairs?" he asked.

"I am she."

"Dr. Wainfleet asked me to fetch you. She's not in her own office at the moment, but she'll be there as soon as she can."

Perfect courtesy, yet no feeling. Who was he?

"Who are you, sir?" she asked in polite tones.

"Walter Jenkins. I'm Dr. Wainfleet's aide."

"A pleasure to meet you, Mr. Jenkins."

After that they walked in silence. Jenkins settled Delia in a comfortable chair, brought her a mug of coffee far superior to most institutional brews, and would have left her to peruse the journals on the coffee table had she not lifted a friendly hand.

"What does Dr. Wainfleet's aide do?" she asked, smiling.

His face registered no emotion; more, thought Delia, as if a few gears had to click around before the answer came up.

"Coffee, first and foremost," he said, but not in a joking manner. "I have memory skills she finds a great help—she says my memory and hers dovetail, and that their collective power is actually more than the sum of both added together."

"Isn't that something called a gestalt?"

"Yes, it is. Are you a psychiatrist?" He asked the question without evincing true curiosity, more as if he needed to keep the clicks and the gears going around.

"Dear me, no! I'm in the police."

He nodded, swung on his heel and left too quickly for Delia to continue exploring him.

Two minutes later Jess came in, Walter behind her with a fine china mug of coffee for her. She leaned over to peck Delia's cheek, and gave her aide a brilliant smile. "Thanks, Walter." She glanced at Delia. "Have you got your car keys, or did you hand them over at the gate?"

"I have them."

"Give them to Walter, he can drive your car down here to save you a walk in this awful sun. Is it your Mustang, or an unmarked?"

"A blue Ford in slot 9," she said, handing over the keys, and, as soon as he was out the door, "What an interesting man! I'd love to see what our new police artist would do with him in paints! Hank is heavily into robots."

All Jess's unconscious little movements ceased as if struck by some psychic lightning bolt; the doed black eyes took on a startled, even alarmed look. *"Robots?"*

"No, that's too unkind a word for Mr. Jenkins. I apologize to his receding back, and he doing me such a kindness too!"

"Why did you use the word robot?" Jess persisted.

"His lack of warmth? Or do I mean emotion? He walked in bare feet across melting tar, Jess, and didn't seem to feel pain. Perhaps what he reminded me of most vividly was the perfect soldier—you know, totally brave because totally fearless, unaffected by the niggling weeny things that get ordinary people so down. If you could clone him—isn't that what the genetics boffins are aiming for, cloning?—the U.S. Army would be in seventh heaven."

"You make him sound like Frankenstein's monster."

Delia stiffened. "Is he, Jess?"

"No, but he is an inmate." Jess bit her lip. "There, I've just given you information you're not qualified to gauge or assess. Walter is top secret."

"Your secret's safe with me, but explain."

"Walter was a genuine homicidal maniac, but over the course of four years I've unlocked the key to Walter's syndrome, and I've effected a cure. He still has some way to go, but the Walter you see is a million miles from the Walter who used to be. On my authority and with Warden Hanrahan's agreement, Walter has the run of the Asylum and its grounds—though of course he can never go outside the walls for as long as a millisecond. Everybody knows him and is cheering for him, and my team is ecstatic at my results. The trouble is that the cost of treating someone like Walter is nearly prohibitive, so before I can go any farther with my plans for Walter, I have to develop techniques that are more cost-effective. Todo and his tax dollar reign, and rightly so. But I guard Walter with my life. In a way, Walter is my life. That's why your impression of Walter is so important. You didn't pick him as an inmate, right?"

"No, I didn't. But I knew *something* was different," Delia said, at a loss to explain adequately what she meant. "He reminded me of a slot machine. My asking him a question pulled his handle, but the dollar signs or cherries or clown heads had to clunk into a row before he answered. Always, I hasten to add, correctly."

"He's improving—and that's not wishful thinking!" Jess said. "I can't be technical in my explanation to you, but in essence what I'm doing is forcing him to abandon the pathways his thought processes used to travel, and open up pathways he's never touched before. Our brains are overloaded with alternative routes that seem to be there on a just-in-case premise. So Walter is drawing himself a new road map for his thoughts to travel, and I'm its designer-architect. His old paths ended in horrific dead ends, but his new paths have benign and logical destinies."

Her own mind was spinning, so much so that suddenly Delia knew it was time for her to go. If she stayed, she might end in being drawn too deeply into the controversy she could see around Walter Jenkin's profoundly disturbed head.

"I think I hear my pager," she said, picked up her handbag from the floor, and went rummaging inside. Encountering the pager, she made it buzz, then consulted it anxiously. "Oh, bugger!" she said. "I'm needed, and just when I was settling in."

"At least your car will be closer. Walter will come in with your keys any second," said Jess, delighted to be liberated. Ari Melos had warned her, she reflected, that she was getting too close to Walter to see him in perspective. She should have seen these flaws in Walter, but hadn't. Therefore she was becoming Walter habituated. Only how to dishabituate herself? He wasn't ready yet to go a single day without seeing her; when she had taken her 1968 vacation, Walter had gone back to the Asylum, and it had set him back sufficiently for her to postpone 1969's vacation, speak of putting it off until spring of next year.

When Delia walked out of HI's front door she found her cop unmarked parked there, and Dr. Ari Melos just pulling up.

"Have I missed your presence, Sergeant?" he asked, climbing out of his car without bothering to lock it.

"My beeper went off, alas. Saturday night was wonderful, yes?"

"Emphatically yes."

"I've just met an interesting member of your team."

"Really? Who?"

"Walter Jenkins."

"An astonishing case," Melos said smoothly.

"Ought he to be wandering unsupervised?"

"His papers are marked never to be released, but that, we all agree, means from inside these prison walls. Walter is no longer homicidal, and even in the worst of his furors he was as cold as the North Pole. Guards on foot are collected in groups of five and are armed to the teeth. He is safely contained, Sergeant, I do assure you. In fact, Walter is the best reason for existence that HI could ever have." He looked suddenly perturbed. "You do not, I trust, intend to lodge a complaint?"

"Dear me, no. If Dr. Wainfleet says Walter is safe, then I accept that Walter is safe."

She climbed in and drove away, surprised to discover that Walter, who must almost have amputated himself at the midriff when he tried to slide behind the wheel, had made the adjustments necessary to drive the car himself, driven it, parked it, and then put her seat back exactly where it had been. Few people playing with a full deck did that, she reflected, so whatever Jess had done to Walter's cards, they now certainly seemed the full number.

And Walter, watching her drive back to the gate from his window on the second floor, assessed what he had learned about the tiny, tubby woman who drove it. To all intents and purposes it was her car, he had decided; it didn't have a cop car look or smell to it, whereas its servicing stickers were the Holloman PD garage, so it definitely was a cop car. Nor did she herself fit the standards—height, weight, health—too little on all counts. So what did she have that the head honchos all valued enough to wink at standards? She carried a 9mm hand gun and a .22, probably a little lady's two-shot handbag job, silver-plated and pearl-handled; he found spare magazines and a box of .22s in the arm rest between the front bucket seats, together with a bottle of spring water, two bars of dark chocolate and two folded cloths. The glove box held maps, a first aid kit, a Connecticut road atlas, the car's papers and a spare pair of shoes, each in a drawstring cotton bag. Neat lady, permissibly obsessive. The book she was reading, Carl Sandburg's biography of Abraham Lincoln, lay on the passenger seat. According to her bookmark, she was about halfway through the volume.

She was the Enemy. That status had nothing to do with her cop activities or career; it sprang out of his instinct that Jess was beginning to develop a weird need of her. He didn't know what to name the whatever-it-was Jess was starting to feel, nor could he predict its outcome. It simply *was,* and a part of it was an enormous threat to him. He knew that he mattered to Jess more than the rest of her world put together, and that Delia's threat was outside of his importance to Jess. No, what he sensed was that Delia would pluck at a loose end to remove it as unwanted—and end in unraveling everything. She introduced an unknown factor into Walter's life in a way that Ivy Ramsbottom never had, but it wasn't because she was a cop.

Not yet, for all his copious reading, able to find metaphors for what he felt or how he felt, he had climbed into a metaphor that saw him flying on gauzy wings high above a mass of crawling insects. Jess had enabled him to get this far, she had shown him a world of thoughts, and his gratitude was so great that he would have done anything for her—*anything!* Now Delia Carstairs was moving into his space, and he couldn't discuss her with Jess; he had to work out for himself what her significance was. For if he asked Jess, he would show Jess too much, betray open pathways on his map that she had no idea were open. Was Delia a superhighway bypassing his own desperate efforts to stay flying on gauzy wings? Whatever else he discounted, Walter could never make light of the solitude around him. Didn't Jess tell him every day that he wasn't enough, that she needed at least one other? One other what? He used to think she meant, one other like him, until she began to say he was unique; after that, he didn't honestly know. Did she mean a *Delia?*

Oh, he could see pathways everywhere! But which were the right ones? He couldn't read the street names!

"Walter, are you all right?" Jess was asking as she stood in his doorway.

"I'm having trouble with some of the new pathways," he said.

"May I come in?"

"Sure, please."

She sat in the armchair by his window, one hand gesturing to its mate, opposite. "Sit, Walter."

He sat, but stiffly. "Where will I start, Jess?"

"Anywhere."

"Why aren't I enough?"

"In one way, you're as many millions of enoughs as there are stars in the Milky Way, Walter," she said in the voice she kept for him alone, soft and warm, "but where you yourself aren't enough lies in other people, not in me. I need someone else to prove beyond a shadow of a doubt that what I did to set you straight, I can also do to other people like you."

"But this Walter is enough for you?" he asked tonelessly.

"More than enough! Inside my own mind, Walter, you stand on a high pedestal as the greatest happening of my whole life!" Her voice took on a note of triumph, though to Walter it just sounded louder. "I refuse to give up the search! Somewhere is another person who will serve both our ends, Walter—yours as well as mine! I want to see you granted your freedom, acknowledged as a citizen in good standing of your country."

He had heard it all before, but it had been a while, and with a sinking at the core of him he realized he had forgotten, that he had been fretting over a nothing, a replica Walter Jess hadn't had any luck finding. He *knew* that! What had made him forget it?

"Jess, there are too many new pathways," he said. "I'm at a crossroads all the time. You said they'd be hard to open up, a real struggle. But they're not. Opening them up is so easy that I'm caught in a stampede."

A huge mixture of emotions boiled up in her; she wanted to shout, sing, trumpet her victory, but the impassive face in front of her dazzled eyes forbade it. All that would do was confuse him, he had no idea what he was saying.

"Then it's time we changed our methods," she said calmly. "Between us, we have to work out a system that lets the pathways open up naturally—they're doing that now, but much faster than we anticipated. We don't want to slow them down, Walter, what we want is to enable you to deal with the stampede."

Ari Melos came in; Jess had neglected to close the door.

"A session on a Monday afternoon?" he asked.

"Yes," she said, forcing herself to sound offhanded. "We need some privacy, Ari. Close the door for me, please."

Outside in the corridor Dr. Aristede Melos looked at Walter's door, its complex lock, and stood frowning. The atmosphere in there had been electric. Jess was making another breakthrough, but he wouldn't know what it was until he read about it in her next Walter paper. Secretive bitch!

TUESDAY, AUGUST 12, 1969

When Delia walked into her office she found Carmine Delmonico in her chair, his feet propped on her work-table, and the ugliest dog in Holloman, Connecticut, sound asleep on the floor beside him. He was in his work clothes, a fine white cotton shirt open at the neck and with its sleeves rolled up, a pair of dun chinos, and rough suede desert boots.

His eyes were open, and twinkling at the expression of huge joy busy writing itself on her face. Then she pounced on him to give each cheek a smacking, lipsticky kiss, while he adroitly transferred her to her chair and himself to a spare one, ignoring the dog's semi-hysteria at seeing Delia.

"When did you get in?" she asked, thumping the dog.

"Yesterday's Red Eye, but I slept on the plane—Myron put me in first class."

"It does make a difference. Why are you here?"

"I'm surplus to requirements in California, Deels. It took me one day to see how right Sophia was about Desdemona, who dived into the life like a man dying of thirst into a mirage that turns out to be real. Sophia was also right about the kids, who think they've arrived in toddler heaven. It took me two days to see that Myron and Sophia between them could set up world peace, if only the world were sensible enough to grant them the authority. Desdemona has absolutely nothing to do except amuse herself in whatever way she fancies, and the kids are at the center of a heaving mass of helpers, entertainers, you name it. Myron had found a great niche for me as his gofer at the studios, and I was enjoying being ordered around." The big shoulders shrugged. "Then the shit hit the fan for Myron—some movie deal, don't ask me. He had to fly off to London and couldn't take me along.

"By the seventh day I realized that a rudderless Carmine was a handicap to a wife in need of a few weeks in Sybaris or some other place riddled with hedonism, and in no shape to compete for his sons' attention with Bozo the Clown, Buck the cowboy, Tonto the Indian, Captain Kidd the pirate and Flash Gordon from Mars. So I flew home."

Delia drank in his beloved face. "You're a sensible man."

"The animals were grieving, so I figured I'd be welcome— Winston actually lost a pound after a week at the kennels, poor guy, and Frankie was a zombie," Carmine said, rolling his feet across Frankie's belly to its groans of pleasure. "How about lunch at Malvolio's?"

"Definitely."

"Frankie, mind the house," Carmine said, escorting Delia out. "You can fill me in once we find a quiet booth."

Nothing loath, Delia recounted the events of her August to date, ending with her visit to HI to see Jess Wainfleet, and her own odd reaction to Walter Jenkins.

"Yeah, that guy." Carmine sipped his coffee, frowning. "You don't know about him, of course, whereas I know him about as well as you can know anyone without actually meeting them. I was on the panel that agreed the Asylum could take him as an inmate—he's an out-of-state lifer, and then he was very rare—the mania never let up for a second. Dr. Jess Wainfleet had just put HI together, and she wanted Walter exactly the way he was. The Asylum facilities plus HI and some hefty grant money saw Walter an inmate. I guess no one thought anything would come of Walter as a guinea pig—he'd killed a total of nine of his fellow lifers as well as three guards. Terrible crimes! Yet Dr. Wainfleet has made a kind of human being out of him."

"Walter is the HI blue-eyed boy," Delia said, "but I confess I didn't take to him. I described him as a robot, which quite upset Jess. She teetered on the brink of taking offense."

"HI and Jess Wainfleet do good work, according to the people who should know. The unadulterated maniacs like Jenkins are few and far between. Wainfleet's papers on him are cagey, she never really advances a hypothesis. Some psychiatrist pals of mine maintain that she's stalling for two reasons—one, that she hasn't mined all the gold out of Jenkins yet, and the other, that she's looking for a second Jenkins to confirm the first." Carmine smiled. "But enough of that! What about the Shadow Women?"

"Abe's been far luckier with his starvation victims, but I don't want to steal his thunder."

"You can't. I've already seen him."

"What do you think of Hank Jones's paintings?"

"They're the way of the future. I must meet him. Cease the side-stepping, Delia! The Shadow Women?"

"Oh, Carmine, I'm not sidestepping! The truth is that there have been no developments capable of shining any light on a really impenetrable darkness," said Delia, misery personified.

Winston's large bowl of raw meat was licked clean; when Carmine put Frankie's dinner down he smiled at the sight of it, but did not relent by giving Winston more. Not that he intended dieting an animal, which he regarded as cruelty; more that it boggled the mind to think of Winston's going a week actually leaving food in his bowl. That was the minus side of keeping pets; when you had to board them out, they fretted, no matter how luxurious the kennels. Who would ever have dreamed Winston would grieve?

When he settled himself in his over-large armchair, he had Winston on his lap and Frankie squeezed into the seat alongside him; he also had a stack of files on the table and time to think.

It had been Desdemona sent him home. Where would he be

without Desdemona, his glorious ship of the line, her bows cleaving the sea as she forged ahead at full sail? Well, she needed time in dry dock, he went on inside his metaphor, and a long overhaul could not be accomplished with a husband to worry about, or two kenneled pets.

"You're going home, dear heart," she said bluntly. "Miss Monson has your tickets and the chauffeur will call at her office to pick them up en route to the airport. Concita has packed your bags, so all you have to do is pack your briefcase." She dropped a kiss on his brow. "I feel so well, but experience has taught me that unless I stay here in this palace long enough, I'll flag as soon as I get home again. You've made love to me so many times in a week that I'm dizzy, so I'll survive without it better than you will, I suspect. *Go home!* Apparently Holloman is peaceful, but Hartford isn't, with a war brewing between the Comancheros and the Puerto Ricans. We may have watched our astronauts skip around on the Moon, but North Hartford is rapidly becoming a moonscape we don't have to fly a rocket to walk on. So you might be needed. Abe's case is blowing sky-high, even if Delia's isn't."

His amber eyes had studied her wonderful face with its big nose and big chin, amusement glittering in their depths. "Who's the little dicky-bird sings you these songs, wife?"

"An anony-mouse, not a dicky-bird, husband."

"I love you, I'll always love you, and I'm going home."

Now he studied Hank Jones's paintings in wonder. After so long in No Man's Land, the Does had names and identities.

Abe had more work to do with Rha Tanais and Rufus Ingham, but had already outlined his future course: Tony Cerutti the bachelor would go on the road to interview parents, schoolfriends, history prior to joining Rha Tanais—named after two rivers in an atlas of ancient times, yet! Liam would deal with the accountant, Nicolas Greco, and bureaucratic data.

However, the case that most intrigued Carmine was Dr. Nell

Carantonio, whose body had never been located. The first thing he found fascinating was her medical degree, very rare for a woman in 1921, the year she had graduated from Chubb Medical School, another coup—*Chubb* graduate a woman doctor in 1921? In a social climate seething with prejudices against women in any profession, Dr. Nell seemed to have led a charmed life. Her student years must have been stuffed with all kinds of cruelties and denigrating plots, but no record of them had survived, and she graduated in the top five of her class, which plain didn't happen. Women's papers were marked down, their clinical work sabotaged; some of the worst and most ruthless bigots were their professors. But no, Dr. Nell graduated high. Following which she was allowed to intern at the Holloman Hospital in numerous fields; her final choice of anesthetics seemed to have been a personal wish, as she had been offered residencies in general medicine and pediatrics as well. Once in Anesthesiology, she had been well respected and never short of surgeons requesting that she administer the gas for them. The entire twenty-seven years of her life had been pursued as she wanted, and with success. Then—poof! She vanished into thin air.

The wealth had been in the family for three generations, its source being complicated little machines that did chores previously in the purlieu of human beings; the savings in time and money had enabled Antonio Carantonio I to build a small empire his son and then his grandson had continued to build. Antonio Carantonio III had just the one child, Eleanor called Nell, and had sold out his company interests for want of an heir. If Nell wanted to be a doctor, it was fine by him. He gave her his blessing and two million dollars safely invested in blue-chip stocks. Even the Great Depression, endured while the courts waited to see if she were dead, did not affect the fortune. Then Fenella Carantonio had parlayed the two million into ten million, simultaneously preserving her mansion and the secret of her only child's paternity. Rufus Ingham, also known as Antonio Carantonio IV. The homosexual business partner and personal lover of Rha Tanais.

" 'O what a tangled web we weave, when first we practice to deceive!' " Carmine murmured. "I wonder who gets what when Rufus is no more? Nor is Rha the kind to have progeny."

Dr. Nell's body could be anywhere, and Rufus's father might still be alive. Carmine picked up the portrait of Un Known and examined it very closely. The background was a landscape reminiscent of Louvain after the Kaiser's war machine had rolled through it, all smoke, crumbled medieval walls of niches once occupied by statues, a fire-torn sky. . . . Did it have some significance, or was it just the first circle of Hell? And the eyes—he reached for his magnifying glass and thrust the portrait under the central spotlight of his lamp, then held the magnifying glass above it. No, the eyes were not black. Their pupils were widely dilatated, but around their edges he could discern a ring of dark blue. Blue! Blue, not brown! This would have to go to the artist for cleaning—who knew what other secrets it held?

How old would Un Known be now? Rufus was forty in November, so was Rha, and what kind of man would have appealed to Fenella in the days of her limbo waiting for Dr. Nell to be declared dead? In 1930, say, she was twenty-two years old, so—not a man in her own age group, someone at least ten years older. Make Un Known forty in 1930, and that would make him around eighty. Then he was probably dead. It was all there to be learned, and Carmine wanted to learn it all. An ideal project for himself, one that could be run in tandem with Abe's case, without stealing any of Abe's limelight. An attitude of mind only Carmine cherished; he knew his detectives were neither jealous nor defensive, therefore it was up to him to watch out for their professional welfare.

Malvolio's was always where the dickering went on between members of the same police unit. It wasn't so much that walls had ears, as that office chats could be interrupted, phrases overheard out of context, phones ring, people dragged off to do something perceived as more urgent. Whereas food and the partaking thereof were sacred; only the direst of emergencies could intrude on them.

Carmine tipped twenty-two pounds of cat off his lap and put the phone there instead, then dialed Abe's home number.

"Breakfast in Malvolio's at eight?" he asked.

"Betty thanks you. The boys have been nagging for pancakes, and I hate them. You've just made the Goldbergs very happy."

WEDNESDAY, AUGUST 13, 1969

At eight in the morning Malvolio's was full, its largely cop custom in desperate need of what they mostly couldn't get at home: a solid breakfast of eggs, crisp bacon, hotcakes-and-syrup, or, if desired, meatloaf and mashed potatoes; for the graveyarders, this was dinner, not breakfast. The powder-blue-and-white Wedgwood decor went well with cop navy blue, especially the roomy padded seats of the booths, upholstered in navy-blue leather that fifty years of serge-clad bottoms had kept polished and supple. Luigi, the owner/proprietor, dreaded the thought that one day his granddad's Italian leather would finally give up the ghost, but so far it hadn't. His granddad had bought the very best.

Abe was already in a booth, a two-man, sandwiched between an end wall and the four revolving counter chairs that finished in the waitress's gap. The booth was extremely private, the four chairs unpopular because of the waitresses; this morning all were occupied by Nutmeg Insurance workers.

"Good spot," said Carmine, sliding opposite Abe. "How goes it, Merele?" he asked the elderly waitress, already filling his coffee mug.

"Busy," she said with a beaming smile.

Having ordered eggs-over-easy with plenty of bacon and hashed browns, the two men drank their coffee, unwilling to talk seriously until after they'd eaten. The food came quickly; they ate quickly.

"I know we talked yesterday, Abe, but I need an extra word this morning," Carmine said, pleased to note that Abe was hanging on to his resolve to quit smoking; even the delectable aroma of a Nut-meg Insurance cigarette wafting right under his nose wasn't costing him exquisite pain, just a bearable agony. "Do you foresee needing Delia?"

"No, the three of us can handle it, though it would be a help if you okayed Tony's travel applications a.s.a.p."

"Consider it done. What I want to talk about is our oldest open case—Dr. Eleanor Carantonio."

The mild grey eyes widened. "Dr. Nell?"

"Yep, Dr. Nell. I know it kinda brushes against your own case, but not, as far as I can see, in a way that would make it—or me!—a nuisance if I investigated it for what it is."

"Nor can I. Frankly, to me it's more a red herring than a contribu-tor to our case, and I'm not willing to waste my time on it, that's for sure. So go to it, Carmine. But why?"

"Call it a hunch. I took the file home last night and read it thor-oughly. Maybe it's forty-four years of hindsight prodding me, but whatever it is, my hunch says it might pay to take a new look at her disappearance. I'd work it together with the weird non-appearance of the Un Known."

"What on earth do you suspect?" Abe asked, fascinated. It was never sensible to dismiss Carmine's hunches, they had a habit of pro-ducing results. "Come on, Carmine, give!"

"I don't know how or why, but my hunch says the John Does are connected in some way to Dr. Nell's disappearance. The root cause lies in the events that happened between 1925 and 1935." His face took on a heroic resolution. "In fact, I guess I'm here telling you this morning because it may be that you and your team should be doing the investigations. Common sense says it's all one case, and I have qualms about horning in."

Typical Carmine, thought Abe. Having seen some kind of light himself, he didn't want to take over Abe's case now that it was going somewhere thanks to Abe's team's efforts. And that was a great feeling, to know that the boss was not greedy for the glory, *but* the case came first, not individual egos. "No," Abe said in a firm voice, "you won't be horning in, Captain. I have more than enough to do following my present leads, and if there is a connection between the two cases, it's better to start at either end. I'll keep to my end, you take the antique end, and whoever needs Delia can grab her." He smiled ruefully. "Poor old Deels isn't having any luck with the Shadow Women."

"Tell me about it! The odd thing is that I keep thinking the answer has already been found—something Delia said to me yesterday triggered it, but then it slid back under the sludge before I spotted its shape. That means she knows it too."

Dr. Eleanor Carantonio's file had yielded the name of her law firm: Gablonski, Uppcott, Stein & Stein. It was still practicing, and the names of the partners hadn't changed according to the Yellow Pages. His not knowing it meant that none of its members were in criminal law—it would be a family-style business more concerned with wills, trusts, conveyancing and civil disputes. A phone call informed him that none of the partners dated back as far as 1935, but that Mr. Uppcott's father had been there from 1923 until his retirement in 1961. Yes, the present Mr. Uppcott was still with the firm, and could see him within the hour, as an affidavit interview had been canceled due to the heat wave.

The offices were on Charles Street, a narrow thoroughfare between Cromwell and Cedar Streets—a five-minute walk. Taking a last breath of ME cool air, Carmine emerged onto Cedar Street in something close to 100°F and near-saturation humidity. Five minutes later he entered an elderly office building that proved to hold, on its third floor, his destination. Outside the glass-paneled door Carmine paused to roll his sleeves down and put on his Old Chubber tie, then went into a waiting room that gave away no hint of its calling, as likely a podiatrist's or a vendor of things in plain brown wrappers as a law office. The receptionist, hammering away on an IBM golfball typewriter, paused to speak through an intercom, then went back to her work.

"Captain Delmonico? Come in," said a deep voice issuing from a tall, portly man in his early fifties.

Carmine walked into a little heaven of chilly air, his hand outstretched to shake the one being proffered.

"John Uppcott. How may I help, Captain?"

Uppcott too wore an Old Chubber tie: Carmine's instincts had been right.

Keeping it brief, he explained that he was re-opening Dr. Nell Carantonio's case.

"I know she left no will, but what I'm hoping, even after so long, is that I can locate some people who knew her well," said Carmine, sounding relaxed and only moderately interested. "This firm handled the intestacy and the presumption of death, but I imagine the only Carantonio you knew personally was Fenella."

"Yes indeed, I knew Fenella well," Uppcott said, something in his tone suggesting that it hadn't been a joyous experience. "However, the one you should speak to is my father. He can tell you all the Carantonio dirt."

"Would it be possible to see him?"

"He'd be over the moon. Dad is barely seventy. My mother died fifteen years ago, and he's been having a ball ever since. Not that my wife and I worry about acquiring a stepmother! Dad is far too fly to get caught in *that* trap. He likes very pretty young women around nineteen or twenty, lavishes presents on them, gets all the sex he asks for, and everybody's happy."

The two Old Chubbers smiled at each other broadly.

"Him, most of all," said Carmine.

"Definitely. What I love most about him," said his pragmatic son, "is that he knows down to the last cent how much he can afford to spend, and never dips into the red."

"When would it be possible to meet your dad?"

"How about ten tomorrow morning? Do you mind if I come along to kibitz? I'd enjoy hearing him on the subject of Dr. Nell too."

"Be my guest."

"No, you be ours. I'll bring fresh raisin bagels and brew the coffee," said John Uppcott. "Your car, I'll be navigator."

Carmine slid his card across the desk. "The number on the back is my home phone. Just in case you have to switch the time or the date."

And that, he thought, was too easy. His tie in his pocket and his sleeves rolled up again, he walked back to County Services.

Next on his list was Mr. Hank Jones, the new artist; with him Carmine brought the portrait of Un Known from Fenella's boudoir.

"The Man himself!" said Hank Jones, eyes gone yellow. "What can I do you for, sir?"

"Carmine will do for me. Interesting taste in wall art."

"Flowers are nice, but I like 'em growing in a garden or a field. Walls are for *statements*."

"And flowers can't be statements?"

"Not for my walls, no. Unless it's a pitcher plant, maybe."

Carmine unwrapped the portrait. "Have you seen this?"

"No," said Hank, inspecting it. "Brilliant brush work, but dirty as an old broom. I'd like to clean it."

"That was what I hoped you'd say. Will it take long?"

"No, it's not old enough for the grime of centuries, just the smog of this one. I can wipe it clean with my magic elixir."

"How old is it, Hank?"

"Several decades, maybe around five . . . It's in oils, but none are hand-ground and mixed, yet there are no really modern pigments either." Hank wiped the canvas lightly in one corner and examined his rag, an old handkerchief of fine cotton. "I'm safe with this. Won't be long, there's nothing ingrained."

By the time he was finished the handkerchief was uniformly dirty, and the portrait had leaped into life. Pale skin, and an undeniably blue ring around each enlarged pupil. No writing or lettering had appeared in the background, which was impossible for Carmine to pin down as a specific location.

"Leave it with me and I'll ask Photography to make some good copies," Hank said, fascinated. "Is he a John Doe of way back?"

"I don't think so, in that he doesn't appear to be linked to our Doe case. Yet in a different way he's definitely a John Doe."

The elfin face looked gleeful. "I knew it! What's his name?"

"That's just it. He has a name, but it means John Doe. His first name is Un, and his last name is Known."

"You're kidding!"

"Nope. All we know about him is that he's someone's father, and his name on the birth certificate is Un Known."

"Cool!" said Hank.

As Carmine prepared to leave, he found Hank between him and the door, face a mixture of apprehension and determination.

"Uh—sir—Carmine?"

"Yeah?"

"Delia told me that you live on East Circle in the house with the tall square tower, is that right?"

Eyes twinkling, Carmine prepared to hear some proposition as bizarre as individual. "Spit it out, Hank," he said, grinning.

"Well, it's like—uh—after midnight, when all the lights except those permanently on have been switched off—and when there's no wind, the harbor water is glassy—and the Oak Street hydrocarbons farm is blazing with lights—uh—it's gorgeous!"

"I have noticed these phenomena," Carmine said gravely.

"Sir—Carmine—if I was quieter than a pussycat, could I maybe sneak into your front yard after midnight and paint all the lights across the water? *Please?*"

"It turns you on?"

"Like Saturn seen from an outer moon!"

"With some modifications," Carmine said. "First off, there's a pit-bull in residence, and you'd have to know him very well. Secondly, if you set yourself up on the deck outside my back door you'd have the best view of all. So I suggest that you and Delia bring some Chinese food next Saturday night about eight. We'll eat, you can meet Frankie the dog and Winston the cat, look at my deck, and if the night's right for your needs, you can paint."

Then he was gone, leaving Hank to stand, gasping, unable to credit his luck. He'd seen the view from East Circle itself on one of his two a.m. prowls, been blown away, then realized that from public land there was no clear sight of what his imagination was piecing together; it would have to be the land belonging to the house with the tall square tower. When he'd told Delia, she informed him that her boss, Carmine Delmonico, lived there, and she'd prodded him to ask Carmine now he was back from California.

What he hadn't expected was such a warm response; thus far life hadn't been all that kind to Hank Jones, the quintessential foster child with sinews tough enough not only to survive the system, but actually get something out of it.

Hot damn! When the picture was finished, he'd give it to Carmine, on condition he could hang it when he held his first exhibition.

Time to see Commissioner John Silvestri, who was closeted with the Captain of Uniforms, Fernando Vasquez.

"We're all worried about the situation in Hartford," Silvestri said as Carmine sank into a chair.

"Any sign of its spreading our way?" Carmine asked.

"Not so far. The Comancheros don't have a big presence here, as you know, and they're in the thick of it."

Carmine grinned at Fernando. "No sheet of relevant paper?"

"Why do you always harp on my bureaucratic tendencies when you know they're necessary?" Fernando demanded wryly.

"Am I paying you a vacation salary, or a working one?" the Commissioner asked Carmine.

"A working one, I guess, as of this morning. Your new artist is a great find, John."

"Stan Coupinski in Chubb Anatomy told me to grab him. He'd earn a fortune in commercial art, and hate every minute of it."

The three men passed into a discussion of what was going on in Holloman, a difficult town for Black Power militants to exploit thanks to the two-mile separation between its ghettos, one to either side of downtown and the main Chubb campus, therefore with a tendency to be at loggerheads rather than united. The Hispanic element was small and as yet not infiltrated by any of the fierce Hispanic gangs of bigger cities.

All in all, Holloman seemed likely to survive August in reasonable shape, unlike Hartford.

"Good," said the Commissioner, and closed the session.

THURSDAY, AUGUST 14, 1969

Carmine packed everything he could imagine he might need into his briefcase: copies of Hank Jones's portraits of John Doe Three, John Doe Four, James Doe, Jeb Doe and the hypothetical Doe the Desired. To them he added a copy of the cleaned painting of Un Known, and the same painting with pupils of a normal outdoor size, allowing wide, vividly blue irises. Fenella had two pictures: the head and shoulders from the staircase masterpiece, and a Richard Avedon photographic portrait in black and white. And the photograph of Dr. Nell from her police file. Of police files there were five, commencing with her disappearance in 1925, and ending with presumption of her death late in 1933. He doubted there was any other case in the Holloman PD files so rich with pictorial history. Mr. John Uppcott was bringing his law firm's files, but—no pictures!

Uppcott was waiting outside his building, carrying a fat briefcase and a big bag of fresh raisin bagels, and stepped into the passenger seat of Carmine's beloved Fairlane as soon as he had deposited his burdens on the back seat.

"I suppose you never get a parking ticket, even in this tank," he said, enjoying blasts of cool air.

"Not unless the cop who issues it feels like spending the rest of his career in our version of Outer Mongolia."

"Sheer curiosity, but what is the Holloman PD version of Outer Mongolia?"

A wide white grin flashed Uppcott's way. "Manning the North Holloman station—nothing ever happens there."

"Well, Captain, I guess you have to have some perks for what I suspect is a lousy job." Uppcott stripped off his tie and undid his shirt collar. "Thank God for that! My wife and I always go on vacation in June because it's more comfortable people-wise, but the office in August is only bearable because of my A/C unit. I'd put one in Rosemary's reception room, except that old Mortimer Gablonski, the senior partner, won't hear of it. Subordinates must suffer, the old bastard says."

"Does that mean you pay personally for your comfort?"

"Yes, and gladly. The Steins are no problem, and we've got it all worked out. Morty retires next February, then we're moving to the Nutmeg Insurance building—full A/C, even for Rosemary."

"Any special directions how to get to your dad's?"

"No. He's on Inlet Road at the point end."

They drove then in a pleasant silence through the leafy streets of Carew, turned onto Inlet Road and emerged into what Carmine privately thought one of the prettiest coast villages Connecticut could boast—tranquil, well kept up, an antique row of shops, prosperous houses except for the one little tower of apartments that had so upset the locals they promptly banned any structures over two storeys in height.

John Uppcott Senior lived just three houses short of the park that formed Busquash Point, in a white-painted New England saltbox house with dark green shutters and a shingled roof. It stood in a generous half-acre of carefully maintained gardens, its sole trees several dogwoods and a magnificent North American birch with four trunks, its flower beds filled with roses. The owner was obviously a passionate rose fancier.

The son looked older than his father, whom he clearly admired as much as adored.

"Call me Jack," said Uppcott Senior, shaking hands.

He was shorter than his son and in much better condition: flat belly, broad shoulders, supple movements. A magnificent head of fair, wavy hair set off a handsome face endowed with a pair of permanently laughing green-blue eyes that few women could have resisted. What a legal lion he must have been in his day! A pity his day had been so short on lady lawyers; he would have swept all before him. Though he probably had anyway. Carmine made a mental note to pump Judge Thwaites for information—those two would have loved each other.

"No teenyboppers dropping in, Dad?" Junior asked.

The eyes danced. "Son! Would I do that to a captain of detectives? Go make us some coffee and put the bagels on a big plate, like a good guy," said Jack, leading Carmine to a shaded loggia that overlooked the park and Long Island Sound.

"Doctor Nellie!" the youthful old man said on a sigh. "I never knew her, though I joined the firm in June of 1923 and she didn't disappear until October of 1925. Stonemeyer was the senior partner, and even he hadn't set eyes on Dr. Nell. Since her portfolio was blue-chip and she never speculated on the Market, she didn't use a broker. We kept her scrip and papers, and after tax began to come in, we retained a tax accountant for her and other big clients. After she disappeared George Stonemeyer handed everything to his son, Norman, who was useless. Norman co-opted me as his full-time assistant, and dumped the whole Carantonio mess in my lap. He was killed in 1926 literally skating on thin ice to impress a local Clara Bow, and his father sold out of the firm. My own father had died and left me a bundle, so I bought in as second partner on condition that I kept Carantonio in my purlieu. You see, Carmine, by then I was hooked on it, and the last things I wanted were the headaches of the senior partner. Sy Gablonski bought the senior partnership for his son, Mort. As far as I was concerned, everything came up roses. Until the end of 1933, I handled nothing except the Carantonio affair."

John Uppcott came out bearing a tray of coffee and bagels, performed the duties of a waiter, then sat and listened.

"Did you cherish any ideas of your own about Dr. Nell's sudden disappearance, Jack?" Carmine asked. "There's no interview with you in the police files."

"My only ideas were suspicions without foundation," said Jack, sinking his excellent teeth into a bagel, "but here they are, for what they're worth. There was a man involved, I'd bet a lot on *that*. Dr. Nell never lived much at Busquash Manor—the house called Little Busquash always held a caretaker, a man named Ivor Ramsbottom, who I gather the police enquiries cleared totally. But Antonio III had sent her to boarding school when she went into high school, though she lived at home through her university years—U-Conn and then Chubb Medical School. I can solve the mystery of her easy medical career—Antonio III bought it with enormous endowments that were kept what we'd call now, top secret."

"Fascinating," said Carmine, enjoying both bagel and story. "In not interviewing you, Jack, the cops missed a bonanza."

"I agree," said Jack complacently. "When Dr. Nell went into her clinical years at the Holloman Hospital as well as the Medical School, she bought a three-family house on Oak Street not far north of where the Holloman Hospital is today. The cops knew all about it, but I think missed its true significance. She lived on the middle floor, installed a housekeeper on the top floor, and—at least I believe— not a bodyguard on the bottom floor, but a lover. The neighborhood back then was on the slide, but it was still lower middle class white— why a bodyguard? To me, it didn't make sense. By the time that the detective got around to investigating the house, both the woman on the top floor and the man on the bottom floor had packed up and left the state. As far as I know, neither ever surfaced."

"You're right, neither did. Any theories about the lover?"

"Oh, sure!" said Jack, reveling in this late chance to air theories ignored at the time. "For one thing, he didn't really *live* in Dr. Nell's bottom apartment, according to the neighbors. He came and he went, always with a bag—a suitcase, I mean. My theory? He was married."

Carmine was leafing through the fat first file, and found what he was looking for. "According to the neighbors, a big guy in his middle thirties, and something of a looker—one witness calls him extremely handsome—female—and another, a fine man. It strikes me that a progressive thinker like Dr. Nell would have been bored by guys her own age, so if she did have a lover, the so-called bodyguard would fit for looks and age."

"My interpretation exactly, Captain! How cheering, that the Holloman PD detectives are also evolving!" said Jack slyly. "He must have been married. Otherwise, why the subterfuge? Dr. Nell was a marital catch—brains, beauty and two million dollars. I think he was a surgeon."

"Not a fellow giver of gas?" Carmine asked.

"Yes, it was a rather limited field back then—mostly good old nitrous oxide. But no, Carmine. Similar field, conflicting schedules. An allied field, like surgery."

Carmine extracted the photograph of Dr. Nell. "I know you never saw her, but does this face ring a bell?"

"It fits Dr. Nell's description. Look at the fire in those eyes! Some woman," said Jack, sighing.

"Fill me in on her cousin, Fenella. The second Nell."

"Antonio Carantonio III had a younger brother, Angelo," Jack said, pausing to savor his coffee and choose another bagel. "Not unusually, they hated each other, a feeling that blazed higher after their father, Antonio II, left absolutely everything to the older son, Antonio III, who was the father of Dr. Nell. Angelo had always been the black sheep—he was shiftless, a compulsive liar, and an adept at forging checks on the family bank accounts. In 1903, about ten years after inheriting, Antonio III dealt with his brother and the business in one fell swoop. He sold the business and invested the proceeds in blue-chip stocks, nothing else. His income from these investments was paid directly into *one* bank account so well protected that Angelo couldn't get at it by hook or by crook."

A lull fell; Carmine took the moment to absorb the scene. A cool breeze was blowing gently inshore, it was a Thursday and in consequence no one was mowing lawns, the air was filled with birdsong. He put down his empty coffee mug, smilingly shook his head to the offer of another bagel, and reflected that there were worse places to be right now than here, listening to a spry old man's story, delivered with lawyerlike crispness and some humor.

"What happened to Angelo?" he asked.

Jack blinked. "Typical Angelo! He married a rich woman."

"Poor thing! Life married to Angelo must have been hell."

"While it lasted, it undoubtedly was, but in 1908 there was issue—Fenella. Of course Angelo had wanted a boy whom he could call Antonio IV—the Carantonios were Sicilian and girls weren't considered proper heirs. Fenella was born early in November, and Angelo left the house cursing his new daughter as well as his wife. He was also drunk. There were plenty of automobiles around in cities, but Angelo's automobile was pretty rare on the back roads around Holloman. He stopped in the middle of 133 to take a swig of booze from his bottle, but it wasn't a good place to stop because he was straddling the main Boston railroad line." Jack shrugged, grinned. "The locomotive had a full head of steam up, and it was still doing sixty miles an hour when it ploughed into Angelo broadside." Another shrug. "The best way to describe it was strawberry jam—automobiles were frail in 1908."

"Was he identified?"

"Oh, yes. His briefcase was hardly marked, pitched a hundred yards away alongside the body of his pooch, also hardly marked."

"So in 1908 Antonio Carantonio III assumed responsibility for his sister-in-law and his niece," Carmine said.

John Junior spoke, his face angry, his eyes snapping. "Oh, no, not that bastard! He disowned them. In fact, no mention of their existence ever passed his lips, so Dr. Nell—and we, her lawyers—had no idea that she had an aunt by marriage and a first cousin by blood."

"That's some brotherly hatred," Carmine said. "What else happened between 1908 and 1925, Jack?"

"Just Antonio III's death in 1920. He never lived to see her graduate a doctor of medicine. His will left everything to Dr. Nell, never mentioned Fenella or her mother."

"What do *you* think happened in October of 1925, Jack?"

Jack Senior was smiling at the antics of a very inexpert adolescent trying to get his Sunfish out of the inlet. "I do know that the Holloman PD wasn't rich in detectives of your quality! I remember a Sergeant Emilio Cerutti at the head of enquiries—a nice enough guy, but no Sherlock Holmes."

Carmine's lips twitched. "He was my great-uncle," he said.

"Well, not everybody who picks up a violin can play it like Paganini," said Jack, unabashed. "Dead now, of course."

"Years ago."

"Man, I love the Carantonio case! Law is as boring as bat-shit, a fact you are aware of, so you can imagine what it felt like to be a bloodhound on a leash, straining and drooling like mad. And I'm not being fair to Sergeant Cerutti—it was hello and goodbye, no talks or interrogations." His eyes sparkled as he visibly tensed at the memories flooding back. "Bear in mind that we had no inkling Fenella or her mother existed. After Dr. Nell vanished, all my energies were focused on finding her, as we were convinced she had no heirs."

Out came the pictures of Un Known with and without unmistakably blue irises. "Have you seen this man?"

Jack Uppcott studied them pensively. "In general terms, the one with blue eyes looks like the description of the bodyguard, but farther than that I can't go. I never saw a picture."

"You never encountered a surgeon or even a physician who looked like this?"

"No, never. Never," said Jack emphatically. "If I had seen him, I'd have sooled the cops onto him straight off. Whoever he is, he killed Dr. Nell."

"How did you go about finding Fenella?"

"When the cops hadn't turned up anything in three months, I decided to start looking at law. That meant I advertised heavily and consistently in the law journals and major national newspapers—

and kept on advertising month in, month out, year in, year out. The Carantonio estate could afford the expense. I asked for any information about Dr. Nell or a Carantonio relative."

"You're a bird dog, Jack," said Carmine, grinning.

Mr. John Uppcott Senior looked modest. "It was such a shame to see all that money and property in a legal limbo. Of course I had done—and continued to do—all the things that would make it as easy and rapid as possible to have Dr. Nell declared legally dead after seven years. But by the time 1928 had gone, I knew in my heart that Dr. Nell was dead, body or no body. My search for relatives occupied me more and more, but the thought of New York City was so daunting that in the end I hired a private detective—a guy with good references." Jack gave a dazzling smile. "I should've done it sooner. He found Fenella."

"Bingo!"

"I wired him his fee and a bonus, and asked him to give the extra hundred included to Fenella to cover her expenses when she came to Holloman." He shivered. "I was so excited, Carmine!"

"I bet. Did she make you wait long?"

"She was sitting in the waiting room when I came into the office the next morning—so young, so beautiful, so shabby in her years-old flapper dress, a moth-eaten fox fur with a bald tail around her neck like a sansculotte draped in a dead rat. I saw her thus because she was wearing a battered bonnet like Madame Defarge, right down to a tricolor cockade."

"The second Nell," Carmine breathed.

"She was definitely that. She'd brought more than enough documentation—her birth certificate, Angelo's marriage in a New York registry office to Ingrid Johanssen, letters from and to Antonio III and Angelo that made the whole quarrel clear, and a letter from Antonio III to the widow refusing to help her or her daughter. She had a cardboard box full of papers."

"What did you do with her?" Carmine asked.

"No matter what Antonio's opinion of his brother and his niece might have been, I had certain duties—either find Dr. Nell and re-store her estate to her, or, failing that, to find her next of kin," Jack Uppcott said with dignity. His mouth turned down. "Books by their covers, Captain! My initial impression of Fenella Carantonio was about as wrong as an impression can be. The sweet little sansculotte was Madame Defarge to the core—a bitch. Once I had assured my-self that her documents were genuine and I had told Fenella what the stakes were—"

"How did she take the news?" Carmine interrupted.

"Knocked the breath out of her. I hadn't told the detective there were millions involved, and I guess she and her mother were hoping for a thousand," Jack Uppcott said, eyes back on the kid trying to sail his Sunfish.

"I thought you said she was a wealthy woman?"

"She was, but by the time Fenella appeared in my office, the mother was dead and her money had gone. And once Fenella had assimilated the fact that there were millions involved—about fif-teen minutes—the pathetic act went out the window. Even though there were still at least five more years to wait for legal presumption of death, Fenella demanded to be maintained as the heir until she could inherit. She demanded to see Dr. Nell's stock portfolio—what a mind for figures! Faster than I can do it on my adding machine, she determined to the last cent what the annual income was, and professed herself satisfied to be housed in Busquash Manor and paid all the income except my firm's fees and expenses. Frankly, I didn't think it was worth antagonizing her by attempting to block her. I just bit the bullet, and if I did, my partners took the hint. She was a tiger! No, a cobra. *Dripping* venom."

"She can't have had an easy life, with that father, even if he did die the day she was born. The mother can't have been much chop either. And she would have been pregnant?" Carmine quizzed.

"She never said she was pregnant, and she didn't show any sign of it. That was June of 1929, but when I saw her in July, she was show-ing." His face creased into laughter lines. "No guts, no gifts! I asked if she was pregnant, she said she was, I asked if she was married, she said she wasn't, I asked if she intended to marry, she said she didn't, I asked who the father was, she said that to all intents and purposes it would be a virgin birth. End of subject." He laughed aloud. "A formidable woman, even if she was only a scrawny little thing." Reflection replaced amusement. "I daresay the disease was chewing away at her even then, and she was just the woman to be aware of it."

Carmine lifted the picture of Un Known. "According to legend this is the father of Fenella's child."

"If he was—or is—then I've never seen him, and the firm still cares for Rufus Carantonio's affairs. Nice guy, not at all like Fenella in looks or nature."

"Were there any hitches in declaring Dr. Nell dead?"

"No, none. It was just very slow. The court decided in December of 1933. No reported sighting of Dr. Nell had ever been lodged, unusual in itself, and it was a kind of the final nail in her coffin. The estate had weathered the Great Depression just fine, I should add. Then the new owner decided that with all the fiscal changes F.D.R. was busy making, it was time to revamp her portfolio. Which she did herself, using brokers only as she needed them, and switching them frequently. She bought blue chip too, but blue chip of the future, in fields to do with electrical gadgets, or pharmaceuticals, or aeronautical products. Once she'd finished her revamp, she'd parlayed her fortune from two million to ten million. But that's chickenfeed. I'd have a heart attack merely thinking what the Carantonio estate must be worth today."

"Interesting, that money follows money," Carmine said.

"Oh! Rufus and Rha's money, you mean. True, Rufus doesn't need Fenella's money, but it's also good to know that eventually it will go to better causes than maybe Fenella envisioned."

The kid with the Sunfish had lost the breeze and decided to cool off in the water; far overhead a contrail said someone, probably packing nukes, was flying at military heights; a family had arrived to take possession of the choicest picnic spot on Busquash Point; and Carmine suddenly wished with all his heart that Desdemona and his sons were on the one-and-only, *proper* coast.

He rose to his feet, put his briefcase on the table, and tucked his exhibits back inside it. "Thanks for a very pleasant interlude," he said, shaking hands. "I'll call you with the news if ever I get any. You've been a help."

And I wonder if there's anybody at home at Busquash Manor? he asked himself as the Fairlane growled down Inlet Road. When he came to Millstone Road, he made a right; he was in the neighborhood, so why not try? People who slammed the door in a cop's face were stupid, and he didn't think, from what he'd learned about them from Delia and Abe, that Rha and Rufus were stupid.

He'd never had reason to call on Rha Tanais or Rufus Ingham, nor could he remember ever meeting them, probably because his was the Holloman of Chubb University, various manufacturing industries and community services; its theater and homosexual worlds were two that had not thus far professionally concerned him. Rha Tanais had genuine international fame, Rufus Ingham did not, yet Carmine knew enough to understand that the anonymous half of the duo was not merely a boyfriend/lover. Rufus Ingham *contributed*. Therefore he must be an interesting guy, to accept his anonymity without, apparently, resentment or expectations.

Even stripped of four acres, Busquash Manor was imposing, a Newport-style palace with a cunningly concealed parking lot and, tucked in a far corner of the grounds with its own vista of the Inlet and Long Island Sound, a charming house that he presumed was Little Busquash. Now inhabited, he had learned from Abe, by Rha's older sister, Ivy Ramsbottom. And what had that been all about, to try to pass Rufus off as other than Antonio Carantonio IV? Except that Abe had liked both men. As did Delia. Not bad guys, then, but what?

Having parked his Fairlane in a slot marked for visitors, Carmine walked through a gap in the hedge that put him on a flagged path toward the mansion's front door, one of those with a large oval sheet of beveled, part-frosted glass embedded in it. There was a bell; he pressed it.

After a shortish wait, the door was opened by, from Abe's description, Rufus. A knockout, was his immediate reaction, but coupled with a tinge of sadness at the eye make-up—still, there could be no doubt that even eyes that magnificent benefited from a touch of mascara and eye-liner. Though the hair, a stunning copper, owed nothing to a dye-bottle or skilled scissors, it was simply a natural head of great hair.

"Mr. Ingham? I'm Carmine Delmonico, Holloman PD. Would it be possible to have a word with you and Mr. Tanais?"

"The Chairman of KGB himself!" said Rufus, clearly delighted. "Come in, Comrade General, please! We're in the theater, and almost through for the morning. Would you mind watching us put the goldfish through its last gasp in an empty bowl?"

"Not at all, Comrade Art and Culture. It will be a change from the noises of the Lubyanka cells."

He was led through an extraordinary place of opulent yet bizarre furniture and furnishings, then down a curving ramp, and into the naked stage area Abe had described. Rufus's hand eased him into one of a row of seats, nearly next to the longest pair of legs he had ever seen, clad in narrow black trousers and flung outstretched to end in feet as big as scuba flippers. The upper regions of these tree trunks were hidden in shadows, but the head was tilted back to listen to whatever Rufus whispered into one ear. Then Rufus sat down on Carmine's other side, hemming him in. He concentrated on the stage.

All the light percolating into the vastness was focused at the front of the stage, where a slim, middle-aged man in a gold lamé tunic and sporting a gold crown on his head was dancing and singing through a cascade of weightless gold discs the size of coins. He looked extremely uncomfortable.

"My darling Servilia has left me
Bereft me
Cleft me
In twain!
How can I bear the pain?
The bitterness of memory's lane?"

His accompaniment, an upright piano from the sound, sat out of sight somewhere; even translated by such a pedestrian instrument, Carmine could sense that the music was clever enough to make the lyrics sing reasonably and fittingly. What rendered the performer unhappy was the dance expected of him; the choreographer had blocked out a routine for someone younger and more athletic.

"If Sid can't manage this, Roger never will," Rufus murmured.

"Tell me about it!" Rha murmured. "There has to be an answer somewhere, though I refuse to ghost it with younger dancers."

Rufus began to sing in a falsetto that rang around the rafters.

"Poor darling old Sid!
You're no longer a kid!
At best you're a"—he launched into coloraturas—"pra-ha-ha-ha-ha-ha-ha-ha-prancer, never a dah-ha-ha-ha-ha-ha-ha-dancer!" The coloraturas ceased. "This hit is total *shit!*"

The "shit" came out like the hiss and crack of a whip; as a way of expressing displeasure Carmine had never heard its like, and found himself grinning. The singer/dancer on stage stood smiling and nodding, while another man in the same age group erupted onto the stage radiating fury. Clearly he was a dancer.

"Fuck you, Ingham!" the angry one yelled.

Rha's voice boomed, pure *basso profundo*. "Todo, stupid Todo, you're an utter dodo! Not so much punch, and let's break for lunch."

Rha Tanais beamed at Carmine and extended a hand. "Sorry for that," he said affably. "Choreographers never take encroaching old age into account because they always stay fit themselves."

"Oh, I loved your lyrics. Extempore is an amazing gift."

"Not really," said Rufus. "Lyrics are a mind-set—a part of the job, you might say. How about a bologna sandwich?"

"We have a great choreographer in Todo Satara," said Rha as they walked, "but right this moment he's battling both his temper and his inner conviction that he's wrong."

They settled in a booth in the dully glowing stainless steel kitchen, he and Rha comfortably ensconced while Rufus fixed the sandwiches, which would have been banal were it not for the fresh and crusty loaf forming their basis. No supermarket pre-sliced bread here! Nor, with an English wife, did Carmine mind butter instead of mayonnaise.

"Abe Goldberg tells me that you've identified four of his John Doe people," Carmine said, lifting his glass of sparkling mineral water. "Your accountant, Mr. Greco, has been helpful too."

"So I should hope," said Rha, who didn't, Abe had told him, engage habitually in "gay" repartee. "How may we further help?"

"By telling me more of the history of Busquash Manor. I'm taking another look at the disappearance of Dr. Nell Carantonio, who would be your close cousin, Rufus?"

"First cousin once removed, or some such thing," Rufus said, sawing bread. "A local socialite built the house in 1840, but it didn't come into Carantonio hands until 1879, when Antonio II bought it. His son, Antonio III, inherited it when he died, and Dr. Nell, an only child, was born in 1899."

"What happened to Dr. Nell's mother?" Carmine asked.

"She died giving birth to Dr. Nell," Rufus said. "It saddens me to think how many years Antonio III lived here virtually alone. The place was different in those days—gloomy and dark. Fenella and then we are responsible for how it looks these days. But Dr. Nell's father was a misanthrope, tended to hate everyone. That went double for his brother, Angelo, and Angelo's daughter, Fenella."

"Was his death a coroner's case?"

"In 1920? No," said Rha, taking over. "By then my father had been a fixture in Little Busquash since 1908, when Antonio III bought two automobiles and my father as chauffeur and—I guess you'd have to say, general factotum. Ivor Ramsbottom—no award for thinking it wise of me to change my name! Antonio III was a genuine curmudgeon, hated the world, but he loved Ivor. He relied on Ivor for everything from managing the servants to being a weird kind of mother for Dr. Nell, and Ivor was the faithful, devoted servant. From what Rufus and I have gathered, Antonio III promised him that he'd be remembered in the will. And he was! Just not the way he'd counted on. He was left tenancy of Little Busquash until Dr. Nell died."

"So in 1925, when she vanished, his tenancy hung in the balance?" Carmine asked.

Rufus finished serving the simple lunch, and slid into the booth alongside Rha. "The trouble is," he said, sipping water, "that Rha and I weren't born yet. The second of November, 1929 for both of us."

"All Souls' Day," Carmine said.

Rha's eyes danced. "Is that as bad as Halloween?" he asked.

"For a Catholic, I'd think it was a good day, not morbid."

"Good but morbid," Rha said solemnly. "Doesn't sound like us."

"Isn't Ivor a Welsh name?" Carmine asked.

"I don't know, except that Ivor's ancestors were Russian—I mean the original Russians, not invaders from the Steppes. His marriage was shameful in my lights, though I don't remember my mother. Ivy does. Mama's origins were Swedish and she was hugely tall, but that wasn't the shameful part. She was a simpleton, and Ivor knew it. Why he married her I don't know, nor does Ivy, and she had normal offspring, so whatever was wrong with her wasn't inherited, at least in our generation. Still, it sure turned Ivy and me off marriage and children."

"When did your mother die, Rha?"

"In 1931, falling down the Busquash Manor grand staircase. She had poor control of her body, Ivy says."

"And Ivor? What happened to him?"

"He died in 1934," Rha said, sounding reflective. "Funny, that. He wasn't old—fifty at most—but after Mama died, he faded away. I mean that he became more frightening but less visible, if that can make sense. Ivy took the brunt of him, while Fenella had taken me to rear with Rufus. Though Dr. Nell and her father both loved Ivor, we children were petrified of him."

"How old was Ivy when he died?" Carmine asked.

"My sister's sensitive about her age, but I think she was at least ten, maybe twelve."

Time to change the subject. "What was Fenella like?" he asked.

Rufus laughed. "Ah, you've been listening to conflicting stories!" he cried. "An angel, or a devil, huh?"

"You got it."

"She was both. If Fenella loved you, Carmine, you could have no greater friend and ally. If she disliked you, look out for trouble! Some of her churlishness I lay at the feet of her health—it must have been terrible, to inherit all that money, make even more, and then become too sick to do all the things she wanted to, like cruise the world on ocean liners, wine and dine and dance her way from Rio to Buenos Aires—all she could do was show Rha and me pictures in books, and they were in black-and-white. I know I loved Fenella."

"And so did I," Rha said.

"Do either of you think of her as a mother?"

They answered together, strongly. "No."

Something had been growing in Rha's face—puzzlement? "A question, Carmine, if I may?"

"Sure, go ahead."

"The conviction is growing that I *have* seen you, but never been introduced."

"I've picked my wife up from Rha Tanais Tall a couple of times," Carmine said. "She's six foot three, so she shops there."

"Your wife is the Divine Desdemona?"

"Yep."

"Captain, you have *taste!* Desdemona is the most queenly person I know." A giggle escaped. "No offense."

Carmine eyed Rha sourly, but with a twinkle. "None taken. On a queenlier note, did Fenella object to your sexuality?"

"No, it delighted her," Rufus said. "She really thought her malady was inheritable, so anything that meant we didn't procreate pleased her. She was never selfish about us, tried to keep us at home during her last years. I think she preferred our visits, because we always had so much to tell her. We used to try to make our stories of show biz and gays as exciting as the ocean liner cruises she never had." He slid his arm around Rha's waist. "The greatest piece of luck we ever had, Carmine, is knowing each other all our lives. Oh, the success and the comfort are fantastic, but they're not what Rha and I are all about. We are about a very great love story."

"That, I can see," Carmine said, sliding out of the booth. "My thanks for the candor and the clarification. So many deaths!"

"Mostly from natural causes," said Rufus, letting him out. "A world minus antibiotics and skilled obstetricians was a harder place to survive than today's world. I mean, pneumonia was the biggest killer on the planet."

He returned to the theater and sat down next to Rha.

"How do you think it went?" Rha asked.

"Straight story-telling. He's just information gathering."

Rha had had enough Carantonio family history, and went where his mind was dwelling. "I think we have to bring Roger up to go through his numbers. If he still wants to play Broadway leads, he's going to have to suffer an occasional day or two up here away from all his friends. If Todo doesn't work the routines out with him personally, it will never come right. Why won't dancers admit that singers with great voices don't dance like Fosse?"

"Fred Astaire proved the same point twenty-five years ago," Rufus said. "Roger Dartmont may not be Fosse or Astaire, but he can sing both of them into the back row of any choir."

Rha began to sing.

"All is not gold despite its glitter, dodo!
Let's prevent our work going down the shitter, Todo!"

FRIDAY, AUGUST 15, 1969

Paper, thought Dr. Jessica Wainfleet, will be the death of me yet. She was sitting at her desk entering notes into one of the files dotted in neat stacks around it, taking care never to untie the striped ribbon around a stack until the stack preceding it had been tied up again. It had been a routine day and therefore not an exciting one; no patient had manifested evidence of change for better or for worse, and the chimpanzee Ari Melos had planned to use for stimulation and implantation of electrodes tomorrow had developed "the miseries" as he called them, not knowing how else to describe an inarticulate primate sickening for something not fully emerged. Whether it was a cold or some other bug, the animal most definitely would not be undergoing neurosurgery this weekend!

Her phone rang just as Walter Jenkins came in; she gave him a brief smile and answered the imperious summons no modern person seemed capable of ignoring; the power this inanimate thing owned fascinated her. Nodding, Walter sat down opposite her, noting her growing exasperation as if it were some alien disease—which it probably was to him, Jess thought wryly.

"Goddam grant committees!" she snapped, banging the receiver down. "NIH needs me to pinch-hit tomorrow in Boston."

"I'll be okay," he said, it seemed reading her mind. "I don't need knocking out or sending back to the Asylum. My road map is getting bigger every day—I can see around corners now."

Startled, she stared at him intently for long enough to have unsettled an ordinary person; but not Walter Jenkins, who simply waited for her to finish whatever it was she was thinking. "When did you realize what happens to you if I go away?"

"Dates come hard, Jess, that hasn't changed. A while is the best I can say."

"But you realize what happens?"

"Sure. If it's a weekend, I get doped up and locked into my room here in HI. If it's longer, I go back to the Asylum. They don't treat me bad, but I hate that place."

"Do you know why it's done?"

The aquamarine eyes flashed scorn. "I'm no dummy, Jess. If you're not here, they worry I might revert to the Old-Walter."

"And what do you think about that, inside yourself?"

"The Old-Walter is dead. They know that too, but knowing it can't kill their fear of the Old-Walter. He was bad news."

She couldn't help it; Jess beamed at him, a mixture of love and admiration so entangled with self-love and self-admiration that she couldn't quite locate where one ended and the other began. "Walter, you're doing splendidly!" she exclaimed. "You're deducing—and correctly! These are pathways you've opened up yourself, and they're logical. There's even a possibility that these new self-opened pathways are ethical. Do you have any liking left for the old Walter?" She spoke it as noun qualified by adjective, having no idea that to him, it was a two-part proper name.

"The Old-Walter is beneath contempt," he said, finding a use for that phrase, read in a book and esteemed. "I have a better name for him, though."

"You do? May I know it?"

"Walter No-brain. He belongs in the Asylum. Walter Big-brain belongs in HI, even if you're away in Boston."

"I think that too, and by this stage in your career, Walter, I think your panel will vote to keep you in HI. How much freedom from being locked in your room or medicated I can't predict, but it's possible the verdict will be only if necessary. And it won't be necessary, will it?"

His relaxed pose didn't alter, nor his eyes deviate from fixation upon hers; he lifted his chin, yet still held her gaze. "I'm trying to stay on my road map, Jess, I really am. If I can discern which is the correct road to take when I come to a fork, I travel down it, even when the other road I didn't take looks very pretty. That's when I tell myself I'm in real control."

"Who is this 'I'?"

"This mind. This Walter Big-brain."

"And what did you call the old Walter?"

"Walter No-brain. The non-Walter."

"You don't really need to damp your language down, do you?"

No emotion answered her question, but everything else was present. "That's true," he said. "I can talk on a higher level about myself— what I was, what I am, what I will be. But it's better to keep it low level because of the others, I always feel. If I were to spout neuroanatomical terms, I'd frighten people all over again, and worse. Am I wrong to think that?"

He had just demonstrated a stunning breakthrough, but also betrayed that it wasn't particularly new. Was she neglecting him, or was he outstripping her? In the meantime, he was waiting for an answer to his question.

"No, Walter, you're not wrong. People always have expectations about the nature of outcomes, and they can only credit so much as the truth. Your instinct to dumb yourself down is right on, my friend. Even our world isn't quite ready for Walter Big-brain."

"Ari will want to lock me in my HI room."

"Ari doesn't have the last word," Jess said firmly. "The last word belongs to me, and I say you should be allowed out and about during my absence. However, if after I've gone to Boston Ari, Fred and Moira decide to lock you in, I need your assurance right now that you'll submit."

His head nodded through the unpalatable part of this, his mouth firm but tranquil. "My map has expanded enough to see what you mean, and why. I don't want to be locked up, but I understand it. Yes, I'll submit without a murmur."

"It won't happen, Walter."

He demonstrated another stunning breakthrough. "The old Ari was a great guy, but he's gone. There's a new Ari, and the new Ari was born when Rose Compton married him. Rose is a weakling; you misjudged her when you appointed her head nurse. It's not like you to fall for brownnosing, but maybe it's Rose's sex makes her brownnosing harder for you to see. Rose wants two things. The first, is you discredited, and the best way to do that is to show everyone that I'm not cured, that I'm a monster. The second thing she wants is Ari as Director of HI."

Her breath caught, she visibly stiffened. My God! she thought, how many new pathways is he opening up, and where do they go? He has just informed me that I fell for a professional confidence trick, and he's absolutely right! Yet he called Rose a *weakling!* He's right again, only a weakling would hatch such a futile plot.

Weakling. Where did he learn that word? Or when I ablated—that is to say, destroyed—did I miss some micro-clusters of subcortical grey matter no one dreams exist? Old brain stuff.

I am the best in the world at this, but how good is best? Oh, Walter, Walter, you are my testament to life, my triumph! All I need is another like you to repeat the procedure, and my entire world will genuflect. Don't let me down!

She paused to assess him again. Let there be no rage in him as a result of his deductions! If he's angry, then his prognosis plummets into an abyss. But there was no anger: not one iota. Rather, he demonstrated a kind of clinical interest in Rose's plots.

"Ari won't take your place, Jess," he said flatly.

"Why?"

"He's not in your class, and everybody but Rose already knows that. Most importantly, Ari knows it."

"You're exactly right, Walter."

"At least I can see you for dinner tonight."

Her face fell. "Oh, Walter, I can't! I'm dining out. But I'll be there for breakfast at seven tomorrow."

Dinner that evening was at Delia's condo, and consisted of pizza with a side salad and a bottle of chilled sparkling wine.

"The wine snobs say Cold Duck is rubbish," said Delia cheerily as she poured from the champagne-shaped bottle, "but I really like it—sweet, fizzy, pure Keats."

Jess eyed her friend warily. "I'm not going there, Delia, so don't try to lure me. Though I do agree with you—I love Cold Duck, no matter how the snobs put it down."

"Have you ever partaken of a thousand-dollar bottle of wine?"

Jess blinked. "Never."

"We dealt with the theft of a thousand-dollar bottle of wine once," Delia said dreamily. "Its owner had bought it at auction, and never intended to drink it—my personal theory at the time—it was my first case in Holloman—was that he simply got carried away at the auction the way people do. He certainly wasn't a wine collector!"

"Beaded bubbles winking at the brim!" Jess cried.

"Eh?"

"That's your Keats lure, ha ha ha!"

"It is too! But the thousand-dollar wine is now at issue!" Delia said, a little put out. "Who took it?"

"His wife put it in a Beef Burgundy," Jess said.

Delia looked disgusted. "Oh, you party-pooper!"

"I bet the marriage was rocky for a while."

"No, he was too nice a guy." She peered at Jess. "However, a bit of light-hearted badinage has done you good. You were looking quite bothered when you came in tonight, Jess."

"I was feeling it too, but a dose of Delia and Cold Duck has fixed me right up."

"Can you talk about the problem?"

"Oh, yes. The NIH has me on their list of inspectors of some grant applications. They don't usually involve weekend trips, but there's a maverick in Boston, and I'm a last-minute substitution member of a committee going to Boston tomorrow morning. It kills my own schedule, but that wasn't the real problem. Walter was."

Delia lined up olive pits on the edge of her plate. "I'm changing my pizzeria—pits, yet! What's Walter's peril, dear?"

"He can get upset if I'm absent overnight, though I can't equate him with a small child in any way, including how his mind works," Jess said, glad to have an outside ear. "Right at this very moment he's decided to make breakthroughs in all directions—Delia, it's so *exciting!* The last thing I need is an upset Walter, and he's so aware that I think he expects Ari Melos will send him back to the Asylum as soon as my back is turned."

"Is it likely?"

"No, I really believe he's safe. If Ari decides to lock him up anywhere, it would be in HI, not the Asylum—he hasn't shown any need for Asylum-style confinement in—oh, three years!"

"Then why don't you lock him up before you go? You say he trusts you. I may be getting the wrong message, but it sounds as if it's the Asylum Walter's afraid of, far more than being locked in his room at HI. Can't you talk him into letting *you* lock him in? Or have I got it wrong?"

"No, you're right. The trouble is, I promised that he'd be free while I was away. I'd have to go back on my word to him."

"Then it's a good test of his ethics," Delia said shrewdly. "If he's making all these exciting breakthroughs, he ought to be able to cope with a disappointment or two as well."

Jess accepted another glass of Cold Duck. "Oh, Delia, you're asking for a lot! I didn't choose the road map metaphor for no reason—he and I are journeying through utter terra incognita, and I don't call his brain unknown country for nothing. On many levels Walter's thinking is highly developed, even sophisticated—he can read and understand technical, factual books, and has a deep appreciation for classical music, though popular music bores him, I think because it lacks mathematics. Yet on other levels his thought processes are vestigial, even alien. For instance, he slavers at Shakespeare's use of language, but can't appreciate any of the core emotions behind Shakespeare, like Hamlet's Oedipus complex or Othello's jealousy."

"An intellectual competent but an emotional imbecile?"

"It's not as simple as that, but . . . yes, something like."

"So if you leave Walter free, you're not one hundred percent positive that he'll survive. Though I think it's other people you don't trust far more than lack of faith in Walter."

The long, serious face lit up. "Yes, exactly!"

It had been another hot, windless day that left a brown bank of smog hovering over the Sound, as smooth and glassy as a sheet of polished steel; the two women sat, chairs turned to the huge window and its view, and said nothing for some time. Old Father Reilly from St. Mary's at Millstone came wandering along the stony beach with his two ancient beagle dogs, a sign that all was right with his world; a pity, that worlds like Jess's were newer, vaguer, more unpredictable.

"Jess," Delia began, choosing her words, "far be it from me to teach you your incredible job, especially when at the moment I'm at an absolute dead end in my own job, but I have a nagging feeling that you should at least confine Walter Jenkins to his HI room while you're away. Perhaps, since you believe he now possesses a lot of reasoning power, you could find the right words to reconcile him to a very temporary detention in quarters he seems to regard as a home rather than a prison? Don't give him any drugs to damp his emotions or what pass for emotions, that way he'll be alert enough to see that you haven't lied to him about anything."

"You've inferred a lot from very little implication."

"Detectives excell at that, Jess!"

All the way home to HI, crossing the main roads rather than using them, Jess debated. She had promised him freedom while she was away, now she was contemplating shutting him up. Was he capable of seeing that what she was really doing in shutting him in his room was safeguarding him?

He was waiting in her office, clad in his T-shirt and shorts uniform, always grey; he was atrociously color-blind, and thought his grey was an entrancing shade of green. But how do any of us know what we see is red, or green—or grey? How he managed the colored stripes of her coded file ribbons she could only guess at; he never got them wrong, and insisted he did see colors. Just not the colors she saw. But how did he know they were different? What was his standard of comparison?

"Don't work too late tonight," he said, with that quaint authority. "Are you driving to Boston?"

"No, I'll take the commuter from Holloman airport."

"I've been thinking," he said, busy opening the safe.

"Thinking what, Walter?"

She had pushed her chair to one side to let him deal with the safe more comfortably; now she swung the chair to stare at him fixedly, her dark eyes wide.

"How about you lock me in my room here at HI while you're in Boston, Jess? If the no-Walter appears, the most he can do is to wreck a room. I don't expect the no-Walter, he's lost in the old dark, but I'd rather be sure than sorry. Please," said Walter, twirling the disc as he spoke.

"One day, Walter dear friend, I *won't* be here. But that's for the years to come, not this weekend. I'll probably be back quite early on Sunday evening."

"Lock me up, Jess, please!"

"Amazing!" she said, drawing the word out.

"Will you lock me up?"

"Since it's your own idea, Walter, yes, I will. Gladly!"

SATURDAY/SUNDAY NIGHT, AUGUST 16–17, 1969

I t looked like accommodation in a luxury hotel, complete with an en suite bathroom with
a large shower stall and a jacuzzi tub. But be-
hind the tasteful lime-and-ultramarine fabrics and white-painted
wood lay the kind of wall construction no hotel of any grade would
have possessed: inch-thick steel bars, very special electrical wiring,
and, separated by six inches of vacuum, two window panes of ar-
mored glass so thick the outside view was yellowed. Once its occupant was inside and the day's code was punched into its lock, he was
inside until the lock was disengaged, and that included an alarm like
an ocean liner's foghorn.

There was nothing Walter Jenkins didn't know about his room,
which had been specially created for him over two years ago after
Jess ended the actual intervention treatments and banished the old
Walter. His progress and his promise of future improvement rendered a cell in the Asylum undesirable to the point of posing a threat
to progress and improvement; Jess had gone to battle for the money
to incarcerate him within HI itself, and won. The Asylum nowadays
was not to make Walter safer, but to make those who fraternized with
him feel safer. With a record as appalling as Walter's, people found it
extremely difficult to credit that the monster he had been was truly
no longer there. Ari Melos and the Castigliones were believers, but
HI ran on nurses, aides, technicians and various domestic staff, and
it was among these people that vestiges of terror lurked. While Jess

was in-house, it was quiescent; when she went away, some staff were uneasy.

Facts of which Walter was aware, and dealt with in ways no one, including Jess, had ever spotted. Like the time during which the men built his room. In his T-shirt and shorts, with his military look, those workmen had taken a liking to him when he hung around; he had become part-mascot, part-apprentice, for he demonstrated a remarkable manual dexterity, and when given some chore, did it well enough to be admired. As the degree of his technical ability grew more apparent, he was allowed the run of the on-site workshop. Limited in its comprehension of abstract concepts, Walter's mind couldn't gauge other people's reactions as naive, but such they were, and that went as much for the psychiatrists as it did for the builders who constructed his new quarters.

Walter took what Walter wanted, understanding what "want" was. So he hung around to watch, would trot off to fiddle with wires and solder in the workshop, then tender his efforts knowing they would be accepted. For they were helpful and beautifully made. Because it was done en bloc at the very last moment and tucked behind a steel bar, none of the workers noticed him introduce a bypass that both opened his door and cut off the alarm; the contractors were running dangerously near penalty rates for lateness, and by now they treated Walter like a workmate. Cameras and microphones were also installed, but there was no way he could bypass them. However, when he had lived in his luxury cell for six months he went to Jess and formally objected to his complete lack of privacy. It retarded his progress by inhibiting him, he said—weren't six months enough of it? The panel met, and agreed that visual and acoustic supervision of Walter Jenkins were unnecessary. His sensitivity in reaching that conclusion was *so* exciting! Walter covered lenses and devices with plasticene just to make sure, and if anyone tried to watch or listen, no one admitted to it.

Imprisoned since childhood, he had never driven a car or a stick-shift truck. Ari Melos thought of offering Walter a treat and using it as an opportunity to see how well Walter's reflexes would work while his mind was occupied in controlling a heavy mass of metal moving at speed. And Walter excelled; whatever the damage to his forebrain and its subservient pathways, his controlling and driving skills were superb. So superb that Ari brought in his Harley-Davidson motorcycle and examined Walter's skills riding what he jokingly called his "hog."

"A Harley is a hog because it has grunt," he explained.

Walter knew what hogs were for the same reason he knew what most things were: he had seen them on television. Books were static, just pictures, but TV *moved.* If Ari's jest was no jest to him, that lay in his lack of a sense of humor. Even Jess couldn't provoke a smile, nor had anyone ever heard Walter Jenkins laugh. The subject of a hundred and more conferences, Walter remained an engima to those who studied him, including Jess. Where were his limits? Was he capable of feeling?

"Tabula rasa," Ari Melos had said. A blank page.

On a motorcycle Walter proved to be so good that, after some negotiations with Warden Hanrahan and Asylum Security, a section of internal roadway had been cleared of all traffic and Walter permitted to ride the Harley at speed for a total of twenty miles—fifteen minutes. That the experience thrilled him was beyond doubt, but he didn't smile, and his heart rate had never increased at the end of his ride. It had only happened the once, ten months ago; Walter had never expressed a wish to repeat the experience.

At eleven, Walter turned his lights out. Inmates' lights were centrally extinguished at nine-thirty, Walter alone exempted; only he decided when to go to bed, no matter how late the hour. With Jess away, he was locked in; she had done it herself before leaving to catch the Boston shuttle at six Saturday morning, her own eyes checking that he had sufficient reading material. The big television screen was permanently on, volume usually a murmur, and he was connected to cable networks; he liked natural history shows, scientific documentaries and all kinds of films.

Disengaging his door lock and alarm, he opened the door. The overhead lights were off, the hallway well lit near floor level by inset lamps; it was empty, silent, tucked up for the night. Good! The green ON bulb was glowing above his door combination, telling the curious that the lock was engaged, he was inside. His was the only inmate room upstairs save for the hospital sector, which held no patients at the moment. The night staff would be drinking coffee or tea in their wardroom at this hour, fresh from their first rounds, girding their loins for the next patrol.

Still in his grey T-shirt and short shorts, Walter raced down the corridor toward the bright green EXIT sign, and there punched in Saturday's code to open the door into the escape stairwell. Not four seconds later he was through it, down the stairs five at a time, and at the bottom. No need to open the inside door; he had the correct code to open the fire door that led outside. That was one little item of information he hadn't confided to Jess—his scary ability to remember codes and numbers.

The I-Walter hadn't announced his presence very long ago, though Walter knew he loomed there like an insurmountable pinnacle of rock; but when, less than two months ago he stepped from his pinnacle, Walter looked into the face of the I-Walter, and knew it as his real one. Nothing had made sense until then, not the memory or the ability or the fate or Jess. . . . But the I-Walter and his layers gave it all meaning, and every single day an opaque sheet between two of his layers would fall away, dissolve into purpose. He didn't know yet what the I-Walter's purpose was, just that the I-Walter was the real Walter. And tonight, with Jess away in Boston and his room locked, he was out and about to serve the I-Walter.

On this back side of HI's oblong mass all was quiet and dark, no searchlights licking luminous lacework across the night, which sometimes happened if Warden Hanrahan thought his guards were getting sloppy and needed an exercise. The reality of an inmate escape had never happened, never ever. Walter checked out the Asylum itself, equally dark and quiet. The watchtowers were positioned to be of maximum strategic and tactical assistance to the Asylum blocks, which meant that at the far, narrow end of the teardrop-shaped walls, only one watch tower was manned. When the immense reconstruction of the Asylum had taken place between 1950 and 1960, the plan had been to amputate the end of the teardrop, paying for a fairly small section of new outer wall by selling off the land—then the State ran out of money. Dr. Wainfleet's needs had taken precedence and costs were way over budget, with the result that in 1969 the Asylum was divided into two parts: the blocks housing inmates and research facility clustered inside the gate, and a tapering, progressively narrower section of deserted parkland containing in one again constricted area, the sheds and outbuildings no one at all went near after dark.

Like a Belgian leech or some other flat, slapping worm, Walter was through the fire escape door and prone on the parched grass in one liquid movement; lifting his head just enough, he saw that everything was as it should be, then got to his feet and ran like a hare for the deep shade of the Asylum's only grove of trees. There was no moon and thunderheads bulged muttering in the distance, no pallid outriders of wispier cloud to pull them this way; the storm cells were vanishing into Massachusetts.

Here, the grove of trees inside the Asylum wall met the forest on its outside, and here, buried in a thick clump of mountain laurel, was the rounded bulge of a watchtower that had never been erected above the top of the wall, so was not drawn on the plans as a watchtower, nor noticed thanks to the dense shrubbery. And in the wall just beyond the roundel of the aborted watchtower was a door. Walter's door. He had found it on one of his illicit, unsuspected night excursions a full year ago.

It was the size of an ordinary door and wall-colored, a relic of an earlier time that inexplicably had gone unnoticed: a non-door. Pilfering what he needed gradually, he had removed its rusted hinges and simple latch, fitting new ones that he kept well lubricated. Inside the door, he discovered, the wall was hollow and had a similar door into the external forest. More hinges, another new latch, and he, who would become the I-Walter, stepped into the free, untrammeled world. He, who never remembered a time when he hadn't been imprisoned, was free. The realization provoked no elation or sense of triumph, but he did feel *something*, and he fully understood that he was an intruder rather than a native. Perhaps because of that, he took his time, time never having been an entity Walter thought about as others did.

Confinement breeds infinite patience.

With television to tell him what the real world was like, he had thus far made two forays into it.

On his first, following a deer path through the forest, he chanced upon Route 133, and skulking in the shadows that loomed right up to it, he found a house and a shed, then more sheds, and an old, non-customized Harley-Davidson motorcycle. It had been someone's beloved workhorse rather than a gang bike, for it had a pannier on either side of the rear wheel and a big pillion box connecting them. One pannier held a basic set of Harley tools, and draped between the handlebars was a black Viking helmet. He wheeled the bike the five miles home and put it inside the wall in the circular swelling of the roundel, which he was busy fitting out as a kind of a bolt-hole, a place that really belonged to him. The I-Walter. Pressure lamps, camp cooking gear—it was amazing what was squirreled away in the Asylum sheds! Examination had revealed that the bike's gas tank was full, but one of the things he couldn't find was a supply of gas for it.

On his second foray three months later he had wheeled the Harley (already equipped with as efficient a muffler as the emissions would tolerate) far enough not to alert wall or tower guards on Millington, which meant way down 133. Late at night held additional perils when it came to noise, but he could hide a bike, never a car. A trip to the library had seen him memorize the Holloman County road map and locate the whereabouts of the things he needed. So when he set out he knew exactly where he was going: to a group of shops on the Boston Post Road that included a motorcycle emporium. Thirteen miles there and back again—did he have enough gas? He could only hope he did, based on his television experience, and that said he had plenty. He had no money to buy gas or anything else, though if he had to, he could siphon.

For Walter, busting into the emporium without triggering the alarm was child's play. He found black leathers that fitted him well, including boots, took two empty plastic containers that would fit inside the pillion box, and, out of a glass-topped counter, a handy hunting knife. When he opened the cash register, all it held were checks. But he left no fingerprints, having sheathed his hands in a pair of surgical gloves. Television again! If the prints of one of the most dangerous prisoners in the nation turned up a few miles away, they'd start looking for his door. So he took special care when choosing a pair of black leather gauntlets. Except—no cash. *Where can I find money?*

Tonight, after a long wait familiarizing himself with the Harley and tuning it even better than its erstwhile owner had, he was going out again. The I-Walter had struggled out of his opaque sheets and displayed all his layers, and the I-Walter wanted to ride the Harley. The pathways kept opening up, a source of calm well-being that the I-Walter liked. But he needed money, and that was difficult for a night-man to contend with. Banks were closed, so were shops. The shops that were open, his television told him, were staffed by foreigners who were always a problem in one way or another. Walter decided that his best bet was an area of small factories and workshops like the one marked on his map behind Holloman City Hall; he could crack a small combination safe by sound and feel if the room was quiet enough, and at this hour on a Saturday night, who would be at work? What he hoped for, television fueled, was a cash box or two. He didn't need a fortune, just money for gasoline.

As he rode downtown under the speed limit, Walter and the I-Walter finally came together. It wasn't like that fool movie about the three faces of Eve, because different people couldn't live inside one and the same body, it didn't make sense. No, what happened on that ride was an understanding, that it had taken over two years from the end of Jess's operations to part the sheets of mystery; his made-over brain had been one set of curtains after another, and now they had all vanished he could see what Jess had made of him: the I-Walter. Only the I-Walter was his secret. Knowing about the I-Walter would make Jess a basket case, at least until she could be made to understand, as Walter understood.

He never saw a squad car or a highway patrol as he rode. Facing the magnificent Green, City Hall was imposing, but behind it lay a different world, one that suited Walter perfectly. No dwellings, just premises. Killing the bike in a pool of darkness fairly close to the back of City Hall, he listened to its engine tick as it cooled off while his eyes roamed in every direction. Then, satisfied that the bike was safe and the area deserted, he moved off into an alley, examining the doors of the buildings as he went.

Someone moved; Walter froze against the wall, fused into it. If there were neighborhood kids the street lamps would have been shot out long ago, but an occasional lamp was lit in a privacy pattern the prison inmate Walter had no way to understand: loiter under the lamp, move into the darkness for an against-the-wall fuck. The loitering woman was a light-colored African-American, mini-skirted but knickerless, and talking with her was a burbling, bopping black man counting the bills she was handing him.

"Yo' done good, Hepzibah," he said, ceasing his dance.

"Sattidy night, Marty—mah big night."

"Get yo' ass back on yo' beat, woman!"

"Fuck that," she said. "Home fo' me." And melted away.

Marty Fane resumed his burbling and bopping in Walter's direction, pleased with the night's takings. This was his patch, had been for so long that it never occurred to him anyone might try to take it off him. As pimps went, he was a good one, in that he cared for his girls, made sure they were clean, didn't beat them up for the fun of it, and gave them enough to pay for their habit or their kids, though both was a hassle Marty preferred to avoid by kicking the real hags off of his patch.

His car, a moderately old Cadillac pimpishly embellished, was parked in an area adjacent to City Hall's rear end. As Marty undulated gracefully along, Walter paralleled him, insubstantial as cigarette smoke reflected off a polished table. At the car Marty paused, eyes busy, ears listening; he unlocked it, walked around to the passenger's side, opened that door and knelt on the seat to rummage in the glove box. A hand snaked over his mouth and yanked him to his feet in the same movement, then two hands went around his neck and he collapsed onto the road, unconscious but not seriously harmed.

Walter saw the path on his cerebral plan divide, but the decision as to which branch he would take was made in a flash. Flipping the inanimate form over, he drove the knife, absolutely centered, into the base of Marty's throat, then ripped the blade upward to the chin before pulling it free. As he'd imagined, not much blood in the midline, but the guy would drown in it, voiceless.

He extricated a roll of bills from Marty's pocket; there were two more rolls in the glove box, as well as a .45 semiautomatic and a spare clip. Everything was stowed in Walter's jacket, but all of that was done absently; Walter's mind dwelled on Marty's eyes, which had opened just before the knife went in.

He was back inside his wall, not a spot of blood on him, at three in the morning. By the light of his lantern he counted his takings, mostly fives and tens: nearly fifteen hundred dollars. Now he could buy gasoline!

At three-thirty he beeped his room intercom.

"Hi, it's Walter. I know the night isn't over, but could I come out for a while? I've been in here now for almost a day, and my legs are seizing up. Just a walk, please!"

Jess answered. "Guess who's back early? Like a game of poker or chess? Or—after that walk, of course!—like to talk?"

"Walk, then talk," he said. "It's been so boring."

Another breakthrough! Walter knew what boredom was.

SUNDAY, AUGUST 17, 1969

Wondering why Marty Fane had been parked there too long, the crew of a routinely patrolling squad car had found Marty lying beside it in the road at three a.m. This was the true witching hour, when even the cats and cockroaches had done their thing, when Marty's girls could expect no further customers, and Marty himself was back home in his little Argyle Avenue palace.

Carmine took the case himself with Delia as backup; Abe and his team were moving on the Does. Donny could handle the street stuff, Buzz was on vacation and Delia so frustrated over her Shadow Women that she'd probably think processing parking tickets a boon.

The murder of the long time pimp caused a universal sensation, and if grief were not mentioned nor tears detected in official eyes at the news, nonetheless it provoked shock, concern, a definite and complex sorrow. For Marty Fane had gone on long enough to become an institution of sorts, and his particular world, deprived of his steadying influence, was in for all the troubles that went with a vacant patch, rudderless girls, greed, and violence. Despite his history he'd been relatively young: a mere forty-five. Certainly not old enough to have seen any sharks cruising in the periphery of his patch waiting to close in. Now there would be a turf war fought through the dog days of August.

"He died quite slowly, poor fellow," said Gus Fennell in the autopsy room. "Interestingly unusual technique, not something taught in a Quantico boot camp or anywhere else I can think of."

"But silent," Carmine said. "No voice box."

"True, but think for a while, Carmine. First, his attacker got Marty around the neck and part-throttled him—he'd have been out cold for a minute or two. Then—this! Initially bloodless because it started the way you'd do an emergency tracheostomy, puncturing the airway below the swallowing reflexes. Had the attacker stopped there, Marty could well have lived, but he didn't stop there. Instead, he drove his knife deep enough to make contact with the ventral side of the spinal column, and dragged it upward to the under-jaw without severing anything capable of bleeding out fast. No spray, no huge lake. I estimate that Marty regained consciousness about the moment the knife tracheostomized him, so he endured the rest awake. I mean, the notochord—the fetal tube—folds over and closes in the front midline, hence the lack of major blood vessels and nerves there. I ask, did the attacker know that? I must presume so, but anyone with that degree of anatomical sophistication would have other, better ways to kill, including with a knife."

"Are you implying a torture element, Gus?" Delia asked.

"I don't honestly know, Delia. The most I can tell you is that the attacker had fantastic control over the knife—the cut was absolutely straight, no matter what structures it bisected."

"Paul says he wiped his knife clean on Marty's fake-fur upholstery," Delia added.

"And wore gloves—no prints anywhere," Carmine said.

"And that's it as far as I'm concerned, Captain," said Gus. "A very resourceful and individualistic killer."

The two detectives set off upstairs grim-faced.

"I'll have to brief Fernando," Carmine said, plodding up the stairs one at a time. "The uniforms are going to be busy until the whore-pimp equation solves itself. I liked Marty because he got on well with his girls and kept them clean. When his best girl was murdered a few years back, he was genuinely grieved."

"A world wherein no one needed to pay for sex and therefore no one peddled it," said Delia with a sigh, "would be an ideal answer to the Marty Fanes, but unfortunately it doesn't exist. There are always more people wanting sex than there are people willing to give it out freely."

Carmine laughed. "Muddled thinking, Deels, but true for all that. Time to go to the scene of the crime."

Its being a Sunday, he reflected, was a great help; Carmine and Delia walked the area behind City Hall secure in the knowledge that the entire tangle of streets and alleys was cordoned off, and that he had been called in early enough to ban an invasion of squad cars and uniforms. No insult intended to Fernando Vasquez and his boys, but it had meant that Paul Bachman could send someone to go over a fairly pristine murder site. As this had been done, he was free to go where he pleased.

The 1964 Cadillac hadn't been towed away yet. Sitting with her long legs planted on the roadway and a cigarette in one hand, Hepzibah Cornwallis waited in the shotgun seat of a lone squad car, rather pleased with herself; she had categorically refused to ride in its caged back quarters, since she was a cop witness, and had wallowed in the pleasure of seeing the female squaddie ride in the cage while she rode shotgun. Another part of her was devastated at Marty's death—what would happen to her now? She was Dee-Dee Hall's replacement, her speciality blow jobs, so she was a big earner, a valuable whore.

She eyed the couple walking toward her in some amusement; they belonged together about as much as a lion belonged with a miniature poodle. The guy was Carmine Delmonico, who she knew was a shit-hot cop, but that couldn't sour her feminine appreciation of his dynamic attractiveness. Tall, bull-necked, flat in the belly, always dressed like a Chubber, with black hair fighting curls by a short cut, eyes a kind of goldy-brown, and a face she had a weird feeling should have been a king's. A real lion, leader of the pack or whatever a harem of lions was called. The woman was that Brit bitch Delia Carstairs, ugly as sin, clad today in loose pajamas of tie-dyed cotton in every color that clashed.

"Hi, Hepzibah," Carmine said, smiling at her. "I'm sorry about Marty, I really am."

"I'm sorry too," said Delia warmly.

"Yo' ain't sorry like me. Why yo' bring me here?"

"I thought you might be of more help here than down in County Services," Carmine said easily, and keeping to the singular; it didn't escape him that the whores detested female cops. Taking the hint, Delia wandered off into the distance. Carmine indicated the Cadillac. "There's not much blood, so it won't be a horrible ordeal, but if I ask you very nicely and politely, would you look at the car with me? If anything's missing, you'll know what it is."

"Fo' you, honey, I would go down on the Pope. An' fo' my Marty too. Anything I can do, I do. Jus' catch this motherfucker fo' us, Cap'n."

"When did you last see Marty?"

"Around two. By then, he closin' shop. I went home."

"No customers in the neighborhood?"

"Nope. Place was stone dead."

Carmine extended his hand and pulled Hepzibah out of the car with what struck her as courteous respect, and walked, hand under her elbow, to the Cadillac. In honor of Marty's death she was wearing knickers, but her skimpy mini-skirt of cherry-red satin fully displayed her quite beautiful legs as she paraded on Captain Delmonico's arm; at twenty-five years of age and an expert in the art of fellatio, she still had a long career ahead of her. Eat yo' heart out, female cop!

"Tell me anything different about the car," Carmine said.

Avoiding the blood puddle, old and browned, she went for the glove box immediately, flipped it open. "Marty keep the world in here," she said, rummaging but not removing anything. "Money's gone. So's his .45 gun an' a spare clip. Nothin' else."

"Do you think his attacker was someone moving in on his turf?" Carmine asked as they moved away.

She thought—and she could think, as she earned to support two children, not a drug habit—then shook her head. "Nope, no one movin' in on Marty. The mother-fucker wanted his cache."

"And got it. Why would the attacker have killed Marty? Our doctor says he didn't need to kill."

"'Cos he bad news, Cap'n. He kill fo' fun."

"Have you girls gotten a plan?"

The big, tear-filled eyes widened, the white teeth flashed in a smirk. "We's jus' ho's! *Ho's* plan?"

"Hepzibah, you're a natural leader. Remember, the best way to defend is to attack."

"I remember that. Yeah, us ho's might have a plan, but it depend on things. Yo' got a suggestion?"

He installed her in the shotgun seat of the squad car, and shook her hand. "Get in first, Hepzibah. Choose your own pimp."

The squad car sped away.

"The beautiful part about murder scene interrogations is that they're impossible to immortalize on tape," said Delia demurely. "Choose your own pimp indeed! They'll end in getting their own throats cut. Compared to Otis Fly-by or Chester the Pollack, yon dead Marty Fane was a pushover."

"No, Marty's stable is all superior girls. That's why he lasted so long in a cut-throat business. I'll back his girls if they're well led and get in first. Hepzibah has a brother."

"That's insider trading!" Delia said. "Whoever their pimp ends up being, the girls will be exploited."

"Yes, they will. However, not all lashes inflict the same degree of punishment. Some cats are kinder than others."

"Touché!"

They walked the ground together then, using a powerful beam from a flashlight as a precursor that banished shadows, penetrated niches and cracks, bounced off tiny objects that an overhead and flatter light would have missed.

In what at night would have been a smallish section of dense blackness under the lee of a garbage Dumpster they found a hint.

The nocturnal concealment would have been complete, but in daylight it could be seen that the area was a carpet of vegetable matter from the same Dumpster, littered there each time it was emptied; dark in color, a trifle oily, and tamped down by time's heavy hammer. The source of the Dumpster's contents was a little factory that made frozen egg rolls for the grocery trade. So venerable was the carpet that it didn't even smell.

"Hello, what's this?" Carmine asked as the flashlight beam hit the squashed litter.

Delia crowded up; they examined the ground together.

"Someone parked a motorcycle here last night, and this is a very strange place to leave a big bike. It is big—see the tire width? A Harley-Davidson, maybe?"

"A customer for the whores?" Delia asked.

"Not parked here, I hazard a guess. This bike was hidden, intentionally hidden. There are confused marks around it that could be footprints, though nothing definite. No oil leaks. . . . If it belongs to our killer, then he's riding, not driving," said Carmine, pleased. "So he's very mobile and potentially elusive. Deels, I don't like this guy. He's new to Holloman, and for reasons too murky to grasp, he decided that the best way to get hold of some cash was to rob a pimp. Except he went further—he murdered the pimp. Hoods don't pick on the guys who run ladies of the night, they've all killed to get there. This is Mystery Man, in more ways than one. Why a pimp? Why Marty? Why kill? What would his take have been? Relative peanuts, I can answer that question. He sets a low value on murder, and hoods are generally smarter than that. Connecticut doesn't execute, but the sentences are long and the parole boards tough."

"You're making a case for a psychopath," Delia said.

"Yeah, I think I am. If so, then he just blew into town on his bike. Let's hope he keeps on going."

"Rubbish!" Delia exclaimed, snorting. "You want him to stay just long enough to nab him."

*   *   *

He wasn't late home to the house with the square tower on East Circle in East Holloman; The Sunday *New York Times* as a consolation prize and a long, weakish bourbon-and-club-soda as an additional prize, Carmine went out onto the deck behind his house and settled to watch the late afternoon bleed away into dusk across the reaches of Holloman Harbor, which lapped at his front boundary. Windless conditions and a long heat wave had bronzed the sky, its edges somber. Holloman was a working port, especially by the tankers filling the reservoirs of the hydrocarbons farm at the end of Oak Street; there was plenty of industry in the region, from howitzers and jet engines to instruments for microsurgery, so the cargo ships continued to come and go, but these days they were too big for the Pequot River.

He was missing his family terribly, and caught in that old, rusty-toothed trap that forbade him to let his plight show to Desdemona and the kids when he talked to them by phone. What he wanted to do was scream and yell and howl and holler "Come home! Come home!" Yet he didn't dare; did he, Desdemona would be back in a flash with all her precious rest-and-recreation leave imperiled. No one knew why some women got the blues after childbirth, except that their hormones were out of whack, and it had happened to his wife after the birth of Alex. If he left her in Sophia's and Myron's tender loving care for another month or six weeks, she'd be okay—provided there were no more kids. Which could best be ensured if he had a vasectomy. As far as he was concerned that was no sacrifice; he had a girl and two boys. But he wasn't sure Desdemona would agree, and he was still marshaling his arguments. Still, time had a way of sorting problems out if no one pushed too hard, he had to insert that fact in his calculations. A dog and a cat were great, but they were a flea bite on a mammoth's ass compared to the presence of his wife and kids. He missed them so!

He had left it so late to marry the right woman and sire the sons of his heart; nor was Desdemona a spring chicken anymore at thirty-six. Nowadays he absolutely wallowed in what family life a demanding job permitted him, his enjoyment enhanced because Desdemona, rarest of wives, understood his ethical commitment to his job; he must never short-change either family *or* job, and that was quite a juggling act. A professional herself, Desdemona took the brunt of domestic life as if she had never run a research institute, and he knew that wasn't fair to her. Days went by if he was busy or away when she never heard any but baby talk. Enough to drive anybody into a depression! Maybe her breakdown had been a manifestation of resentments she couldn't even admit to herself?

And now, missing her, and Julian, and Alex, and her superb cooking, it looked like he was lumbered with a biker psychopath. A new man in town. He *had* to be a new man! Such men were like all human fruit; there had to be a growing and ripening process before the fruit attained maturity. Were he a Holloman man, he would already be marked and noticed.

"I don't suppose," said a voice below him, "you'd have another of those bourbons, and you'd let me snitch a section of your paper, and then later I could buy us a pizza?"

Fernando Vasquez, who lived shorefront a few doors down, was standing in the humble-pie of jeans and a checkered shirt.

"All of that can be arranged," Carmine said, "provided you don't want Sports. I didn't realize you were a bachelor."

"Solidad has taken the kids to Puerto Rico. I am so fed up with my own company I could spit snake venom." He climbed the steps. "You can give me any part of the paper, I don't care."

"If my midnight until dawn visitor wasn't so shy, there might be three of us, but after his introduction to the animals, he went invisible. Frankie goes to welcome him, but I never see him."

"You mean Hank Jones, the artist?"

"Yeah, he's painting my night view."

Fernando following, Carmine went inside to fix a second drink. Then, very glad of the company, the two men enjoyed the last of the day on the deck before darkness drove them in.

MONDAY, AUGUST 18, 1969

Commissioner John Silvestri called a breakfast meeting in his big eagle's aerie office atop the tower the architect had intended to give his late-1950s bureaucratic erection some distinction. Quite a vain aspiration was most people's verdict, but it did permit John Silvestri to look down on all his fellow public servants.

The company was a trifle thin, due to two absences: Buzz Genovese was on vacation, and Tony Cerutti was on the road. Which left Carmine, Abe, Liam, Donny and Delia. Neither Gus Fennell nor Paul Bachman was there, nor was the new artist. That no one voiced any objections to this seven a.m. call-out was properly thanks to Silvestri's position, but went a long way farther than that, even embracing the food and coffee. No fresher donuts, bagels and Danish existed, and the coffee was freshly filtered finest.

Silvestri was, besides, an excellent boss. Though he wore the pale blue ribbon of the Medal of Honor for exploits as a soldier during the Second World War, he was a born desk cop who had only once fired his side arm on police duty—to telling effect, thus proving his eye hadn't lost its ability to see a concealed target and plug it dead-center. Though his last name was Silvestri, most of his blood was Cerutti, which made him genetically related to more than half of the Holloman Police Department, including Carmine Delmonico and several other detectives. Delia Carstairs was an Englishwoman from Oxford, but she was also his niece; her mother was Silvestri's sister, who had foolishly thought she could escape her cop roots by marrying a scholar of old English in a different country. But where was her only child now? A cop with Uncle John!

His wife, Gloria, had held the title of the best dressed woman in Connecticut for years, and when the Silvestris appeared together it was generally held that the only other couple as handsome and elegant was M.M., President of Chubb University, and his wife, the divinely wafty Angela. That Gloria was not just a beautiful face was manifest in her owning a Master's degree in Renaissance history from Chubb and in her having splendidly reared three sons.

None of the Silvestri boys was a cop. John Junior was a major in the United States Marines; Anthony was fast-tracking a career in particle physics at Berkeley; and Michael was well on the way to becoming yet another contentious Jesuit. So the Silvestris had a soldier, a scientist and a religious stirrer, as well as five grandchildren from John Junior, including two idolized girls. They were intensely proud of their Italian-American ancestry, and they hated the Mafia as disgracing a fine immigrant input for America.

Under ordinary circumstances Silvestri had a wicked sense of humor, but it was not in evidence this morning, despite the rare luxury his tower enjoyed—air-conditioning. Outside its walls the temperature was up to 89°F already, and no end in sight.

The death of Marty Fane had upset the Commissioner, whose darkly handsome face was stern. "A turf war?" he asked.

Carmine answered. "Almost a hundred percent no, sir," he said calmly. "If I thought it was a turf war, I'd have asked for Fernando, Virgil and Corey this morning, because the uniforms would be in the thick of it. It may come to a turf war, but Marty wasn't killed to start one."

"Expound," Silvestri said.

"I think we have a new man in town, sir, and this new man put paid to Marty. But not to take over his patch. Whatever he is, he's not into prostitution."

"Then let's leave it for the moment. Our plethora of missing persons first, I think. Abe, what progress on the John Does?"

"We've identified the last four, sir—John Doe Three, John Doe Four, James Doe, and Jeb Doe. All physically very good-looking kids about nineteen or twenty years old, and all employed for varying time spans between a week and several months by the designers Rha Tanais and Rufus Ingham. They worked out of Busquash Manor, which contains a theater stage," said Abe.

"Homosexual elements?" the Commissioner asked.

"Yes, sir, though I'm not convinced homosexuality had much to do with their murders," Abe said steadily. "Indications are that each Doe was kidnapped, then castrated and starved to death. Now that we know who the kids were, it seems likely that the Rha Tanais/Rufus Ingham connection provides a pool of candidates for the killer. The kind of work allied to the sexual freedom around Rha Tanais and his pal attract dozens of kids of both sexes in any year—it's a honeypot for this killer, sir. I'd say in all certainty that John Doe One and John Doe Two were also scooped out of this pool. Tony Cerutti is on the road talking to relatives and friends of the identified victims, and it's becoming clearer by the day that the perpetrator is either a central part of the Busquash Manor zoo, or so close he can masquerade as center."

Silvestri's face lightened. "Good news, Abe! You've made real progress since our last meeting. So where do you plan to go from here? Anything you can share?"

"Tony should be on his way home tomorrow or the day after, sir. Then the three of us will start putting the people of Busquash Manor under a cop microscope, starting with Rha Tanais and Rufus Ingham." Abe frowned. "I'd like to add, sir, that I don't think either of those men is the perpetrator. However, it's very possible that they know more than so far they're telling. I intend to *grill* them."

The Commissioner turned his dark eyes on Delia, a twinkle flaring in their depths.

She was wearing a loose, floppy pajama suit of the weirdest print anyone present had ever seen; on a pea-soup-green background paraded dozens of cats and dogs with toothy smiles, caricatures and cartoons of cats and dogs in lurid colors and worse designs—spots, stripes, zig-zags, checks, curliques, squares, triangles. It was blinding as well as mesmerizing, but none of it rivaled her gigantic purse, the front end of a cat joined to the front end of a dog, and opening along its top from the set of feline ears to the set of canine ears. Not only did it hide her usual arsenal, it probably had room inside it for a small mortar and plenty of shells.

"I'm afraid, sir," she said in her pear-shaped Oxford voice, "that I'm at the opposite end of the earth from Abe. I haven't advanced my case a scrap. The missing women are still shadows."

"Well, Delia, if you can't find a loose string in the tangle, no one can," Silvestri said with as much cheer as he could summon. "I can't imagine you're at a complete standstill."

"Not quite, sir," she said, smiling to show lipstick on her teeth. "I chanced upon a book at the weekend, and it's providing some illumination—just, unfortunately, not in the direction of solving the case."

"Carmine?" the Commissioner asked.

"Delia goes back to her book and her missing women, while I concentrate on the new man in town. He rides a big bike, but he's not part of a biker gang, and he prefers murder to assault. His MO is unlike anything we've seen, which is why I think he's just blown into town from somewhere out of state. The death of Marty Fane was shameful, in that there was absolutely no need for it, and seasoned hoods have more sense than to prey on old-stager pimps like Marty, who would have killed his first rival before his voice broke. That says our new man in town doesn't care about his own skin the way hoods usually do. Or else he's supremely confident of his own ability to get in first."

"You're talking psychopathic loner, Carmine."

"Yeah."

"Okay," said Silvestri, sighing. "Let's eat."

*   *   *

With a charming apology, Delia gathered up several fruit Danish on a plate and carried it downstairs to her own office, regretting the much poorer coffee, but too anxious to dive into her book to consume her sugar binge upstairs in Uncle John's aerie.

The book was highly technical and on most levels beyond her understanding, but she could just manage to get enough of it to make reading it worthwhile. It hadn't come from the municipal library, or even from the five-million-volume main Chubb library; its source was the Chubb medical library. She had gone there on Saturday to see if she could find material that would help her grasp what Jess Wainfleet did, her peculiar and super-specialist psychiatry, and with the help of a bored librarian, she had found what seemed a promising book. Then had come Marty Fane, and any chance to spend a quiet Sunday reading.

As she read, the quality of her coffee forgotten, memories began to stir and then to roil, of an era after the Second World War but before the great advances in psychiatric chemotherapy. . . . Fascinated, she read on, skipping the pages and pages of gibberish in search of the passages that unlocked at least a part of her case beneath her very eyes. Shortly before one in the afternoon she closed the book, conscious that her head and neck and shoulders were one mass of aches and pains from a nervous tension that had escaped her notice until she was done.

Book in hand, she went to find Carmine, whom she tracked down in Paul Bachman's laboratory. On seeing Delia, he thanked Paul and walked upstairs with her to his office.

"I have some thoughts on my Shadow Women," she said, sitting in his visitor's chair.

Carmine's hand, which had been pulling his dog's silky ear, went suddenly still; Frankie sighed and flopped prone on the floor, aware that the attention was over.

"Expatiate, Deels."

"Something called a prefrontal lobotomy, or leukotomy," she said, "depending on how the surgeon described his operation. If he thought of its ultimate purpose, to sever the prefrontal grey matter cortex from its connection to the rest of the brain, then—lobotomy. If he thought of how he was going to sever the connection by cutting its white matter pathways, then—leukotomy. Lobotomy is the most drastic measure taken to neutralize frightful behavior disorders. Before lobotomy, savage, dangerous animals. After lobotomy, flat and emotionally unresponsive human beings."

Her bright brown eyes, fenced in by spikes of mascara, glowed at Carmine. "But then, luckily, psychiatric chemotherapy arrived, too soon to fill our psychiatric hospitals with lobotomized zombies. I found this marvelous book, Carmine, that outlines the entire history of dangerous behavioral dementias from ancient times right up to 1965. If one leaves the red herring of the studio portraits out of the Shadow Women, those who encountered them during their six months of tenancy all describe flat, rather unresponsive women. Well, to me their mood is no longer a mystery, whatever else about them may be. I think they were all heavily dosed with a mood- or mind-altering drug like chlorpromazine."

"It's a very good point, Delia, but where does it get you?" Carmine asked.

"It says that in order to keep each woman tractable over the period, she had to be chemically reduced to a sort of a zombie."

"If it's part of a murder MO, it's in the realm of science fiction," Carmine objected. He thought. "Or science fantasy."

"I want to interview Jess Wainfleet," Delia said, "here in County Services, and in tandem with you."

One black brow flew up; he grinned. "Is she suspect?"

"No, but I need more information, and I'm more likely to get it in a formal setting divorced from her own bailiwick. Ideally I would like her to be unafraid yet not at perfect ease, unable to plead a sudden emergency or parade Walter Jenkins under our noses. She has a huge ego and she can be arrogant. We can play on the ego by humbly begging her to see us in County Services, as we don't want our plea for her help known at HI," Delia said.

"How has your thinking changed on the Shadow Women?" Carmine asked, reluctant to foist his own theories on her just yet. She had distinctive ways of looking at things, and must be granted the time necessary to decide purely for herself whether her ideas had merit. Personally he put her up there with Abe Goldberg, so . . .

"Drugging them to achieve an emotional plateau only an inch above sea level says more about the mastermind than it does about them," Delia said slowly. "A lot of patience, no impulses to draw close to any of them emotionally—he's very cool, I think, though I don't know if he's cold. Really, I need a Jess Wainfleet."

"Don't be disappointed if she doesn't work as well as you hope. For myself, I'd go for Dr. Aristede Melos," Carmine said.

"Good thought. If Jess doesn't work, I'll try him. Thank you!"

Carmine was relieved to see that Delia had dressed down for this entirely informal interview; had Delia greeted her today in yerterday's dogs and cats, Jess might have been excused for thinking *anything*. Room 1 was larger than Room 2 and had better ventilation; Delia had even attempted to humanize it with a vase of summer flowers.

The escorting uniform showed Jess in, no more; it was left to Delia to seat Dr. Wainfleet in the most comfortable chair, and perform the introductions when Carmine walked in. A flicker of surprise showed in Jess's eyes—clearly he didn't look as she had expected. She wore a burgundy pant-suit and a pale rose-pink blouse in cotton fabrics as a concession to the heat; both face and body were relaxed, though the smile on her lips didn't reach her guarded eyes.

"At best, Dr. Wainfleet, this is a semi-formal procedure," Carmine said from the corner where the tape recorder lived, "and the reason we asked you to come to us is purely selfish. Our recording setup is tried and true, and the subject so foreign that we felt it had to be recorded for our archives as well as our present case. As far as we have been able to ascertain, Dr. Wainfleet, you are our nearest premier authority on neuroanatomy, and it is in that capacity that we wish to talk to you. To the best of our knowledge, you are not embroiled in the case of six missing women currently being conducted by Sergeant Delia Carstairs, and therefore stand in no need of an attorney-at-law, but if you have reason to believe or know that such is not the case, then you are entitled to ask for legal representation. If you waive your right to an attorney-at-law, you are free to invoke it at any time in the future," said Carmine.

Jess's eyes danced. "For an informal interview, Captain, you have managed to endow it with all the portent of the Pythoness at Delphi!" she said, smiling. "However, I understand. What's more important to you, I waive my right to an attorney this morning."

"Then let's make ourselves as easy as possible under the circumstances," Carmine said with an answering smile. "The coffee is Malvolio's, freshly made every half hour, and it's not milk, it's half-and-half. Okay?"

"I thank you for your consideration," Jess said. "Do you mind if I smoke an occasional cigarette?"

Delia reached behind her and produced a clean glass ashtray, then hard on its heels the six studio portraits of her Shadows. "Do you recognize any of these women, Jess?" she asked, geared for the inevitable denial.

But what Jess said, almost instantaneously, was "Oh, yes!"

"You *do* know them?" Delia said on a squeak.

"Certainly," Jess said, removing a cigarette from her pack and lighting it. "They were all patients of mine."

Carmine was staring at the psychiatrist in a mixture of awe and anger at his own sheer stupidity in not perceiving that there might be a connection between a group of women displaying the same symptoms and a psychiatrist conceivably treating them. They had all demonstrated a flatness of mood typical in clinical depression, yet it hadn't occurred to him to canvass Holloman's thriving cluster of psychiatrists. Admittedly he wouldn't have flushed Jess Wainfleet out of hiding, as she was a public servant in charge of criminally insane patients, but it would have made her more visible. As it was, she had been drawn to their attention purely as an expert in a different field.

Delia spoke. "When did you see these women, Jess? Did you see them separately, or together as a group?"

"Separately," Jess said, voice unconcerned. "Each of them was my patient." She frowned, looked at Delia. "I don't understand? I thought I was here to give you help with neurosurgical details, not identify people."

"So did we, Jess. This comes as a terrific surprise," said Delia. "It never occurred to anyone in the Holloman PD that these six missing women were HI patients, or in the Asylum—for that matter, we didn't think there were any female prisoners there."

"There aren't," Jess said blankly. "They were all my own private patients."

"Private patients?"

"Yes, of course. I am permitted to treat private patients," Jess said, looking surprised. "Each of these women was a private patient." She laughed, apparently at their naiveté. "It was all aboveboard, and it's all in the HI records."

"Starting with Margot Tennant in 1963?" Carmine asked.

"That is correct, yes."

"Was there a time span for each woman?"

"As far as I was concerned, yes," Jess said. "January second of the relevant year, without fail." She touched each photograph as she spoke. "Donna Woodrow in 1964. Rebecca Silberfein in 1965. Maria Morris in 1966. Julia Bell-Simons in 1967. Elena Carba in 1968. She was the last."

"And that's it? Just January second of each year?"

"Yes." Jess leaned forward a little, took a sip of coffee, then folded her hands on the table, not thrown off balance in the least. "Actually I'm pleased that your investigation has been revealed to me—I have concrete examples to illustrate the procedures you want to know about. Let me take the second woman, Donna Woodrow, in 1964. She was referred to me suffering from an intractable behavioral psychosis that made her a danger both to herself and to others. The alternative for Donna was to undergo a crude bilateral amputation of *all* her pathways to the prefrontal lobe. Or Donna could undergo my kind of surgery.

"I consider crude amputation abhorrent. It turns an uncontrollably manic patient into an oafish and shambling zombie—a creature stripped of its very *soul!* It's irreversible because brain tissue doesn't have the ability to regenerate. So no future recovery can ever happen. These poor creatures have lost their humanity. So why is it done? To turn a rabid wildcat into plant matter, soulless and subhuman.

"The best I can say about it is that it saves the State both money and manpower. But, Captain and Sergeant, I firmly believe that no one on earth has the right to strip a human being of his or her soul. Better to kill them than do that."

Passion had flowed into the voice and animated the eyes; this was Jess Wainfleet fighting like a tiger for the Walters of the world. No wonder she valued him so much! He, whose history had been a horror story of violence and murder, was proof positive that amputation of all connections between the brain and its prefrontal cortex was not the only way to treat the underlying causes.

"What I did to each of those women was to modify the procedure so that the patient kept her human soul. Each woman emerged able to enjoy some kind of basic human life—read, watch television, listen to and absorb a radio news broadcast, keep herself clean, fed, and fit to move about in society, if not to relate to it on a very adequate level."

Her voice ceased, her explanation apparently over.

"So you rented the women apartments and supervised their post-operative progress," Carmine said.

The slim figure stiffened. "I most definitely did not!" Jess snapped. "Each one came to me for an operation, then returned from whence she came with specific instructions as to what must be done and a request for a full outline of that progress for my records. I had no knowledge on the patient before the relevant January second, nor after it."

"I'd like to digress," said Carmine. "What did your own operation on these women entail?"

"As the brain has no ability to feel pain," Jess said, answering in a way that told her audience she was used to such questions, "provided the invasion is relatively small and benign, one doesn't need to worry about sequelae—sorry, after-effects—due to the invasion itself. It's *vitally important* that the patient be fully conscious! I need general anesthesia only for fixing the stereotaxic frame's calipers into the bone of the skull—the skull must be rigidly fixed, and the calipers do that. Of course the patient is strapped immobile as well. I leave no scars because the burr holes for the calipers are surrounded by hair, and I raise no bone flap. Instead, I go in through the orbits—the two round holes in the skull where the eyeballs reside. It's easy. I simply retract each eyeball—what's the matter, Delia?"

Delia had gone white. *"You pull the eyeball out?"*

Jess laughed. "No! Retract means I push the eyeball very gently just enough out of the way to let me insert my instruments around or behind it. The eyeball itself is quite unharmed, really! On the other side of orbit bone lies brain, and with good stereotaxy plus my own knowledge, I can drill through orbit bone, maneuver my microelectrodes, and be where I want to be in the patient's brain. With the patient awake, I electrically stimulate, guided by her answers, until I find the areas I must ablate—that is, destroy. Even though she may not have spoken logically for years, she does when I stimulate. It's a very long, taxing procedure."

"How can a demented person answer logically?" Delia asked.

"The dementia falls away as the pathways are adjusted."

"What do you mean by adjusted?" Carmine asked.

"I destroy some pathways, and as I do so others, freed from the malign influence of those I have destroyed, actually begin to function as they were intended to," Jess said, matter-of-factly.

"What is stereotaxy?" Carmine asked.

"It's a mathematical plotting of the brain." Jess said, "akin to the navigation co-ordinates of the world, but different. Externally, the stereotaxic device renders the head immobile and possesses mathematical co-ordinates that have been calculated from many brains in what is called a stereotaxic atlas. Having the stereotaxic atlas enables me to place my electrodes and other invasive tools in exactly the right place. There are limitations, unfortunately," she said in the same tone of voice. "The atlas was prepared using skulls of a common kind, skulls those six women owned, and that many own, including males—it's possible to extrapolate simple enlargement or diminution on the skull, provided its proportions are identical—Walter Jenkins, for example, has this skull, merely larger."

"So not all candidates for your kind of surgery are suitable?" Carmine asked.

"Correct. I have to see every kind of X-ray, plain or with the addition of dyes or air, plus a specific set of measurements, before I can decide."

"Do you mean these requirements could be—well, posted to you in the mail?"

"Why on earth not? Together with blood tests and other relevant information."

"How long did each woman remain in your care, Doctor?" Delia asked, light dawning.

"Admission was at six a.m. and discharge at nine p.m., January second of the years between 1963 and 1968, inclusive," Jess said, "but I first saw each one at seven, and paid my last visit at six p.m. So I myself can state that I saw each woman for a total of eleven hours. Nine of those hours were on an operating table. None of the patients exhibited aftereffects, so each was discharged per ambulance as arranged prior to operation."

"Who assisted you to operate, Doctor?" Carmine asked.

"A professional neurosurgical technician named Ernest Leto. He and I had worked together at the National Hospital, Queens Square, in London. Since 1959, he's freelanced so he can work with the surgeons he admires."

"I'll need his address," Delia said.

The thin black brows lifted. "I fail to see why, but good luck! I placed an ad in the *New England Journal of Medicine.*"

"I see. Considering the gravity of the surgery, Dr. Wainfleet, you think a fifteen-hour admission adequate?"

"The post-operative course for this kind of surgery isn't plagued by the usual bugbears—hemorrhages, wound infections and extreme pain. I operate scrupulously cleanly in a scrupulously clean environment, and have never had a wound infection. Any pain takes the form of headache, but is nothing like, for instance, the pain of migraine. Over-the-counter medications relieve it."

"Did you use an anesthesiologist?" Delia asked.

"No. I acted as my own anesthesiologist, with Mr. Leto as my assistant. This was possible because Mr. Leto is expert at positioning the stereotaxic frame. I left him to do that while I administered the general anesthetic and injected the local anesthetic in both orbits. Once the stereotaxic frame was in position, I could rouse the patient. Mr. Leto then kept custody of a syringe of general anesthetic he could inject through the IV line very rapidly if the patient became violent. As they had been adequately pre-medicated, they never were uncooperative," Jess said, her pride obvious.

Carmine stared at her a little grimly. "Dr. Wainfleet, we brought you in this morning to get a lesson on the possibilities of brain surgery for psychiatric reasons, but I confess I didn't expect you to solve—partially, anyway—a missing persons case we've had on our hands for some years. Candidly, I'm staggered. Before I decide what to do with you, I'll have to ask you more questions, but if in answering you incriminate yourself, you should have a lawyer present. It's your choice. We can conclude this session now and reconvene when you've found a lawyer, and I'm warning you that you might need one; or we can continue without you having legal representation."

"Let us continue," she said, seeming unconcerned. "I've done nothing wrong, and can't incriminate myself, as you put it. Ask your questions, Captain."

"Were you aware of police interest in the six women you operated on, Doctor?"

"Absolutely not. Each was a patient a year apart."

"Even though you have social contact with Sergeant Carstairs?"

"I knew she had a missing persons case, but we don't discuss our work when we meet, Captain."

"Doctor, you must have some idea what happened to your patients after you operated on them. Surgeons don't operate and then fail to follow up—it's not Hippocratic."

Dr. Wainfleet sighed, her hands moving as if she was holding onto her good nature. "You want details I can't give you, sir, because I don't know them," she said slowly. "The cases were not American. The patients were not American. The referring agency was not American. It happens every day, Captain! Someone in a particular country is the best practitioner in his or her field—usually medicine, but there are other fields—and gets referrals from abroad. Well, these six women were all referred to me from abroad, and came to this country so that I, an expert in the field, could operate on their brains."

"Then there will be records of that with the I.N.S."

"I have no idea how the patients were processed, but I presume they were processed. It was my understanding that they left the country a week after surgery."

"But you didn't follow up on that?"

"My contract was specific. Just the operation plus a very detailed description of postoperative care for six months."

"Can you produce that contract, Doctor?"

She looked haughty. "Of course."

"Then we require you to produce it." Carmine paused; the more he was in Jess Wainfleet's company, the less he liked her, but he knew Delia was fond of her, which put him in an awkward position. "Do you really expect me to believe, Doctor, that you knew nothing about the six months each of your patients spent in Holloman living quiet but normal lives?"

"I knew they would be *somewhere*, but I assumed it would be outside America. There's no point in—er—*grilling* me, because I genuinely don't know one thing more about these women than that each was my patient for a much-modified lobotomy of the prefrontal region of the brain. I saw each woman on the day of operation, and that is the end of the matter."

"I need the name and location of your referring agency as well as your contract, Doctor."

"No, I can't give you that," she said flatly.

"The name at least will be in your contract."

"True, but good luck tracing it."

"Dr. Wainfleet, you're a medical scientist with what I gather is an unparalleled knowledge of neuroanatomy—I have your word for it that your reputation extends far enough abroad to attract foreign patients," Carmine said, laboring to penetrate her veneer of self-righteous confidence. "Do you honestly expect me to believe that you didn't follow up on your surgery?"

"Oh, but I did! Just not in person, as I understood my subjects had returned to their countries. The reports I received indicated recovery to the extent I had hoped for—indeed, in two cases, Silberfein and Bell-Simons, the recovery was superior to all my expectations. I think you fail to understand, Captain, that these women were institutionalized, certified insane. The legally insane have few rights and little redress. They are at the mercy of their keepers, who unfortunately tend to be unaware of emotions like compassion. I am not in the business of destroying souls, for I believe a soul is that vital spark inside the brain that makes an organism human rather than animal. To produce a zombie is an offense against Nature. It is purely a cost-effective measure, and I don't deal in such measures. I have done nothing wrong, and I defy you to prove that I have."

Delia had played little part in the interview, which rolled down on her like a slow landslide; a trickle of small, troubling things that kept increasing in magnitude and frequency until it swept her away, overwhelmed. How could she look at this woman who had been such a good friend in any way approaching the old way? Oh, she would try, but she was too rational not to know her efforts would be in vain. No, she wouldn't tell Carmine, but she herself couldn't overlook some of the conversations that had occurred between Jess, Ivy and her, Delia. The names of the Shadow Women had been spoken, she was positive of it. In which case, Jess had deliberately suppressed the fact that they had been her patients. Knowing her friend, Delia could grasp at why the secret had been kept: Jess would simply have told herself that nothing she knew or had done would advance the case. The only proof would be the production of the missing women alive and, apparently, much better than before the surgery. But that she wasn't willing to do. *Why?* All Delia could think was that Jess herself didn't know who they were or what had happened to them postoperatively.

It was all forgivable between true friends, but her career was affected; she was put at a disadvantage by the conduct of one who called herself a friend, and she disliked the sensation.

Carmine was speaking again. "Do you realize, Dr. Wainfleet, that you are now a suspect in a case of multiple murder?"

Jess smiled and clicked her tongue. "Nonsense!" she said crisply. "What I've told you should be sufficient to close your file as solved, Captain. The chances that my patients have been murdered are millions to one. Clearly they survived some kind of social adjustment test that followed my recommendations, and have returned from whence they came. To prove murder without a body is extremely difficult, but to prove six murders without one single body is so difficult it would be laughed out of court."

"You're quite right, Doctor," Carmine said. "You're free to go. However, there is one more matter I'd like to clarify, if I may?"

"You may ask," she said stiffly, at liberty now to display her outrage at the turn events had taken, and not looking at Delia.

"Walter Jenkins. How does he fit in? Is he yet another triumph for your kind of surgery?"

She couldn't help herself; her face lit up. "Absolutely!"

"Did he suffer the same kind of disorder?"

"The only similarity was in antisocial behavior, and even in that the differences were as many as the leaves on a tree. Walter's syndrome was unique. I am still looking for another of his kind, but thus far I've had no luck. Good day." And she swept out, taking, thought Delia, all the honors of battle.

"That taught us our place," Delia said to Carmine.

"I'm very sorry, Deels. She's your friend."

"Was, more like, though I'll persist, chief. She can't just virtually confess to six crimes of some kind and expect us to take her word that she's committed no crimes," Delia said firmly. "She awed me, which means she turned me into a puppet and pulled my strings for some purpose I don't know. Or that's how I feel after this morning. I don't *know*, Carmine! Do you honestly think Jess could murder six inoffensive women? And why, if she did palliative surgery on them? It doesn't make sense."

"You're right, it doesn't. Except that she's a fanatic of some kind. For all our sakes, I hope it's the legal kind. She's going to go back to HI and dig out the contract, plus operation reports on six women. All aboveboard, try to prove otherwise."

Carmine ejected the tape from the recorder and tucked it into a special pocket in a cardboard file folder he proceeded to label WAIN-FLEET, DR. JESSICA with a felt marker; the result was so neat and regular that it might almost have been machine done.

"Your first conflict between duty and friendship," he said.

"One expects a first for that, does one?"

"One should, but never does," he said gently. "That's why it hurts so much. If you want off the Shadow case, Delia, then all you have to do is say so."

"No, boss, I'm not as wimpy as that. If she has done anything wrong, she'll be very hard to catch out, I can tell you that. I think I'm developing an aversion for people whose professions start with 'p'— psychiatrists, priests, paper-pushers, politicians."

His mouth twitched. "What about police? Starts with a p!"

"It's c for cop," she said gruffly. "I forgot to ask her about the studio pictures of the women."

"Immaterial," he said. "You may be a little stiff with Jess for a while, but you've still got Ivy."

Delia brightened. "Yes, I do. But she's terribly troubled, Carmine, and I don't know why. In all honesty, neither one may prove a lasting friend."

He frowned. "Well, you've got family, and family never ever changes. The pains in the posterior continue to be pains in the posterior, and the gems shine as bright as your eyes."

Said eyes glowed at him; he was right, as always. What she really needed was tea with Aunt Gloria Silvestri.

SATURDAY, AUGUST 23, 1969

When the spirit moved her, Ivy could cook very well; the trouble was getting her into the right spirit. The heat wave had broken in a terrifying cluster of storm cells that hung over Connecticut for two days, unleashing their fury one by one, and making the inhabitants wonder how any place this hot could possibly get that cold in winter. For Ivy, the proper stimulus for an orgy in the kitchen—just not her Little Busquash kitchen. If she cooked, she used the stainless steel perfection of Rufus's home next door. All of which was well and good, though none of it answered Ivy's moving spirit.

The real cause was her worry about Jess, who had gone for an interview at the Holloman PD on Tuesday morning and refused to discuss it in any way. She wouldn't even tell Ivy who had been present!

Therefore, a dinner at Busquash House on Saturday with a severely limited guest list: Rha, Rufus, Jess and Ivy. Not a handsome waiter or assistant in sight. Extreme privacy and three loyal, loving friends ought to do the trick, especially if the food were out of this world. Oh, gastronomy didn't work on *Jess*, but it set a mood, and it certainly worked on two of the most charming men in existence; if Jess could resist Rha and Rufus combined and properly briefed, then it would be a first, even for Jess. No one knew better than Ivy how a united front of several intelligent, resourceful people could bolster the efforts of a lone fighter. Time that Jess was made to see that she wasn't as solitary as she imagined. The specter of Walter Jenkins rose before Ivy's mind as she busied herself in the kitchen, and she had no idea whether to laugh or to shiver: Jess's relying on Walter as sole ally was both brilliant and disastrous, but it was definitely, definitely inadequate. Jess needed allies—allies in the plural.

For a first course Ivy was serving a seafood salad of small pasta bows, chunks of lobster and chunks of jumbo shrimp, all mixed in a pink mayonnaise and horseradish cream dressing; she garnished it with tissue-thin slices of varicolored bell peppers and tendrils of crab. After it would come something that looked dull and boring: a steak-and-potato casserole whose appearance belied its stunning taste.

As she worked, Ivy thought, trying to see a way out for all of them. The trouble was that no one could accurately see what the future contained, even though at the time the future had loomed ahead unmistakably, couldn't go anywhere else. Then you found that it did go somewhere else, despite its looking identical on the surface—it was the layers, and how they tilted the planes into geometrical shapes that were not what they seemed at all—looking straight and perfect, but up close and in reality skewed, twisted, jumbled. Like getting old, thought Ivy, who was getting old. Her eyes were the perfect example of how one looked at the future: everything looked perfect because her lenses didn't focus as well as they ought anymore. When a merciless magnifier was put on what seemed smooth, it was a lava field of obstacles.

Rha and Rufus, Ivy noted when she came in at six o'clock Saturday night to add the finishing touches, were looking more cheerful than they had in some time; both were wearing black trousers, but Rha was sporting a blue lamé pullover shirt, and Rufus a magnificent pirate's shirt in dark red silk, its extremely full sleeves pulled and gathered into long, tight cuffs. *King Cophetua* must be okay.

"What's happened on the *King Cophetua* scene to make the pair of you look like cats in cream?" she asked.

Rufus eyed his surrogate sister affectionately. She was in fine form herself tonight, he was thinking—who would ever guess her real age? Her dress was a simply cut reddish-purple tunic under a gauzy tabard of paisley droplets in toning colors; its resemblance to a chasuble gave her the air of a priestess, an image he knew she enjoyed giving. Not a line on her face, even at the corners of her eyes or her lips! Whatever the genes Ivor Ramsbottom had owned, they were youthful ones.

"We dragged Roger Dartmont up from the Big Apple, kicking and screaming the whole way—he actually accused us of kidnap! Darling, we should have done it weeks ago!" Rha said, handing out drinks. "It's a flimsy plot, but aren't they always? Writers live in lofts, darling, what do they know about *life?* The good part turned out to be Roger's age—we decided to play Cophetua as a silly old sugar-daddy, and Servilia as a KGB major rather than as a consumptive Bolshoi ballerina. *Silk Stockings* gone wrong. The librettist is coming up this week to make the changes."

"Will he buck?" Ivy asked.

"Thetford Leminsky?" Rha laughed. "He's a pussycat."

"What's with tonight, Ivy?" Rufus asked, settling in his favorite chair with a glass of red wine.

"I suspect Jess is in trouble with the cops."

"Ohhh!" said Rufus, grimacing. "What do you need from us?"

"We have to make her see she has friends over and above that awful monster Walter Jenkins. She's so alone in the world!"

"How do you know that, sis?" Rha asked quietly.

"From what she doesn't say. I have never heard her mention her family, where she comes from, even which medical school she graduated from," Ivy said. "We all have secrets, and I'm not trying to dig up any bodies she may have buried—"

"Unfortunate metaphor, Ivy," Rufus said dryly.

Ivy went on as if Rufus hadn't spoken. "I just want her to know some of the security I feel every day of my life because I have two brothers on my side no matter what. Jess isn't as tough as she makes out she is, and those psychiatrists of hers I would *not* call friends.

Ari Melos wants her job, and the Castigliones—well, maybe they're not cruising sharks, but they could well be the scouts for a school of piranha. We three rejoice in each other's successes, but I don't get those vibes from Jess's shrinks. As for Walter Jenkins—he literally *is* a monster."

Rha got up and went to kiss his sister's brow. "For what it's worth, Ivy, we'll try to help." His head tilted. "There goes the doorbell. I'll be back."

Jess arrived in a black pantsuit and black cotton sweater, her body more an adolescent boy's than a mature woman's, though privately Rufus considered it devoid of any sex, and wondered if perhaps when intellect was poured out in such huge quantities, one of the penalties might be dehumanization. With a different personality, Jess Wainfleet had Audrey Hepburn potential—that gamine face, those alluring dark eyes . . . Instead she repelled, she repulsed. Taking her to bed would be like coupling with a hybrid of Medea the sorceress and Medusa the stonifier.

Rufus adored Ivy, one of the truly stabilizing influences in a strange life, but gazing at Jess, her friend, he admitted yet again that she impaled him on the horns of a dilemma, for he just couldn't like her. How then could he do as Ivy wished, support her? And support her in what? A general, moral support, apparently.

For Rha, Ivy's blood brother, it was simultaneously harder and easier than it was for Rufus. Understanding the lyricism and romance in Ivy that she was utterly unable to bring to the surface, he knew too that Ivy was in love with Jess, though she experienced no sexual desires. What grieved Rha was Jess's unsuitability as an object of love; feeling no soft emotions herself, Jess never saw them in others. If only Delia had been there all those years ago! But she hadn't, it was Jess at the center of Ivy's dreams. Juggernaut Jess, said Rha to himself, rolling and grinding over everyone she encountered on her voyage to fulfillment.

So, as the four of them sat down in comfortable tub chairs to enjoy a superb meal, Ivy had no idea that her brothers didn't like Jess, and cared not a scrap for her welfare. It was Ivy whom they set out to protect and cheer up, not Jess.

The conversation was merry and appreciation of the food in center stage as the meal progressed; no one had yet mentioned Jess's visit to police headquarters, Rha and Rufus content to leave the broaching of that subject to Ivy or Jess.

"Let's stay here," said Ivy when the remains of the casserole were cleared away. "Anyone for coffee?"

No one was; out came the cheese board, fresh fruit and the after-dinner liqueurs, while a curious tension began to steal into what had been a pleasant, satiated, relaxed mood.

"What happened when you saw Captain Delmonico?" Ivy asked.

"Oh, I see! I have to sing for my supper," Jess said.

"You won't turn me off with answers like that, Jess, and you know it," Ivy said sternly. "Everyone at this table is a friend of many years, and friends confide in each other, stick together, circle their wagons when they have to—but *never* split their own ranks. As a psychiatrist you know better than most that it's not wise to bottle up your feelings. As a person you know perfectly well that no one here tonight has a prurient interest. So cut the injured innocence crap and tell us."

A silence fell; Jess studied the bubbles in her glass of sparkling mineral water, her wide mouth compressed, hooded lids down to hide her eyes. After a while she shrugged.

"Why not?" she asked, but to whom she put the question, not one of the other three knew, for each felt it was directed at someone else. "Why not? Has anybody got a cigarette?"

Rufus stood, went to the sideboard and returned with a box. He opened it for her to take a cigarette, then lit it.

"That's better. Sometimes a cigarette helps my thought processes. She lifted her eyes, gleaming derisively. "It appears that I am the main suspect in a series of six murders."

"Delia's Shadow Women?" Ivy asked, astonished but not surprised.

"Yes." Jess blew a stream of smoke.

"But why on earth would they think that?"

"Because I performed neurosurgery on each of them."

Three pairs of eyes were riveted on her, though only Ivy spoke.

"You operated as a group? Or one at a time?"

"One at a time, over a period of six years."

"Were they inmates at HI?"

"No, private patients. I saw each one only when I operated."

"Why do the police deem you a suspect?"

"Because they're desperate, and I link the six missing women to-gether. Unfortunately my professional ethics don't permit me to give them an A to Z of each woman, and it's police mentality to assume guilt from refusal to answer all questions. Delmonico won't believe that I saw these women only for surgery, and genuinely know noth-ing else about them. He thinks I must be lying, whereas the truth is that I have no more to tell him. That's why I never spoke up about the Shadow Women. I knew speaking up would achieve only one thing—my own obvious guilt," Jess said, her voice calm, quiet and matter-of-fact.

"Are they going to *charge* you?" Ivy asked, horrified.

Jess looked scornful. "Of course not! They have not an atom of proof that I did murder, and since I didn't, nothing can come of their suspicions. What's more, I was absolutely open and candid about op-erating on the women—the police had no idea until I told them that the women were psychiatric cases. In reality, I imagine each woman is, at this moment, alive and well, and mentally calm enough to enjoy some kind of ordinary existence."

Rha spoke. "The cops had no idea you operated on them?"

"None," said Jess. "To me, it was no concern of the police's or anybody else's that I had performed surgery on their brains—*before* their renting Holloman apartments and then disappearing, I empha-size. I'm innocently entangled, as I knew I would be if my involve-ment were to become known."

"Can they prosecute you for withholding information, or else contempt of court or obstruction of justice?" Rufus asked.

Her cigarette finished, Jess Wainfleet got up. "Let them try!" she said militantly. "However, I might need a good attorney."

"Anthony Bera is the best," Rha said. "He could get you off if you shot your husband dead in a very public arena, so I guess your case would be a sinecure."

"Then I shall retain him." She smiled. "Thank you for a magnificent dinner, but even more for your obvious concern."

Ivy conducted Jess to the front door. "I wish there was something positive I could do," she said, on the verge of tears.

Jess's face softened. "You're here, Ivy, and that's a huge comfort. It's nice to know I'm not alone."

Rha and Rufus sat wordless until Ivy returned.

"A great dinner, but the offer of help went down like a lead balloon," Rufus said. "She's Kipling's cat, if ever I saw one."

Ivy sighed. "She won't confide in us, will she?"

Rha laughed wryly. "She leaves me in the dark, does Jess."

"What we do know is that she's suspected of six murders, and that's *serious*," Ivy said. "Poor wretch! If only she weren't so proud! Chin up and face the world, that's Jess."

"Don't cry, Ivy darling," Rufus said, fluffing out his handkerchief and giving it to Ivy. "The slur will be hard to get rid of, but the charge will never stick. I think Jess knows that too. She's no dummy, guys, never forget that!"

"You're right, Rufus love, but there's even more," Rha said. "All that really matters to Jess is her work, and she sees the cops as imperiling her work. That's bad—for the cops." His voice became musing, as if he were dredging up his thoughts from buried layers of his mind. "Psychiatrists are like the Catholic confessionals or the tribal shaman—a receptacle of secrets. Things that weigh on the spirit have to be confided to at least one other person, and if there's no family to listen, then he who is weighed down will seek a trusted confidant. In the old days these confidants swore sacred oaths to keep the secrets— priests still do, and I think psychiatrists do as well. And if Jess keeps secrets, nothing the cops can do will force them out of her."

"You mean she might not be the murderer, but she might know who the murderer is?" Ivy asked.

"Exactly!" said Rha.

"Do you mean that Jess can't tell us anything because the cops might question us at some stage?" Rufus asked.

"Think about it! We're not professionally bound by any oath of secrecy, but we are bound to answer cop questions truthfully. Jess *can't* confide in us, and that doesn't make her guilty."

"Yes, I see," Ivy said.

"So do I," said Rufus.

"I don't think Jess is in much danger, and I also think she knows it," Rha announced loudly. "What worries her is how much of the odium will stick after the fuss dies down. Say Captain Delmonico decided to charge her with six counts of murder, put her under arrest, and the D.A. sent her for trial. No matter how suspicious her conduct might look, what solid evidence could the Prosecution produce to convict her? All they've got is her refusal to explain herself on grounds of professional ethics. No jury would buy into it. In fact, no D.A. would buy into it."

"There are no bodies," said Rufus. "Doesn't habeas corpus mean you have to produce a body? Like, 'I have the body!'?"

Rha clawed at the air with taloned fingers. "Oh, Rufus, really! The body you have to produce under habeas corpus is the body of the accused, and it had better be alive. It means the Law has to try you in a court before it can imprison you. In other words, no one can throw you in the pokey without a trial first. *Capice?*"

"Clever bird!" said Rufus.

"Stupid turd!" said Rha.

*   *   *

Walter was waiting in her office when Jess walked into it shortly after eleven. How well he looked! was her first thought, followed by the guilty realization that as yet she hadn't sat down with him for that exhaustive interrogation aimed at discovering how many new pathways he was opening up. His eyes, her disobedient mind went on, were the most beautiful she had ever seen, between their amazing aquamarine color and the lucent glimmers in their depths, both heightened by his long, thick, crystal-fair lashes. Am I experiencing the Pygmalion syndrome? Is he my Galateus? No, I cannot let that happen! I *must* not!

"A good dinner?" he asked.

"Oh, yes. Ivy is a superb cook."

"What did you eat?"

"A unique seafood cocktail, then a beef casserole."

"I had mac-and-cheese."

"With vegetables, I hope?"

"No, I didn't feel like rabbit food."

"Where did you hear vegetables described as rabbit food?"

"Television."

"Is that what you did tonight? Watched television?"

"Only a movie on Nine or Eleven, *On the Waterfront*, with Marlon Brando. It was good. But most of the time I sat at my window looking at the dark and thinking."

"Thinking about what?"

"I was trying to remember what it was like before I knew you. What it was like to be a maniac and a monster."

"I've told you before, Walter, that the staff call you things they don't even begin to understand. May I offer you some advice?"

"Yes."

"When you're in the mood to look at the dark and think, don't direct your mind backward into the past—that's wasted effort. The past and who you used to be can never come back again. One of the things I hope I gave you was the ability to think ahead—to plan. It's forethought makes a man far more than a mere animal, and you're so lucky, Walter. You have a clean page to write on, to fill with brand-new plans. Forget the past, it's irrelevant. You're Walter Jenkins, a thinking man, and you have a lot to think about. You're relatively young, and it's possible that before you grow old, the review panels will be enlightened enough to offer you a chance at life outside in the world. In the meantime, life inside HI can be planned. You should think about the things you like to do, then work out a schedule that fits them in enjoyably. For instance, you're very good at wiring things up, at electronic gadgets—maybe you'd like to do a course by mail in electronics? Whatever, I'm just throwing things at you. You're very good at architectural drawing, I'm sure we could find a correspondence course in that. The important thing is, do you see what I'm driving at? Do you understand how important it is to keep your brain occupied and interested?"

He had listened to this speech—long, for Walter—with eyes fixed on her face, and comprehension in them. "Yes, I see what you're driving at, and I do understand how important it is to keep my brain occupied with interesting things."

"Have you any preferences?"

"Lots of them," he said solemnly. "I have to think longer and harder before I can tell you anything." He rose to his feet. "Coffee? I just ground it before you came in."

Her face lit up. "Oh, I'd love some! It was the one thing Ivy didn't serve, and I have to work tonight."

Waiting for her coffee, she put the last few minutes under a second review, and knew disquiet. There was *something*—yes, there was something going on, and Walter wasn't being entirely frank about it or himself. Looking at the dark . . . Why did that ring alarm bells? Because it didn't mean the dark outside his window. It meant the dark inside his mind. And why did he want to seek the dark? It was where everyone's monsters dwelled, even the sanest of men's, and this was a man had known his monster with the intimacy of a sadistic killer—no laws, no limitations. He had come so far, and at a speed that awed her; now she found herself wondering exactly how much she knew about the progress of this psychological triumph. All the tests had been applied, and didn't really apply; his I.Q. was phenomenally high, but she was responsible enough to assume that beneath the monster he had always been the brilliant man. His abilities were astounding, from his manual dexterity to his ambidexterity, but again she had to assume that they had always been there below the monster. What a tragedy! she had thought each time a new facet of his mental physicality appeared; what might Walter Jenkins have been if the wiring of his brain hadn't banished all his gifts behind the door flung open to liberate the monster?

The coffee mug and the aroma arrived together; she blinked, gave Walter a specially warm smile.

"I heard something today," he said, sitting with his own mug of coffee. "I'll help you with the files in a minute."

"What did you hear?" she asked placidly.

"That the cops accused you of six murders."

"No, they didn't. They can't, they have no evidence. Just ignore the gossip, Walter. That's all it is."

"No one will arrest you, Jess. I wouldn't let them."

A laugh escaped her; were he anyone else, she would have put an affectionate hand on his arm, but Walter's personal space was inviolate. "Thank you, but it's not necessary," she said. "I've committed no murders, and the police know that very well. What they're really after is information about the victims I don't have, but they're convinced I do. The situation is like many of life's situations—time will prove it a dead end. They'll realize that, and abandon the theory that embroils me."

"They'd better," he said grimly, "because I won't let them hound you, Jess."

"Rest easy, Walter, I'm in no danger. You have my word on it," Jess said, gazing at him sternly.

"I'll rest easy, I promise." He fell silent, then suddenly asked, "Who is this Captain Carmine Delmonico?"

"A long-time and very senior Holloman policeman. A detective. However, he's a member of the panel that reviews your progress, and therefore he's important to you. Thus far he's been an excellent choice for the panel—he never lets his personal prejudices get in the way of his panel decisions, and he accepts my professional opinions in the same way as a Senate Committee would the opinions of Richard Feynman on something atomic."

"A friend at court."

"Yes, Walter, definitely. Which is why this business with the six women is such a nuisance. It undermines his respect for me."

Walter rose, came round the desk, and hunkered down to deal with the safe combination. "We can't have that, Jess," he said, his tones absorbed. "No, we just can't have that."

MONDAY, AUGUST 25, 1969

Since Walter Jenkins had no pathway leading to frustration, but had many leading to an ability to plan, he set about his task in a calm and unhurried way. Having no true comprehension of the multiple-layered nature of Jess Wainfleet's problem with Captain Carmine Delmonico and the Holloman PD, he had decided that the correct answer was also the most direct: remove Delmonico from his position of leadership and deflect the rest of the Holloman PD into an avenue of investigation that had nothing to do with Jess. Therefore, he reasoned, a simple elimination would not work; he had to do something that suggested Delmonico had about-faced, had found something new and important.

He had spent all of Sunday in the HI library, which luckily had a microfiche facility that covered all Connecticut major crimes; HI was an institute for the criminally insane, and its senior staff liked to be able to consult newspaper or magazine reports on its speciality. Thus he had learned about Delia's Shadow Women, and opened up a few more pathways as he did so—pathways that would have greatly thrilled and dismayed Jess. He also sampled the high end of Carmine Delmonico's profile, and had a half dozen superb photographs of the Captain into the bargain, though he had to process them from negative to positive before he really saw what he had to contend with. Delmonico was well into his forties, but not yet past his prime. . . . Then Walter found an article in a local magazine on the Holloman PD, a recent, lengthy piece that featured other important faces, like Commissioner John Silvestri, Captain of Uniforms Fernando Vasquez, and Sergeant Delia Carstairs, whom the journalist found fascinating because she was the Commissioner's niece, from Oxford in England, and whose plain clothes were anything but plain. It also featured the radically new style of the young police artist, one Hank Jones, and how his modern approach had identified a series of bodies labeled "Doe."

Walter wallowed in movies. He had watched hundreds and hundreds of them on his road back from insanity, and almost all he knew of the world was movie or television fed. Consequently he saw at once that he could accomplish nothing by attacking head on. That would be like planting the briefcase bomb inside Hitler's "Wolf's Lair"—someone could move it to the wrong side of a solid oak table leg. No, he had to be more subtle than that!

The moment that resolution clicked into place, Walter threw out any idea of a daylight foray, and felt a thrill of emotion that would have transfigured Jess. His medium was the night, in which he could move more stealthily than a predator after prey, and no one would suspect his absence from a high security prison.

The plan! What ought it be? First, it had to deflect the Captain; second, it had to remove all suspicion in the Shadow Women case from Jess Wainfleet; and third, it had to replace Jess with a different, unconnected suspect.

Let it look as if Delmonico was the killer! The time was still August, if a little late, so the woman could have done her disappearing act halfway through August, as the others had. Maybe Delmonico kept her a little longer, if she was a special kind of woman? Such a special kind of woman that, having killed her, Delmonico suddenly realized he only had one course—to put his gun in his mouth and make a meal of a bullet. Yes! Yes, that made perfect sense! He had a wife and two kids, but he had heard Jess on the phone to Delia, and one of the subjects was Delmonico's family, vacationing on the West Coast for some time to come. He must be at home alone. Ideal, ideal!

Then the identity of the woman hit him, and his breath hissed out

188

of him like air out of a compressor valve, sharp and loud and vicious. It had to be her kind, even if she wasn't the renting kind, the disappearing kind. The Captain had grown bored, that was it, he'd moved on to a spicier, juicier, tastier kind of woman. Well, they did, these multiple killers, wasn't that so? There must be a note, and the note could explain it all. Delmonico was well educated, everyone said, so the note would have to reflect that. Businesslike yet poetic . . .

Brimming over with joy, Walter perfected his plan—Jess would smile in triumph, if only she knew how well her subject was planning! Logic wasn't hard, it was easy.

Would he do it in two stages, or three? As many as it demanded, decided Walter. My plan is flawless.

At eleven-thirty he was on the road. First stop was to gas up at a station that had gas pump jockeys; he asked for five dollars' worth, got it, handed the money over, and was gone before the kid manning the pump even noticed his face. Still easing back on the throttle so as not to irritate folks in the houses nearby, Walter concentrated on the left side of 133, not wanting to ride by the high brick wall when he came upon it. Two or three little shops, and there it was, punctuated in its middle by an archway surmounted by a cross. Speed slackening, he rode well past it before steering the bike off the road into the encroaching forest. A few yards in he killed the engine and dismounted, then reached into one pannier and removed the tools of this particular trade: a roll of duct tape, a pair of thin rubber surgeon's gloves, and a roll of picture wire. Diagonal pliers-cum-cutters, screwdrivers and scissors resided in one of his jacket pockets.

The high brick wall was for 133 alone; the property's fences on its three forest sides were chain-link topped with barbed wire; not a problem for Walter, who produced his diagonals and cut a neat rectangle in the wire, which wasn't rigged with any kind of alarm. Once through the fence, he found himself in carefully tended grounds, many of the larger lone trees ringed by a wooden seat. There were two separate buildings, the farther one clearly a school of some sort.

The spacious grounds held tennis courts, basketball courts and what he suspected was a gymnasium. Unacquainted with schools, Walter didn't know that the air of demure quietude it emanated was a powerful indication that it lacked both boys and men. The nearer, much smaller building, of two storeys, was Walter's target. He moved to it quite briskly, but kept one hand on his knife in case of dogs—but there were no dogs.

The front door he opened with a small steel spatula attached to his screwdrivers—so easy he knew the inhabitants weren't worried about security. The place was silent and dark, a tiny flame in a red glass bowl showing a faint ruby glint beneath a statue of the Sacred Heart of Jesus in the front hall. No one was moving, and he didn't need a flashlight to see even into the blackest corners, for darkness was his natural milieu. Up the beautiful old staircase to the second floor and its sleepers.

These nuns each had a big room to herself, which made his task simple. Five doors down on the right, he struck paydirt. A sleeping woman in her late twenties or early thirties, smooth of face, smooth of skin, slender of body; her arms, clad in fine fawn cotton, reclined one to either side of her as she slumbered on her back. Closing her open door, he inched up the edge of her little single bed until he was level with her chest, then put his hands around her throat and jerked her upright, her scream no more than a sigh. A pair of terrified eyes, rolling white, goggled up at him, a black shape in a black room, as he leaped to straddle her, one knee at each of her shoulders, the weight of his rump settling onto her chest as he lay her down again, his face inches from her own. While his fingers around her neck tightened remorselessly and her legs drummed and threshed vainly behind him, he watched the life go out of her. It was delicious. It was like sucking her animation into himself and becoming more than both of them put together. It was an act of God. It was the ultimate experience, and the I-Walter called it ecstasy. For he was the I-Walter, and finally he knew what the I-Walter wanted. Ecstasy. Nothing but ecstasy.

To be absolutely sure, he remained sitting on top of her with his hands around her throat for several more minutes—was this what Kris Kristofferson meant by "coming down?" So much he didn't know, unless he gleaned explanation as well as exposition from television, movies or radio, and he really did feel as if he was coming down from a much higher level. He found another popular word: transcendental. He thought that one applied too.

But there were things to be done. He lifted the limp form onto the floor and loosely remade the bed; nothing else was disturbed. Up she came to be draped around his neck; Walter Jenkins quit the scene, closing the door of her room after him. Out by the bike he laid her down to inspect her by flashlight, and was immensely pleased. Clad in a modest fawn cotton nightdress from wrists to neck to feet, she was quite pretty in the face, though her brown hair was cropped as short as a marine's, and no cosmetic had ever marred her skin. Out of the other pannier came a smallish rubber body bag he had pilfered from HI, and into it went the body of the nun. He looked at his watch: two a.m. Best head home.

The body bag strapped across pillion and panniers with its contents face down, the whole forming a large U, he kicked the bike into life, eased it to a low growl, and poked the front of it onto 133. No traffic moved; the big trailer trucks that drove all through the night preferred I-95 or I-91, and the locals were at home in bed. He rode the few miles to the vicinity of the Asylum without encountering a soul, turned into the forest, and killed the Harley not many yards from its destination. Walter was growing bold. Provided he didn't roar, no one on the walls noticed.

Safely inserted within the wall, the motorcycle stood on its prop with the body bag still lashed across it; there was no need to remove it, as it would remain there until rigor mortis had passed off, and would therefore be flexible when he needed to move it during the next phase. He wouldn't gas up from his plastic containers until then either. In the meantime he had to be sure there were no signs of his bike or feet outside, so back outside he went to straighten bent grasses and ground things, straighten bent branches or shrubs, break off broken twigs. Only then did he change into his HI uniform of grey T-shirt and shorts, and commence the walk home. If someone saw him, he had his story all ready—restlessness, headache, boredom. Jess was hooked like a fish on boredom, but the I-Walter knew he couldn't tell her that the most boring aspect of all was Jess herself.

Walter wasn't a happy person.

TUESDAY, AUGUST 26, 1969

The nuns of the Sacred Heart School for Girls said their first prayers of the day at six a.m.; when Sister Mary Therese Kelly wasn't present, Mother Perpetua Gonzales discovered she wasn't anywhere to be found. A thorough search of the convent, school and grounds produced no sign of her. At seven a.m. Mother called the Holloman PD and was put through to Captain Carmine Delmonico.

"I'm coming," said Carmine. "Don't touch anything."

Siren on and messages out to Delia and Donny to join him, Carmine raced through traffic building up to rush hour and reached his destination twenty minutes later.

When Mother Perpetua had taught a six-year-old Carmine to read with enjoyment she had been a skinny little nun not far out of her teens, endowed with a genius for instilling love of learning in kids; a whole career as a primary school teacher had stretched before her. Now that she was into her sixties she was principal of her school and a force to be reckoned with. Vocations had fallen off drastically, so much so that many Catholic schoolteachers these days were lay-persons, but Mother Perpetua was still capable of drawing vocations. Once a nun was under the shade of Mother Perpetua's wing, she seemed to take to the life as if made for it, and its problems, shared, always seemed to have an answer.

Mother Perpetua was waiting outside the convent door, pacing up and down, when Carmine arrived, Delia and Donny in his wake.

"Forensics won't be long," said Delia tersely.

"Delia, you take the school buildings. Donny, check under every twig and leaf on the grounds. If you're done ahead of me, I'll be with Mother Perpetua."

It took Carmine many, many minutes to cross the front hall and ascend the lovely old staircase to the rooms on the floor overhead; there was no third storey.

"Are bedroom doors ordinarily closed?" he asked at Sister Mary Therese's closed door.

"Not unless privacy is required, and that you may imagine why."

"Had she asked for privacy?"

"Definitely not. That was why we were so surprised this morning."

Carmine produced a magnifying glass and examined the knob. "The prints are smeared—the last hand on it wore a clammy glove." He opened the door and went into a large but unostentatious room, a kind of a home, though the bed was single and the furniture unfashionable. A big desk, well lit, shelves of books, a lounge chair facing a TV set, a cork board festooned with pieces of paper. Delia and Donny came in as he summed up a busy, useful, happy life complete to a small shrine to Our Lady.

"I don't think there's much here for us, guys," he said.

Mother Perpetua spoke. "Then come and have breakfast and coffee with us. You must be famished."

"He remade the bed," said Delia.

"How old was Sister Mary Therese Kelly?" Carmine asked at the end of an excellent breakfast.

"Thirty-four next May," said Mother Perpetua. "Most nuns look younger than they are. Conventual life keeps the spirit youthful because our troubles are shared. She was a marvelous teacher of arithmetic."

"Did she enter straight from high school, Mother?"

"Yes. She took her degree from Albertus Magnus."

"Her relatives?" Delia asked.

"One brother a parish priest in Cleveland, Ohio, and another an insurance salesman, married, with two children. No sisters."

"I take it Father Kelly is the head of the family," Carmine said. "Would you like me to contact him?"

"If it's at all possible, Carmine, I would prefer to do it?"

"Mother, it's one job I don't mind handing over, believe me!" Carmine said fervently.

"Have you any idea what might have happened to her?" Mother asked as she walked them to the front door.

"As yet, no," Carmine answered, keeping his voice casual. "It's too early, Mother, and kidnapping seems unlikely—I mean, why her when there were better candidates closer to the stairs? Though I have notified the archbishop, just in case there's a ransom demand."

Delia waited until the front door was closed and she, Donny and Carmine were alone. "I very much fear that Sister Therese is dead."

"Why?" Carmine asked with a premonitory shiver.

"This is Mystery Man—the out-of-towner on the big bike."

"No one heard a bike," Donny said.

"Or saw one, I know. But it's he. I don't care what you argue to the contrary," Delia maintained. "What's more, he's working to a plan. This chap is a loner, and I'd be willing to bet that he's not fixated on nuns. Sister Mary Therese is essential."

Walter had discovered that he could mirror-write as easily as he could write in the ordinary way; it only meant, as he called it now, "shifting gears" to turn a very sharp corner, and—hey presto!—he was through the looking glass. Right and left, side to side, had always confused him, whereas the points on a compass did not; now he reasoned that it had something to do with two different worlds, the linearity of right and left, the circularity of north, east, south, west, and back to north. The trouble was that explanations bored him. If he told Jess, she would insist on hours and hours of dissection and discussion. The I-Walter was not even remotely interested in the Jess-Walters because the Jess-Walters were a mish-mash. The I-Walter was the whole entity, and was complete in himself.

He knew what the I-Walter's purpose was, though sometimes it still came in patches, or was befogged and twisted. That frustration never occurred was the result of a kind of infinite patience that only a lifetime prisoner could endure.

His plan was working, he could see that clearly, and once he had written his mirrored note and read it through, he smiled. Jess was right: when a good feeling invaded him, he was more and more tempted to betray that fact by smiling. *Not* a good idea! The smile vanished immediately. Time to feel the pleasure-thing after it was over and he could confirm that it had worked. There were dangers in too many pathways; events were starting to go too fast. He couldn't slow down events, but he could set a guard on himself.

"What did you do today, Walter?" Jess asked him at dinner.

He'd lead his mentor somewhere he knew she found alluring. "Remember when I discovered I could write just as well with my left hand as with my right?"

"How could I forget?" Amusement gleamed in her eyes, but not, he knew, a contemptuous emotion; Jess thought the Walter she had created was a wonder of the world. "Don't tell me you've taught yourself something new?"

"No, not new. My toes, remember?"

Her amusement fled. "You mean—?"

"Yes, I can write with my toes now."

"Right foot, or left foot?"

It was as if he had neatly caught her amusement as it vanished and installed it in his own eyes. "Both."

"What provoked you to try, Walter?"

"Ari Melos said I had prehensile toes, so I looked up 'prehensile' in Webster's and found out that it means capable of gripping an object. A pencil is an object, so I gripped it in my left toes and wrote."

"You're amazing, Walter," she said hollowly.

"Will you put it in my notes?"

"Of course."

"I'm tired," he said. "I think I'll try to sleep."

"Since sleep is the state of being you find the hardest, I won't delay you a moment longer."

"Do you think I'll ever be able to control my dreams, Jess?"

"If you could do that, I'd win a Nobel Prize."

"Is that important?"

"The most important thing that can ever happen to a doctor."

Jess kept Walter's notes in her handbag—or rather, kept the meaningful notes there, the ones she didn't want Walter to see; he read everything on everybody, especially himself. But he had one extraordinary idiosyncrasy, given his amorality: he refused to open or delve into the contents of a woman's handbag. Jess's private theory about this put its cause before his thirteenth year, during one of Walter's brief, infrequent periods in foster care. Whatever the woman who found him rifling her purse had done to him, Jess had no way of knowing, but it had been terrifying enough to survive mania and two hundred hours of neurosurgery.

So Walter would find a few bland lines in his file folder when he had a look, but only her eyes would ever see what she wrote and deposited in her handbag. The many dozens of these slender exercise books had accumulated over the thirty-two months of his postoperative career, and were stored in the basement of her house, some among anonymous thousands.

While Walter slept, Jess filled ten pages of his notebook, then dropped it into her handbag; time now for other patients.

By half after eleven he was inside the wall, topping up his gas tank from a plastic container; tonight he didn't dare go near a gas station on his way home. Sister Mary Therese had passed out of rigor—not that it made any difference, as he had stored her bent exactly as she would be over the additions to the back of his Harley. At midnight he opened the door to the outside world and wheeled the motorcycle out, frowning at the thought that perhaps two nights in a row might leave a track. But the ground was still wet from storms and short deluges, the grass was actively growing. After he came back tonight he'd have to spend some time outside obliterating the marks of his passage. If anyone found his door, he was over and done with, kaput.

A full mile away he kicked the bike into life and grumbled down 133 a very short distance before turning onto Maple, a long, winding street that traveled across Holloman from its outskirts on Route 133 to downtown, sheltered by the trees after which it was named, his burden draped across the pillion box and panniers no burden at all to a Harley-Davidson. Whenever he saw flashing lights from a patrol car he pulled over into dense shadow and waited; police presence was up tonight, after the nun's abduction. Once through downtown he headed for East Holloman and a street called East Circle that followed the curve of Holloman Harbor on its east side, providing its houses, each on an overly large allotment, with views both interesting and beautiful. Wardroom scuttlebutt had informed Walter that the most enviable house on East Circle, adorned with a tall, square tower owning a widow's walk, belonged to Captain Carmine Delmonico, of the Holloman PD. He doubted anyone would remember who dropped the name into that particular chat!

Hank Jones had every reason to be delighted with the address; he had turned up after the Captain had turned in, been welcomed by an ecstatic but relatively noiseless Frankie, who received a yummy snack as reward. Then, in harmony with each other, youth and dog set up Hank for a night at the easel, a portable one, unfolded a card table, and put Hank's tiered box of paints and brushes down on it. As soon as Hank became more interested in what sat mute on his easel than what sat panting at his feet, Frankie heaved a huge dog-sigh and went back to his basket in the bedroom hallway upstairs—a lonely place with only Carmine for company.

Given the constant police presence, Walter decided to leave the bike under the east pylon of I-95; the west pylon lay at the end of a long span that arced over the factories and Holloman airport. Which left North Holloman Harbor and the Pequot River much closer to the east pylon, built right on the shore.

There was, however, a track worn scant feet above the high tide marker; Sister Mary Therese around his neck, his left hand gripping the wire between her wrists and the butt of his hunting knife, his right hand gripping the wire between her ankles and the butt of his .45, Walter saw the house he was aiming for as soon as he emerged from the blank blackness under the pylon. Ah! Easy! He'd follow a line just up-water from the rear ends of boat sheds—crappy little things that housed rowboats with outboard motors, or canoes, or kayaks—no millionaire craft here!

When Walter moved with intentional silence, it was like listening to the night breathe, so the sleeping dog's inbuilt alarm never sounded until the first foot put weight on the bottom step leading up to the deck: the dog cried terror with four stiffly upright legs and a cacophony of roaring barks.

The sudden eruption of Frankie's savage barks enhanced Hank's profound horror as the apparition rose up in front of him, the Creature from the Black Lagoon with something draped across its shoulders. He couldn't help himself: Hank screamed.

Brushes, paints and palette flew everywhere as Hank scrambled on all fours along the deck away from the Creature. It threw whatever it was carrying far from it to crash against the easel like a reflexive gesture the moment Frankie began barking and Hank screaming. The noise from the dog rolled thunderously in the quiet night, Hank's screams adding an eldritch quality of terror. Then something emitted a single roar that was even louder, and became entangled with blue-white pain in Hank's lower back; the screams turned into howls.

Dog and cop erupted out the door onto the deck together, Carmine in shorts, arm up and Beretta extended. It gave its crashing roars four times, but the intruder had gone and there was at least one casualty on the deck. Frankie had set out in pursuit; a high whistle brought the dog back at once.

Lights came on in other houses, and Fernando Vasquez leaped up the steps, in shorts and brandishing his own side arm.

"Jesus, Carmine!" Fernando said, going to the light switches and throwing the scene into high relief. "Jesus!" he repeated.

"Ambulance, now!"

Sister Mary Therese was sprawled amid the wreckage of an easel; one glance, and Carmine stepped over her to reach Hank, lying in a growing pool of blood, all his mind concentrated on a pain more awful than any he could ever have imagined.

"Try not to move, Hank," Carmine was saying. "An ambulance is on its way, and you're not going to bleed to death."

From somewhere Hank found an answer. "I might wish I had died, I might wish I had! I can't feel my legs, but the small of my back is agony! Oh, Carmine, help me!"

"I won't leave your side until the ambulance crew make me, then they'll be with you. The first thing they'll do is give you a shot to ease the pain." Carmine's eyes met Fernando's. "I can't ride with you—I'm a cop needed at the scene of the crime, but as soon as I can I'll send you Delia. Do you have anyone I should contact, Hank?"

"There's just me," Hank whispered, weeping the tears of sheer shock and agony. "Oh, God, it hurts! I'm just hopin' for no pain!"

"That's first priority, soldier. What happened?"

"I can't! The pain! The pain!" Hank wept.

"Sure you can, soldier. It gives you something else to think about.

"I was painting, sir, nothin' else in my mind than the black water and the shimmering lights across it—I'm nearly finished. It hurts, it hurts!" Hank lay whimpering for a moment, then continued. "And the Creature from the Black Lagoon rose out of nowhere in front of me right as Frankie went into bark mode—I was so scared I started hollering, and couldn't stop. The thing was carrying a woman around his neck, threw her away—I'd crouched down for protection. Then there was an explosion, I was knocked all the way down like a kid by a car—*boom!* I guess it shot me, the Creature, huh?"

"He did, but you're in a very good town for docs, thanks to the Chubb medical school. Nobel Prize winners a-go-go."

*   *   *

The ambulance took less than five minutes to reach the patient, and had a physician's associate aboard. Hank was given a shot of morphine that reduced his pain to bearable, and was taken off, siren wailing, to a waiting ER. By the time he arrived, the spinal team, complete with neurosurgeon, was assembling, the chief of the unit coming under a police escort.

East Circle had sustained other disturbances over the years since Carmine Delmonico had bought his house, but this was the loudest and most intrusive, happening at an hour when those still in town were peacefully asleep. However, the Captain's popularity far outweighed these disadvantages, so no one complained. After all, there were *two* primary policemen on East Circle, and that held many advantages.

"Our only choice, really, is to wait until morning, and pray it doesn't rain," Carmine said to Fernando.

"It won't rain, and our luck is improving," Fernando replied, sipping his tea. "The wind is dropping to nothing." Something occurred to him; he looked up. "Why did you whistle Frankie back?"

"He's the beloved pet of two little boys, Fernando, and the guy had a gun he wasn't afraid to use. Desdemona and I keep Frankie as a watchdog, and he's brilliant. Tonight he gave me time to put on a pair of shorts, get my gun, take the safety off, and prepare for anything. Hank was the unknown factor, poor guy, As for the dog, I'll not let him go in harm's way."

WEDNESDAY, AUGUST 27, 1969

They met at ten a.m. in Commissioner Silvestri's aerie to discuss the stunning turn this raid on Carmine's house had meant. Though his team was not actively involved, Silvestri had asked that Abe, Liam and Tony should attend, so the room was crowded; Gus Fennell and Paul Bachman were there, as were Fernando Vasquez and Virgil Simms from the Uniform Division. Delia had yielded her place at Hank Jones's bed to Simonetta Marciano, who had survived her husband's retirement as Captain of Police without any diminution in her sources of gossip. Upon hearing of Hank's plight—*no relatives!*—she had insisted upon gathering her women friends together and taking the matter of companionship for Hank unto herself. Knowing Netty of old, Delia was sure she was just the person to manage Hank, and went back to her own world with a sigh of relief.

"First of all, how's Hank?" Silvestri asked.

"The news is better than feared at first, sir," Delia said. "The projectile had lost some oomph on a ricochet before it hit Hank, which was the saving of him. It shattered part of the right pelvis at a level too low to damage the spinal cord directly. The collection of smaller nerves called the cauda equina sustained damage, but the worst injury was to the right buttock. He's in the care of neurosurgeons and plastic surgeons, and the neuro boys have already operated to remove bone fragments and reduce spinal cord swelling."

"Will he walk again?"

"Yes, sir, he will. How well is on the lap of the gods."

"A long period in the hospital?"

"Yes, sir. Eventually he'll be transferred to Professor Prarahandra for extensive grafts to give the poor little chap a right cheek to sit on as well as a left."

Silvestri heaved a huge sigh. "For which, we may be very thankful. Sounds as if it could have been worse."

"It could have been," Paul said grimly. "The projectile had been doctored with mercury, but the shooter bungled the job."

"Carmine, what exactly happened?"

"Someone, identity unknown, walked onto my property about one in the morning carrying the body of Sister Mary Therese, who went missing yesterday. I think he intended to leave her on my property—inside the house, not outside. Hank Jones was on my sun deck painting a nightscape, as he called it—he'd been there every night from midnight on for a week. According to the little he was fit to tell me, the guy rose up in front of him and gave him a helluva fright. Frankie started barking, Hank started screaming, the intruder literally threw Sister Mary Therese's body at Hank, then fired a single shot. I came out the back door in time to see a vague shape drop off the deck and run. I fired four rounds after him, then ceased for fear I'd hit a neighbor coming outside to investigate."

"Did you hear a car? A bike?" Abe asked.

"No, nothing," Carmine said.

"Gus, what can you tell us about Sister Mary Therese?"

"She was a well nourished, healthy female with no reason I could see why she shouldn't have lived to be ninety," Gus said with a slight tremor in his voice. "At time of examination, she had been dead about thirty-two hours. Cause of death was manual strangulation—very brutal and powerful. There are no signs of trauma to suggest he clipped her on the chin or otherwise tried to knock her out, just extensive contusions around the anterior aspect of the neck. From carotid to carotid. I haven't done the full autopsy yet, this is from preliminary examination."

"Paul?" Silvestri asked the head of Forensics.

In answer, the bony-faced technician put a folded piece of ordinary writing paper on the table, then inserted two slides into the vacant wings of a wall projector. "This note was found in a plastic bag, folded exactly as it is, and pinned to Sister Mary Therese's nightgown. There were no fingerprints, marks or stains that could help elucidate the note's nature or presence. It said *that*"—and up onto the wall sprang a half-intelligible jumble of mirror-writing. "*This* is the translation."

DO I HAVE TO TELL YOU EVERYTHING?
THERE IS NO MISSING WOMAN THIS YEAR.
SEVEN WOULD BE SELF-INDULGENCE.
SIX WOMEN ARE PLENTY!
EYEBALLS PEELED LIKE BANANA SKINS
TONGUES TIED WITH RED TAPE
TALKING HEADS IN A VACUUM.

"That's the weirdest note I've ever seen in a long, varied career," the Commissioner said. "The guy's cuckoo!"

"Or else he's trying to make us think he's cuckoo," said Abe. "That note is *constructed*, but it's also artificial."

"Written in two unequal halves," Carmine added. "He takes fine care to tell us that Dr. Wainfleet has nothing to do with the Shadow Women, and that there will be no more Shadow Women. Then he tacks on three lines of not particularly clever nonsense."

Delia looked a little sick. "You don't think he means to switch to *nuns?*" she asked.

Silvestri answered her. "I doubt it, niece. Carmine?"

"The poor little nun was a one-off, Delia. The guy was looking for a certain type of woman," Carmine said, more for John Silvestri's sake than for Delia's. "As I see it, his intention was to disgrace me by implying that I was having a love affair with a nun. Either her dead body was to be found on my sun deck, or in my bed—the latter, I suspect. Of course he also intended to kill me, as if, having killed my lover, I was overcome by remorse and ate my gun. The headlines would have been juicy."

"No one would believe it," Delia said stoutly.

"Luckily it's not an issue," the Commissioner said. "Hank must have come as a big shock."

"Not to mention a pit bull dog, sir," Carmine said.

"What exactly *was* his motive?" Fernando Vasquez asked.

"To deflect the whole PD away from the Shadow Women, is my guess," Carmine said. "It was a clumsy effort, bunches of mistakes."

"Like wiring Sister's wrists and ankles together," Donny said. "Still, he wasn't expecting a reception committee."

"I agree that the Shadow Women are at least a large part of the reason for the note," Delia said. "In fact, they may be the entire reason for the note. But if he's telling the true story, then he's the Shadow Woman killer, and Jess Wainfleet can't be implicated."

"One thing for sure!" Liam Connor said suddenly.

"What's that?" the Commissioner asked.

"The guy has a colossal ego. I don't mean the usual big one killers have, I mean an ego way up in the stratosphere. This guy is in an ego class all on his own."

"Invincible, inviolable, invulnerable and invisible," said Silvestri. "He's running rings around us."

Determined to get her point about Jess Wainfleet across before these bulldogs of men discarded it, Delia ploughed on. "Well, whatever or whoever, Jess Wainfleet is *not* a part of it!"

"You're correct, Deels," Carmine said. "Paul, what's the chance that he's left you anything remotely like hard evidence? It's possible he made mistakes after he found Hank on my deck."

"His gloves never came off, that's for sure, but I can tell you what you've probably already deduced for yourself—he's an extremely strong bastard. He managed to pitch a hundred and twenty pounds of dead weight ten feet effortlessly. We found his cartridge casing, correct for Marty Fane's .45 semi-automatic. An honest opinion? He's better with his hands than he is with a gun. His problem was Sister

Mary Therese," Paul said. "He didn't take a bullet from your Beretta, Carmine. We found his escape route, but no blood anywhere."

"Did anyone find signs of a vehicle?" Carmine asked.

Virgil Simms answered. "Nothing, Captain. He stepped on to sealed road at the top of your slope, and his trail vanished. My guess is that he left his transport under the I-95 flyover on the north side of the Pequot. With the all-night truck traffic, no one would have heard him."

"So no extra points for concluding that's what this Samson did," said Carmine, and looked at the Commissioner. "That's it, sir."

"Thank you, gentlemen. Most illuminating! Dismissed," Silvestri said. "Carmine, a word before you go."

Carmine stood as the rest filed out, faces grimly set and downcast, then sat opposite his boss. "I feel awful, John."

"No worse than I. That poor young man! To think I picked him for his talent, only to see this happen."

"He'll walk again. It's the months and months of plastic surgery— muscle grafts, skin grafts."

John Silvestri pulled out his handkerchief and wiped at his eyes. "A tragedy!"

"But he won't want to retire, John. His is a sedentary job, and we should get him back to it as soon as possible," said Carmine, pretending not to see the handkerchief.

It helped; the Commissioner stiffened. "I'm hounding the insurance company already. The worst is, he has no family."

Carmine rose. "He has us, John. Whether he likes it or not, he also has Netty Marciano and her troops."

Despite the presence of the artist on Captain Delmonico's deck, at first Walter was convinced that his foray was a big success. He did much work around his outside door, making sure the forest was unmarked. Now he would lie low for some days at least, while the Holloman PD combed the entire county looking for a killer who was already, did they know it, a lifer prisoner behind bars. Though he didn't see it as a joke, Walter did sense the irony in his situation, and felt a certain glee whenever he thought of his incarceration. If only they knew they had their killer in custody the whole time!

Of course he expected to see his exploits emblazoned in the *Holloman Post* at least, but not a word about them appeared in print or over the radio or television news; apparently the captain had the power to suppress publicity. Then, late in the afternoon, Delia Carstairs visited Jess at HI, and Walter found himself privy to what had gone on among the cops after all—what a gift!

"I know Chubb Neurosurgery is one of the best units in the world, Jess," said Delia, "but I also know you are the world's very best when it comes to brain anatomy. Is there anything you can tell Chubb neurosurgeons that might help poor young Hank? It's appalling to think he may never walk properly again, if at all."

Walter sat a little back from the table, the gentle and tractable soldier Jess had made out of a raving lunatic, present to refill their coffee mugs, produce files or articles, and put them away again. It did not occur to Delia to ask Jess to send him away; she knew how much Jess meant to Walter, and how he fretted when he was banned from conversations he couldn't follow anyway.

"You're talking about a lower motor neurone world, Delia, and that's one I'm no expert in," Jess said with real regret. "Sam Kaminowitz is the best there is, and Hank's lucky he's under Sam in Holloman Hospital. They're performing relative miracles these days, in no small measure due to that horrible war in Vietnam, where soldiers get their asses shot off every day by bigger projectiles than .45 bullets. Sam perfected his skills on the first Vietnam victims. NASA research helps too—science is a great circle that can often benefit from some stupid political mistakes. Nothing is ever totally bad, including war and space races. It's amazing to see machines designed to kill eventually yield machines designed to heal, but it happens."

"I see that. You're telling me to be optimistic."

"For next year, rather than tomorrow. Remembering that the most stupid of all politicians are those who cut science research in the budget. But that's a personal soap box, and not what you came to hear. What happened last night?"

Delia told her story crisply and without embroidery; at one moment she glanced toward Walter, to see those beautiful eyes fixed on a world she couldn't see—was he even listening? No, she decided, he wasn't. "We think he may ride a Harley-Davidson or some other grunty big motorcycle," Delia concluded.

"Isn't there a police registration list?" Jess asked.

"They're registered with Motor Vehicles in County Services subsidiary to Connecticut registration, and we've gone through them with a fine-toothed comb," Delia said. "Nothing's come out of it except several stolen bikes and a dozen stolen cars, none of which have ever come to light. It's a two-edged sword."

"I'm sorry I can't help you. Ari Melos rides a Harley."

"Long discounted." Delia laughed, albeit wryly. "At least your security is a model to everyone."

"It had better be, or we're in trouble."

"Thank you for your precious time, Jess, and thank you for the delicious coffee, Walter," Delia said as she got up. She gave Jess a special smile. "And, most of all, Jess, thank you for the information. A terrific help."

Jess saw her visitor out, then returned to her desk.

"What was that all about?" Walter asked.

"A young man, a very gifted artist, was shot in the back last night. He's still alive, but his legs may be paralyzed—won't work, I mean. Sometimes maiming is as bad as killing."

His head went to one side as Walter considered this statement. "No, it isn't ever as bad. When someone is killed, the lights are switched off for good. It's eternal night."

"But you don't remember killing!" Jess cried, startled.

"I must, because I do."

And what was she to make of that?

*　　*　　*

It was almost six o'clock in the evening before Carmine finally walked into Hank Jones's area of Intensive Care. The curtains around his bed were pulled back and he was lying, eyes closed, in a Gulliver-esque web of cords, tubes, wires and thin cables, with machines indicating everything from an EEG to an EKG, plus two waste bags and two bags of liquid nutriments dripping steadily. His eyes opened suddenly to lock on Carmine; a huge grin appeared.

"If it ain't The Man!" Hank said in a strong voice.

"It's just a man," Carmine modified, putting a chair in a spot where he judged it wouldn't be in the way. "See what happens when people engage in nocturnal activities? The night time is *not* the right time, my man. How's tricks?"

"I got pins and needles in both feet," Hank said proudly.

"Hot damn! Elvis is entering the building, and the crowd goes wild. You got steel balls, man."

"Well, sure, I know that! But why, in your exalted opinion, has the metal infused my rounded bearings?"

"Because, my man, you have survived a day of Delia Carstairs and Simonetta Marciano. Steel *cajones!* What color was the big satin bow in Netty's hair today?"

"Emerald green. Does she always look like someone out of a World War Two movie?"

"Always, but more in the style of Betty Grable than Rita Hayworth. Beautiful legs!"

"I had no idea that the Commissioner has a bastard half brother who is a full-bird colonel in the U.S. Army!"

"That, Hank, is merely the tippest tip of Netty's gossip iceberg. By the time you walk out of here, you'll know the dirt on everyone in Holloman. Netty is an oracle," Carmine said, smiling.

"She's a doll too. As far as I can tell, she's marshaling food or a chocolate malted from all the troops who visit me." The cat's eyes gleamed. "And I *will* walk out of here, Carmine, I *will!* The docs reckon I got a good chance."

"I managed to rescue your painting," Carmine said gravely. "As far as I can tell it didn't suffer in spite of the fracas. No change in the night foreshore has been announced, so you'll be able to finish it later. And don't worry about money. The Commissioner is doing a deal with the cop insurers, and I'm doing one with mine. Delia will be in to see you tomorrow morning after you're rested, and you can tell her what you want done with your apartment."

"Cool!" Hank said, and fell asleep.

That left Carmine to wander off in search of a neurosurgeon who could tell him how Hank was really doing. Having found one, he listened intently to a tale pitched in layman's language, and was grateful for the young doctor's consideration.

"Hank has a marvelous spirit going for him, Captain, so he won't just give up and give in. The slug did a lot of damage, but too low down to prevent such a determined guy from walking again. We've removed all the bone splinters and reduced cord swelling; now we have to get the branches of the cauda equina—a kind of horse's tail that forms the bottom end of the cord—to sit properly in what bone canals and channels remain. The longest job belongs to the plastic surgeons, who have to build Hank a right buttock to replace what the bullet's exit wound tore away. It's going to take quite a while."

Equally important, Carmine had to think through how much he would tell Desdemona, who mustn't be allowed back on the East Coast yet. Some ideas were shaping inside his head, and he needed to nut them out too. Myron? No, Sophia. That was it! He'd call his daughter and tell her what was going on. Sophia wasn't his daughter for nothing, she would know the right plan of action. When dealing with women, it was always best to leave things to a woman.

SATURDAY, AUGUST 30, 1969

Perhaps due to his rather special lines of women's clothing, or perhaps due to his well-known bloody-mindedness about said lines (he refused to say), Rha Tanais always held a fashion parade on the Saturday before Labor Day. If asked, he would explain that he based it on a Buckingham Palace garden party, though the very few who had sampled both venues voted the Tanais turnout more generous in its refreshments. It was also more exclusive; he rigidly banned all persons he disliked, no matter how important they were. So when the invitations were sent out and your rank absolutely demanded one, and you didn't get it, you just curled up into a ball and *died*. The Queen didn't have the power to do that: Rha Tanais did. There were wails of rejected woe from the Hudson River to the Canadian border (Rha Tanais thought New Jersey was a figment of the imagination).

If anything were needed to put the finishing touches on a warm late summer's day, Delia decided, it was the sight of Shirl (Simonetta) strolling the grounds of Bushquash Manor clad in the most exquisite wedding dress anyone had ever seen, complete to a trailing bouquet of white orchids and a veil looking like mist.

"Such a hot and horrible month," she said to Rufus.

They were sitting in what he called a summer house and she called a folly; a small round open-sided temple some distance from the mansion, and it afforded a splendid view of the comings and goings in the garden as well as all Busquash Inlet.

COLLEEN McCULLOUGH

"I met another Simonetta today, when I called in on Hank," Rufus said. "Ravishing, straight out of World War Two."

"Netty Marciano. Her husband was a cop," Delia said. "She was known as the gossip to end all gossips. But people thought she'd lose her title without her cop source. Hah! She has eyes and ears everywhere, from the Hartford Capitol through Electric Boat and Cornucopia to the most sequestered college at Chubb—and then some! CIA and the FBI both use her as a consultant on Holloman and Connecticut affairs. Netty is amazing."

His eyes, gone quite khaki, gleamed. "You're pulling my leg, Delicious Delia."

"Anything but!"

"Something good came out of August."

"I wish I could say that!"

"I'm sorry you can't say it! Rha and I met you."

She blushed. "And I met the pair of you."

"We think we may have a clue for you."

"About what?" she asked absently, eyes on Shirl.

"We think we know who the current John Doe prisoner is."

Delia jerked around to face Rufus. "Tell me—*now!*"

"Case Stephens, but his real name is Chester Jackson. Shirl reminded us about him this morning shortly after six. We were tagging her dresses—you know, telling her when to change, which one to wear next—it would have been half after six by then. She was in a foul mood, but she always is at the crack of dawn, when she's tagging. And she said she'd like Case Stephens as her groom! I told her not to be an idiot, that Case had gone two months ago, and she said he couldn't have, because his dog was still here! I reiterated my opinion that she was an idiot, she reiterated her conviction that Case was still here. She kept on and on about the dog—a ratty little thing named Pedro—and insisted she'd seen it that morning as she came in just before six. It was rummaging through the garbage. Such a mood! If Shirl wasn't such a gorgeous bride, we'd get rid of her, but she's inimitable."

212

"Did you believe her, Rufus?" Delia asked urgently.

Rufus considered the question. "I think so, yes. She really did believe Case was there because of the dog. Case adored the scrawny little thing! He carried it everywhere in a cute little wicker shopping basket lacquered blue—the dog sat in it like a teeny prince, and people made fools of themselves over the sight. And in one way I could understand why Shirl was convinced Case was still around—he and the dog were inseparable."

"You did the right thing, Rufus dear, in telling me." She got up, looking sheepish. "It's the little girls' room for me, alas!"

And off she went to the house, one of the privileged few who didn't have to use the portable outdoor toilets. Into the house, down the hall past the grand staircase, and into Rufus's studio, which she knew better than any of Rha's rooms. There she picked up the phone and called Abe's home number.

"Goldberg."

"Abe?"

"Yes, Delia, it is I. What's up?"

"Oh, thank God you're there! Abe, I'm at the Rha Tanais garden party, and Rufus has just informed me that a young man who was in their employ some months ago has apparently left his dog behind, and it isn't in character. The dog's name is Pedro and the young man's stage name is Case Stephens. Real name is Chester Jackson. It's a zoo here today, but if you were here at the crack of dawn tomorrow, you might find the dog. It must either be extremely shy, or sticking to its master. Look for a chihuahua or something similar—small and ratty is the general description. Find Pedro, and you've grounds for a search warrant everywhere on this property." A vision of Ivy Ramsbottom rose in front of her; Delia swallowed painfully. "Make sure your warrant includes Little Busquash and Ivy Ramsbottom."

"I owe you one, Deels. Thanks a million."

When she returned to the folly she found Rufus gone, but Ivy waiting for her. Feeling a traitor, Delia sat down.

"Desdemona would so enjoy this," she said.

"Captain Delmonico's wife? One of the few who can look me right in the eye," said Ivy, smiling. "Very tall women have an extremely hard time of it."

"Male or female, anyone who differs from the herd has a hard time of it," Delia said. "Too short, too tall, too fat. The odd thing is that too thin is now a desirable state of being, thanks to wearing clothes. What a reason! It doesn't seem right."

"If it flies in the face of what Nature intended, then it definitely isn't right," Ivy said.

SUNDAY, AUGUST 31, 1969

Someone had already cleared and tidied the grounds of Busquash Manor, Liam Connor discovered when he walked casually onto the property at half after five in the morning. If animals were involved, Liam was usually the one in charge, and after several phone calls late on Saturday afternoon, Abe had decided to send Liam in alone to look for Case Stephens's little dog.

"Evidence says it's timid, so a search party might panic it into fleeing the neighborhood, at least for a while. Delia says it was seen in the bushes that conceal the cottage from the mansion, so start looking there," Abe had said to Liam over the phone. "If you can't find the animal—its name is Pedro—by ten a.m., then we'll send in a major search party."

But there it was, the same tannish-brown as fallen autumn leaves, huddled under one of the bushes that grew in a straight line thirty feet from Ivy Ramsbottom's end windows. Liam went close to it, but not threateningly so, and hunkered down. A long-haired chihuahua, he decided, not quite as ratlike as the ordinary ones. He fished a baggie out of his pocket, opened it, and broke off a small piece of cooked white meat.

"Hey, Pedro," he said, smiling. His hand came out holding the chicken. "Try this, guy, it's better than garbage."

Two enormous brown eyes stared up at him; as is characteristic of chihuahuas, it was shivering with anxiety, but the combined smell of man and meat was welcome, and the smile said the stranger was good people.

Liam fed the dog all of the chicken, which it devoured ravenously; it was thin, the Tanais trash apparently not yielding much edible, but, significantly, it had not roamed farther afield in search of sustenance. The reason for that, Liam suspected, lay in some smell of its beloved master lingering in this spot, nowhere else. What was different about here, then? Only what might have been the top part of a finely netted birdcage just behind the dog's position under the bush. *A ventilator? Jesus! This couldn't wait!*

He was on his car radio in less than a minute, asking Abe to get that warrant. "It's not only the dog, Abe—there's a ventilator! Case Stephens is at the other end of it!"

From then on it went very quickly. Confronted at her door by Abe Goldberg, Liam Connor and Tony Cerutti, with ambulance paramedics waiting behind them, Ivy Ramsbottom sighed and held the door wide open, then found herself handcuffed.

"Where is Case Stephens?" Abe asked.

"Go through the door in the kitchen that doesn't lead outside, and you'll find a room with a chair elevator in it. When you sit in the chair, press the DOWN button. To ascend, press the UP button," Ivy said calmly. "It is the only way in and out."

"Tony, stay here with Miss Ramsbottom. Liam, with me."

It was a very large chair that took the two slight men with space left over. The ride was smooth, the stench in the padded chamber below more bearable than the sight of what remained of Case Stephens. Feeling as if his ghost was passing through Auschwitz, Abe knelt to ascertain that the heart still beat, the vital spark lived on, while Liam returned up in the chair calling for the paramedics.

"Why?" Abe asked Ivy when he ascended again, the last to leave save for the forensics team, which would stay.

She stood, an immensely tall, immaculately turned out woman in her thirties, hair lacquered into place, dark red lipstick following the curve of a generous mouth faithfully, and blue eyes wide in bewilderment. Asked the question, she made no reply.

"Why?" Abe repeated. He phrased it a different way: "Why did you do *that* to them? What had they ever done to you?"

The calmness, the lack of surprise and the immediate request to retain the legal services of Mr. Anthony Bera on behalf of Ivy all told Abe that Rha Tanais—and Rufus Ingham—deemed Ivy guilty.

"We ought to tape this and make it official," Rha said, his gentle face sadder, his eyes bright with unshed tears, "but I am so big, and I believe interrogation rooms are tiny. We have a recording studio here—could we use that, with your own people manning the machines and perhaps even some drinkable coffee?"

"I'll check with the captain" was as far as Abe would go; the answer turned up in the person of the captain, and Delia armed with notebooks, files, pens, pencils.

Neither man was insensitive enough to attempt to treat Delia as the dear friend she was, Carmine noted, nor to attempt to drop her hints as to what they would like her or dislike her to do: indications that they genuinely knew nothing of what had gone on at Little Busquash?

"The studio's ideal," Carmine said after closely inspecting it. "Room for all of us to sit inside comfortably, plenty of microphones, and, so Charlie Watts informs me, an electronic hook-up to rival anyone's." His white teeth flashed. "In fact, it's technically much better than anything in County Services. Charlie and Ed can man the recording booth alone."

It didn't take long to set up; things probably didn't if Captain Delmonico were in command, Rufus thought. Rufus sat next to Rha, and facing Delia, on the timer and taking the notes. Oh, poor little baby! He tried to send her a telepathic message, and—she got it! Her eyes met his, wrenched with pain, and fell.

"Before we get the signal to start, Captain, how is Case?" Rha asked. "Is there any chance he might live?"

"Professor Jim Pendleton says there's a chance, and he's a world authority on anorexia nervosa. Same kind of thing, different path and radically different cause, of course, but starvation is starvation. Case had fresh, clean water to drink, so his kidneys haven't packed up yet, the Prof says. Oh, he'll never be the same strong, perfectly healthy young man he was—organs and systems heal, but there are scars, and they don't. Because of the water, he may have continued to survive for another week or ten days. As it is, he couldn't be in better hands."

"I don't understand how you discovered what was going on when we've been right next door and not suspected it," Rha said.

"The model who wears your bridal gowns saw his dog—Pedro. At six in the morning, yesterday, so you told Delia, Mr. Ingham. She recognized the dog's significance. After that, things were easy," Carmine said. "The dog could smell his master. That meant Case was still alive, and that meant straight to Judge Thwaites. He won't issue a warrant unless he can see a genuine need for it. Today, he saw the need."

"What's happened to the dog?" Rufus asked.

"Pedro's in Holloman Hospital Animal Care, being well fed and pampered. He's already been taken to see his master several times," said Abe. "Strictly speaking, dogs are forbidden visitors for human patients, but the rules have been slightly relaxed for Pedro, who's disinfected regularly."

"Poor Pedro!" said Delia, sighing. "Unless they're water retrievers, dogs loathe being bathed."

Carmine had had enough. "Okay, are we ready to record?"

"Roger!" came from the control booth.

"Then let's roll. Mr. Tanais, your full name and any other names by which you are known? Please spell them."

"My professional name is Rha Tanais"—he spelled it—"and my given birth name is Herbert Ramsbottom"—he spelled it. "I was born on November second of 1929, at Busquash Manor."

"You have a sister?"

"Yes, I have one sister, Ivy Ramsbottom. She was born at Busquash Manor on December fifth, 1910."

"One moment, please" Delia interjected. "1910? You said 1910?"

"That can't be right, sir. 1910 would make the lady almost sixty years old," Carmine said.

"Yes, Ivy is almost sixty. She's a youthful looking woman anyway, but she's also had a series of face lifts and other kinds of plastic surgery."

"Then you lied to me when we talked some days ago. You gave her a birth date of 1920, the year Antonio III died."

Rha shrugged. "Needs must when the devil drives, Captain. You have to take our word for it whichever date we give, because Ivor Ramsbottom never registered Ivy's birth. She's a non-citizen."

"Were you lying when you described your and Ivy's mother as a simpleton?"

"No, that was true. Our father had"—Rha drew a quavering breath—"peculiar tastes, Captain. I gave you a second false date, as it happens. Ivor was hired as chauffeur in 1903, not in 1909. By 1909 he was in complete control of everything, including Antonio III. Except in the matter of the money. That, he could never manage to get his hands on." Rha shifted his body in his chair restlessly, then turned to look at Rufus. "You tell them, Rufus. I—am—tired."

"The one who could tell you most is Ivy," Rufus said in level tones, one hand on Rha's, "but she won't. Not now, poor thing. Of the three of us, she suffered by far the worst—we were too young, and what we know comes from her. Ivor started sexually molesting her when she was six years old, and by the time she had her first period, she'd been raped a hundred times or more. Ivor was a monster who didn't look like a monster. He looked like an angel, heaven come down to earth."

"Ivor was the Un Known?" Abe asked.

"Yes. That portrait was his, except that Ivor had blue eyes, and we thought that the man in the painting had black eyes. So we gave him a different title—No One."

COLLEEN McCULLOUGH

"Was he involved with Dr. Nell Carantonio?" Carmine asked.

"Who wasn't he involved with? Yes, he was her lover, but he wanted to marry her to get his hands on her money. She refused."

"Was he aware of the laws for bigamy?" Liam asked. "Unless his children's mother was already dead?"

"No, she was still alive when Dr. Nell disappeared."

"Was he married to your mother, Mr. Tanais?" Delia asked.

"There was a wedding certificate saying he married Uta Lindstrom in Wisconsin in 1910," said Rha. "Ivy told us he had to marry her—she was pregnant."

"Rha has the certificate," Rufus said, "though Ivy never understood why he never harmed or killed Uta. As far as Rha and I could reason it out, Ivor just liked tormenting and killing the people in his life."

"Including Dr. Nell?" Carmine asked.

"Oh, yes!" Rufus shivered. "That was diabolical. She was terrified of small spaces and feared death by drowning."

"What happened to her, Rufus?"

"Ivor locked her in a tightly lidded steel trunk, put heavy chains around it, put it in a dinghy and rowed out of the Inlet one night. Then he tipped the trunk into the water. It sank like a stone," Rufus whispered, looking sick. "She was seven months' pregnant, but she wouldn't marry him."

"When did he meet Fenella?" Carmine asked.

"She was a child," Rha said, looking like death. "You don't know our worst secret, but we have to tell you. We just ask that it not be spread far and wide. If it were, nothing of benefit to anyone could come out of it. Rufus and I are half brothers. Ivor Ramsbottom fathered both of us at much the same moment in time, since we were born within an hour of each other. No one can possibly know how it feels to live in a body half of whose chromosomes belonged to a devil enslaved by cruelty and murder. But we know how it feels. Every morning the first thing we remember is that our father was a Caligula. And we shoulder the burden of that knowledge, desperately trying to prove that mere chromosomes do not make the man, that our mothers gave us true goodness. Not for anything would we have betrayed Ivy had we known, if only because we know what her life has been like." Rha sat up, eyes stern. "We do not apologize for misleading you. Sometimes family wins."

"But you'll never reproduce," Carmine said.

"Vasectomized as soon as it became available, just to be completely sure," Rufus said.

"What happened to Ivor?" Liam asked.

"Ivy killed him in 1934, when it became obvious that he was wearing Fenella down. Looking back on it, we suppose too that she did the math and realized Ivor would soon start molesting Rha and me," Rufus said. "Yet one more debt we owe Ivy. No matter what crimes she committed, she's a good person at heart."

"Was the padded cellar there then?" Carmine asked.

"No, but the cellar itself was. Antonio III had grown fed up with his staff stealing the contents of his wine cellar, and built a new one attached to Little Busquash. No one got past Ivor, who, whatever else he was, was not a drinker. Ivy lured Ivor to the cellar on some pretext—it was empty at the time, between Fenella's gyrations and Prohibition's dying throes. Ivy stunned him and then took the elevator back upstairs and locked it. She told Fenella that Ivor had grown tired of waiting for his money and skipped town for parts unknown. When Ivor had been in the cellar two months she went down into it again, gave him ether, and castrated him. Then she left him to die. Rha and I were old enough to remember Fenella constantly weeping while Ivy chanted like a Greek chorus that he was gone for good."

"How long was Ivor in the cellar?" Abe asked.

"Until the gun emplacements on Busquash Point were poured in 1942," Rha said. "By then he was bare bones and Fenella ill. Ivy tipped him into the six-yard concrete mixer. No one even noticed."

Rha and Rufus were both looking better, as if sharing the secret of their paternity had lifted a gigantic weight from them.

I wonder, thought Carmine, whether we have the whole story

now, or if they're still hiding the finishing touches? But that didn't grieve him; what did were the innocent lives ruined by forces beyond their control—by the power of a parent. *A parent!*

Two hours later, Carmine called a halt. Nothing further had come out, nor would continuing the process produce results. Denying any complicity, Rha and Rufus stuck to their story. More important, they hadn't tripped themselves up in any detail.

Ivy Ramsbottom, they learned on their return to County Services, was in the lone woman's detention cell, and refusing to apply for bail. The bed was too short and narrow for her, and another was being located; Anthony Bera had paid a visit to see his client in an interview room, and there was nothing else in the report.

Delia had elected to remain at Busquash Manor with Rha and Rufus, unsure what to do or say, but inwardly convinced that she still owed them more than a police presence. She had, besides, one vital question to ask, a question that couldn't be asked in front of a half dozen instinctively turned off cops.

"How much home life did you have after Ivor died?" was her opening gambit, delivered over a cup of tea and little cakes.

Rha had lapsed into an anxious silence; very worried for Ivy, she guessed accurately. But Rufus, for some reason, wasn't nearly as concerned; he had a kind of forethought Rha lacked, so why wasn't he more upset?

His carefully painted eyes gleamed, their expression an odd mixture of contentment and—sorrow? "Good for the first eight years," he said. "Fenella kept us at home, and while she wasn't a motherly person, she cared a lot for us. We were looked after."

"Then you were sent to boarding school?"

"Yes. A very good one. It was hell."

"Why, Rufus?"

He laughed. "Oh, come, Delia! Look at us now, and imagine what we looked like at twelve."

"Different."

"That's putting it mildly."

"Were you preyed upon? Molested?"

"No. Oh, that was looming, but we scotched it by blatantly advertising our preference for each other, and increasing our eccentricities. Everyone from the headmaster down decided to leave us alone in our own little world," Rufus said.

"Yes, yes, *yes!*" Delia cried, beaming. "I'm right!"

"I wondered where this atypical third-degree was going! Right about what, Delia?"

"You and Rha are brothers, not lovers. You've never been lovers, have you?"

Shocked out of his reverie, Rha stared; Rufus prolonged his laugh. "Bull's eye!"

"I think I see your motives, but tell me anyway."

"Gays are accepted in artistry, theater and fashion," Rha said, breaking his silence. "As boys, Rufus was too pretty and I was too ugly-ungainly. School was a crucible that we survived by living on our wits. We never hinted that we were brothers, and never told anyone we had been raised together. Whatever our chromosomal inheritance is, sex was rather left out of the mix. Rufus and I are neither homo nor heterosexual. We're asexual." He heaved one of his huge sighs. "It's so comfortable, Delia!"

"Indeed it is," said Rufus.

"I think Captain Delmonico knows," Delia said.

"He's a very smart cop," Rha said. "Oh, poor Ivy!"

All her theories confirmed, Delia led the conversation away from Ivy. Rha and Rufus had weathered all else; in time, they would also weather Ivy.

MONDAY, SEPTEMBER 1, 1969, LABOR DAY

Carmine drove to Delia's condo for dinner, even gladder of the company than the thought of good, home-cooked food; he had been promised potato pancakes for starters and a main course of Lancashire Hotpot, whatever that was. Nothing good for either arteries or figure, knowing Delia, but dining at Delia's was a rare occurrence, and he was keeping fit. Frankie came with him; Winston preferred to lounge at home.

"Do you think we'll ever get the Busquash Manor bunch to tell the same story twice in a row?" he asked, crunching his way through a delicious little pancake and washing it down with a gulp of icy beer.

"Rha and Rufus at least probably don't even know the true story." said Delia, looking out her huge plate-glass window at the pebbles of a suddenly deserted beach. Amazing, how summer literally packed up and departed on the last day of August! From now until November would be halcyon, with any luck they'd have a long and perfect Indian summer while the trees prepared themselves for winter hibernation in a blaze of colors.

"Harkening back to Abe's description of how Rha and Rufus reacted when they first saw Hank's paintings of the Does, I'm inclined to think that on that day, and previous to it, they had absolutely no idea what their sister had done and was still doing," Carmine said, a part of his thoughts on the West Coast with his wife and children. "The sight of the paintings knocked them—uh—sideways."

"For a row of shit-cans, you mean."

"Well, okay, yes. They hadn't known a thing, then Abe woke them up in a hurry, and they were caught in the usual family trap. I guess, especially given the age difference, that Ivy was as close as they ever got to a mother. They're screwy genes whichever way you look at it, though. What's the opposite of an Oedipus complex?"

"An Electra complex, though I can't see it. Electra hounded her brother into killing her mother, she didn't do it herself."

Carmine grinned. "And ain't that just like a woman?"

"If I didn't know you were baiting me, Chief, I'd castrate you. Seriously, those two poor men are pure victims."

"That's what I meant by screwy genes. I don't think I'll ever forget Rha's explaining how it felt to wake up every day knowing that half of his genes came from a sadistic murderer of the worst kind, then spend all day doing something good while still carrying the burden of knowledge."

"I doubt they've ever harmed a fly," Delia said gruffly.

"Nor ever will. It's the sorrow, Deels! The children do inherit the sins of their fathers, metaphorically anyway."

"I concede that, Carmine, but in the case of Rha and Rufus at any rate, one must say they're heroes in the real sense."

"Interesting, that they decided not to reproduce."

"Inevitable, for heroes."

"The media are going to have a field day."

When the phone rang, Delia frowned—not Jess, oh, please, not Jess! Nothing had leaked to the media yet, so how—?

Carmine transferred his attention to the window, where the dusk was closing in; a few powerful lights on Long Island shone across the waters of the Sound—a night ball game of some kind?

"That was Corey Marshall," she said, coming to sit down.

He stared, astonished. "What did he want?"

"He's holding the fort for Fernando today. Ivy Ramsbottom managed to commit suicide this afternoon."

"Jesus!" On his feet, Carmine had already started to walk to the door when he balked, stopped. "Oh, Jesus!"

"Sit down and have a real drink, Carmine," Delia said, a glass in one hand, the bourbon bottle in the other. "There's nothing you can do until tomorrow, Corey's got it well in hand."

Carmine took the drink, a stiffer one than he liked. "How did she manage it?"

"Said she was desperately tired and wanted to sleep. They had just found her a bed that fitted her—she'd passed an uncomfortable night on the one in the cell—so no one was surprised. Where she'd hidden the razor blade no one knows, because none was found on her at search, including full body. She changed into a nightgown, got under the covers, and asked to be tucked in. The woman uniform on duty obliged, turned off the overhead light, and sat in a corner with a table lamp, reading. Ivy cut both her wrists under the covers—the uniform never noticed any movement. Then she lay there and bled to death without a moan or a sigh—it must have been eerie. Apparently the uniform's book was good, she didn't go to the bed to investigate until she'd finished it some hours later. By then the mattress was soaked and the blood was dripping onto the floor. As you may imagine, all hell broke loose. The uniforms hate having women prisoners, they insist it means bad luck."

"It sure did for Ivy," Carmine said with a sigh. "She was bound to do it, wasn't she?"

"Too proud not to," Delia said.

"And no field day for the media."

"For which, I'm sure, her brothers thank her." Suddenly Delia looked inspired. "Her hair! I'll bet the razor blade was tucked under a curl—she wears lacquer, so her hair feels stiff—who would notice? One looks for laces, sashes, belts."

He went to dilute his drink with club soda. "Well, what's done is done, I hope the poor soul is at peace."

"I hope she's in a kinder place than here," Delia said.

TUESDAY, SEPTEMBER 2, 1969

I t had fallen to Rufus to break the news about Ivy to Dr. Jess, but it hadn't been high enough on his list of priorities to have happened before the news of Ivy's suicide was relayed to him and Rha. When Anthony Bera called not ten minutes after Abe had come in person to tell the brothers, offering his services in a law suit against Holloman County for criminal negligence, Rufus had taken the call.

"Mr. Bera," he said in a tired voice, "go fuck yourself," and hung up quietly.

A retort that Abe was able to pass on to the Commissioner, as he was still present when Bera phoned.

It had puzzled Jess that Rufus Ingham, of all people, wanted to see her, but she wasn't particularly busy, and told him that he was welcome anytime. Her surprise increased when he arrived shortly thereafter, conducted down from the wall office by Walter Jenkins, who had difficulty finding a slot to fit the guy in, between the make-up, the grace of movement and the unconscious air of aristocracy. When the guy insisted on privacy with Jess, his hackles rose, but clearly she knew him well and liked him; Walter retired to his suite and thought of other things.

Jess wept bitterly, facing a lonelier life.

Having shed all his tears, Rufus comforted her as best he could, then waited for the first paroxysm of grief to pass, as it had to. With Jess, not such a long wait; she was controlled, her head would always rule her heart.

"It was by far the best solution," he said.

"Oh, yes. I suppose I'm crying for her pain."

"As have all of us who know. How much did she tell you?"

"Enough. But I do think her death is a way of sending you and Rha a message."

His face brightened, he sat straighter. "Tell me, please!"

"That she's expiated the guilt. That the pair of you should stop thinking about who and what your father was—yes, she knew Ivor fathered both of you! The only way you can betray her now is to continue living in guilt because your father was an evil man. In November you're forty years old—that's enough years, Rufus. Wake up each day shriven, not befouled. That's her most important message."

"She *did* tell you everything!"

"I think for a while, many years ago when we first met, Ivy hoped that I'd find a little scrap of brain tissue and label it FATHER'S GENETIC INHERITANCE, but I had to disillusion her by telling her that the code is in every single cell of the body, and cannot be extirpated after the egg is fertilized. It was a blow—she loved the pair of you so much!"

"Yes, that we do know." Rufus blinked hard.

"So this is how she finally decided to extirpate the genes. Not by any process of reason, or even of fantasy. I believe Ivy took all the old sins on her shoulders and tried to negate them, ultimately by destroying them along with her life. You and Rha have to live on as innocents," Jess said.

"There's no sense in it!" Rufus cried.

"There doesn't have to be. What is, is."

After Rufus left Jess didn't buzz Walter's room; she didn't feel up to coping with Walter until her own emotions were under better command—oh, Ivy! It wasn't difficult to understand why Ivy had chosen to kill in that manner; it inflicted great suffering over a long period of time without shedding a drop of blood. Even the castrations were relatively bloodless. Like all large people, she had grown in rapid spurts that demanded big quantities of food, which her father had denied her. Ivy's childhood had been one of perpetual hunger; the only substance Ivor didn't ration was water. One day, thought Jess Wainfleet, I will write a paper about Ivy Ramsbottom. It will contain facts neither her brothers nor the Holloman PD know, because it was to *me* that Ivy confided her life, her loves, her hates and her murders. She gave a sour grin. Fancy those ridiculous cops thinking she, Jessica Wainfleet, would ever betray a professional confidance! They'd have to rack her first, and no one in law enforcement did that anymore, though there were two inmates of HI who had.

"The theory of torturing a suspect to get a confession is so ludicrous it's comedic material," she said to Walter with a smile when he brought her a mug of coffee.

"Is it?" he asked, sitting. "Tell me more."

"In other times, suspects were submitted to ordeals of pain to wring confessions out of them," she said. "It didn't seem to occur to those inflicting the torture that physical agony produces more lies than truth, though my own theory is that they knew that already. They just liked to inflict torture. People confessed just to stop the pain." She smiled. "The rulers knew that all they were doing was encouraging the growth of vermin who mentally and physically enjoyed the act of torture. It's only recently that torture has fallen into disrepute."

"Is there any reason why torture could be good?" he asked.

"Absolutely none, Walter. To enjoy torture is one of the primary signs of psychopathia."

"Is that why anesthetic is given before an operation?"

Jess snorted. "You know that perfectly well. Where are you going, Walter?"

"Oh, I don't know," he said vaguely. "I just wondered."

"The answer lies in human kindness, and in education."

"You believe in education?" he asked.

"Completely, no holds barred."

"Because of God?"

She wanted to laugh, but kept a straight face. "God is a comfort-myth, my friend. If there is a God, it's the Universe. Reward and punishment are human concepts, they're not divine."

"That's why Rose hates you."

"How interesting! I didn't realize she did."

"There's lots you don't realize, Jess. That's why I try to join the wardroom coffee breaks. Except for Dr. Melos, they all think I'm just a wacko, and speak freely."

"Clever Walter!" she said admiringly. "When I have more time, you can fill me in on your impressions."

His face lit up. "That would be good, Jess."

A stab of guilt smote her; she smiled at him ruefully. "Oh, my dear, dear friend, I *am* neglecting you! I wish you were my only patient, but there are around a hundred others, none of whom carries your importance or interest for me."

Then he did it—Walter smiled! A broad, unmistakably wide grin. Stiffening in her chair, Jess grinned back.

Walter smiled! The floodgates were open, thundering a deluge down what had been an utterly dry and useless gulch; not only thoughts but emotions were cascading out, intermingled exactly as they should—how did triumph acquire a superlative? Because she had regarded Walter as a triumph for over thirty months by now, thinking that he had attained his peak, would grind to a stop. The smile said he hadn't stopped, and the sophistication of some of his recent actions said he might even be exponentially evolving.

"You're happy now," Walter said.

"If I am, Walter, it's entirely thanks to you."

Ivy Ramsbottom's cellar hadn't been an air-conditioned surgical paradise; that it had sufficed was astonishing in one way, but logical in another. It didn't gel with Ivy's fastidiousness, yet she had enough Ivor in her to construct a workable crypt.

Paul Bachman thought that Ivy, a skilled seamstress, had had it connected to the water and sewer, then padded it with her own hands. The vent was as old as the cellar. She had also changed the tiny elevator into an oversized chair, apparently so that she could descend and sit watching her victim suffer. From the contents of a bathroom that contained the chair just off the kitchen, the forensics team had deduced that Ivy regularly had put her victim to sleep, brought him up to the bathroom, then cleaned, bathed and shaved him, even to touching up the roots of his hair. Once the victim grew too weak to cooperate at all she abandoned her ministrations. Finally she transported the body to a site where trash was being illegally dumped, and threw him away like a dead animal.

"The cottage was isolated enough that no one ever heard the screams," Abe said to the Commissioner, "even though there was an open vent under the hedge line. I had Tony stand in the cellar and screech his loudest, but surprisingly little noise escaped. We think the acoustic dampening is due to the fact that the cellar and bathroom upstairs are not underneath the main house. They're off to one side, the bathroom area is small, and the cellar covered by two feet of soil and turf on top of a concrete lid. No echo chamber effect. The only way in or out is the elevator chair."

"How is her last victim?" Silvestri asked.

"Hanging in there, sir," Carmine said. "He has a very long road to recovery, but I'm assured he won't die. The worst is that he's burned up most of his muscle fiber in staying alive, so there's more involved than merely feeding him. He'll need phsical therapy and psychotherapy."

"How's his dog?" Liam asked.

"Pedro is taken up from Animal Care on frequent visits," said Carmine. "Rha and Rufus are picking up the hospital and treatment tabs, and I understand will send him home funded with a pension."

"Moving on, what's happening about the guy who raided your house and shot up young Hank?" the Commissioner asked. "Will Hank be okay?"

"He'll walk normally by the end of a year, sir, so I'm told. The spinal damage was virtually nonexistent, though part of the pelvis had to be reconstructed. It's muscle and skin grafts will keep him in the hospital a good while yet." He drew a deep breath. "As for the guy who did the shooting—zilch, sir. Nothing. We've found no trace of him anywhere. In fact, we don't even know if he drives a car or rides a motorcycle, though instincts say it's a big, powerful bike. He dresses in black, that much we got from Hank, who thought they were leather, but won't swear to it. Except that Hank is sure his face skin was white. The guy wore some kind of helmet, but neither a brain-bucket nor a *Wehrmacht* style. Pointed, according to Hank, whose eye is more for unusual than ordinary detail. I don't think he belongs to a biker gang."

"A maverick, then?" Silvestri asked.

"It's my hunch that he's always been a maverick."

"Not to mention a monster."

Everyone nodded.

The Commissioner pronounced. "A nun killer is beyond any-thing," he said, voice harsh. "We have to catch this evil bastard, and soon. No one in Holloman is safe, even the most innocent, until he's behind bars. Fernando, I want your uniforms on the qui vive day and night. If he does ride a bike, patrols stand a good chance of spot-ting him."

"Yes, sir," Fernando said.

"Good," said Silvestri, then, whispering, *"A nun!"*

FRIDAY, SEPTEMBER 5, 1969

She hadn't known quite how hard it was going to be living in a world devoid of Ivy. The shock had taken two days to dissipate, and it was followed not by depression, but by something worse; apathy. To Jess Wainfleet, psychiatrist, there was a difference between the two. Yes, depression could mean flatness of mood, but deep emotions continued to exist far down—there *were* pain and suffering. But not this time: Jess felt only an awful apathy, a total absence of any sort of suffering or pain.

Of course it had one advantage. She could work—and work well, efficiently, swiftly, unerringly. Grateful for that, she took her hundred cases out of the safe and ploughed through them one by one, suddenly shown the insights those traitorous emotions had masked. To bury oneself in work was a universal panacea, a technique she preached to her patients and to her staff—even preached to Walter, whose concern for her, she was aware, was steadily growing. The excitement this realization would have provoked only days before was utterly lacking, but she knew it would return as the vacuum in her life created by the death of Ivy began to fill up, as vacuums did; then she would turn to Walter with renewed energy and enthusiasm.

"Bear with me," she said to him, "just bear with me for a few more days, Walter, then we'll embark on some really fantastic stuff together, I promise. You're the center of my whole world."

The aquamarine eyes studied her intently, then he nodded.

No more was ever said about it, or needed to be said. Walter took himself off to the workshop to build something, while Jess kept on looking at her hundred cases.

She was groping through the labyrinth of words again, still convinced that the clue to those elusive pathways lay in words, and fascinated by the phrase "I want!" Corpus callosum, globus pallidus, rhinencephalon, hypothalamus, substantia nigra . . .

"Jess?"

Startled, she glanced up to see Ari Melos in her doorway, an odd expression on his face.

"Yes?"

"Captain Carmine Delmonico is here, asking to see you."

An explosive sigh escaped; she looked down at the files, at striped and coded ribbons. "Oh, damn the man!" she said. "Ari, offer him two alternatives. If he can wait half an hour, I'll see him then, or he can go away and come back later to risk it again."

But she knew what he'd answer; when Ari came back to say he had elected to wait, she was already retying the files, and when Jenny Marx her secretary ushered Captain Delmonico in, the safe was closed, every file gone.

"Captain, I apologize to have kept you waiting, but my desk was littered with confidential files when you arrived, and they had to be put away—by me."

"No trouble," he said cheerfully as he sat down again, for she was smiling too and he wondered if he would ever receive a truthful answer—why this winning smile? "It's a rare waiting room offers reading material like *Scientific American.*"

Simultaneously she was wondering how she had failed to notice the Captain's amazing attractiveness—had she honestly been that keyed up during her interview with him and Delia? He was dynamite! Had it been Delia blinded her? Or her mood that day?

Some men, she reflected, whether by accident or design, fell into their proper professions, the only ones they were properly suited to do, and this man was one such. Highly intelligent without the spark of genius, well educated without being entrapped by Academia, nigh infinitely patient, rational to the core yet subtle, emphatic when it suited him, and endowed with an analytical brain. A policeman by nature who might successfully have done a dozen things for a living, but had lit upon the one he was made for. His masculine appeal was undeniable but not a part of his arsenal because it didn't loom large in his own idea of himself. Unaware she did so, Jess Wainfleet licked her lips and swallowed, her mind girding itself for battle.

"I've come to talk to you," Delmonico said, "understanding that I'll get no answers worth their salt, but rather to see if you're the kind of person I can wear down, literally and metaphorically. You will never be free of me. Just when you think I've given up, I'll be knocking at your door again. You see, I *know* that you murdered six women in cold blood, and I'm not going to let you get away with it. Commencing with Margot Tennant in 1963, and at the rate of one per year, you killed six women. Why? is my chief question, and the chief reason why I refuse to let you go. What could possibly be the answer? I serve you warning, Dr. Wainfleet, I'm going to find out." The unusual eyes bored into her. "No. I won't let go!"

She sighed. "Captain Delmonico, there is an entity called harassment, and what you propose sounds very like it. Rest assured, I'll be telling my counsel, Mr. Bera, what you're threatening to do."

"Nonsense!" he said. "I'm very well known, Doctor, and *not* for harassment. I wish you luck proving that! Why did you kill Margot Tennant? Or Elena Carba, for that matter? Julia Bell-Simon?"

"I have killed no one," Jess Wainfleet said, voice obdurate.

Carmine shifted in his chair; somehow it came as no surprise that he also shifted subject. "Ernest Leto . . . A most elusive character. In fact, he seems to have no existence apart from work he did here in the Holloman Institute. He has a social security number, and according to the Internal Revenue Service paid tax on unspecified work he did here between 1963 and 1968. Part-time only. We have a description of Mr. Leto, furnished by HI staff: about five feet eight inches tall, thin and whippy in build, with black hair and a swarthy complexion. That could be Dr. Ari Melos, don't you think?"

"It could be, but it isn't!" she snapped, eyes flashing. "Ari Melos is a fully trained and qualified neurosurgeon who served his time at Johns Hopkins! If you look at the amounts Ernest Leto was paid, you'll see they're a pittance compared to what a Johns Hopkins neurosurgeon would ask. Ernie Leto was paid a technician's fees."

"Did Dr. Melos ever operate here?" Carmine asked.

"Naturally!" Wainfleet said haughtily. "He has his patients in the prison, two of whom are with him in HI at the moment, and he takes an occasional private patient, just as I do myself."

Carmine put an envelope on the desk. "This is a subpoena for the records in your possession pertaining to Ernest Leto," he said. "It's a duplicate, actually. I've already served the original on your director of personnel."

"We will endeavor to help in any way we can," she said in colorless tones. "Is there anything else?"

"A hypothetical question," he said.

Her brows rose. "Hypothetical?"

"Yes. Unlike the hypothetical situation Sir Richard Rich posed to Sir Thomas More, my question isn't designed to trip you up in a court of law."

"I am intrigued," she said lightly, feeling her curiosity stir. "Ask your hypothetical question."

"First, Mr. Leto," the Captain said. "He's a very difficult man to find. Your staff have verified that he does exist, that he came here to assist you on a number of neurosurgical interventions which the pair of you did alone, but that he did no other work here. What concerns me is that he assisted you in not merely six procedures, but forty-eight. That's a multiple of six, so were the forty-eight operations all on the six missing Shadow Women, or are there as many as forty-two unknown patients Mr. Leto helped you with? His IRS records list eight periods of employment per year, totaling in each year sufficient to live quite comfortably provided he doesn't have twelve children. Does he?"

"Does he what?" she asked blankly, her mind fixed on the hypothetical question.

"Have twelve children?"

Her hand slapped on the desk. "Oh, really, Captain!" she cried.

"I take that as a no," he said, writing in his notebook.

"Mr. Leto has no children—or a wife!" she snarled as he continued writing. "Forty-eight procedures sounds correct, given the number of years. I always used him for stereotaxy."

"What kind of stereotaxy do you do, Doctor?"

"Obviously, more than prefrontal lobotomies," she said tartly. "Operations in keeping with my interest and training. Walter Jenkins is my most ambitious project to date."

"Yet you didn't use Mr. Leto for Jenkins?"

Her brows rose. "When did I say that?"

"So you did use him for Jenkins?"

Her patience snapped, but not explosively; more, Carmine thought, like the final severing of a piece of very old elastic. "Enough!" she said. "Mr. Ernest Leto is very much alive and well, wherever he may be at the moment, and you, Captain, are groping in the dark. Either desist, or charge me with a crime."

"Then I'll desist. But I'll be back."

"Like summer influenza, you imply."

"As a metaphor, Doctor, it will do."

She laughed. "A waste of time for both of us. In my kind of surgery, bleeds and seizures are the major hazards, not cops. Talk to the Chubb Chairman of Neurosurgery, he'll tell you that no one ventures into the wildernesses of the brain without plenty of help on hand, from an anesthetist to instrument assistants. There had to be an Ernest Leto."

Carmine frowned. "You're saying that no one at HI has ever objected to being denied a hand in the cookie jar? Ernest Leto, says the IRS, received two thousand dollars per operation. If they were genuinely non-American patients, I'm going to say ten big ones. Leto probably took four and declared two. Plus travel expenses."

This time her laugh was a snigger. "Your imagination is really amazing, Captain!"

"Not at all," he said cordially.

"Why don't you ask your hypothetical question?" she asked.

"A good idea, Doctor. Let us say that a frantically busy, over-worked psychiatrist at a famous institute for the criminally insane decides she needs a hobby—my hypothetical psychiatrist is a lady, I forgot to say—and espouses photography. Her duties stifle her, hence her need for a hobby. She takes head-and-shoulders portraits of youngish women who have all mysteriously disappeared. She knows she won't see them again. Interestingly, among her patients are six women who have mysteriously disappeared. Oh, they don't belong to her official institute! They're private patients she doesn't need to see again. My hypothetical question is: do the six studio portraits belong to the six women who have mysteriously disappeared?"

The dark eyes considered him as he sat, so comfortably en-sconced, gazing at her blandly. While she fended him off, his eyes told her scornfully that she was losing the battle.

"Hypothetically," she said smoothly, "I have no idea what you're getting at. Oh, I believe you know where you're going! It's just that I don't." She looked at her nails. "Sorry, Captain."

"Don't be," he said, getting up. "Hypothesis will become reality."

Walter had used his time in the machine shop to good purpose in more than one way. If anyone approached to breathe down his neck and see what exactly he was doing, they would have been rewarded by the sight of two deft hands shaping a piece of soft steel on a metal lathe, the end result a complex, convoluted sculpture any discern-ing person would have delighted to display upon a prominent shelf. Oppositely, if anyone sneaked undetected into the workshop and observed what Walter was doing, they would have noted an ugly, lumpish chunk of iron like a shoddy imitation of a Moore. But if a fly had buzzed in and lighted on the wall, then crawled inside a locked cupboard, the fly would have seen that Walter was making a silencer for the .45 semi-automatic, and popping a little mercury into a box of .45 projectiles.

All research units had workshops: they had to. No professional inventor could dream up in his wildest fantasies the one-off Rube Goldberg devices that laboratory researchers demanded as if asking for a new toaster; then he breathed down the engineer's neck until the Rube Goldberg was finished. Most of the work was exquisite. Tungsten or glass microelectrodes with tips so fine they could be seen only under a microscope sat in the appropriate storage; there were micro pumps capable of delivering a drop of a drop each hour; whatever was needed had to be produced, almost inevitably in the workshop. There was only one proviso: that it not be "large" in any functional way. What was large? A pound or a half-kilogram in weight, a foot or a third of a meter in length, breadth, or depth.

With Jess Wainfleet and Ari Melos in a non-operative phase of their research, the artisan who ran the workshop had been granted a three-month furlough with pay to travel abroad and study techniques in other laboratory workshops. This left the shop entirely to Walter Jenkins, who, should anything come up, could turn to with a will and produce the item required. No sweat, as he said laconically.

He loved Marty Fane's pistol, a custom job right for a pimp; it was gold-plated and had a mock-ivory grip, and it blew a big hole in its target. After each projectile had been doctored by a plus of mercury, it blew a much bigger hole. The I-Walter was very pleased with it.

He was feeling emotions these days—or at least he thought he was feeling emotions. The only judge he had of truth or falsehood was himself, for Jess was in terrible trouble of some kind, and it had driven the I-Walter from the foreground of her mind. That didn't kindle anger or grief, if what he read about anger and grief were true; rather, it set off a paroxysm of payback against the people who were upsetting her.

The first welling up of this payback feeling had pushed him into deciding to kill Captain Carmine Delmonico—and what a fiasco that had been! He'd chosen a nun as his female victim deliberately, intending to put her in the Captain's bed, imply they were lovers, then have it look as if Delmonico had shot her before shooting himself. And it had all gone so wrong, though just afterward Walter had deemed it a triumph, not understanding his mistakes. But they had come to him upon reflection, and ruined his sense of triumph. So many mistakes! Like wiring her ankles and wrists together; easier to carry her, yes, but it left red welts on her skin. And he hadn't done enough surveillance, so didn't expect that fool of a kid to be on the Captain's deck—*painting*, for God's sake! All hell had broken loose, the kid screaming, the dog barking—what a fiasco!

A bell rang, a warning system he had devised; Walter put the gun in his cupboard, the bullets after it, closed the door and locked it. Casually, as if weary of it, he picked up the sculpture.

"You do the most beautiful work, Walter," Ari Melos said as he breathed down Walter's neck. "Gorgeous!"

"Remarkable," said Rose, not knowing what else to say.

"Thanks," said Walter, unlocking the lathe clamps and holding the steel up to the light. "It's not done with yet—see those?" He indicated a section where the silky steel was marred by tangled scratches. "That happened early, before I got the hang of it. I was going to smooth them out, but now I have a better idea. I'm going to work them into a pattern, transform them. Chased, like."

"I see what you mean," Melos said. "When it is finished, are you giving it to Dr. Jess?"

Walter shrugged. "Nah, wasn't going to give it to anyone."

"I'll give you a hundred dollars for it," Melos said quickly.

"Okay," said Walter, surprised, "but only after it's finished."

Turning, the pair went out. "I've known for a long while that he has talent," said Melos, his voice floating back. "Some lunatics are incredibly gifted, and I think Walter is one of them."

Fuck being incredibly gifted, Walter thought. Your eyes will give me your soul when I throttle you, and you won't be any different. I *should* rig it to make it look as if you strangled Rose, then hung yourself, but it's too much fun to strangle. Let the cops think an outsider did them both.

There were no memories to return, Jess had ablated every last one, but the I-Walter who was emerging from the old manic shell was a thinking being, and the I-Walter was acutely aware that he was starting to enjoy the act of killing. It had been there faintly when he had killed Marty Fane, but it had a reflexive flavor to it, as though when the knife went in, there was only one direction for it to go: onward and upward and clear down to the bone, very bloodless and very fast. No real thrill at all.

Ah, but when his hands had closed around Sister Mary Therese's neck! The first factor he encountered was her eyes, rolling in terror, and from that moment until finally he had climbed off her lifeless body, he had looked into her eyes. Sitting on top of her was simple asphyxiation, his weight preventing her straining lungs from pulling in enough air, even had there not been any merciless fingers on her trachea. A crude parody of the sex act, which he had never experienced in all his life; the first prisoner to try it died very bloodily; or so they had told him. It was one of those vanished memories.

To look into Sister Mary Therese's eyes was the ultimate bliss: Walter was sure of it. Most important, the I-Walter was sure of it. The expressions in her eyes! To witness those expressions change as she ran the gamut of those genuinely terminal emotions! He had to see them again and again. . . . Even now, merely thinking about it, back came the wrenching vividness; he saw panic, terror, horror, despair. And then the look turned to submission. While he, who inflicted all of it upon his suffering victims—yes, he, the I-Walter— soared through the act of watching the eyes into full-blown ecstasy.

All the Walters, even the most pathetic of the Jess-Walters, understood now what the purpose of his existence was—*ecstasy!* He threw the sculpture at the wall, hungering to hurt someone—no, strangle somebody!

Schemes and plots and plans crowded in on him, but he couldn't make sense of them; one part of himself knew that he had to seem the ordinary Jess-Walter, whereas most of him roared and screamed to do nothing but produce the look in eyes—anyone's eyes, everyone's eyes, from panic and terror to submission. . . .

"Oh, Walter!" came Jess's aggrieved voice. "Have you honestly forgotten we're eating in the senior staff dining room?"

The quiet soldier looked contrite—so many kinds of looks in the world, most of them designed to conceal or mislead.

"I'm so sorry, Jess, and I was looking forward to it too."

She laughed, linked her arm through his. "My dearest of all helpers, it doesn't matter! I knew you'd forget, so I came searching in plenty of time."

The menu in the senior staff dining room, patronized by eight or nine persons, was superior, and had two waiters. To dine in it if you were not senior staff was rare.

Jess chose a shrimp cocktail and pork spare ribs, but Walter went more French, with a country terrine and a beef burgundy.

"Are you feeling any better?" Walter asked her.

"If you mean, about Ivy, I'm recovering from the shock. But that's not significant. What is, is that I've neglected you quite disgracefully. But be of good cheer! Very soon now I'm going to sit down with you and go through these new pathways you're opening up at such a rate. It's quite wonderful."

"I can feel it myself, Jess."

"Do some things make you feel particularly good?"

What would she say if he told her, yes, strangling people?

The good soldier answered instead. "I sold my sculpture to Dr. Melos for a hundred bucks. It made me feel really good."

"Walter, I'm delighted for you! Coming from Ari Melos, it's a rare compliment. If he didn't think you had true talent, he'd never part with his precious money."

"That's nice to know," he said, looking satisfied.

"Can you describe niceness?" Jess asked.

Frowning, he digested this. "I'm not sure. . . . Happy, I guess. Like seeing a really beautiful butterfly?"

"Then what you felt was more than nice. You were thrilled."

"That's it!" he exclaimed. "Thrilled." He ate beef. "Are there better words than thrilled, Jess?"

Astonished, she laughed. "Heavens, you are fixated! Better than thrilled. . . . Uplifted. Ecstatic. Inspired. It depends what you're discussing, Walter," she labored. "The right word is the one that fits the situation or state of mind."

"Would I be uplifted if my Rube Goldberg worked?"

"Probably not."

"What if I sculpted something crash-hot?"

"You'd either be uplifted or unduly critical."

"Unduly critical?"

"Artists are rarely happy with their work, Walter."

At the end of the meal, just as Jess was settling down to a real talk with him, Walter began to blink and look uncomfortable, shifting in his chair. "Jess, please excuse me."

"What's the matter?" she asked, alarmed.

"I'm starting a migraine aura."

"Describe it," she said tersely.

"A big boomerang shaped thing high up on my left side. It's made up of glittering purple and yellow darts, and it's creeping down."

"Oh, God! It is a migraine aura, Walter. The headache will be left-sided, and start any time, but if it's usual, you've got about twenty minutes. Get off to bed immediately."

"I know, I've had them before. I'm going to lock myself in."

"I'll make sure you're left in peace," Jess said. "Nothing is worse than having people peering at you in the dark and disturbing you just as you have the headache under control."

His face gladdened. "Oh, Jess, thanks! You understand."

"You're right, I understand. I have migraines too."

SATURDAY, SEPTEMBER 6, 1969

He had pulled the migraine stunt shortly after nine, which meant Walter had two and a half hours to fill in before he needed to move; the best way to do this was to lie on his bed in a completely darkened room, neither writhing nor moaning. Any kind of movement, even that caused by a moan, is agony to the migraine sufferer, who lies as immobile as possible and tries to sleep. For Walter, whose brain had been invaded, there could be no shot of morphine. For him, it was sleep or agony.

He used those two and a half hours in trying to remember what he had told Jess was happening to him, and what he had kept a secret from her. Like his doors, his hollow wall, its contents, his expeditions into the outside world and what he had done during them, what he had done in the HI workshop, and, most secret of all, the utter fascination of watching life die out of a pair of eyes. They were all things that belonged to the I-Walter, who was a separate entity from the confused mish-mash of Walters he suddenly recognized, in that darkened room, as the Jess-Walter. The I-Walter hadn't appeared at Jess's bidding—in fact, he would appall her. How he knew that, he didn't know, just that he did. So which Walter was the right Walter? The I-Walter, always the I-Walter. *Secrets!* How he loved secrets! Then, lying flat on his back on his bed, a tiny stabbing pain behind his eyes, he threshed up and down, back and forth on the pillows— WALTER, YOU HAVE BEEN HERE A HUNDRED TIMES

BEFORE! You know all this, you have already reasoned it out! You're the oxen on the tow-path, feet worn down to nothing.

Ari and Rose Melos. Delia Carstairs. Yes, they would be the first three. But only after I have treated myself to a binge. *I deserve a binge!*

I am the I-Walter, but Jess doesn't know about the I-Walter. Even in despite of that, she thinks I am the center of her universe. Poor, deluded Jess! Psychiatrists are so easy to fool; they talk themselves into the right answers.

Inside his wall by half after eleven, clad in black leather and a conical helmet he intended to equip with wings later on, Walter Jenkins consulted his map by the light of a new pressure lantern—there! Out beyond South Rock, surrounded by State forest, two miles from the nearest main road. . . . Perfect!

The Harley-Davidson's panniers and pillion box were stacked with gasoline containers; he didn't dare go near a gas station tonight, no matter what, and that included unexpected detours.

He opened the external door and wheeled the bike out along a new track; the earlier ones had all vanished, and this one wouldn't be used again for months to come. Oh, pray it was a green winter this year! Snow would imprison him completely.

Though the leaves wouldn't begin to turn for three more weeks and some of the days would be quite hot, there was a slight nip in the air, an initial harbinger of Fall. The sun was growing tired of rolling northward; in less than twenty days it would grind to a halt, exhausted, and start rolling down-globe on its southward plod, while behind it everything shivered.

Walter Jenkins shivered too, but not from the chill wind as his bike roared westward; his was an anticipatory shiver. Some miles away he turned southward, but didn't take the tunnel through South Rock. Instead he veered west again to circumnavigate the basaltic pile, then picked up a very minor road through country devoted mostly to apple orchards. Spying trees loaded with big Opalescents, he stopped the bike, raided the nearest tree and wolfed down two apples, eyes closed in simple pleasure. *So sweet!* Then on again, the lingering taste of ideally ripe fruit in his mouth, an unexpected bonus.

And there it was, a single-storey sprawl in white clapboard, surrounded by well-kept gardens in which stood groups of chairs and tables, and adorned with a verandah that spread right across its front, where no doubt in good weather the folks could sit or lie about. The Harley-Davidson was up by an open gateway impeded by a deep pit across which steel bars had been laid to keep out horses or cattle or sheep.

Avoiding the verandah, Walter stole around the back, found the kitchen and the night staff clustered around its table, about to have hot drinks and food. He had timed his arrival perfectly, and entirely by accident. The article in the *Post* had been fair and correct, he soon discovered; the inmates each had a private room and bathroom, and judging by the number seated around the kitchen table, the nursing staff was indeed ample.

It seemed to Walter that he physically entered inside a dream of such formlessness that it had no name, no finite being; it enfolded him in one pair of eyes after another, a twinned pathway of vital sparks fading away into nothing, and he was the cause of it, his the hands that administered it, his the brain that drank it in like a starving dog a puddle of blood.

From room to room to room Walter went.

The screams began to erupt from the nursing home ten minutes after Walter kicked the bike into life and tore away, heading now for Millstone Beach. It had taken him fifteen minutes to strangle three bed-bound patients, the youngest seventy-one, the oldest two days short of ninety.

Delia woke confused and fighting, but not to die. The I-Walter was temporarily sated, and the Jess-Walter had plans for her. A piece of duct tape was already across her mouth, her hands were being bound behind her back ruthlessly tight, and before she had a chance to focus her eyes, they too were covered by duct tape. Her nightgown was decent but feminine, made of artificial silk with lace around the arms and neck, but whoever it was—the Mystery Man, she was sure—bundled her across his shoulders with no additional clothing to protect her from the cold. Yes, a motorcycle! He mounted it and draped her across the front of his legs, then drove off at a pace well below the speed limit, for Delia, in next-to-nothing, a freezing ride.

By now the shock had worn off and she was wide awake, her mind trying desperately to make sense out of this senseless kidnapping—why her, why a sergeant of police? How far was she being taken? Whereabouts? No shoes—she couldn't flee. Did he care for her welfare? She wasn't a child, she wasn't wealthy, she wasn't political. Despite her calling, she hadn't done anything to anyone. A cold and uncomfortable ride, but not a long one, she assessed; ten minutes saw the bike stopped, and her on her feet. Under them she felt a forest floor.

She could feel him touching her right arm where it was pressed against her back and on top of her left arm near the wrist; a cord bit into it above the elbow, and she knew he was raising a vein. Something pricked and hurt a little; her head swam, her knees buckled, and the lights went out.

Disorientated and groggy, she woke in an almost intense darkness to the sound of soft sobbing. Remembering herself bound, gagged and blindfolded, she found herself now freed, though her face and mouth hurt from the gag and duct tape. Wherever she was stank of decay, but faintly. And the soft sobbing went annoyingly on. . . .

"Who—is it?" she croaked, suddenly aware she was thirsty.

The sobbing stopped. The voice that answered belonged to a man—not the weeper, someone else. "We're Ari and Rose Melos."

"Delia Carstairs."

"The cop with the hideous dresses?" squawked a female voice.

"Where are we? Who took us?"

"I have no idea," said Aristede Melos. "We were at home, fast asleep. The next thing we knew, we were bound and gagged. Such a shock! He took Rose here first—I was demented! Then he took me, it was a little better. But it's so mortifying!"

Delia discarded them to assess the situation. One ankle wore a fetter, to which a chain about three feet long was attached; if she moved in a circle at one point she could touch a wall of some kind, and in the opposite direction she could see a black outline of the Meloses, Rose still sobbing softly.

"Oh, for pity's sake, woman, cease your grizzling!" Delia shouted, at the end of her weepy-woman tether.

"How dare you!" Melos snarled. "My wife is in a state of shock!"

"Codswallop!" snapped Delia. "Your wife is doing the petrified little wife act! She'd do better to shut her bloody mouth and let me think how to get us out of the situation."

She was chained to a stone embedded in the floor, not to the wall, and presumed that the same was true of the Meloses; there must be a reason why, perhaps lying in the risk of being heard?

Rose was at it again, an eternal spring that gushed on and on.

"*Shut up!*" Delia growled.

Silence. How blessed quiet could be! She could think. And, thinking, realized she had to examine the fetter. Pulling her nightie under her rump, she sank down and discovered that a band of steel went around her ankle. Where its ends met were two flanges that kissed each other and were punctured by a hole; through the hole was a steel rod bent like a U—a padlock! Whoever had made the fetters was limited in his tools or facilities, so all he could manage was to curve his steel to fit the ankle and then give it a sharp, right-angled bend. That meant a hole and a padlock. But why, her mind went on, have we been abducted? A member of the police I can understand, but two psychiatrists? It has something to do with HI, that glares like a searchlight, but *what?* Her thoughts leaped to Walter Jenkins, who didn't make sense either; he was, besides, a prisoner, unable to get out. No, leave him be for the moment. More important was how to escape.

Behind the Meloses was a stone wall that didn't belong to her: an opposing one, perhaps? She could see them distinctly. "We're getting plenty of air—don't you dare start grizzling again, woman!" she yelled at Rose, whose preparatory sniffles stopped at once. "Rose, you're a senior member of your profession, and you're as tough as old army boots! This weak and trembling female business is an act to impress your new husband, nothing else, and if he doesn't see through it, I do! Put what passes for your brain to how to get out of here. What are you wearing?"

"Nothing," Ari Melos whispered. "Absolutely nothing."

"Hair curlers," said Rose on an audible swallow.

"Can you see me at all?" Delia asked.

"Yes," Rose answered, apparently having decided to abandon the weak woman persona. "You're a black blob against the opposite wall."

"So there is an opposite wall? Do you know where we are?"

"We're inside the Asylum walls," said Ari.

"Ah! Is there any way out?"

"Until this, I wasn't aware there was a way in," Ari said.

"Hmm. That makes it harder," said Delia. She thought for a moment. "Rose, can you throw me a curler?"

There was a scrabbling sound, a pause, then a plop as a curler hit Delia's foot. A minute later, it was in her hand, a plastic cage of cylindrical shape, with a clip-fastened plastic bar down one side to hold the hair in place. Delia sighed. "I don't suppose you have anything like a bobby pin?" she asked.

In reply, she found herself showered with around a dozen hefty bobby pins, three of which actually landed in the slight sag her nightgown made across her thighs. Seizing one eagerly, Delia bit in nibbles at the plastic-cushioned tips. Once they were bare metal, she used them to key the padlock. It was a long and tormenting struggle, but eventually the thing lurched open. With a squeak of triumph, Delia forced the U clear of the hole, then managed in a savage burst of strength to bend the thin cuff apart enough to free her leg. She was at liberty!

Gasping, she stood at full height. "I'm free, chaps!"

"Now free us," Ari Melos commanded.

"Bugger that! You'd slow me down, and that frightful woman would sniffle and screech. I'll come back for you."

"You fucking bitch!" Rose blubbered.

"Ditto, brother smut."

Feeling steadier by the moment, Delia debated.

From her left emanated that stench of an old decay; no, it wasn't the way out, it led to further horrors. She spoke aloud: "He's like a spider, storing his prey for later," she said to the Meloses, struck dumb by her refusal to free them. "Truly, you'd slow me down too much, all three of us would be recaptured. He won't return in a hurry, but I will. There must be a way out! He wants you for some purpose connected to the Asylum, otherwise you'd be dead already. If he does return, use your wits."

Rose was sobbing again, but Ari Melos had listened.

"I still believe we're inside the Asylum walls," he said, "so you may have a long walk."

The darkness had lessened, so her eyes were still adjusting. Delia could see the outline of the Meloses quite distinctly now, and judged that they were being held inside a roundel. The dim light came from her right, and within several yards the space had narrowed to a passage about two yards wide. Using one hand on the wall as a prop, she inched along, the noise of Rose's sobbing diminishing—thank God for that!

"Shut up, you silly cow!" she yelled. "The more racket you make, the quicker he'll come back to cut your throat."

Silence again. With any luck, Ari Melos had strangled Rose.

Delia traveled with painful slowness, the light insufficient to tell her what lay on the floor; that, she had to find out by using her feet as exploratory instruments, sometimes encountering what at first seemed deep ditches and other perils that turned out one pace farther to be illusory. The main constituent was gravel, but there were knotted roots, dead leaves, insect carapaces and rat skeletons. In one place the floor was strewn with slivers and splinters of glass; aware that her feet were now cut and bleeding, she kept on going regardless, and lost the glass two paces on.

Her face was on fire, her heart pounding; all the chill had quit Delia's body during this inexorable and frantic effort. What drove her on was the nameless horror of running into her captor coming the other way to check on his store of prizes.

And then she emerged into a rounded cavern that was lit from above, where several stones had been removed and a sunny day poured in. A Harley-Davidson motorcycle rested on its stand, a collection of objects were stacked on shelves, and, beyond the round cave, a door sat in either wall.

Which door led out, and which in? Eyes hurting from the light, Delia looked at the wall with the stones removed, and decided that was the outside wall. Its door led to freedom.

When she turned its handle she discovered it wasn't locked; Delia stepped out into a thick clump of mountain laurel, with a sun-soaked patch of grass away to her right. Heedless of her feet, she ran as fast as she could away from that terrible imprisonment.

A squad car found her on one of the ceaseless patrols that Commissioner Silvestri had ordered ever since the tragedy at the Hazelmere nursing home had been reported.

SUNDAY, SEPTEMBER 7, 1969

Within minutes of the squad car's reporting Delia's escape, cops were swarming through the forest around the "out" door in the Holloman Institute's wall, under orders to keep the noise down.

Carmine, Abe, Liam and Tony, together with Fernando and six hand-picked uniforms would be the only ones to enter the wall, but first it was imperative to get the Meloses out alive. Carmine took Abe and Tony, Abe carrying a powerful light instead of a drawn pistol, and traversed in five minutes what it had taken Delia an hour to walk. The passage was about two yards across, and widened into a roundel where a watchtower had been built; at those places it was about seven yards in diameter. The roundel containing the two doors was on the plans as a watchtower, though none had been built there, the why unrecorded.

Dr. Aristede Melos and his wife were very much as Delia had left them, except that Rose was spitting in fury at Delia's gall in leaving them behind. Blanket-shrouded, they were taken to the hospital for observation. Once that was out of the way, the pace slackened to a rate dictated by the forensics team, enthused at the prospect of dissecting such a pristine multiple killer's den.

Carmine himself returned to headquarters, where, sure enough, he found Delia waiting. Blinking, he assimilated the full glory of a Delia unharmed—nay, *healed*. Pink bunny slippers to cover the bandages on cut feet. Sheer yellow tights over pallid pink legs to give an impression of overripe bananas. A miniskirted dress of orange and green stripes to which were attached large, electric-blue satin bows. Oh, thank you, dear Lord Jesus!

"You ought to be resting at home," he said, feeling he must.

"Rubbish! I'm a box of birds, and full up to pussy's bow with tender, loving care! You can see that for yourself. Are the Meloses all right?"

"They'll recover. The most serious injury they sustained was to their self-esteem—being found stark naked. Rose Melos couldn't seem to stop crying."

"Tell me about it!" Delia giggled. "I called her a silly cow. Have you any idea who our abductor is?"

"Beyond his being an inmate of the Holloman Institute, none that will hold water. Apart from a fuss out on 133 shortly before dawn, nothing's happened to alarm anyone inside, and I don't intend to tell Dr. Wainfleet a thing for the time being. Or the security guys and Warden Hanrahan on the straight prison side."

"You have your suspicions," Delia said shrewdly.

"Don't you?"

"Oh, yes. Walter Jenkins. But you've never met him, Carmine—how on earth did you light on him?"

"From reading Wainfleet's papers. He's contained, now that we've found his way in and out, but I don't want to tip our hand until after I've seen Dr. Wainfleet under what will look to Walter like routine circumstances. I know he's armed and it's a risk, but less a risk than barging in with guns drawn and a cacophony of noise. Walter's not your usual criminal."

Delia adjusted the bow over her bosom. "What happened last night to put so many patrols out? My good luck, but—!"

"Your abductor strangled three harmless old folks in the Hazelmere nursing home. We had no idea he'd also kidnapped you and the Meloses," Carmine said, tight-lipped. "Finding you and learning about the doors in the HI wall was a revelation that led straight to Walter, in my mind anyway. I wish I knew why he took you and the Meloses, but it's as big a mystery as he is."

"I believe I can answer a bit of it, dear," said Delia. "He has decided that we—I in one way and the Meloses in another—threaten his relationship with Jess Wainfleet. She's the fulcrum, the basis. Assuming her as the cause, I worked backward to the inexpressibly creepy Walter." She shivered. "Jess actually thinks him cured, whereas I thought his actions and reactions were robotic. How that upset her! But you got it from reading her papers? I confess they're up with the astronauts as far as I'm concerned, but they're simply scientific dissertations."

"Oh, they're a little more than that, Deels. In a way they read like eulogies. I inferred from them that some kind of miracle had taken place. When the physician doing the treating starts waxing lyrical the way she did about Walter, any cop worth his salt gets suspicious." Carmine shot her a keen glance. "You know Jess Wainfleet well. Can she honestly be living in ignorance of Walter's guilt?"

"Oh, yes. Of that, I'm positive. He's her child."

Delia really was, Carmine reflected, a superb detective in the true sense of that word: she could take a bunch of unrelated facts and deduce from them. It was for that reason he had given her the Shadow List, and if the last piece of evidence had come from him, that was only because of their contrasting educations; he had seen the neurosurgeon in Jess, whereas she had seen the psychiatrist. But the case wasn't closed yet, it had simply hit another brick wall that one or the other of them would find a way around. That both of them were necessary was yet one more argument in favor of his kind of detective force—men and women with varied skills and educations. Chance and luck played roles too. If he hadn't been lonely and domestically rudderless, he wouldn't have had the time to read all those scientific books and magazines that had alerted him to stereotaxic neurosurgery and research. Though his reading wouldn't have taken the slant it did had Delia not sought enlightenment from a police artist about similar skulls. One hand washes the other. . . .

Walter had emerged from his migraine shortly before dawn on Sunday, to find Jess wakeful and pacing her office.

"What's up?" he asked, bringing her freshly brewed coffee.

Her face lit up, the profundity of her relief written on it, and showing too in trembling fingers as she took the mug.

"Oh, I am so glad to see you! Something about your headache frightened me, Walter. When you went to bed last night, you seemed—oh, I don't know—*changed*."

"It was a very bad headache. Left-sided. Like you said, I lost my speech for a while. Couldn't calculate either."

Sagging into her chair, she waved at the other one. "Sit down, please. I want to talk to you."

He sat, the obedient soldier, chin up, eyes fixed on hers.

"Do you know what I did when I performed all those operations on you, Walter?" she asked.

"Yes. You mended me."

"Well, okay, I did do that, but it's not what I mean. You've progressed so much since the day thirty-two months ago when I did the last operation! Now I can explain on a more complex level than I have to date. Do you know what a short-circuit is?"

"Yes, it's basic. The electrical current that should flow along a preordained pathway of wires finds a way to jump from 'in' to 'out' that bypasses the path, cuts it short. So all the current is lost, the circuit is burned up in a fiery flash of energy, and the work is ruined."

"I like your choice of words. Preordained—wonderful!" Jess drank her coffee deeply, still recovering from the worry of wondering if Walter's headache had been a warning of—? "So imagine that vast numbers of these pathways have suddenly short-circuited at the same moment, and that together they are your whole brain. Because of the massive short-circuit, the flash of energy has utterly destroyed all of your brain's pathways. What becomes of your brain, can you tell me?"

"It becomes a no-brain."

"That's correct. I took you, Walter no-brain, and I put many hundreds of tiny terminals throughout the shell of your no-brain. Each terminal was inside a cluster of cells I'll call a battery. And each battery was wired through pathways to many other points all over your no-brain. Remember, nothing worked anymore!"

"I hear you," he said steadily.

"The new terminals I put in, I then turned on by giving each of them the tiniest imaginable zap of electrical current. The current cut through the burned-out wreckage and reconnected each battery to its pathway. As I did this over and over, I built a new brain on top of the wreckage of the no-brain. The new brain is the new Walter—the Walter *I* created!" Jess cried shrilly.

"You did it," he said woodenly.

"Darned right I did it, Walter! Why? Why is that? Because I am the only one who knows all the brain's secrets! I just needed a framework, and I found it in the burned-out husk of your no-brain—a perfect frame! I gave Walter No-brain the brain of a sane, kind, decent human being! I might call you Walter Jess-brain."

His upper lip lifted in naked contempt. "Horseshit! Utter horseshit! You speak as if to a dim, dull-witted child. But I am not a child, and I am far from dull in my wits," he said.

She let out a bellow of laughter, one of those involuntary, amazed, I-can't-believe-my-ears laughs that mask a total paralysis of thought, driven out of the mind by a colossal blow, the rudest of shocks. Jaw dropped, mouth agape, eyes staring wide and stunned, she sat looking at him emptied of any comeback.

"You make me sound like an exercise in Meccano parts," Walter said, "as if inside my pathetic cranium lies the nuclear wasteland after detonation. You built *nothing*, Jess! What you did was to implant dual tungsten microelectrodes in my brain using the specific stereotaxic co-ordinates your atlas told you were correct. Then you zapped the neurones in between the two tips of a pair of microelectrodes: It was a work of genius because you knew whereabouts to put your ultrafine electrodes and how much current to apply, but it could only succeed if you had an experimental animal—Walter Jenkins the homicidal maniac. But who says where the accolades should go? To you, who did the hack work, or to me, whose brain belongs only to me? Your part ended thirty-two months ago when you performed the last neurosurgical intervention. It's I whose pathways have kept opening up, more and more and more. The man sitting here this morning has nothing to do with you. The man sitting here this morning is the I-Walter."

It never occurred to her to be frightened. As the power to think returned she had listened enthralled, staggered by the ease and familiarity of his delivery—never in a million years would she have dared to hope for anything approaching what he was airily showing her, a peacock spreading his gorgeous cerebral tail—!

"Your vocabulary is amazing," she said.

"I feel things these days, Jess. I've found things to enjoy and things to dislike," he said in dreamy tones. "If intensity of feeling turns like into love or dislike into hate, then I'm not there yet, though there's one thing I do that lifts me high into pleasure. All my feelings belong to the I-Walter."

"And *you* have built the I-Walter," she said.

"Yes. The I-Walter worships you."

Now where was he going? Was this area still in regression? Certainly he gave off no emanations of sexual desire, which led her to presume that the pathways to his erotic nuclei and cortex were either still closed or at most unimportant. The I-Walter!

Third person, or first person? First. . . . "Can you describe how you feel when you worship me, Walter?"

"I feel that were it not for you, I would not exist."

"You feel for me as your maker, your creator?"

The magnificently blue eyes flashed in scorn. "No! I made myself, I created myself. You gave me the framework on which to build, Jess. Haven't I made that clear?"

"It needed the elucidation of words, that's all. Words are vital, never forget that! Without words, we go back to the animal, we can't make our wants, needs, desires and wishes crystal clear. Don't forget how many kinds of 'clear' there are, from a pane of glass smeared with the filth of a hundred years to a pane of glass polished five minutes ago. Both clear, but what a difference!"

"I worship you too because you teach."

"What do you mean by worship?"

"I mean that I would protect you from all harm, make you as happy as happy can be."

Her knees felt weak, her head was spinning; knowing the signs, Jess got up. "My blood sugar's right down, I need to eat breakfast, or lunch, or whatever the cafeteria is serving. May I lean on your arm?" Jess asked.

He was at her side immediately. "Still breakfast. Come on."

Protesting bitterly, Delia was refused permission to continue at work, and Carmine knew exactly how to ensure obedience. He made a call to Rufus Ingham, gave him the barest bones of Delia's ordeal, and half an hour later handed her into Rufus's Maserati at the Cedar Street entrance to the police station. Whether she liked it or not, she was firmly anchored for at least a day.

That done, he went back to the door in the HI wall, where the forensics team had made many discoveries. The interior was lit up like day, displaying Walter's circular base of operations and the narrow passages going in opposite directions away from it. Already processed for prints and other evidence, the motorcycle had gone back to Forensics for further examination, its gas tanks drained. Abe was in command.

He and the others had found Marty Fanes's .45 Colt semiautomatic and a spare clip as well as a box of .45 projectiles.

"Just as well he didn't dare keep the pistol with him," Abe said, proffering a magnifying glass. "He's put quicksilver in the tips—beautiful job too."

A hunting knife had also been found, washed but still bearing traces of blood around the junction of hilt and tang.

A shelf held warm black clothes, a set of black motorcycle leathers hung neatly from hooks driven into the mortar between the stones of the wall, and, in pride of place, a black helmet. A case of bottled Italian water, assorted imperishable foods, a first-aid kit that included suturing needles and silk thread, various tools and a home-made workman's bench indicated that Walter had perhaps planned for a last-ditch stand inside his citadel.

Aerie duty, involving a lookout on top of the wall in the watch-tower under which Delia and the Meloses had been kept; if Walter was seen crossing toward his bolt-hole, the lookout was to ring an alarm bell; radio signals didn't penetrate inside the wall. That meant four uniforms on guard just inside the "in" door, all armed with semiautomatic pistols as well as their .38 police special Smith & Wesson revolvers. Carmine himself packed a Beretta 9mm semiautomatic firearm these days, and Abe had followed suit; the flatter depth of the gun was more comfortable than a round-barreled revolver, and the magazine held more bullets.

"There's something else," Abe said, drawing Carmine away from the four uniforms on guard.

"What?"

"Up here."

Abe led the way toward Delia's prison, the passage lit up, gloomy rather than terrifying. The floor of packed earth, Carmine noted, was liberally dewed with debris from 150 years of enclosure: rodent skeletons, empty insect carpaces, living roots even—how did they get in there?—dead leaves.

"I hope they dressed Delia's feet well at the hospital," he muttered, steering around a dead rat.

"I phoned to make sure as soon as I had a look," said Abe.

"Good man."

In Delia's prison he saw the relics of their incarceration—manacles and chains, a smell of urine. And the faint stench of an old decay. The passage beyond, he saw, was also lit.

"What's up there?"

Abe grimaced. "The icing on what might be a different cake, Carmine," he said.

A hundred yards farther, and there they were, six headless skeletons stapled to the outside wall by bands of steel nailed straight into the mortar with flat-headed spikes.

"Jesus!"

"The Shadow List Women, you think?" Abe asked

"I know," Carmine said. "They never went anywhere, Abe."

"Paul is aware what's up the passage, but we're sitting on it for the moment—Walter is enough to go on with. Unless you feel otherwise?"

"No! No, no . . . What difference can a day or two make now?" Tears filled his eyes; he turned his head away from Abe, and swallowed convulsively. "Even robbed of permanent rest, the poor ladies. Coming and going on the stairs, unnoticed . . . Of course they were zombies, how couldn't she see that?"

"Worse than Walter," Abe said. "They were done in ice-cold blood."

Turning, Carmine walked back to the roundel, where he could face Abe with neither the living nor the dead to eavesdrop.

"Our strategy, Carmine?" Abe asked.

"What time is it?"

"Eleven twenty-one."

"Right. We keep the four uniforms here in case Walter makes a run for it. He's a never-to-be-released killer, so as lives are at risk the orders are to shoot to kill. Fernando's issued the same orders. Our authority is the commissioner himself. I'm seeing Warden Hanrahan right now, it's arranged. You, Liam, Tony and Donny should go on up the road to Major Minor's and grab some lunch. I'll hope that the Warden takes pity on me. Then at one p.m. we'll meet outside the Asylum entrance. Once inside there, we head for HI. I will see Dr. Wainfleet while everyone else waits for me still outside the entrance to HI. If Walter appears, you will arrest him—*full* manacles, hear me? Feet as well as hands, all connected at the waist. If he doesn't appear by one-thirty, I'll join you."

"Let's pray it finishes soon," Abe said.

"I'm going back into the forest. See you at one."

Warden James Murray Hanrahan had suffered atrociously at the whim of Dr. Jessica Wainfleet over the years, or at least as he painted it to Carmine during the first twenty choleric minutes of a long and impassioned interview. Stomach grumbling from lack of food, the captain of detectives resigned himself to a litany of complaints, on the theory that, if unopposed, Hanrahan's tirade would cease more quickly, its deliverer somewhat purged of his ire.

"This is what happens when inexperienced public servants try to graft two disparate things together ass-to-ass!" the Warden roared. "Instead of letting me run a maximum security penitentiary properly, I'm forced to take a back seat to to an obsessive-compulsive fool with no correctional training! The power she's accumulated in D.C., Hartford *and* Holloman mystifies me! I am just her animal care facility, her source of well-fed experimental subjects. I tell you, that woman is dangerous!"

"I know," said Carmine, giving the warden his sweetest smile, "but, Jimmy, look on today as Deliverance Sunday, and on me as your own Archangel Gabriel. Leave things to me, and HI will be put in its proper place. Act independently, and you'll fall flat. You're not without friends, Jimmy, and they're working quietly on your behalf. Dr. Wainfleet overestimates her power, whereas you underestimate yours. Just sit still, and all will be resolved."

The Warden's reply was perhaps inadvertent, but to Carmine it sounded wonderful. "Do you like egg salad?" he asked.

"I *love* egg salad," Carmine said fervently.

"Then we can eat while we talk. It's only sandwiches, but the bread is fresh. If I don't eat, I'm afraid my stomach acids will chew another hole in my belly."

Sometimes, reflected the captain of detectives, the most ordinary of queries can provoke the most delight.

"Make sure you have reserved your best padded cell in complete isolation, as well as maintain maximum security from the moment I leave," Carmine said somewhat later. "Walter Jenkins must be taken dead or alive, I hope at the hands of the police, but otherwise, by yours. Most importantly, after he's caught, you must ensure his isolation is preserved—no visitors, including Jess Wainfleet."

"It will be done, Captain, you have my word on it."

Jess and Walter lingered all morning in the cafeteria, then decided to eat lunch there before moving. The long silences between them were quite usual, though over this particular meal the paucity of their conversation was not due to any of the normal reasons.

Jess was still shaking off the last vestige of her shock at discovering exactly how far Walter had come—and how well he had concealed his progress. Nor had he told her all of it yet, she was positive; there was a lot more to make public, and she was dying to know what. In one aspect her ego was so enormous that she saw herself as a mighty sun alongside Walter's dying ember, yet in another way her ego was so small that she saw Walter as a supernova alongside her own wan moon. She had no genuine concept of God, especially a God imaging her own species; she tended to think God was the Universe, and so she was a part of God. In which case, she reasoned, how then to classify Walter, who saw with diamantine clarity that he had created himself? Did that mean that Walter was the Universe, that *Walter* was God? A God who had created himself, but had needed the vital spark she gave him?

Walter sat wrestling with the knowledge that something inside him was slipping the way a snake swallowed its tail, the insatiable jaws and the coils of muscle behind them already beginning to digest the engulfed tissues of his disappearing tail into nothing. But that made no sense! He didn't know what, or why, or where, or how. What he *felt* was a sensation akin to pain yet was not pain. Somewhere inside himself everything was going around and around, swirling and churning, but he had no idea of a name, or a function, or a reaction to pin on it. And ever and always came memories of the ecstasy he was driven to seek, to repeat. Though he had a name for the idea of ecstasy: the I-Walter. He, Walter, served the I-Walter.

He gave a grunt of exasperation and ran his hand over his aching forehead, screwing up his eyes, grinding his teeth.

"Walter! Walter! What's the matter?" Jess was asking.

He stared at her, eyes clouded and distrait. "A headache," he said. "I looked up the word 'ecstasy'."

"That's an interesting word to look up! Why?"

"I feel it when I become the I-Walter."

"Tell me first what you think ecstasy means."

"Lifted out of myself in a pleasure so great I yearn for it to happen over and over and over again."

"Is it a reaction inside your body? A part of your body?"

"No, it belongs to the spirit."

"When does the ecstasy happen?"

"When I become the I-Walter."

Is he regressing or progressing? Jess asked herself, at a loss. "Tell me what the ecstasy consists of, who the I-Walter is."

"It happens when I watch the life-spark die in a pair of eyes," Walter said, the only emotion in his voice a faint pleasure. "But it took a while to find the right way."

"What is the right way?"

"I put my hands around its throat and squeeze while I'm either sitting or lying on top of it. Then its eyes are very close, I can see right into them and watch the life-spark die." He rushed on with his explanation, it seemed forgetting that she sat there. "I can get in and get out of here, I stole a motorcycle. Oh, I have a *headache!* I find it asleep and I put my hand around its neck and I squeeze all the life out. Ecstasy!"

Her howl brought all talk in the cafeteria to a paralyzed halt; every face turned to look at Dr. Wainfleet, on her feet and howling like a dog, and Walter Jenkins, scrabbling backward in his chair.

"No! Jess! Jess!" he cried.

The howling rose to shrill yammers; Walter finally leaped to his feet, both hands to his head, then, without looking toward Jess Wainfleet again, he ran out of the cafeteria into the hall, and headed for the fire stairs.

At the bottom he forgot the back fire door, erupted into the front hall and sprinted for the glass doors. The shrieks had alerted the small group of detectives outside; they went for their guns.

No shots were fired. Five paces from the doors Walter's back arched and he emitted a solitary scream of agony that ripped through brick and plaster as if it were made of tissue paper. Still in mid-stride, he pitched forward to the floor and lay on it, motionless.

Beretta out and safetly off, Abe Goldberg approached the body slowly, cautiously, searching for the eyes. Only one was visible, staring at Abe's right foot, its pupil fixed and dilated. Abe relaxed a little, came close to Walter, then knelt and groped for a carotid pulse.

"He's dead, but we don't disregard instructions," Abe said to Liam and the rest. "Manacle him properly. He's a brain case, and I'm not taking any chances that this might be some kind of trance or catatonic state. Once he's manacled, he's safe."

Carmine arrived, breathless, a minute later, Warden Hanrahan in tow, to find the lifeless Walter Jenkins as per instructions, in full manacles.

The Castigliones were at the top of the main stairs, forbidden to descend; Carmine joined them.

"What happened?" he asked.

"You tell us!" Moira Castiglione snapped. "Jess was having one of her eternal chats with her precious Walter, when she suddenly—I don't know!—came apart, disintegrated, went into hysterics—God knows what, because I sure don't! She started making weird noises like an animal yowling. She was standing, Walter was still sitting, but apparently he was the cause of her state because he began backing his chair away from the table looking as guilty as sin. I *think* he appealed to her, but if he did, she took no notice. Then he jumped up and ran away in the direction of the fire stairs. Jess collapsed. We put her in the room she uses here for resting if she works late, and when doesn't she?"

"Did you sedate her?"

"No. We figured she might be needed to answer questions."

And you hate her guts into the bargain, Carmine thought to himself. Lots of would-be directors of HI around here.

Carmine leaned over the landing railing. "Abe? Could you join me up here, please?" He thought of something else. "Warden Hanrahan? Many thanks, but your cooperation won't be needed now. I'll call you tomorrow with the full story."

Jess Wainfleet had recovered from whatever Walter had said or done to trigger her hysteria, though both Carmine and Abe had a fair idea what the trigger had been: the monster had informed his Dr. Frankenstein that he was out and about the countryside murdering for the thrill of it rather than from ignorance.

"Which doesn't alter our original dilemma," Carmine said to Abe outside Jess's makeshift bedroom. "Is this the right moment to hit her with the rest of it, or do we concentrate on Walter?"

"Let's play it by ear," was Abe's advice.

"Okay by me." Carmine knocked, was bidden enter. She had changed her blouse to a fresh one in a color he had never seen her wear—a dismal mid-grey—and primped at her hair and face to some effect. But the eyes she turned upon the two men were lackluster, devoid of warmth or any other feeling. Yet they were not defeated eyes: they were wary eyes.

"I take it, Doctor, that you were not aware what Walter Jenkins was up to?" Carmine asked gently.

"That is correct," she said mechanically. "I had no idea."

"Did finding out dismay you?" Abe asked.

"The word I would use is devastated, Lieutenant."

"He rode a Harley-Davidson motorcycle, we presume stolen from someone nearby who hasn't missed it, and killed a number of people in cold blood. Most of his murders seem to have been as the result of a homicidal psychopathia and undertaken for the fun of it, if I may be pardoned for what sounds a facetious phrase? His victims would have cooperated gladly, but the pity of it is that he discovered he enjoyed the act. Once he learned that, there could be no turning back, he actually sought to kill," Carmine said. "You presumed that he was cured of his psychopathia, whereas the truth is that no cure had taken place."

"The evidence supports my hypothesis," she said stiffly.

"Except that all your so-called evidence was negative, Doctor. You were not, and never have been, in a position to infer a cure on positive evidence. The first positive opportunity resulted in the first murder. There can be no getting away from that."

"I have no reason to get away from anything, Captain. It is not my fault that Walter Jenkins, cured or uncured, was permitted to roam the streets of Holloman County murdering innocent people! That is the fault of a system which does not take its duty anything like seriously enough. I mean that the security precautions supposed to keep Walter Jenkins imprisoned within a facility for the criminally insane were totally, utterly, inadequate. Anyone reading my papers on Walter knew that his I.Q. was extremely high and his ability to reason much better than that of most free men." Her chin went up, her eyes kindled. "I was shocked literally out of my wits today when I learned that my patient—a lifetime felon from seven states—has been allowed to run amok thanks to the slipshod methods of the man responsible for the security of the Holloman Institute for the Criminally Insane—Warden James Hanrahan!"

"Are you prepared to go on record as testifying to that, Doctor?" Carmine asked, staggered.

"I most certainly am!" said Dr. Wainfleet.

Fascinated, Carmine and Abe watched her visibly change mental gears; a bright smile appeared. "Now, if you please, I would like to see my patient Walter Jenkins."

Neither man answered; they looked at each other.

"I insist!" Jess Wainfleet said through clenched teeth.

Again, she was answered by silence. "*I insist!*"

Carmine spoke. "Doctor, Walter Jenkins is dead."

She rocked. "You're lying!"

"Dr. Wainfleet, what price my lying? Walter Jenkins came down the stairs to the front foyer like a bat out of Hell, his head grabbed between his hands. Then he screamed and fell to the floor. By the time Lieutenant Goldberg reached him, he was dead. His body has been taken to the Holloman County Morgue for autopsy. We have no idea why he collapsed and died."

She was rigid with shock. "*Autopsy?*"

"Naturally. It's required by law, Doctor, you know that."

"You can't! I won't let you!"

Carmine had had enough. "Madam, I am tired of your constant obstruction," he said, keeping his voice calm. "You may be the head honcho of this little corner of our state and municipal world, but in the performance of my duties I outrank you. So does the State of Connecticut bench, to which I will appeal if I continue to be obstructed. The corpse in question is both a federal and a state prisoner, diagnosed criminally insane, with a cause of death yet to be established by the legal authority, the Coroner/Medical Examiner of Holloman County. He is Dr. Gustavus Fennell. If you wish, you may apply to him to witness the prisoner's post mortem examination from the observation gallery, which is as close to the corpse as you may come, given your relationship to the living man. That is all I have to say on this subject. Is that quite clear?"

All color had drained out of her face, leaving it bleached to pure white; as a result, the eyes were obsidian—stone, not living matter.

"Thank you, Captain, it is clear," Jess Wainfleet said. "I would respectfully ask that autopsy not begin until I am present, and that there be voice communication between Dr. Fennell and me. If this request is honored, his task will be easier."

"Then I suggest that you make yourself available right now. I've asked Dr. Fennell to proceed at once."

It was like, yet unlike, an operating room. Since sepsis was not a risk, no sterile precautions were taken beyond those to protect the living tenants of the room, and Walter Jenkins had not been suffering from any known infection: in fact, he had been thought in the rudest of good health.

His naked body lay on the overly large and long stainless steel table, which ended in a sink and drains beyond the feet, and was surrounded by sufficient of a ditch and fence to keep fluids from running off its surface onto the floor. He had been washed, and bearing no visible injuries, looked asleep save for the agony frozen on his face.

Apart from Gus Fennell and his assistant, two others stood on the autopsy room floor: a technician who would label the specimens as commanded, and Carmine Delmonico. Looking down from the gallery were Dr. Jess Wainfleet and Abe Goldberg. The gallery could be sealed off from the autopsy room by a series of electrically operated glass panels, but today it was open so that Jess Wainfleet could speak to Gus Fennell.

"One request, Dr. Fennell," she said before the preliminaries began. "May I have the brain once you've done with it?"

His nondescript face, tilting upward, wrinkled in thought. "What is your reason, Dr. Wainfleet?"

"I spent a total of two hundred hours in twenty periods of ten hours each performing micro-neurosurgery on this man's brain. I wish to do a complete anatomical and histological study of his brain to see what I can verify and what discard from my technique," Jess said in even tones.

"Then when I am finished, you may have his brain. If I find cause of death before dissection of the brain becomes necessary, you may have it intact." He smiled up to someone he had no reason to suppose was any but an ordinary colleague. "If I do have to cut into brain, I'll try to be economical."

"Thank you!" Jess said with real gratitude.

"This is a very curious autopsy," Dr. Fennell said for the benefit of his idly turning tape recorder, "in that no short cuts of any kind can be taken. To establish cause of death unequivocally is my directive, which means excluding surface insults, particularly injection sites or scratches drawing blood. . . ."

And so it went for several hours of painstaking searches of skin, scalp, nail beds, tear ducts, salivary glands, and so on, until Gus could categorically rule out an external agent introduced other than by mouth. Then came the examination of internal organs, the many body fluids and tissue samples that were sent to Paul Bachman for detection of toxins, the examination of arteries for bruits, fat or air emboli, plus veins, lymphatic channels, and glands, ductile or ductless. Clots? No. Nothing, nothing, nothing.

Finally came the head, the grotesque peeling off and away of the face to reveal the skull's rictus, and then, ultimately, the saw shearing through the cranium to lift a huge lid off the brain.

"Ah!" Gus exclaimed. "A subarachnoid bleed!"

Jess Wainfleet spoke at last. *"An aneurysm?* Impossible!"

The brain was coming out, its surface empurpled, blackened, reduced to pulp in places. Gus swung a massive magnifying glass over the brain's base, held upward in his hand.

Jess was babbling. "I did every conceivable test on him! I did *everything*, I tell you! Pneumoencephalograms—right *and* left carotid arteriograms—his arteries filled beautifully, each side was a perfect tree!" Her fist pounded. "There was no aneurysm!"

"My dear, there was," Gus said gently. "See for yourself! See? On the basilar artery right at the cerebellar-pontine angle—just before it bifurcates into the vertebrals, see? Messy, but visible. The one place that hardly ever fills satisfactorily, yet the site of his aneurysm. From the look of the areas south of the Circle of Willis, I'd say he's had an occasional tiny bleed ahead of the catastrophe itself. Cause of death is evident. I won't need the brain itself. Do you still want it, Dr. Wainfleet?"

"Yes," she said tiredly. "And thank you."

It was nine o'clock on Sunday night, no one had eaten since lunch, and John Silvestri was demanding to be fed information immediately. The Commissioner gathered Carmine, Abe, Paul and Gus, and marched them into Malvolio's for a late dinner.

"The first thing I need is a bourbon and soda," said Carmine.

"Ditto," said Abe.

"I'm an abstemious man, but I have earned a red wine glass full of ruby port," said Gus. "At least none of you smokes."

Consumed with curiosity, Luigi elected to wait on this booth of heavies himself, sitting with them whenever he wasn't needed; a fellow classmate of Silvestri's in St. Bernard's days (and a cousin), he would have donated several crushed knuckles before singing of what he heard, as everyone knew.

After two glorious gulps of his bourbon, Carmine spoke. "Gus, the first thing is, explain the autopsy result, and why it upset Jess Wainfleet so much."

"Two hundred hours of neurosurgery!" Gus said on a squeak. "It boggles the imagination. Jess did twenty procedures on Walter, each ten hours long, I presume in some kind of attempt to rewire his brain. Well, you don't put in that amount of time unless you make sure your patient has a physically perfect brain—no silent tumors or scars or—aneurysms. Aneurysms are the toughest to find, as you have to do a dangerous test, the arteriogram, to see an aneurysm. What is it? A weakness in an artery wall, like a bubble. As long as blood pressure remains stable, the bubble is okay. But if blood pressure rises, it can develop a tiny hole, and leak. If there's a huge increase in blood pressure, it bursts and blood goes everywhere. Whether it's on the aorta or in the brain, death ensues. Jess did arteriograms. That is, she put a needle full of dye into the carotid artery and watched the dye travel through the brain arteries. On both sides of the brain. She was convinced Walter was free of aneurysms—they're not very common, and people usually have only one. But Walter's aneurysm was on the one artery of the brain that doesn't always fill with dye completely. That's how she missed it," said Gus, taking bird-like sips of his port. "Most unfortunate!"

"Why was she so anxious to have his brain?" Abe asked.

"Oh, she'll sit at a microtome and slice it so thinly that tissue paper is a brick wall by comparison," Paul said. "She'll want to know what effect her two hundred hours of microsurgery produced. She's a scientist."

"Grisly," said the Commissioner.

"It's not finished yet," Abe said, "but before I explain what I mean, I'm going to order dinner and another drink."

Luigi got up, flapping a hand for more drinks. "Place your orders, gentlemen. Everything's on, but there are no specials."

By the time that meals were consumed and the hot chocolates (Luigi made great hot chocolates) were ordered, tomorrow's plans had been worked out. Paul would do the fluid and tissue analyses from the Walter Jenkins postmortem, John Silvestri would retire to his aerie, Gus would go back to less urgent work, and the two detectives would meet with Delia, Liam, Tony and Donny at eight in the morning in Carmine's office.

MONDAY, SEPTEMBER 8, 1969

Delia had had a delightful Sunday held captive by Rufus and Rha, who kept her mind off criminal matters by teaching her to write witty song lyrics, limericks, and all kinds of zany verse. As a technique it was inspired, for it couldn't be performed with a mere segment of a mind; the whole intellect was involved. And it made everybody laugh, sometimes to the point of near-hysteria.

Thus to learn of the later events of yesterday came as an utter shock, one she was very glad not to have participated in; she could have contributed nothing to success while enduring a great deal of personal anguish.

"I hope to conclude the whole sorry business today," Carmine said, ending his narration of events. "Dr. Wainfleet is a very slippery customer, adept at taking what seems an indefensible position and turning it into an advantageous one. Our constitution was tailor-made for her. Every time she's seen, she must be fully warned of her Constitutional rights all over again, is that clear? Delia, I'm sorry to have to drag you in today, but a woman must be present at each interview, and she's too smart for me to use a woman uniform. I'm aware that you have 'friend at court' status with her, but it can't be helped. It's purely to make sure she doesn't cry rape or physical abuse. If you need to wear slippers, then wear them, okay?"

"Thank you, Chief, but my feet weren't badly punctured. If I wear thick socks and long trousers, my nun's shoes will be bearable."

"Then let's go."

"Why not Abe and his team rather than me?" Delia asked as the Ford Fairlane growled toward Route 133.

"What a diplomat you are!" Carmine said appreciatively. "It has to do with your friendship with Jess, actually. She doesn't like men. By that I don't mean she's a man-hater. This is far different, far colder. Men are the enemy in a war situation, and she sees herself as on the side of the angels. Nothing could ever convince her that, were she not a woman and therefore held back, she isn't qualified to rule the world. I don't know whether megalomania is a certifiable illness or not, but she's definitely a megalomaniac. What she'd condemn in anyone else, she can excuse in herself as her inalienable right to stand above the laws that bind and tie the rest of the world. The trouble is, her crimes are so well concealed that she can't be called to account for them."

"I see," said Delia, seeing indeed. "We have to obtain a confession."

"Exactly."

"But how?"

"I have no idea, except that we play the cards as they come and be prepared to bluff."

"No, let's not think of it as a card game, it's too complex for that. It's a piano sonata we have to play by ear."

"Okay, Beethoven, it's a piano sonata."

Jess Wainfleet stared through the transparent wall of the glass jar holding Walter Jenkins's brain, beginning to feel that two or three additional changes of the preserving solution would be sufficient; the liquid in the jar was still a reddish-pink, but it was translucent. She donned heavy-duty rubber gloves and tipped the jar until the reddish-pink stream into a bucket became a trickle, then she refilled the jar and looked again. A much paler pink that would deepen in color, but not yet, and not nearly as richly as the last lot.

The base of the brain was on top, its spindling threads and tatters all that were left of blood vessels and tissue envelopes covering it. And there, insofar as she could ascertain, was the Circle of Willis, the brain's brilliant internal safety valve to ensure that, in the event of blood supply to one side of the brain being cut off, blood from the flowing side could cross via this ring of tiny bridges and give the starved side blood. That it was so difficult to pinpoint lay in the devastation caused by the rupture of the aneurysm on the basilar artery, which ran off the back of the Circle of Willis toward the top of the spinal cord.

Walter's blood pressure must have been through the roof. When the aneurysm ruptured it sent blood out of itself at huge pressure, part of the jet down to bone, part of the jet up into butter-soft brain at the pons and medulla. All the cellular nuclei that governed heart rate, breathing and other bodily functions were hosed into mush by that jet. Walter died screaming in agony because that was how subarachnoid hemorrhage victims died. The pain endings were in artery walls outside the brain.

And she grieved terribly; why, or what for, she barely grasped. Never her lover, even in her imagination. He was far more her child, she decided, her gestated creation. Though not gestated in her belly—there was nothing visceral about Walter. He was the child of her mind, she had carried him through twenty separate procedures that saw him change from a raving maniac to a creature bounded and determined by thought. Walter dead was herself dead. The grand experiment had been terminated by a weakness she hadn't suspected existed. *An aneurysm!*

The vultures were gathering: the Meloses, the Castigliones, Jim Hanrahan. . . . To avoid the smirks on their faces, she had phoned every last one of them before midnight last night to tell them of Walter's unsuspected aneurysm, making it very clear to everyone that these things happen, and are no one's fault. Those among them who had medical degrees got the message at once, and those in ignorance soon became enlightened. Jim Hanrahan was in deep trouble over the secret doors in the Asylum walls, and no one attached to HI itself was strong enough to spill her.

The real crunch was the only immutable, and immutable it was: time—the years—age—call it what you will . . .

I haven't enough time left to start again. I am nearing fifty years of age, and Walter's death is a cut wrist in a warm bath. My vigor is leaching away like the hard hot deluges of monsoon rains soaking into thirsty barren ground.

Oh, what are we here for, if our time be so short, so sourly brief? I am too old to do it all again! My supernova has fizzled to a dim, brown old shell. I am defeated.

Then she bethought herself of something and phoned HI.

"I am afraid I won't be in today," she said to her secretary, a meek creature named Jenny Marx who had long taken an inferior position to Walter Jenkins, and certainly wouldn't be a problem now. "If the police should need to see me, tell them I'm at home and will be glad to see them here at any time."

There. That was it. *An aneurysm!*

Like most scholarly persons who had chosen a solitary life, Jess Wainfleet's home was centered around the room she called her library, though it was not a room visitors ever saw. They were accommodated in a kitchen breakfast booth.

The library was shelved from floor to ceiling wherever no windows intruded, and provided with a broad-stepped, bannistered ladder anchored in tracks on the floor; it held a Barcalounger, an upright easy chair, a desk with an office chair behind it, two console tables and two lecterns on wheeled stands, one holding her stereotaxic atlas of the brain. The floor was black carpet, the ceiling a uniform cloudy brilliance from inset fluorescent tubes overlaid with milky plexiglas. The kitchen, a bedroom, a bathroom and a door to the cellar opened off a hall.

When Carmine and Delia arrived at Jess's front door, she led them straight to her library.

Its furniture had received two additions: a pair of stern hard-backed chairs facing the office chair across the desk.

"Please sit there," she said, taking the office chair.

Delia sat; Carmine walked about a little at first, his manner polite, patently awed.

"Everyone from Voltaire to Thucydides," he said, smiling at his hostess, "and you've had your *Scientific Americans* bound in leather year by year. I used to do that until I married, then I couldn't afford it anymore."

"Has married bliss been worth the pain of loss, Captain?"

His face registered genuine astonishment. "Good God, yes! Infinitely. I can still afford the annual subscription, and by the time my sons can reach the shelves where they're stored, they will be pulling them out to read, not to rip."

"A miracle!" Jess exclaimed.

"Excuse me?"

"You are a thinking parent, a luxury I never had."

"I'd rather call a thinking parent a necessity than a luxury."

"And what may I do for the Holloman police?"

"Why did you take their heads?" Delia asked, setting the tape recorder on the desk, its innards already in motion.

This time it was Jess astonished. "Oh, really!" she cried, exasperated. "All I needed from the pathetic creatures were their brains, and it's a great deal easier to extract an intact brain from a cranium if the entire body isn't attached."

"Margot Tennant was the first, long before Walter Jenkins came on the scene," Delia said, keeping her voice neutral. "Perhaps you would explain to us what happened to her. From the beginning, I mean. Where did she come from?"

"I reiterate, she was a private patient from another nation signed over to my care by her relatives, who were financially exhausted and emotionally quite beyond caring what happened to her. I reiterate, all the Shadow Women, as you so aptly named them, were from foreign parts," said Jess Wainfleet.

"It would be a great help if you told us your source, Jess, and also more about Ernest Leto," Delia said.

"Oh, I'm sure it would be, but I'm afraid I can't do that. Modern authorities make it so difficult for people to rid themselves of intolerable burdens because modern authorities never seem to experience one iota of the pain or the hardship of caring for the hopeless. All that interests them are the pieces of paper, and pieces of paper inevitably end as ass-wipes. I know the pain, I know the hardship. Therefore I refuse to join the bureaucratic conspiracy. You will learn what I choose to tell you, nothing else."

"Then let's see what you choose to tell us," said Carmine. "Margot Tennant was acquired. What did you do next?"

"She became the first of six experiments on a neurosurgical technique, the prefrontal lobotomy. You know this because I have already described the operation to you. However, I followed the patient's progress through six months of her apartment life. At its end I put a photograph of her in the apartment that served as a trigger telling her it was time to go. She obeyed by leaving at once to come to this house. I went to the apartment and cleaned up, knowing I had six weeks' leeway."

Jess lit a cigarette and continued. "I returned here and sacrificed my subject by perfusing her brain with my own fixative solution through both carotid arteries. Death is absolutely instantaneous. Once the subject was dead and the fixative given enough time to suffuse through all the brain's tissue, I amputated the head and then removed the brain.

"Without sacrificing my experimental animal, you must realize, I know nothing. But after studying the effect of my neurosurgical intervention, I learned everything there was to learn. And I was correct. Six subjects were sufficient."

Never had Delia come so close to vomiting during a case; she felt her mouth go dry, felt the first premonitory retch, and fought to keep her gorge down. That she succeeded felt no victory; was Jess Wainfleet *human?* Detached, impassive, pitiless . . . And I had fun with this woman! I liked her!

"How did you dispose of the bodies?" Carmine asked.

"I bought a huge chest freezer—it's still in the basement. After I succeeded so fantastically with Walter, I brought him here to my house four times to remove the first four frozen bodies. The task was beyond my physical capabilities, but no one checks my car when I drive into HI. I don't know what Walter did with any of the bodies, including the last two, which I gave to him unfrozen and on site, so to speak. I presume he buried them somewhere."

Carmine too was having trouble assimilating the degree of utter coldness, and a part of him had room to grieve for Delia—poor, deluded, betrayed Delia! *That* hurt. The rest just revolted.

"Are you saying, Dr. Wainfleet, that you deliberately made use of an inmate to conceal your personal activities?" he asked.

"Yes, yes!" she snapped, goaded.

"Their skulls are missing," Carmine said.

"I *know!* I had Walter crush them in a vise, then pound the pieces to powder. He worshipped me," she added in a confiding voice, "absolutely worshipped me!"

"Dr. Wainfleet, I must arrest you on six charges of murder in the first degree. Anything you say or do may be taken down and used against you in a court of law. You are entitled to legal representation," Carmine said.

The handcuffs came from inside Delia's spacious purse; Jess Wainfleet held out her hands without comment, even after her arms were repositioned at the small of her back before the cuffs were clicked into place.

"I didn't think you'd give in without a fight," Delia said.

"Were I ten years younger, I would have fought with every ploy known to the law," Jess said, looking wry. "I'm too old to do it all again, even if I had another Walter to work on. But I don't. Walter was a rare bird."

"One the world won't miss," Carmine said. And nor, he added silently, will the world miss you, Dr. Wainfleet. I'm hard put to decide whether Walter was the worse monster, or you are. Whatever else he may have been, Walter was a dupe—your dupe. You used his capacity for murder to conceal your own murders, then condemned him for getting a kick out of killing.

By noon it was all over.

Dr. Jessica Wainfleet was in that sole woman's cell that had seen so much, with a woman uniform right inside it with her, even when she used the bathroom. No suicide was going to happen on his watch, vowed Lieutenant Virgil Simms.

"Well, swoggle my horns!" said Commissioner Silvestri to his captains over lunch in his aerie. His black and sparkling eyes traveled from Carmine to Fernando and then back to Carmine, scant humor in them, which was almost unbelievable. "This has been a spooky and horrible case from start to finish, guys, not to mention two cases rolled in one—kinda. As my Aunt Annunziata used to say, 'The sins of the flesh are the hardest to be rid of.' I know it's only lunch, and normally at this hour my eagle's nest is as dry as a water hole in a drought, but today, gentlemen, I am moved to offer a snifter of X.O. cognac squeezed out of Napoleon's boot."

Nothing loath, the gentlemen captains accepted this rare accolade. "And tonight," Silvestri said, swirling his balloon, "we are all invited to Busquash Manor for dinner, including all wives and children down to newborns. The older kids will be screened first-release movies, and the younger ones will watch a pantomime-style concert. Infants will have lullabies."

"That's what I call civilized," said Fernando with a grin; he was the father of a ten-year-old boy, an eight-year-old boy, and a five-year-old girl, so sitters were usually a nightmare.

Despite the darkness of Ivy and Jess lingering web-like still, it was a joyous gathering that evening at Busquash Manor. The kids were spirited away to environs that pleased even the most fussy among them, including beds as well as skilled entertainers, which meant the unexpected treat of freedom for parents, fed the most delicious foods and drinks. Rufus played Chopin, Rha sang Russian folk songs in a voice that went from soprano to bass, and then everyone lounged around in comfortable chairs to talk.

Carmine participated, but as an outsider. A rare privilege for one from a large and closely knit family. The Brothers Carantonio, he reflected, had subtly changed, thanks, according to Delia, to Jess Wainfleet's one good deed. She had told Rufus to stop atoning for their father's crimes, and he and Rha had seen her logic. Rufus, of course, was flirting with Delia, while Rha had captured an extraordinary duo: Betty Goldberg and Gloria Silvestri. If anything good had come out of this business, it was a steadier foundation for Rha and Rufus.

Stomach pleasantly full, Carmine leaned back in his chair and listened to John Silvestri on the subject of funny farms.

He must have fallen asleep, and Silvestri had compassionately moved away to let him doze in peace; when a hand rested lightly on his shoulder, he jumped.

"Phone, Captain," said Rha.

Carmine got up and followed Rha down one of the Manor's halls to a jade-green and citrus-yellow room where a phone was lying off its cradle.

"Delmonico!" he barked, not pleased to be aroused.

"Carmine, listen," said a beloved voice, "I'll have no arguments! I am well, I am rested, I am in an uplifted mood, I am as fat as butter, and I am bored to dry sobs. The boys are missing Frankie and Winston desperately. I am flying home tonight on the red-eye. Phone you from Kennedy." Clunk.

Blinking, he emerged into the hall.

"Is everything okay?" Rha asked anxiously.

"My wife's coming home on the red-eye."

"That," said Rha, "calls for a drink."